The Perfect Pafko

Robert Booth

Bugle Books
7956 35th Avenue SW
Seattle, WA 98126

First Bugle Edition 2005

Cover Design: Nate Whitehill
Use of Topps 1952 card of Andy Pafko on the cover
is by permission of Topps Company, Inc., and Mr. Pafko.

ISBN: 0-7795-0101-2

Acknowledgements

While working on this project, I relished those occasions when it was necessary to go to school on the expertise of others. Part of that enjoyment came from the looks on their faces as they had to wonder, "Why on earth does he want to know *that*?"

In Georgia, I am indebted to Scott McDonald, animal control officer extraordinaire, Bob Rice and Tommy Cathey, for their patient explanations of the poultry and egg businesses, Steve Schaefer, for his primer on Georgia history, John Shockley, for his friendship and inspiration, and Marjean Meadow, for helping to pin down a variety of details.

I appreciate the support and encouragement received from Bobbie Carter and Joe Guidry, in Florida, Tass Bey and Zina Bennion, in Utah, and Gail Goeller, in Washington. In Milwaukee, I am grateful for the generosity of South Side native Mary Liner, Dave Martinsek's polka knowledge and the warm hospitality of Susan and John Gleysteen.

While much of my learning was informal, I also benefited greatly from the critical observations of my three advisors in the MFA in Creative Writing program at Goddard College: Darcey Steinke, Neil Landau and Jeanne Mackin. In addition, I had the privilege during this project of working at two wonderful schools—Wasatch Academy and Annie Wright School—and the stimulation of those academic environments aided me greatly.

The critical comments of several readers were especially helpful and came from my daughter, Laura, Cynthia Beebe, Cheryl Jordan, Paula Morgan, Ron Richardson, Emily Lambert and Anne Winebrenner. Each made excellent suggestions.

Last and most profoundly, I am deeply indebted to Kathy Keller. It would be hard to imagine a more exacting and inspiring editor.

All of the above were most generous with both their time and their talent. There are scores of people whom I have known over the years, both in and out of Georgia, whose influence is felt here in ways both large and small. Any errors made in translating their wisdom to the page are, of course, entirely my own.

Robert Booth
May 15, 2005

1

Brady Greer stood on the small foot bridge arching above the fish pool in his back yard, gazed at the Japanese carp below and wondered how long they would last if he introduced piranha into their tightly ordered little world. Thirty seconds? A minute? There was no way to actually know, unless…

No. That chewing was best left to the mind. Acting it out would create a mess and that was something especially frowned upon in the tidy high society of the Deep South.

The pool, surrounded by a rose garden, was the centerpiece of the compact back yard of the Reynolds House, built by Col. Rupert Reynolds, a local cotton dealer, in 1849. Its stately exterior walls were three handmade bricks thick. The landscaped grounds included two huge live oak trees in the front yard with boxwood bushes and a garden of daffodils and geraniums outlining the front porch. It sat 50 feet off Main Street on a half-acre lot and was not one of the bigger homes in town, but its history was authentic and that counted most in Midian, Georgia.

Though the Reynolds House had been the home of Brady and his wife, Beth, for less than two years, they were preparing to put it on the market and move again to what would become their third home in six years. Her hobby was renovating old houses, selling them, then finding another project. She looked for historic buildings with good bones, but ones possibly weakened by the telltale sight and smell of sawdust, indicating termites were munching their way through history. The trick was not just knowing what to do with this and other problems to bring back curb appeal, but acting as your own contractor while doing it. After some painful trial and error, she had found reliable masons, carpenters, plumbers and electricians who gave her work top priority, because they knew she could keep them employed on a regular basis.

Beth liked to showcase each project in the annual Tour of Homes just before placing it up for sale and so, to satisfy the Tour's promotional brochure, each home had to include "period antiques and fine reproductions." That was where Brady came in. He provided the furnishings, even though the only period pieces he owned before meeting Beth were a crimson lava lamp and an orange beanbag chair, which were kept well out of sight now...since they were not the sort of period pieces the Tour committee had in mind.

So, the emphasis at the Reynolds House would be on ersatz versions of pieces from the correct era. Brady had checked around and discovered a little shop in the North Georgia mountains that specialized in knock-offs of antiques from the antebellum period and whose reproductions were so good that none of the local Daughters of the Confederacy had been able to distinguish them from the genuine article.

Best of all, this shop would rent its larger pieces to Brady, who was grateful, because positive cash flow was often elusive. His brokerage business had fallen on hard times and it was Beth's knack for renovation that was paying many of the bills and also improving their social standing in Midian, where those who burnished the symbols of the antebellum era found their reputations similarly buffed.

Beth assumed Brady was covering his portion of the

renovation expenses with income from his brokerage business, so she would have been surprised to learn that some of that cash she was handing over to her subcontractors was coming from the pieces of Brady's baseball card collection which he had been dismantling, bit by bit. He felt as though his body was being dismembered secretly, in slow motion, with no one there to share his pain. Watching his prized possession slip away to a dealer up in Athens was bad enough, but of more immediate concern was the fact that the pieces of value were almost gone. Essentially, his bankable reserve was down to a small cache of rookie cards from 1957, some of Sandy Koufax and the others of Roberto Clemente. The great left-hander was now pitching relief here for Brady, while Clemente, who died trying to help the poor, was still managing to contribute cash on Main Street, in Midian.

The Reynolds House was an excellent venue for entertaining and the Greers were about to host a cocktail party. Everything had to seem perfect, so Brady left his thoughts of predator fish and returned inside, where Beth greeted him with a look of alarm.

"What's the matter?" he asked, knowing the answer instantly as he followed her gaze down to his favorite necktie, one displaying a variety of colorful cigar bands from around the world. As Beth shook her head, Brady held up his hand in surrender, then headed for the bedroom to replace it with a fine silk substitute of solid blue, resigned to the fact that clashing is also on the list of things to avoid here in Midian.

Looking into the mirror as he adjusted the knot, Brady suddenly found himself assessing his reflection: The peaking of his hair was becoming more pronounced as it continued to recede on either side…and it wouldn't be long before the dark brown had yielded to the gray enough to demand being labeled "salt and pepper." Though his father still had a full head of hair, each grandfather had gone bald early, causing Brady's continual concern about shiny domes skipping a generation. The rest of his skin made him feel better, since his complexion was just dark enough to tan easily.

Brady swore he could remember his eyes being brown when he was younger, but they were now hazel, like his father's. Could they really change color that much? He had heard for years that sons often morphed into images of their fathers, but had never taken that seriously…until recently, when pieces of Harry Greer began popping up in his son's reflection. Brady still thought of himself as youthful, being a regular at the noon basketball games at the Midian Recreation Center, but the bags beneath his eyes were becoming more prominent and the definition of his chin less certain.

"Oh, that's better, much better," said Beth, snapping his reverie with a quick glance from her vanity before applying her lipstick. "The other would have been dreadful with your pink shirt."

There were only two times when Brady wore neckties, on social occasions and to church, so he did his best then to look as though he belonged, though he could not quite shake the feeling his world was now a drawing room and he was its brass spittoon.

Suddenly, the chimes in the front hall broke into their grating little chorus. I know we could switch that to "Take Me Out to the Ball Game," Brady thought. There must be a way… Beth's voice called out from the bathroom, "Brady, can you get that? I'm not quite ready."

He rose from his leather chair in the den, walked into the front hall, past the beech wood coat rack and turned the brass knob on the red heart pine door.

"Ross! Melanie!" he said to his neighbors from three doors down. "Come on in!"

"Oh, Brady!" Melanie said after a couple of quick air kisses and a glance around, "You and Beth must be so proud! We hardly recognize the place. It looks terrific!"

"Thanks, Mel," Brady said with a warm grin. "You know Beth deserves most of the credit."

"Right you are, Mr. Greer," Beth said with a broad smile as she made her entrance down the staircase. "But you are very helpful."

Brady saw Ross and Melanie socially every weekend, so he did not have to ask what they were drinking. Returning with Ross to his den, he poured a glass of chardonnay for Melanie and a vodka, rocks, for Beth. The men each had a healthy shot of Gentleman Jack, poured from a crystal decanter. The first drink came from the host, then the guests could help themselves. It was Saturday night and the busiest place in town since noon the previous day had been the local liquor store.

As the rest of the guests arrived, Beth showed the women her latest renovations while the men retreated with Brady to admire the Greer's biggest conversation piece in what had been their extra bedroom. It was now The Billiard Room.

On one of Brady's antiquing expeditions, he had come across a dirty, dusty billiard table up near the Tennessee border. It was genuine oak; he could see that much beneath the layer of soot covering it. With a few balls missing and only one cue, the owner was getting tired of it taking up space and let Brady have it for $500.

"Are you out of your mind?" was Beth's first reaction. "We could use that money for furniture we actually need!"

Her tune changed after it was appraised. Turned out it was definitely made before the Civil War, probably before 1850, out of quarter-sawn oak. The table bed was a single piece of slate and the rails had ebony inlaid sights. Brady was able to acquire the three missing ivory balls and another oak cue. The complete package, properly cleaned up, then appraised at $10,000 and its maker, the Brunswick Company, had offered twice that in an effort to reacquire it to display at the home office, an offer the Greers had decided they could afford to refuse...at least for the time being.

The billiard table was the only antique of any value they actually owned, so they agreed it would be used primarily as a conversation piece. Some of those talks Brady had with himself, when Beth was not around. He would cup one of the white, ivory balls in his right hand, then roll it gently back and forth across the green velvet, before a snap of his wrist sent it speeding toward a side rail. Bonk! It was instantly redirected. Bonk! Off it would carom again, toward another rail. Usually, after three banks, it would roll gently to rest. Brady thought of himself as that little ball, hurtling through life, this way and that, suddenly redirected on occasion by an immovable object in his path. *Where and when will I gently come to rest?* he wondered.

One night, over a drink, Brady asked Beth proudly what she thought of the news of the strong appraisal of the billiard table.

Reaching for her bottle of Stoli, she turned to him, shrugged and said, "Luck doesn't impress me."

There was a day when that kind of remark would have incensed Brady. Not now. Since about the time he moved into the

Reynolds House, Brady had been hearing voices, calm and soothing. They grew in strength and frequency to the point where they were now both friendly and familiar, recalling to him Earl Gillespie and Blaine Walsh doing the Braves games on the radio decades before, back in Milwaukee--only these announcers were exclusive, broadcasting on a station only Brady could hear. It was Skeeter and Herb now doing the play-by-play and color commentary on the life of Brady Greer.

Skeeter: *Whoa! She really ran one by his chin there, Herb. But he just dodged it, then stepped right back in. Kinda thought we'd see more of a reaction out of him.*

Herb: *Nope. He's seen that pitch before. He's a veteran, one who knows there are really few things in life worth arguing about. It'll take more than that to rattle him now.*

Brady tried to keep his focus on what he thought was the strength of their relationship: When he was down, Beth was up and vice versa. Their ability to help each other beat the blues was the emotional epoxy binding them together. If that meant one occasionally brought the other down from a high, well…it was the price they tacitly agreed to pay for making sure those lows never became too dark, too distant. In addition, Beth's deft touch with renovations gained Brady a level of social acceptance in Midian unusual for a Yankee.

He especially enjoyed holding up his end of the bargain creatively. One night when she had the blues, Brady suggested they play "Shot Monopoly," taking a drink every time they passed "Go." Another time, he arrived home after work on a Friday with their bags packed in the trunk for the weekend. His idea was to head for the city limits, then flip a coin at every major intersection. They wound up at a cornbread festival in Tennessee.

The talk on this night centered on the hot topic of the day: a local referendum many feared might change the entire complexion of the community. Publicly selling liquor-by-the-drink had been on the ballot a couple of times before and, on each occasion, the local ministerial association had banded together, preaching successfully from pulpits throughout Munson County to defeat it. This time, several hotels out on the interstate were pushing it hard and there was growing concern that passage of the measure might lead to the kinds of sleazy bars and, God forbid, even topless clubs that could be found in the other cities throughout Georgia lacking the courage and foresight to oppose them.

Brady was more concerned about another community, the baseball community. It seemed to him that greed—greedy owners and greedy players—was a virus ever more virulent, coursing through the sport's veins now in the form of a nasty labor dispute between the two sides that might result in a strike before the end of this 2002 season. He fantasized--in fact, he was doing it right now, in the middle of his cocktail party--about the steps he might take as commissioner to end the strife and return the focus where it belonged, to the game on the field.

Having just celebrated his 49th birthday after six years in town, Brady was still having difficulty dancing to the rhythm of Midian, which came naturally to its natives, yet was acquired with greater difficulty by recent arrivals, a category including any new resident appearing in the last 20 years.

His friendship with Ross, a Midian native, was especially important to Brady, because it was his strongest link to local mores and folkways, teaching him that the rural South could be appreciated best by grasping the concepts of loss and recovery. Any consideration of loss led back to The War, perhaps the most-romanticized loss in U.S. history. To ask, "Which war?" was to admit openly to locals that you just did not feel their pain and probably never would. The specter of The War seemed to Brady to hang like a weeping willow over every hamlet in the Deep South.

It still seemed odd to him that Midian was the one town in the path of Sherman's March to the Sea that managed to gain from that notoriety. While the rest of the antebellum era disappeared long ago in a haze of musket smoke and the din of Rebel yells, Midian held itself out as the last, living bastion of a state of mind, a place to which Southerners could repair to confirm their image of past glory. Thousands of visitors from beyond the South arrived each year to record on film a level of serenity and gentility on a lush, verdant backdrop they had previously thought might only be found in fiction.

Soon after he became friendly with Ross, Brady asked about that.

"How can this be? Midian sits squarely on the route from Atlanta to Savannah. Didn't General Sherman come through here nearly 150 years ago, torching everything in his path? Yet Midian's glossy brochures proclaim it, 'The Town Sherman Refused to Burn.' Why?"

"One thing you need to understand about Midian," Ross said patiently, "is that this is where myth has become a mantra masquerading as reality."

Brady could easily see the truth in that, knowing antebellum Midian, the tourist town with its stately homes lovingly restored, was the bright, white picture you saw from a sidewalk on Main Street. Only from a different vantage point, a weedy curb a few blocks away, could you complete the canvas with a contemporary struggle that was often uncivil, for it was there that Midian appeared far more similar to the rest of rural Georgia: poor, dark and uneducated. This was a picture of Midian not touted in Tourist Council brochures, sharing the same zip code with its affluent neighbors, but little else…except the credo of every small town: Even when you don't know what you're doing, someone else always does.

"Here in Munson County," Ross added, "cotton was king for a long time. Then we started getting a lot of dairy farms, but those are both tough ways to make a buck these days, so those folks have been selling to developers or getting into the poultry business."

"Seems like those chicken places are everywhere."

"That's right. Steady income's what they offer. The smell of money must be stronger than the stench those birds make, though it's hard for me to see how anything can be stronger than that."

As 10 o'clock approached, Brady returned to the bar with some trepidation. This was the hour by which everyone generally had enough to drink…but the parties usually carried on until 11 or 12. The result was that someone often said or did something during that hour or two that would haunt them for a few weeks if they were lucky, a few years if they weren't. But it was also the time when people who were otherwise circumspect in that wonderful Southern manner exhaled all the way and spoke with a refreshing candor. With that in mind, Brady worked his way across the room toward his personal sage, Lester Sloat, a longtime resident of Midian with a fondness for fine bourbon and the ability to look good in bright bow ties. Brady wanted to get his take on why that bastard Sherman hadn't torched the town.

"Yes, Midian was spared," Lester said as he contemplated the ice cubes in his glass, "but Sherman was nowhere near us when that happened. The Yankee troops in the area were under the command of General Slocum, not Sherman. President Lincoln had issued Executive Order No. 1, which said, in effect, that no town was to be burned that was represented before The War by a man sympathetic to the North." Lester paused, then looked away from Brady before continuing with a thin smile.

"The fact that our congressman had resigned in protest over Southern secession is not one of the town's ugly little secrets—of which there are many—but it is a subject seldom discussed in polite company.

"By the way," Lester continued as he moved toward the bar for another jolt of Gentleman Jack, "ever wonder why you and Beth were the first ones to restore this house back to its original condition?"

"No, I guess I haven't thought about that."

"Well, the man who built it, the old Colonel, was a Northern sympathizer, too."

"But, how could that be? Wasn't he a colonel in the Confederacy?"

"Nope. He wore blue when he made his reputation fighting the Indians first, then the Mexicans. He was too old for The War of Northern Aggression."

Brady caught a gleam in Lester's eye when he said that, "The War of Northern Aggression," as though he looked for the opportunity to slip the phrase into a conversation, then savored the moment when he did so.

"Then what did he do during The War?" Brady asked, trying hard to pick up the local phrases, even as he fought the temptation to ask why this war was still being waged, 150 years later, in dens and drawing rooms across the South.

Lester took a sip of his malt, letting it linger for a moment on his lips before speaking. "He made money," he said finally. "That's what he did. That particular impulse drove him a bit harder than any feelings he had for the Confederate cause."

"Made money? Doing what?"

"History is unclear on that point," Lester said. "But much more clear on another."

"And that is?"

"People from outside the South often think we're still pining away down here about slavery and states' rights. But that's not what really sticks in our craw."

"What does?"

"Reconstruction—or the lack of it. The Yankees rebuilt Japan and gave Europe the Marshall Plan, even wrote a big check to the Mexicans after that war. We got pretty shabby treatment by comparison, wouldn't you say?"

"Well, I—"

"No offense, by the way."

"Offense?"

"You know, about the Yankees?"

"Oh, no," Brady said quickly, more focused on absorbing his history lesson. "No offense and none taken."

"Anyway, getting back to the Colonel. His presence here mostly reminded people of the Mexican War and of people out to make a buck from the War of Northern Aggression. When you and Beth get ready to sell this place, as I suspect you may be doing soon, the buyer will likely come from outside Midian." Lester smiled as he watched that comment register on the face of his host.

Brady was deep in thought as he headed back to the billiard room. So, it was Honest Abe who had actually saved Midian from a fiery fate. But where was the romance in that? Gratitude to a Yankee--especially the ultimate Yankee martyr--was a tough sell in the heart of Dixie, even after a century and a half had elapsed.

He now understood why the Midian Tourist Council had become creative, encouraging the fable that maybe Sherman was so taken with the beauty of Midian--its magnolias, azaleas and boxwood gardens--that he spared the town...or an old West Point classmate who resided there convinced him to pass on by. Some even speculated that Sherman had a paramour in town who ran out to meet him, pleading in her petticoat to please spare this pretty city. But it seemed to Brady any possible Scarlet O'Hara in Midian's past was eclipsed by the specter of Sherman. Southerners continued to vilify him as a monster of Hitlerian proportions. The fact that Midian escaped his torch, for whatever reason, enabled its upper crust citizenry to affect an air of noblesse oblige.

And it was this small group of present day nobility that

11

finally started to rise and make its way out of the Reynolds House into the warm spring evening. As Beth and Brady said their good-byes in their front doorway, framed by etched ruby sidelights and the transom above, it seemed to be the picture of gracious Southern contentment…until Melanie lost her footing and landed with a "thud" on the porch floor, having dipped just a little too deeply into the chardonnay.

The reaction was practiced and immediate. Every woman present turned away, as though the sight was simply too terrible to behold. The men immediately helped Melanie back to her feet and dusted her off. As soon as she thanked them, the women knew it was then safe to look up again and begin making a fuss about her condition.

"Poor dear," one would say. "It is hard to see in this light."

"Yes," another would chime in, "it does take time for the eyes to adjust after being inside."

In sum, Melanie's mishap would quickly be ascribed to everything short of the tides and her biorhythms—everything, that is, except the real reason why she could no longer function as a biped.

When the hosts were finally alone, they returned to their kitchen, where Brady rolled up his sleeves to address the pile of dirty dishes, while Beth removed her shoes and collapsed into a chair.

"What were you and Lester talking about?" she said. "He looked a little more animated than usual."

"Oh, he was telling me that our boy Reynolds wasn't in favor of The War. Did you know that?"

"No, I didn't. Hadn't heard that."

"He thinks that's the reason nobody fixed this house up for so long. Says we'll have a tough time selling it to the locals."

"No surprise there," said Beth. "But that's fine. That's not our market anyway. It's Atlanta people that want these houses. The antebellum demand keeps getting bigger and the supply gets smaller every time one gets sold. We'll be fine."

"Have you ever thought about who really won The War?" Brady asked.

"What are you talking about?"

"You know. The South lost in the short run, lost big time.

Then Reconstruction was a mess, which made it worse. But look at it now: Lots of towns like Midian, dotted throughout the South. Good weather, low taxes and a sense of history. Great places to live. Then look at the North: bad weather, high taxes and not so much pride in the past."

"Brady, are you drunk?"

Skeeter: *Hmm... Looks like our boy's tryin' out his knuckle ball here...*

Herb: *Good move. Gotta keep mixin' up your pitches.*

Skeeter: *A good move when you can control 'em...but you got to practice that knuckler, or it goes its own way.*

He looked at her, startled. "Why, no, of course I'm not drunk. Why do you ask?"

"Because I'm hearing you telling me the South won the Civil War. Tell me you're not saying that."

"That does sound ridiculous, doesn't it? But sometimes you can't call the winner 'til long after the fight is over. It's food for thought."

"Well, I've seen all the food I can handle for one night," Beth said as she picked up her shoes and checked her tan face and slim waist one last time in the kitchen mirror before heading up the stairs to change into her sweats.

Brady had become accustomed to her habit of running three miles just before turning in for the night, regardless of how much food and drink she had consumed. Beth had the cool, quiet streets to herself then and he was convinced her nightly run--especially with her shoulder-length blonde hair tied into a pony tail behind her baseball cap--kept her looking much younger than the 40 she had turned a couple of months ago. That was a difficult birthday for Beth, so Brady made it a point to remind her how fit she looked. When he did that, she would sometimes reward him with the dazzling smile that first beguiled him...one he had seen less often in the last few months.

As Brady finished the dishes, he gazed out the kitchen window toward the rose garden. Sunday had begun. He would make an extra effort to get his shirt and tie combination right for church later that morning and hoped that would make his wife happy.

2

The following Monday found Brady taking refuge on a rainy April afternoon in his stock brokerage office inside the town's old train depot, his favorite place in Midian. Anyplace else, it would have been just another decayed building, a dump with a dog. But Brady liked to think of his aging depot as a dowager in decline. In this case, the dog was "Louie," a blue tick hound who had been hanging around the depot for years. He had his very own water fountain, rigged up by the railroad workers, to wash down whatever food they and Brady threw his way.

Railroads were once the engine of commerce in Midian, and the sharp burst of a train whistle was still heard there frequently. Passenger trains, though, run where the action is—which meant it had been decades since they had passed through Midian.

In rural Georgia, these train depots seemed to Brady to evoke sharply their privileged past. The one in Midian was the first brick depot between Atlanta and Augusta and still looked to be as sturdy as it had been the day it was completed, shortly after The War. But there was an enormous, diagonal crack in the wall closest to the tracks. Brady wasn't sure if it had been caused by years of vibrations from the freight traffic or from the uneven settling of the foundation. Either way, these cracks were a common sight here in antebellum Georgia, where the locals were fond of saying they were like the lines in your face: gave it character.

Throughout Brady's tenure at the depot, the first-time visitor was always confronted by the singular scent emitting from the Swisher Sweet Peach Optimos he regularly fired up. He liked to say that was his way of supporting the state's peach industry, but their low price was the real attraction.

"I don't know what's worse on your clothes," Beth had told him, "just the smoke or that peachy sweetness." She tried to avoid both and so seldom dropped by the depot. The two small lights hanging by chains to the ceiling gave a dim cast to the office and a murky feel to the room, as though it was better suited to be a poker parlor. The slate shutters were closed, further darkening the interior.

There was a rusted, pot belly stove on the right just a few feet from the door. It was once coal-fired, but now burned wood, which was stacked knee-high along the length of the wall closest to the door. The upper half of the walls was painted a rusty red, while the lower half was beaded wood. The 12-point buck mounted above the oversized desk to the left of the door was much more to Brady than a mere hunting trophy. It represented the highlight in an otherwise stormy relationship with his father, a passionate hunter. Brady had not taken naturally to handling a gun and his father had grown impatient while teaching him.

The other reminders of Brady's father at the depot were the two well-worn wing back chairs in front of the desk. Harry Greer had retired to Florida several years ago with no further use for these refugees from his Wisconsin den. Brady remembered them as the chestnut sentinels they once were in his father's office, even though they now resembled more a pair of slouching soldiers on the verge of expiring right there in their tracks.

Overall, the room felt detached from the rest of town and frozen in the early 20th Century. In fact, it had been the white ticket office before 1970, so black folks native to Midian were still reluctant to enter. The old depot appeared an odd place from which to run a brokerage office, making it well-suited to the man who was doing that.

The stages of Brady's career were marked by how he handled the business channel on TV. As an eager rookie in downtown Atlanta, he had turned the sound down just a little; in the suburbs, where he met Beth, it had been usually muted, though he kept an eye on it, ready to return the sound when the image of one of his favorite stock pickers filled the screen. After his arrival at this depot in the country, an hour east of Atlanta, he concluded that oracles from every point on the financial compass provided no true north, so he muted them all and set their silent words to music.

He initially preferred the mordant humor of Warren Zevon and Randy Newman. Slowly, however, Brady realized the depot was his personal kingdom, the one place where he could express himself freely and without explanation. It was then that he began to slip some favorite accordion music into his CD player.

Since leaving the home of his youth, along Milwaukee's North Shore, and arriving in this place steeped in a history not his own, Brady had sought ways to remain rooted in his native city. Initially, that desire manifested itself in his fondness for bratwurst and beer. Hearing the occasional polka triggered thoughts of his childhood, even though that music hadn't been part of his personal experience. It was a manufactured memory Brady would not expect others to understand, one that became even more real when he heard that polkas and beer were fraternal twins, being born at about the same time in Bohemia.

During an especially blue period right after college, when his friends were as certain of their futures as he was confused, Brady saw pictures of a South Side polka festival. Everyone was smiling, that's what he noticed most. Soon after, a smile became Brady's Pavlovian response to the sound of polkas.

Skeeter: *Sometimes, I think the only thing our stadium organist knows is, "Charge!" A good polka would work for the 7th inning stretch, don't you think?*

Herb: *It would be different, I'll give you that.*

Brady's keen interest in the accordion eventually led him to Buckwheat Zydeco and, most recently, to contemplation of tejano conjunto music, in which his favorite group, "El Conjunto Bernal,"

had popularized the use of two accordions. Brady felt uneasy
sharing his fondness for this music with Beth and was quite certain
any open display of affection for the accordion would brand him
even more of an outcast here in rural Georgia, so it was a secret he
shared only with the empty depot and the muted market mavens on
the screen in front of him.

Being in the train station reminded Brady that the market
always worked on boom and bust cycles. One of the biggest booms
of all had occurred when there were dozens of railroads throughout
the country, followed by the bust that forced their consolidation into
the handful of lines that remained. Since the dawn of free agency,
baseball had experienced a boom that made virtually every player a
millionaire, right down to the end of the roster. Will labor problems
kill the golden goose? That possibility made Brady nervous.

He was lost in this boom-and-bust reverie when his 4
o'clock appointment walked in through the big oak depot door.
Irma Arnold smiled as she stuck her umbrella outside to shake it,
before resting it carefully on the uneven pine floor. Brady loved
the unusual sound of rain beating on the pavement outside during
the drought. The smell of it moistening the floor near the door
tempted him to ask Irma to keep it open, but he decided against it.

"Isn't this rain great?" she said. "Yards will really be green
tomorrow."

"ALWAYS PROTECTING YOUR TURF, AREN'T
YOU?" Brady answered back with a grin, straining to be heard over
the rumble of the 4:05, bound for Atlanta.

Irma, a native of Midian, was a slim, well-dressed woman
in her early 60s. She and her husband had a low six-figure nest egg
and were living mostly off their investments and the disability
payments he was receiving after a car accident--at least that was the
story for public consumption. The nature of one of those
investments was known locally only to Brady and her husband.

As an Army brat, Irma had eight different homes before
settling in Midian. Somewhere along the way—-Brady never
pressed her on where, which she appreciated—-Irma developed
considerable skill playing poker. This latent talent was revived
soon after her husband's accident, when Irma periodically began to
take the proceeds from those disability checks and head for Atlantic
City.

"It's a simple routine, really," she had confided to Brady. "On the first Friday of each quarter, I just slip out of town, drive over to Atlanta and catch a plane for Philadelphia. My first stop is always the Lord & Taylor downtown, which I first visited as a child with my parents, back when it was Wanamaker's. They don't build department stores like that anymore. Its got a 30,000-pipe organ and 2,500-pound eagle statue that are just magnificent, truly inspirational.

"Then, I get on one of those buses to Atlantic City and blend right in with all the other senior citizens headed for the quarter slots. I check into my room at the Trump Marina, take a nap, then arrive refreshed at the poker parlor around 11 PM. Where I play depends on what convention is in town. Could be the Marina, Bally's...any of those places. I always bring along some peanut brittle in my Lord & Taylor shopping bag, which amuses the tough guys around the table.

"But, you know," she adds with a wink, "they're not smiling too much a few hours later, when they're several thousand dollars lighter. First thing Monday, I make my deposit in my Atlantic City bank account, then head back to Midian. A day or two later," she says brightly, "I'm down here at the depot, ready to play the utilities."

Before he had heard this story, when Brady first started receiving Atlantic City checks from her, he gave her a puzzled look, to which she darkly responded, "I'm just taking that Yankee money and bringing it back home."

Herb: *Gotta keep an eye on Irma.*

Skeeter: *What for? Looks to me like she's a loyal member of the team...*

Herb: *Yeah...looks that way, but she's a poker player. Never know when she's playin' cards she ain't got.*

Irma became one of the most influential women in town through deft use of her two-legged power base. This included being the senior member of the city's Historic Preservation Commission, which had to approve any proposed exterior change to a home in the Historic District before it could be made. In addition, she was president of the Tara Garden Club. Every 30 days, it conferred "Yard of the Month" status on some lucky local landowner--a coveted distinction in Midian, one that some people went to great lengths to get. It was awarded to Brady and Beth the last time they stuck a "For Sale" sign in the ground and they still think it helped cut the selling time in half.

"Now, Brady," Irma said with another wink as she settled into one of his wingback chairs. "You know I'm not just happy for the lawns out there. Why, this liquid sunshine keeps all those crepe myrtles, Japanese maples and boxwood bushes healthy."

"Not to mention the daisies, black-eyed susans and zinnias," Brady added casually. Anywhere but the South, he would think Irma was flirting with him.

"I do declare!" she said approvingly. "You are trying, Brady Greer, but don't forget: I do spend a lot of time reading people's eyes and I don't believe you are actually holding those flower cards just yet."

Brady laughed and shook his head, knowing better than to try and run that jive past Irma. Any woman who could overcome breast cancer, the suicide of her teenage son and her husband's accident, while somehow managing to maintain her sunny disposition, had an inner toughness worth saluting. Where did people find the strength to keep moving ahead through all that? She had done what he could not. Problems seemed to cling to him like that Tar Baby Joel Chandler Harris wrote about, right down the road in Eatonton, and Brady was most likely to rail against them, rather than shed them and move on.

Irma and Brady moved in different social circles and each was an important source of news to the other. Whenever she heard an especially juicy piece of gossip, Irma declared with a shriek, "Oh, Brady! Isn't that the limit?" He had made a game out of getting her to say that before they got down to business.

When he moved to Midian, Brady decided to streamline his approach to the brokerage business. As a result, whenever his clients had any investable funds, Brady was happy to help them put it into a company they all knew and loved: Coca-Cola.

"Need a blue chip for your portfolio? Let me tell you about Coca-Cola common. Income? Let's look at Coke bonds. In the mood to gamble? Let's try some Coke options."

"Co-Cola," as it was known in Georgia, has been as much a part of the state as red clay, cotton and kudzu for nearly a century. It was a reassuring name to anyone, no matter their position on the investment spectrum. At Brady's suggestion, Irma had purchased both Coke stock and bonds for her account.

Brady explained to each of his clients that Coke was marketed initially as "The Ideal Brain Tonic," and it had also added pep to portfolios: From its inception as a public company in 1919 until the end of the century, Coke stock paid a dividend quarterly without interruption since 1920 and split 10 times, meaning that a modest initial investment of 100 shares grew through compounding of dividends to nearly 500,000 shares by the end of the century.

To make an effective sales presentation, Brady realized early that he had to personalize those numbers and chose the citizens of Quincy, Fla.--a rural town of 8,000 just slightly larger than Midian--as the best vehicle for doing so.

In 1922, tobacco farmers in the Quincy area brought in a bumper crop and, following the advice of a local banker--Brady's spiritual ancestor--plowed their profits into Coca-Cola stock, which had recently been offered to the public for the first time. Many of those farmers and their heirs never sold. As a result, the town had 25 Coke millionaires. At one point before World War II, Quincy was the richest town in America on a per-capita basis.

"But how much more can it grow?" Irma and Brady's other clients would ask. He loved to hear that question. Brady would then lean back in his antique leather chair, tap his pen slowly on his desk and say, "Well, Coke gets most of its profits today from overseas. China and India have more people than anybody else and Coke's barely made a dent there…"

Right about then, he would reach into one of his side drawers and pull out a couple of quarters from a stack he kept there for that purpose. Walking slowly, over the creaking hardwood floors, to the far side of his office where he kept an old Coke machine, he would say over his shoulder to his client, "I think it's time for the pause that refreshes. Care to join me?"

After that, it was usually just a matter of how many shares Brady's visitor would buy. If his client persisted in wanting to purchase something else, Brady would agree that maybe it was okay to speculate a little on the latest fad--knowing it was axiomatic in sales to "first sell 'em what they want, then sell 'em what they need"--but "Coke is the core" he always counseled, knowing that any Georgian wouldn't lose sleep over owning Coke, however volatile the market.

Thus, he had happy clients, but also ones who tended to simply buy and hold their shares. He knew how to get referrals from those satisfied customers and turn them into more business, but…well, that required a level of energy he couldn't quite summon to the task. The leisurely pace of Midian was an invitation to put your life on cruise control and Brady had accepted that offer. In the process, the repetition of his sales technique had become monotonous of late for Brady, causing him to do a lot of daydreaming about how to inject his life with a little excitement.

As soon as Irma left the depot, he gathered some research reports to read at home, then paused as he headed for the door and called out to his dog, "Louie! Louie! We gotta go now." Laughing as he reached into his pocket, he retrieved a couple of quarters and dropped them into the Coke machine, confident that a bottle of the South's favorite tonic would perk him up for the moment, until he could figure out how to develop a more permanent buzz.

3

Talking flowers with Irma caused Brady to stop on the way home and pick up something for Beth. He liked to say Americans had become lazy, allowing special occasions to be decreed by Hallmark or the U.S. Congress. If you set your mind to it, he thought, any day could be special, especially when garnished with Phalaenopsis orchids, which were Beth's favorite. Before she came into his life, Brady had been mainly moody and withdrawn, aware enough to show up at the office each day and go through the motions, but increasingly brooding about how too many of his contemporaries—-people he felt to be often less talented than himself—-were forging ahead with successful careers while his seemed to be standing still.

Beth changed all that. Soon after they met, the negative energy fueling his downward spiral exhausted itself and was overtaken by her zeal for renovating places…and people. His energy returned as his admiration for her grew, especially over the way she was able to pick up her life and move ahead after dealing with the cancer that took her first husband, though she, too, was still capable of lashing out without warning, as though her demons were sometimes able to pop the cork she had stuck in them. Beth liked projects and Brady became her next one. She saw in him the promise he thought had been obscured and tried to connect with it at about the time when Brady had declared himself a hopeless case.

"Hi, Honey!" he announced to the vacant vestibule as he walked through the back door, unable to find her. "Got something for you."

"In here," she called from the living room.

Brady rounded the corner from the kitchen to see his wife hunkered over the coffee table, renovation magazines all around her.

"I just can't make up my mind," she said. "The people who read these things would be interested in this house. Maybe we should do the advertising ourselves, instead of paying a realtor. I don't know. What do you think?"

"I think I've got something for you," he said with a smile.

A moment later, Beth lifted her head to see the orchids.

"Oh…they're very pretty," she said, still distracted. "There's a vase in the cupboard. Put them in some water, then come over here, okay? There's a lot of money riding on this. We've got to decide what to do."

Brady turned toward the kitchen with a shrug. Phalaenopsis used to be a surefire winner. He made a mental note to surprise them both next time with something more exotic.

Herb: *See what I mean about different looks? Gotta mix those pitches. A change-up woulda looked good right there…*

Skeeter: *But you got to have confidence in a pitch to use it. This Beth is a tough out. If she thought he was gonna change speeds, she'd have smacked that pitch over the fence.*

After Beth had briefed Brady on the pros and cons of the various magazines, she glanced at her watch and snapped her fingers.

"Damn!"

"What's the matter, Hon?"

"I almost forgot," she said with a sudden frown. "My garden club committee's going to Athens tonight. I've got to go; I promised Irma. We won't be late, though. Can you heat up some of that roast from last night? If you wait up for me, we can finish taking care of this when I get back, okay?"

"Sure."

Brady took a seat on the couch. He welcomed the time alone because he felt guilty watching baseball when Beth was around and now was free to settle in and enjoy his favorite rivalry, the Cubs and Cardinals, from St. Louis. Each team had been a regular visitor to Milwaukee when he was growing up there and watching them now was Brady's way of climbing into his own time capsule. The names in the current lineups didn't matter much to him. The uniforms hadn't changed, that was the important thing. After a couple of innings, that allowed his thoughts to drift to Ernie Banks, Dee Fondy and Moe Drabowsky; Stan Musial, Wally Moon and—surely one of the greatest names ever—Vinegar Bend Mizell. To Brady, those were the real Cubs and Cardinals and they would always be playing in his mind. He had collected all their cards and so, after piling Beth's magazines neatly on the floor, he opened up his album right there on the coffee table, to breathe life into the old guard.

Out of habit, he ran the fingers of his right hand lightly over the pictures, as though touching them somehow strengthened his connection to the past even more. It was much tougher on Brady when the Braves were on TV. Though their uniforms were similar to the ones from his youth, the team had moved to Atlanta back in the early '60s, while he was still in junior high, breaking the heart of a city, his city, and he hated them for it. The script "A" on today's Braves caps didn't look right to him--40 years later--and never would. Every time someone asked him to go to a Braves game in Atlanta, he found a reason to be busy and was proud he had never set foot in that stadium.

Brady carefully appraised one card, then the next, with a jeweler's eye. He smiled approvingly. You seldom knew the saints from the sinners in the '50s, because details unvarnished by a club's PR man rarely made the papers. Brady's affection for the old Milwaukee Brave players was stronger than for any other. Warren Spahn, Lew Burdette, Joe Adcock, Eddie Mathews, Johnny Logan…he could still see the whole team quite clearly in his mind's eye. Of them all, his favorite was Andy Pafko, the only member of the original Milwaukee Braves—the team that arrived from Boston in 1953—born in Wisconsin.

Brady leaned back on the couch and let out a sigh. He tried to imagine again what it must have been like for "Handy Andy," growing up in Boyceville, a small town near LaCrosse, not far from the Mississippi River, the product of a Slovak Lutheran household that didn't have electricity until he was in high school. As a player, Andy was always smiling, worked hard and never seemed to complain--even when asked to switch to third base after he became an All-Star center fielder--or groom a rookie named Hank Aaron to take his place in the outfield years later. That clean-cut, hard-working image of Andy Pafko had taken root in Brady's mind a half-century ago and now blossomed more with every new story of a contemporary player's wife beating, drug rehab or illegitimate kids. The happiest times Brady had spent with his father were while watching Handy Andy and the Milwaukee Braves.

Brady rose from the couch, moved toward the fridge and helped himself to a bottle of Rolling Rock, still thinking of Pafko, who wasn't the best player on the old Braves, not with future Hall of Famers Spahn and Mathews as teammates, but was still very dependable. At the heart of Andy's appeal was his persona as a man-of-the-people, immigrant son--and Wisconsin native. Pitching like Spahn or hitting like Mathews might be too much to expect for kids growing up in the '50s in Wisconsin, but Pafko's success seemed to be a product of old-fashioned hustle and work ethic. "Hey, if I can make it," he seemed to say, "then you can, too."

Most importantly to a young Brady Greer, he thought to himself as he returned to the couch, this was something upon which he and his father agreed. Harry Greer was a product of the Depression who had made his own way in the world and he admired anyone else who did the same. Brady recalled with a grin one of the ways Harry impressed thrift upon his son, through a ritual they performed before attending each of their Braves games. Harry would always stop by the Johnston Cookie Company, just a few blocks from County Stadium, to buy a big bag of cookie pieces— not the whole cookies you could buy in the store, but the seconds that never made it onto the shelves.

"What's the diff?" he would say when anyone asked him about this curious habit. "It's the same cookie. You're gonna break off a piece before you eat it, anyway. This way, they already do that for you and it's just a buck a bag. What a deal!"

Those bits of chocolate chip and oatmeal raisin were the peanuts and Cracker Jack of Brady's childhood. The Johnston Cookie Company was long gone now, but he always figured there must be another company somewhere that sold cookie seconds; Brady just hadn't been able to find it. So, it was left to his baseball card collection to be the umbilical cord to his youth, one that no knife could sever.

By 10:30, Brady was fighting off sleep. *Where was Beth? Should have been home by now.* He decided to close his eyes, just for a minute, his face buried in a pillow and his right hand at rest inside a bag of microwave popcorn. Whatever the hour of her arrival, he knew her priority would be to get in her nightly run. Late evening was not only the coolest time to exercise, but also the final opportunity to burn some of the day's accumulated calories, so Beth could continue to tolerate the image she saw reflected in one of her many mirrors.

The sound that eventually woke Brady was a loud rap on his front door. Pushing himself up with his left hand to a sitting position, he glanced at his watch. *Midnight? That's a marathon garden club meeting. Beth must have forgotten her house key.* As he stood, there was more knocking, this time louder than before.

"Damn! Beth," he called out. "Take it easy. I'm coming."

When he reached the door, Brady opened it and was startled to see Ross, his neighbor, and Scratch, the deputy sheriff, two of his funniest friends now looking more solemn than he had ever seen them. Ross reached out and squeezed Brady's arm.

"It's Beth," he said. "There's been an accident. You need to come with us."

"What...," was all Brady could muster, though now fully awake.

"C'mon," said Scratch grimly, closing the front door. "We'll explain it all on the way."

The three jumped in Scratch's squad car and rushed to the local hospital. En route, Brady was told his wife had been hit by a car during her evening run; an out-of-town man was being questioned at the station. She was in the emergency room, the extent of her injuries unknown.

At the hospital, the first thing they saw was a stretcher being loaded into an ambulance. A nurse ran out to meet them.

"Oh, Mr. Greer, I'm so sorry…"

"What is it?" Brady said. "Is that Beth on that stretcher? How is she?"

"Yes, sir. That's Mrs. Greer. She needs a CAT scan and we don't have one, so we're sending her to Athens General."

"Let's go," said Scratch. "We'll follow the ambulance."

"No!" Brady said sharply. "I'm riding with Beth."

Before there could be any dissent, Brady ran to the rear of the ambulance, opened the door and jumped in. Motioning to the attendant, he said simply, "Let's go."

Skeeter: *Looks like we got us a clutch hitter here, Herb.*

Herb: *Could be…problem is, some guys forget the clutch isn't the only time they got to swing the bat.*

As the ambulance accelerated, Brady took his first look at his injured wife. She was unconscious, but appeared to have only a few scrapes on the right side of her face. Reaching out and squeezing her hand, he turned to the attendant.

"How bad is it?" he asked.

"Don't know," came the reply. "Won't know 'til we get to Athens."

Brady cursed the tight-fisted Munson County commissioners under his breath. The hospital had been a contentious local issue for several years. Its debt of over $50,000 per month had been covered by the commissioners until recently, but, with an election approaching, they had decided to tighten the fiscal screws, cutting costs by reducing service. It was now little more than an outpatient clinic masquerading as a hospital.

Twenty minutes later, the ambulance stopped moving, its rear door opened and Beth was whisked down the hall to the CAT scan room. Brady stayed with her as long as he could, before a nurse gently led him to the waiting area. He looked up to see that Irma and Melanie had joined Ross and Scratch.

"Oh, Brady, I'm so sorry," Irma began as Melanie wept quietly while clinging to Ross. "What do they say? How is she?"

"Nobody knows at this point," Brady said with a shrug. "I guess the CAT scan will tell them what they need to know, then…" here, he paused and looked down the hall, "then we'll know what they need to do to...to get her back on her feet."

"Well, she's in wonderful shape," Irma said hopefully. "That should help her pull through."

There was nothing to do now, but wait. Brady tried to tell his friends they didn't have to stay, but they wouldn't hear of it, insisting on remaining with him at least until more was known about Beth's condition.

Brady was a pacer when he became agitated and so began to walk back and forth in the waiting room, with an occasional glance toward yesterday's newspaper or a copy of the "Reader's Digest," Large Type Edition. When he felt that might be making the others nervous, he decided to extend his walk to the admissions area of the ER, which seemed almost as chaotic here as it was on TV. Athens is a small city, but--it quickly became apparent to Brady--one with its share of stabbings, shootings, heart attacks and mental patients. As he returned to the waiting area, Brady was met by one of Beth's doctors.

"Mr. Greer, we're doing everything we can for your wife," he began.

"And what is it, exactly, that you need to do?"

"Well, there's been a lot of internal bleeding. We need to address that first."

"And then?"

"There's some organ damage and she has a fractured hip."

"So, how bad is it? Are you telling me her life is in danger?"

"We have to get the bleeding under control," the doctor said evenly. "That's what they're working on right now. Once we've done that, we can address her other injuries. I'll give you an update just as soon as we know more. Uh...Mr. Greer?"

"Yes?"

"We have a chapel at the end of the hall."

"What, what are you saying here?"

"I'm just saying," the doctor said patiently as he turned to go, "that we have a chapel here, should you care to use it."

Praying? Brady was a regular churchgoer mostly because that was expected in Midian. It was one of the three ways you were identified: your church, your job and your Daddy. Brady was the Presbyterian stockbroker whose people were from...up North.

28

Minnesota? Or was it Wisconsin? Somewhere up there…damn Yankees, at any rate, and that had been a continual problem. When the locals didn't know a man's Daddy, they were less able to take the full measure of the son…and were denied the window into a man's character that knowing him as a youth could provide, which seemed especially important in the rural South. In this case, the fact that Brady had spent his formative years on the wrong side of the Mason-Dixon Line only made it worse.

The lip service Brady had been paying God on Sundays was doing him no good at all on this particular week night. Crunch time has a way of illuminating the truth, so the thought of suddenly trying to summon God's help after years of neglecting that particular relationship was giving Brady a bad case of cotton mouth. He paused at the water cooler and glanced at his friends' expectant faces as he reached for a cup. What should he tell them? How to phrase it?

"She's in bad shape," he blurted out moments later. Melanie sobbed while the lips of the others tightened further. "They've gotta stop the bleeding before they can do anything else."

With that, Brady sat down and buried his head in his hands. He felt someone squeeze his shoulder and it came to him that Midian was at its best when one of its own was in pain. Still, he was chilled immediately at the thought of Midian's wakes and funerals, always a big sendoff to the hereafter, with enough baked goods and covered dishes to comfort the survivors until their numbness began to wane. Was that scenario now awaiting him? He bristled at the thought…certain he would give anything at that moment for Beth to just get up and walk on out of there, so they could all go home and try to forget that any of this had happened.

Everyone took turns glancing at the cheap, institutional black-and-white clock on the wall. After perhaps the slowest 40 minutes in history had passed, the same doctor reappeared and motioned for Brady to join him.

"It's going to be a while longer before we know the full extent of her injuries," he said gently. "There's a motel down the street. Why don't you go get some sleep? We can call you if we need to."

"Thanks, Doc," Brady said. "I wouldn't be sleeping any better there than here, so I guess I'll just stick around."

Brady tried to make himself comfortable in the metal waiting room chair built clearly for brief visits. As he closed his eyes, his thoughts turned toward life with Beth. In the winter, they looked forward to the week they spent each spring on St. Simon's Island, off the Georgia coast. During languid Georgia summers, they would enjoy evenings cooking out in the back yard with small groups of friends. In the fall, the social scene featured Georgia football games, causing them to share intimate jokes about the life-and-death importance Bulldog fans attached to their team's fortunes...never dreaming the reality of mortality would hit so close so soon.

He had about given up ever being able to exchange the me for we in his life, until Beth came along. She had made doing that both fun and profitable. He didn't want to think about life without her, so he rose and headed back toward the ER, looking for relief. *Relief? Short relief. That was a problem for the Cubs this year: Didn't have a reliable set-up man to get to the closer. Damn! What am I thinking?*

Brady shook his head, amazed at allowing himself to think of baseball when his wife remained unconscious, her future—his future—uncertain. Still, Brady had never been one to corral his thoughts. They ran free, like mustangs on the open range. At the moment, they were galloping again away from reality toward baseball, his favorite refuge. The changes Beth's accident might cause in her life and his were too grim to contemplate, but fixing the Cubs? Now there was a world of perpetual hope, one in which he could lose himself for quite a while.

4

      Shortly after Athens welcomed the promising glimmer of a new day, Brady was struck by how a fresh page on the calendar had transformed life inside the hospital. The frenetic activity of the night before had given way to a more corporate atmosphere. A new shift of doctors and nurses, looking crisp and alert in their starched whites, bustled about, but with far fewer interruptions bursting through the ER door. It was now, Brady thought, time to tidy up from the mayhem of the previous night.

      And Brady Greer was one of those loose ends. He was still wearing the same shirt he had slept in twice during the previous 12 hours, first on his couch, then in the waiting room chair. Every time he touched his face, he was reminded that he needed a shave and was glad Ross would be arriving soon with his electric razor and a change of clothes.

      The morning staff had not been able to close the book on Beth because she continued to fight for her life, receiving blood transfusions throughout the night as the doctors kept trying to staunch her bleeding. As Brady recoiled from his first taste of coffee and its thin, cardboard cup from the hospital machine, he looked up to see Ross approaching.

"Any progress?" his friend asked.

"Nope. Bleeding's still the big issue. They're doing what they can to stop it."

"Well," Ross began carefully, "this may not be the best time to bring this up, but, would you like to hear more about the car that hit Beth?"

Brady swung his head around until his eyes were locked on those of Ross. "Yes," he said tersely. "I *would* like to hear about that. What have you got?"

"An elderly couple, the Ma and Pa Kettle type, from over near Covington. They were driving an Edsel."

"An *Edsel*?"

"That's right. Had it for years, I guess. Anyway, Scratch says they got into an argument, something about the guy not being able to see well enough at night to drive. He takes his eyes off the road while he's yellin' at her. Next thing you know, the car veers off and hits Beth."

"From the front or the back?"

"Scratch says it must have been from behind."

"Where are they now?"

"The city's holding 'em until..."

"Until they know if Beth makes it, right?"

"Well...yeah," Ross said softly. "Here. I brought your stuff. Why don't you go clean up? I'll relieve you for a while."

A few minutes later, Brady huddled with the doctor in the corner of the waiting room. When they had finished their talk, Brady turned to his friend with a sigh.

"Well, they think they've stopped the bleeding."

"That's great!" Ross answered, relieved.

"That's just the first step," Brady cautioned. "She busted some bones and they're going to keep her here for a few days, but they've got the bleeding under control. She's pretty doped up, but the doc said I could see her," Brady added as he started down the hall, "just for a minute."

When Brady entered his wife's room, the nurse stepped

away from the bed and Brady approached it. Beth looked much the same to him as she had in the ambulance, the main difference being the salve on her facial cuts and, most importantly, the fact that she was conscious enough to recognize him—groggy, as though she'd spent the night drinking with Ross and Mel—but conscious all the same. When Brady gently took her hand in his, Beth groaned softly, turned her head slowly, opened her eyes carefully, then smiled as much as her pain would allow when she recognized her husband.

"Beth? Beth, I--" Brady felt the hand of the nurse on his arm.

"I wouldn't ask her to talk just yet, Mr. Greer. You might want to let her rest a while and give the sedative time to wear off."

"Yes. Yes, of course," Brady said. Putting his fingers to his lips, he blew his wife a kiss as he departed, then returned to the waiting room.

Ross agreed, reluctantly, to leave, but only after promising he would return late that afternoon. Brady now had a pile of newspapers and magazines to keep him occupied, but opted, instead, to take a walk. Something else had dawned on him besides the new day and that was the realization that any hospital could lay claim to being the city that never sleeps, with hundreds of lives starting and stopping there at all hours, every year. Having been a little too close to the end of the line on this visit, Brady now felt he needed to see some happy faces and so headed for the maternity ward.

As soon as he stepped off the elevator on the fourth floor, he was struck immediately by the change in smell. *What is that?* Then it came to him: talcum powder. Of course! Happy place, happy smell. The entire floor had a different feel to it than the ER. Nurses and attendants bustled about, as they did throughout the hospital, but these were happy people, with smiles to match those of the new dads floating several inches above the tile as they guided the wheelchairs of their beaming wives and snoozing newborns up and down the halls.

Brady made his way over to the large glass window to look in on several rows of bassinettes, each with its tiny, precious package. At 49, he wanted to start a family; in fact, he wanted that much more than he let on. He'd given the subject of parenting a lot of thought and felt confident he could succeed at it--replacing the insensitivity he had witnessed first hand with a nurturing warmth. Ideally, he saw that approach developing a scrappy, confident infielder--one who could do all the little things to help his team win--that would make both his parents proud.

Beth had warmed to the idea of children early in their six-year marriage, but recently ran hot and cold on it, which struck Brady as a bit odd. Most women wanted children, certainly by the time they reached 40. Those who didn't tended to reach that conclusion early. The last couple of times he raised the subject, she dismissed it, saying she felt the timing would be better after they got out from under the Reynolds place and settled in a new house.

Shortly after Brady stepped up to the window of the nursery, a new arrival was placed in an empty bassinet to his left. This was a huge baby, one that seemed nearly twice the size of the rest. As a nurse approached him in the hall, Brady looked up at her, pointed to the window, and said with a grin, "That *had* to be a C-section, right?" Before she could answer, Brady heard a soft voice behind him.

"No, no it wasn't. It was a normal delivery."

He turned around to see a petite young woman, one who couldn't have been over five-feet tall and more than 100 pounds, sitting in a wheel chair and staring at her baby through the window.

"I...I'm sorry," Brady started, not sure of where to go from there.

"That's okay," she said with a slight smile. "Nobody else can believe it, either."

"Uh...his Dad must be a big guy," Brady offered hopefully.

She was silent for a moment, then said softly, "Yes, yes he is."

Glancing up and down the hall, Brady did not see anyone who fit that description. He then noticed the absence of a ring on her left hand, wished her well and retreated back to the elevator.

Skeeter: *Unbridled joy for some, bittersweet for others.*

Herb: *It's luck of the draw, how healthy that baby comes out.*

Skeeter: *How a kid turns out later, though, is a lot more than luck. Good coaching is the key.*

Herb: *But that can only go so far. Eventually, it's up to the player to perform.*

That afternoon, Brady asked Ross for a ride back home to pack his things for a move into an Athens hotel for as long as necessary. Between visits to Beth, he'd drop in on Flaps—the man with the biggest ears he had ever seen—at his baseball card shop downtown. Brady had asked Flaps after they got to know each other how he felt about his nickname.

"Beats what I heard when I was a kid," he said. "Back then, everybody called me 'Dumbo.'"

But dumb he was not. Flaps was from Macon and had attended many minor league games there as a kid. One of the players who had come through on the way to the Majors was Andy Pafko. That was during another war—World War II—and so was a little ahead of Flaps' time, but, after Brady became a customer, Flaps made it a point to bone up on the life and times of Andy Pafko and could now discuss both at length and in detail.

"Didn't play night games in Savannah back then," Flaps would tell a fascinated Brady, "'cuz of the blackout. Didn't want to help any of them German subs off shore."

Flaps had also become an unlikely banker for Brady, loaning him money against certain cards in his collection, with a careful eye for those players for whom Brady had a real attachment and would want back, versus those in whom he had no emotional investment. Flaps had tried to get Brady interested in buying the cards of current players, but found that his customer's clock stopped in 1962, the year the Braves left Milwaukee for Atlanta.

When Brady arrived back home in Midian, there was a young woman waiting for him on the front porch who identified herself as Tammy Davis, a reporter for The Midian Monitor, in search of Beth's story. Though Brady was usually wary of saying anything for publication, he was now quite happy to share the bulletin that Beth had made it through the worst of it and appeared on her way toward recovery.

"Oh, that's *such* good news," Tammy said. "From the looks of the way that car hit the tree over on Fremont Street, a lot of people were thinking it would be much worse."

"Fremont Street?" Brady asked, knowing that wasn't on Beth's regular route. "Did you say, 'Fremont Street?'"

"Yes, sir. The police are saying the car veered off after it hit Mrs. Greer, then plowed into a tree."

The paper wanted a picture of Beth, so Brady reached for the door to get one, when he noticed a fancy tin box at his feet. Bending to pick it up, he pulled off the card taped to the top. "Brady," it read, "I'm so sorry. Gina." He was puzzled at first, but only for a moment. The only "Gina" he could recall was Gina Garrison, a divorced realtor in town whom he barely knew. What had she heard? That Beth didn't make it? He knew realtors could be pushy, but...Jeez! He opened the tin just long enough to identify its contents.

"You like chocolate chip?" he asked Tammy.

"Oh, *yes*," she said. "That's my favorite!"

Handing her the tin, he said, "Here. They're all yours. Enjoy," and disappeared into the house.

In the 10 days that followed, it seemed to Brady as though his life was on roller skates. The first thing he brought Beth was the arrangement of Philaenopsis from their kitchen, thinking it might now be more welcomed. He quickly settled into his new routine, which began with an early morning visit to the hospital, followed by an attempt to track the opening hour of trading on the financial markets as closely as possible by phone. Then it was more time with Beth, discussing whether to delay or proceed with listing the house. She was now adamant that they put it on the market as soon as possible with a local realtor. Brady returned to be with his wife and her visitors in the afternoon and stayed through dinner before heading back to his hotel.

Beth's homecoming return to Midan was a big event, with neighbors gathered 'round to applaud as Brady wheeled her onto the porch, past the giant "Welcome Home!" banner and into the house, where Melanie had supervised a special buffet lunch unattended by the guest of honor, who remained in her room, gazing out the rear window toward the rose garden. All the action was covered by Tammy and featured prominently in The Monitor.

In an odd way, the weeks that followed were happy ones for Brady. The warp speed usually enjoyed by his wife was now downshifted into the first gear befitting a wheelchair. She had no choice but to smell the flowers and did so...reluctantly. She often asked Brady to park her in the back yard, which he assumed was so she could admire the roses and appreciate—for the first time, really—the beauty she had crafted to enhance the home's appeal to prospective buyers.

In truth, Beth was coming down with an acute case of cabin fever. With the time to sit and think about her confinement, she became increasingly irritated and would bark orders to Brady. Meanwhile, his agitation grew as decisions regarding the house suddenly fell to him during one of her lengthy naps. Several times, he attempted to take initiative without consulting Beth. When she found out, she roared her objection.

When they were not at odds over various details, Brady and Beth spent time together engaging in actual conversation, instead of the sentence fragments and grunts that had previously been the norm. Beth found herself asking about his day at the depot, then listening as Brady recounted what had happened in the market a few hours earlier. This was new to them both, since prior discussions had usually centered on Beth, the house or what Beth was doing to the house.

It was after one of these talks that Brady turned the conversation back toward his wife.

"Honey, the police report said that car hit you over on Fremont Street."

"So?"

"Well, you never used to run over on that side of town…"

"I don't run there--or *didn't* run there--all the time," she said, shifting in her chair. "It got boring running the same route all the time, so I'd change it some. What's the matter? Got something against the people over there?"

"Oh, no," Brady said quickly. "Not at all. I just never knew you were running there, that's all."

Neighbors came and went frequently from the Reynolds house, as Midian again proved it deserved its reputation as a town that rallied around those in need. Ross and Melanie were stalwarts; Brady knew he would never be able to thank them enough. Lester Sloat would show up once a week with either sliced pork or ribs adorned with his homemade barbecue sauce, in which he took great pride. As a lubricant for the social machinery in a rural Southern town, a good barbecue sauce was second in importance only to a tumbler of Jack Daniels. This sauce was from the Sloat family recipe, conceived shortly before The War, then passed down lovingly from one generation to the next.

The only problem here was that Beth hated barbecue sauce and the mess that often resulted from eating it. So, each week, Brady would thank Lester profusely for his thoughtfulness, wolf down as much of it as he could, then feed the remainder to Louie. This went on for three weeks, until the resulting methane emissions from the dog grew so pungent they made the house virtually uninhabitable, so Brady convinced Lester he and Beth were ready to resume their own cooking.

Other visitors included the workmen and subcontractors who had been with Beth through several projects. While they had a clear economic interest in encouraging her to return to the renovation business, Brady was struck by the sincerity of their support for her. They would frequently stop by, either for a cup of coffee early in the morning or a Coke later in the afternoon, to keep her current on developments in the latest renovation projects around town. The new arrivals from Atlanta were constantly trying to one-up each other with costly upgrades. Local craftsmen often paused to laugh at them behind their backs before cashing their checks.

One of the Greer's frequent visitors was Rex, the mason they had used on the Reynolds House. He was a quiet guy, in his mid-30s, and Brady was intrigued, because there always seemed to be something new to be learned about Rex.

He had one glorious year as a high school pitcher up in Athens. Threw a fast ball in the mid-80s and was able to mix it up well enough with his change-up to lead his team to the state championship game, where he threw a no-hitter through nine, but his teammates couldn't get him any runs, so the game and the title slipped away in the 10th. The Braves gave him a minor league contract after that, but his arm went dead the following year. Rex knocked around the minors for another season, but couldn't get anybody out, so he finally said good-bye to his dream of pitching in the Majors, came home and took up masonry.

"The guy was a legend," Flaps told Brady, "just from that one year. Unhittable. But that isn't what people remember most."

"What is?"

"Well," Flaps said, "the guy had an attitude, you know? Not a bad attitude; nothing like that. Just a certain look about him, a focus. He'd pick that resin bag up just before each batter stepped into the box, then slam it into the dirt and stare in for the sign from the catcher. The hitters looked like they knew they were headed back to the bench. It was just a matter of how they got there.

Skeeter: *I hope Brady's takin' notes here. There are ways to beat a guy before he even picks up his bat.*

Herb: *Get in his head, he's as good as dead. Brady's a smart boy, he can figure that out.*

"Guys used to call him, 'Ice,'" Flaps said.

"Ice?"

"Yup. And the hell of it is he's made himself into a pretty good mason, even though he never has to work another day in his life."

"What do you mean?"

"Family's loaded; Dad's one of the richest men in Athens."

"And the kid's laying bricks?"

"That's not all he's layin', from what I hear. He's cool with the women, too. A real magnet. They can't get enough of that strong, silent type, I guess."

"A rebel with a trowel, eh? Did he ever get married? Don't guys like that knock up the beauty queen and have a house full of kids?"

"Oh, he had his beauty queen," Flaps said. "Him and Heather Wilson. They were real tight...'til he lost his stuff. Then she disappeared. Now she's got her house full of kids, but it's with some big shot lawyer in Atlanta."

Rex remained a man of few words and they were well-chosen. Though his formal education was limited, he was a student of various antebellum architectural styles and could discuss them in detail and at length, when necessary. Brady, of course, tried on several occasions to coax out Rex's opinions about The National Pastime, but was gently rebuffed on each occasion. When Brady persisted one day, Rex finally stared at him intently and said, "Look, I'm beyond baseball, okay?" and that had closed the matter—for the mason, but not for Brady. *Beyond baseball? Turn your back on your little kid? Why would someone willingly do that?*

Rex's most impressive physical feature was his abs, which he enjoyed displaying on hot days by removing his shirt. They looked to Brady like the base of a chimney, with each brick perfectly placed. *I must have had abs like that myself once,* he thought. *I just can't remember exactly when...*

Brady enjoyed having Rex around, because his restoration discussions with Beth seemed to take her mind off her physical condition, if only briefly. The doc said she was healing nicely and should be out of her wheelchair soon, but the pain from all those broken bones was bound to linger a good deal longer.

In the meantime, as Beth's condition improved, Brady had the opportunity to focus on his work, spending time at the depot, trying to convince his clients that it was okay now to broaden out from their core holding of "Co-Cola" to other well-known Georgia names like Home Depot, Georgia-Pacific and Fuqua Industries. Brady had decided several years before that a broker could extend his "go-with-what-you-know" strategy beyond his favorite soft drink, as long as the other companies included were still familiar and comfortable to his clients.

He had learned this lesson as a new broker while working with a young Atlanta doctor. Brady met with him on three occasions, each time presenting a careful proposal, supported by extensive research, for investing his retirement funds. But the doctor could not make up his mind.

Finally, in exasperation, Brady said. "Look, you grew up in St. Louis, right?"

"Right."

"Well, how do you feel about Ralston-Purina and Anheuser Busch?"

"Oh, *very* good. Those are a couple of great companies."

"Then, let's split your account three ways, using those two and Coke. How does *that* sound."

"Now, I *like* that," the doctor said as a relieved look spread across his face. "I like that a lot! Let's do it."

It struck Brady during his drive back to the office that day that he had just performed an act of financial *ju-jitsu*: taking the emotional energy of his client and giving it back to him in the form of a successful suggestion. In football, they call it the influence block: taking your man in the direction he wants to go. From that day forward, Brady continued to present his own ideas, but always made it a point to hold in reserve an alternative appeal aimed at the heart of his client's comfort zone. He noticed later, during the inevitable market downturns, that clients holding positions in companies previously familiar to them were the ones most likely to ride out the storms without complaint. *"Selling Zen,"* Brady thought with a laugh, *Somebody's going to write a book about that and make a million bucks.*

It only made money, though, when you were able to practice it in front of a lot of people, and that was becoming a chronic problem for Brady. Midian was a very small base from which to operate and he had met all the people there likely to ever do business with him. It was okay to ask current clients for referrals once or twice, but pushing beyond that would start to annoy them.

As a result, the money he and Beth were taking in from renovation projects was more important to their cash flow all the time. He was happy to see her getting more exercise every day, even though it didn't seem to improve her disposition. They were putting that ugly accident farther behind them and getting closer to selling the Reynolds House. Brady thought a new home, a new challenge, was what she needed to start over.

5

A couple of weeks later, they were ready to put the house on the market and Brady figured the day the "For Sale" sign was planted in the front yard was cause for celebration, so he arrived home from work that evening armed for the occasion: a bottle of '88 Krug--good champagne, for a change--some jumbo shrimp, the best duck liver *fois gras* he could find in Athens and a dozen red roses. All he needed to complete the picture was Beth, but she wasn't there. Brady placed his packages on the kitchen counter and saw instead an envelope with his name scrawled on it, written in her hand.

Brady—

What I have to say to you will be hard to take and every bit as hard to say--so hard that I couldn't possibly tell you personally.

Selling the house is going to be sort of like closing a chapter in our lives. I think it's also the time to make a clean break—as clean a break as we can—and move on with our lives in our own way, apart from each other, writing our own chapters. The house will sell—soon, hopefully—and we would be relocating, anyway. We'll just be doing it separately, that's all.

Brady, you were terrific after my accident and I really do appreciate all you did for me. When you get that close to losing your life, you can't help but do a lot of thinking. It changes you in ways someone who hasn't experienced it can't understand. That's what's happened to me. I want a different life now.

There's only one pain I can spare you and that's hearing a story for the first time from the Midian rumor mill, so I'll tell you here: I won't be in Midian when you read this. When I return, I'll be staying with Rex.

    Beth

Still grasping the letter in his left hand, Brady lowered it to his side and stood at the kitchen counter, slack-jawed, for the longest minute of his life. His first coherent thought was not of what she had done to him, but what she was doing with…Rex?

Suddenly, he threw the letter into the sink and reached for the Midian phone book. Flipping through the pages, he noticed for the first time Rex's address on Fremont Street. On the tenth ring, the recording kicked in.

"You son of a *bitch!*" Brady screamed into the earpiece. "YOU SON OF A *BITCH!*" He stood there, staring at the receiver for a long moment before slamming it back into its cradle. What else was there to say? What was he going to do? Threaten to tell his parents? Pitiful, is what that was, and pitiful was how he felt. A real man would confront his rival and have it out with him, man-to-man, but Beth's note made it clear she and Rex had fled the city, probably planning to stay on the lam until the loose tongues around town tired of wagging about this and started clucking about the next sensation.

Brady's mind darted in different directions, aided by one shot of Jack Daniels, then another. Finally, he moved uncertainly toward the back hall closet. Opening the door, he groped through the dark. *It's here…I know it's here…a-HA!* His right hand slipped around the handle of his favorite bat: the 36-inch, 33-ounce H4 Louisville Slugger preferred by Joe Adcock when the old Milwaukee first baseman menaced National League pitchers while becoming the only player ever to hit a home run over the double-decked, left field stands in Ebbets Field.

After stopping back at the kitchen table for another shot of Jack, Brady began tapping the bat on the carpet, like a cane, as he thumped his way up the stairs to the master bedroom and stood facing Beth's dresser. Turning sideways, he stared intently at the mirror above it as he cocked his bat, waiting for a pitch that only he could see. Timing his swing carefully, Brady launched his lumber, the milled northern white ash, from his right shoulder…WHAM! Shards of mirrored glass went flying in every direction. *Extra bases. Gotta be.*

After opening his eyes to admire the destruction before him, Brady noticed the basket of potpourri, which now included cut glass, and nodded approvingly. *Always hated that stuff. It's…edgier now. Might learn to like it.*

He turned and headed toward the stairs to the front hall. *Bottom of the ninth, bases juiced. Full count, so he's comin' to me*…WHAM! Another mirror unsafe at home. *That felt good! Probably cleared the bases there.* Then, it was on to the kitchen, site of the mirror that amazed him most. *Over the sink? Who ever heard of putting a mirror over the kitchen sink?* Brady gave that one two swings, to be sure he completed the job. In a matter of minutes, every mirror in which Beth had ever admired herself was shattered into scores of jagged glass.

Skeeter: *You know…and you can't help but notice this…his form is excellent: good extension, head down, eyes fixed on the…uh…ball…*

Herb: *That's great, Skeets, except the 'ball' here isn't moving…and, when you take out a mirror, you lose the reflection but not the need to reflect.*

Brady's tour ended in the powder room near the front door, where tight quarters demanded a compact swing, one that left three chunks of mirror remaining. As he gazed at them, Brady was startled to see his disjointed, Cubist reflection returned to him as a poor Picasso imitation. Confronted by this crazy image, he backed out of the little room, set his bat down by the Beachwood coat rack in the front hall and retreated to the kitchen.

A moment later, he was reaching again for the telephone, suddenly in need of a conversation with someone, anyone who would verify that he hadn't lost his mind completely. It surprised

44

him that he was about to dial Irma's number. She would understand. Brady trusted her. She knew what it was like to keep a marriage together through adversity and she knew Beth well. Irma would be an excellent sounding board. Best of all, she would offer insight without judgment.

But there was no answer. Brady lightly returned the phone to its cradle, having lost his zeal for taping messages. He sank back into his chair, trying to make sense of all that was suddenly broken in his life. Glancing at the bottle of Jack, he pushed it away. A moment later, he returned to the sink to retrieve Beth's note and, as the last rays of sunlight shimmered over Midian, headed out the front door in search of solace down the street at Ross and Mel's.

"Brady?" Ross said as he opened his front door. "Good lord, man, what *happened* to you? You look *terrible!*"

"Some bad luck, neighbor," he said, "at least seven years of it. I need to come in and tell you about it."

"Uh…sure," Ross said, opening the door wider, "sure, Brady. C'mon in."

Melanie made a fresh pot of coffee and joined them around the kitchen table. When she and Ross finished reading the note, they looked up, speechless. Brady quickly filled the void as a torrent of words gushed forth: "…out of left field on me here…haven't been arguing…okay, here and there…not really fighting…just got done working together...made it through a rough patch…now, *this*?" He pounded his fist on the table. "Something's wrong, let's *fix* it. That's what married people are *supposed* to do." He suddenly looked up to see Ross and Melanie exchanging nervous glances.

"Wait a minute," Brady said, suddenly upright. "Did you two *know* about this?"

"No," Melanie said quickly. "Nobody could have dreamed it was anything serious…but there was, you know, talk…"

"What *kind* of talk," Brady asked acidly.

"It's just the way Midian *is*," Melanie replied.

"Brady *knows* that, honey," Ross interjected helpfully. "Hell, gossip's a bigger industry here than tourism."

"The two of them were just spending a lot of, you know, time together, that's all," she said. "Doesn't take much more than that to get the tongues wagging in this town."

Brady was sure those tongues would soon be in overdrive wherever people gathered throughout Midian. He could almost hear the whispers as various gossips took the latest rumor out for a spin. One version of the tale ascribed Beth's behavior to brain damage, another said the affair had been going on well before her accident. There were no children in the marriage. Was that a problem? Then there was the drinking…

No one knew the truth except Beth and Rex and they stayed out of sight.

Brady did not have that luxury and headed for the depot, not sure what he would find there. He spoke with several clients, straining for any hint of recognition about what had happened the night before, but there was none. It settled into a routine morning at the office, until about 11 o'clock, when Irma walked in. She was forcing a smile, though not bothering to make any small talk. Pulling a chair up close to Brady's desk, she put down her purse and looked him in the eye.

"I heard the news," is all she said. "How are you doing?"

"It's good to see you," Brady said with a sigh. "You're the first person today who's been willing to face me about what I suspect everybody else is talking about behind my back."

"How you holding up?"

"Still in shock. I just got blind-sided. How about you," he added, eyeing her intently. "Did *you* see this coming?"

"No," she answered immediately, leaning back in her chair. "Can't say as I did. Never thought about it much, but I didn't figure Beth for the type that would…"

"Run off with her mason."

"Right."

"But you *did* hear the talk, right?"

"Brady, sometimes that's *all* you hear in this town," she said. "People with no excitement in their own lives love to prattle on about everyone else, whether or not there's anything to it."

Looking out the window toward the train track, he said quietly, "Well, I wish there was less excitement in my own life right about now, that's for sure."

"How do you feel about it right this minute?" Irma asked gently. "If you could get her back, would you want her?"

After staring a moment into a corner of his ceiling, Brady turned to Irma and said, "My instinct is to say, 'Yes! Absolutely.' But I know what I really want is to turn back the clock and have things the way they were—or the way I *thought* they were—24 hours ago. But she's not the woman I thought she was and we didn't have the marriage I thought we did. Now that I know she's capable of running off with some young stud...I don't know..."

Stung by his own description of Rex, Brady sat quietly for a moment, then continued.

"She just isn't thinking clearly, that's all. It's all so...rash, so sudden. The only thing that would make me feel better about this, if that's possible," he said, looking hopefully at Irma, "would be for someone she trusts to try to talk some sense into her."

Irma exhaled and pursed her lips. "I don't know," she said. "I really *would* like to help, but, you have to understand, it would be a long shot."

"And who better to gamble with than an expert gambler?"

"Okay," she said, rising to go. "I'll see if she'll talk to me, but no guarantees, hear?"

"None whatsoever," Brady said as he escorted her to the door.

Seeing Irma always made Brady feel better and never more so than today. She was a straight shooter who could read people whether or not they were sitting at a poker table. Irma had managed somehow to become an influential and respected presence in town, without succumbing to the superficial gentility that characterized so many of its relationships. There were times when people didn't like what she had to say, but her takes were usually on target and always worth considering.

It was time for lunch and Brady had no stomach for the prospect of people whispering around him as he made his way through downtown Midian, so he decided this was the perfect time to take a ride in the country--beyond all the poultry houses, cotton fields and peach orchards--out to Scofield, home of Gator Hater's Bar-B-Cue. Gator's was the best barbecue Brady had ever tasted, but that wasn't the attraction at the moment. The appeal today was that sports was almost always the topic of conversation there. Regardless of the season, you could find at least two or three people ready to tell you why Georgia Bulldogs were simply superior to

Florida Gators, genetically and in every other respect.

Brady's most indelible impression of Gator's had come the day the O.J. Simpson verdict came in. All eyes were on the TV as the picture switched from SportsCenter to CNN. When it was announced that O.J. was off the hook, there were gasps around the room, then a moment of silence as the camera panned from victors to vanquished, then back again. Finally, one of the regulars spoke as SportsCenter resumed:

"He may be a sumbitch, but he was one *fast* sumbitch. Damn! That boy could *run!*"

With that, the genial buzz of conversation resumed, pausing momentarily on the gridiron exploits of O.J. Simpson--impressive, but not enough to eclipse the sainted Georgia hero, Herschel Walker--before returning to the main topic of year-round concern at Gator's: college football in the Southeastern Conference. Brady was confident that here his personal issues would not displace the Bulldogs' upcoming season as the hot topic of talk. Entering the shack through its weathered screen door, he nodded toward a couple of familiar faces, who briefly returned the gesture before resuming their conversations.

Skeeter: *This isn't a restaurant, it's paradise! A world where the worries outside don't intrude. All sports, all the time. Wow! If a story doesn't make it to ESPN, they basically don't know it happened. How great is that?*

Herb: *Easy, Skeets. That's not paradise we're looking at here, more like childhood. Most people get through it, but some folks pull up a chair, then don't know when to leave. You got to get up and go eventually. Longer you wait, the harder it is.*

Brady didn't need memories of O.J. to trigger thoughts of revenge. They were already there. *What would happen if I surprised them in their love nest and shot them both? Isn't the law sympathetic to that? How about a duel? That's it! I could challenge Rex to a duel for Beth's hand! That's chivalrous, no doubt, but he'd get to choose weapons. With my luck, it'd be baseballs and he'd drill me right between the eyes before I'd finished my wind-up.*

"Brady? Brady, where *are* you?"

He snapped out of his reverie with a "Huh?" and turned his head to see Gina, the realtor, standing beside his table.

"I'm not sure where you were just now," she said with a smile, "but it wasn't Scofield. Another solar system, maybe? Mind if I sit down?"

"Uh…no, not at all. Please, have a seat. I've just been…under some stress lately and was doing a little daydreaming there. What are you doing here? You don't strike me as the type who would be a Gator Hater regular."

"I'm not," she said. "More of an irregular, you might say. I just listed a farm near here and thought I'd stop by for a quick sandwich. Say, did you ever get those cookies I left for you?"

"Yes, yes I sure did. Very tasty. Been meaning to send you a note about that, but, well…it's been hectic…"

"Yes," she said, placing her hand lightly on top of his, "so I've heard. If you ever want to, you know, talk about anything, just give me a call. I'm a very good listener."

"That's…very thoughtful of you," he said, with a vacant smile as he carefully withdrew his hand. "I'll sure keep that in mind."

A few minutes later, Brady was back in his car, headed toward Midian, with a new fantasy to ponder. *What if I suddenly found my own squeeze? Would that make Beth jealous enough to change anything? Would it make the break-up look more mutual?*

No. It would be, he concluded with reluctance, the same sort of artifice he had criticized in others. If he was, indeed, now newly single, a relationship was bound to develop sooner or later. If it was natural, fine. But he wasn't going to force it just to spite Beth or for any other lame reason.

His afternoon back at the depot was consumed by the preparation of various reports for the home office. This was a time of the month he usually dreaded, but he found himself welcoming it now, because it required enough concentration to take his mind off Beth, if only briefly.

Glancing at his clock, he saw that 4:45 had arrived before he knew it. As he started to think about straightening his desk up and calling it a day, the door opened slowly and in walked Irma, with a bottle of Jack Daniels and a couple of cups.

"Irma! What's going on? Don't tell me we have something to *celebrate*?"

"No," she said thoughtfully, setting the cups and bottle on

Brady's desk, "that's not the first word that comes to mind..."

"Did you see her? Did you talk to her?"

"No, I didn't see her and I didn't talk to her."

Brady sank back into his chair. "Then, what's *happening* here? I don't get it."

"Brady, I'm going to tell you something and I want you to listen carefully, okay?"

"Sure, go ahead."

"Good. There's been a lot of pain and suffering in the South. Some people say that's what gives it much of its charm. I don't know if I'd go that far, but people here seem to sometimes get knocked down by life more than other folks. If they can figure out how to bounce back, then the locals can...I don't know...empathize with them better."

"And what does all that have to do with me?"

"Well, you're a Yankee. When you were younger, nobody here knew you or the bumps you got along the way that made you the man you are today. This is farm country, where people like to see calluses on your hands—and your life—and know how they got there."

"Oh, I get it," he said. "When your wife takes off, you get a Merit Badge, like in the Boy Scouts?"

"Brady, I believe I do detect some sarcasm creeping into your voice..."

"It's not creeping in, Irma. It sprinted in and it might stay a while."

"Have a drink," she said cheerfully. "Here's to the rest of your life!"

The warmth of the bourbon sliding down Brady's throat suddenly put him in a more relaxed state of mind. "So," he said, "Beth gave me a callous last night and that was my initiation into Club Midian. Is that it?"

"Well, actually, she gave you two," Irma said, pouring him another drink.

"What do you mean, *two*?"

"Well...I didn't speak directly with Beth today, but I did do some checking around. My sources are very good, you know," she said proudly.

"And?"

"First, another drink," she said, raising her glass. After both tumblers were emptied, Brady repeated his request.

"And what did you find out?"

"I found out," Irma said, "that Beth is pregnant and she thinks Rex is the father."

6

How many ways can Beth taunt me? Brady wondered as he pulled into his driveway and immediately experienced a feeling of detachment. He thought he knew the residents here well, but these new people were quite different. The lady--*the harlot*--of the house was a stranger who had disappeared. And the man? Well, he was gone as well, never to return. In his place was a body appearing similar outwardly, but hollow within, certainly devoid of feelings for this building. The house now stood there--had it ever been a home?--stood there simply as an improvement on a lot that Brady wanted to be rid of as quickly as possible.

Checking his phone messages, he heard a series of hang-ups and assumed the telemarketers were again pursuing him for various products he didn't need. Finally, this:

"Brady, I don't know where you are, but we need to talk."

Beth? *Beth*? She hadn't inflicted *enough* pain and now wanted him to take some *more*? Brady walked away from the phone and tried to busy himself, picking up around the house and taking out the garbage, but it was no use. He sat down, began to dial, then returned the phone to its cradle. He could think of nothing--nothing civil--to say to Beth, so what was the point?

After staring at the phone for a couple of minutes, he picked it up again and dialed another number.

"Brady! I'm so glad you called!" Melanie said. "We haven't seen you lately. Are you okay?"

"I'm fine," Brady lied. "Look, I've got a message here from Beth and I thought you might be able to see her and relay one back for me."

"Okay...I'll try..."

"You can tell her I don't want to talk to her. If she wants to communicate, she can write me a letter, okay? Have you got that?"

"Aren't you...even going to talk...about selling the house?" Melanie asked carefully. "Don't you want to talk about *that*?"

"Business deals are done in writing all the time," Brady said as coldly as he could. "In fact, they're all reduced to writing sooner or later."

After hanging up the phone, Brady turned to his old friend, Jack Daniels, to calm his jangled nerves. Picking up a bottle, a glass and his baseball card album, he decided to enjoy them on the back steps under a full moon.

Brady was a card collector long before they became a hot commodity, with prices bid up to ridiculous levels. It annoyed him to think that people would buy cards merely in hopes of turning a profit. His collection was much more than just a cold asset. He could open his binder, turn the pages and immediately bask in the warmth of the summer of '57. That was the best year ever for the Milwaukee Braves and, quite possibly, for the City of Milwaukee. It had earned its reputation as a great baseball town many years before through its strong support of the old Milwaukee Brewers, a AAA team owned at one time by Bill Veeck. In 1953, the Braves were lured from Boston and, just four years later, brought a National League pennant to their new home, followed by a World Series victory over the New York Yankees.

That year might also have been the high water mark in Brady's difficult relationship with his father. Harry Greer was able to get just a single ticket to the '57 World Series and, aware of his son's passion for the Braves, gave it to Brady. Now Harry, a widower for seven years, was zipping around the Gulf Coast of Florida in his golf cart. The two had spoken by phone more often than usual in the past year or so and Brady remained hopeful that, somehow, they would finally sit down together and really get to know each other, perhaps on his next trip to Florida.

The cards of the big stars—Warren Spahn, Eddie Mathews and young Henry Aaron—commanded the highest prices these days, but it was the characters that made Brady smile: Johnny Logan, the feisty shortstop; Hurricane Bob Hazel, the rookie sensation who hit over .400 after being called up in the last half of the '57 season, but got cut the following spring; and, of course, Andy Pafko.

Warmed by both the bourbon and his memories, Brady sat there on his back step, smiling wistfully in the moonlight, until he felt himself caught suddenly in a wave of sadness that puzzled him at first by its intensity. *C'mon, get a grip! These are just pictures, pictures pasted on little cardboard cards!* In just a few moments, though, he realized fully what he had only admitted casually before: This was an album of his youth, each picture becoming its own time machine, transporting him back to bases where he was always safe.

Brady had several other photo albums--covering everything from the day he was born through high school, college and married life with Beth--yet he rarely looked at them. Why? He wasn't sure. Maybe it was the result of a trip he had taken to the Taos Pueblo in his 20s, which helped him appreciate John Prine's observation that, "Every time he clicks his Kodak pics, he steals a little bit of soul."

The actual pictures weren't as important to him as the memories they triggered. Wally Moon, for instance. Looking at the old first baseman reminded Brady of the night he and his Dad sat in County Stadium during a rain delay, waiting for a game with the Cardinals to resume. Conversation is all you've got to fill the void then, as announcers sometimes find to their discomfort.

"You know," Harry had said after a sip of his beer while they both watched the ground crew wrestle with the giant tarp during one of those breaks in the action, "this reminds me of when my Dad would take me to Fenway when I was growing up in New Hampshire." Then, without a hint of irony, he added, "Seems as though we had some of our best conversations then."

"What did you talk about?" Brady asked.

"Let's see…he would talk about his Dad a lot. His Dad—my Grandpa—loved to fish, so they would spend a lot of time in a boat together."

"What did they talk about?"

"Oh, I don't think they talked much. Grandpa said it would scare the fish."

"How're things at work?" Brady would ask tentatively, trying to keep the conversation on comfortable ground for his father.

"Oh, things are fine, fine," was usually all he would get out of Harry, choosing not to delve into the complexities of foundry supplies with his young son. Harry would then change the subject to the weather, or back to the Braves, but the topic never turned to Brady, who remembered that now very clearly.

Looking back at the album, he noticed Harvey Haddix. Brady was listening to Earl Gillespie and Blaine Walsh on his Zenith Royal transistor radio—under the covers, after his bedtime—the night the Braves won in Pittsburgh, even though the Pirates' Haddix threw a no-hitter through nine innings. Brady managed to yell and scream in whispers through that one and the thought of it made him laugh now, realizing it was the most fun he ever had in bed...until his junior year of college.

Every player in the album connected Brady to a time when he was a young man of promise and potential. There is a window of opportunity to deliver on that promise. It closes early for a young ballplayer--later for an old stockbroker--but close it must. Brady's way to keep it open was to revisit often the days of his youth, in hopes of staying connected to his promise long enough to allow himself to score, even if that did turn out to be in the ninth inning.

Skeeter: *Here's a guy who really knows how to throw a pity party. I mean, if you're gonna do it, you gotta get right in there and wallow...and he's very good at it. I admire that.*

Herb: *...and his invited guests are all little pieces of cardboard. Not much risk for animated conversation there. By the way, I like rain delays. Gives us the chance to roll up our sleeves and mine the riches of obscure baseball lore.*

Skeeter: *Right, you are. True fans know today's game was built on generations of trivia and we're here to remind them it's a foundation that's rock solid.*

As Brady sat there on the steps, splashing a little more Jack on the rocks and trying to beat the blues, a musical interlude arrived, provided by the plaintive wail of a whistle from an approaching freight train almost a mile away, but cutting clearly through the muggy Georgia night. It was a sound that had become imbedded in the fabric of Midian life for over 150 years, to the point where it received little notice and almost no comment. Every once in a while, though, Brady caught himself cocking his ear in appreciation of those whistles that beckoned him back to simpler times when life seemed more black-and-white and not infused with the abundance of contemporary gray.

Even though he heard those whistles easily and frequently from his depot office, Brady found he enjoyed them most from a distance late in the evening or early in the morning, times when Midian was otherwise as quiet as a field of cotton. The sharp bursts from an approaching train announced its arrival, while also heralding its departure as the engine of commerce in the rural South.

After the train had cleared the city limits, heading for Augusta, Brady wiped his eyes on his sleeve and started laughing over his sudden descent into melancholy. *Why not go all the way?* He ran up the stairs to the master bathroom and searched the drawers and medicine cabinet. *Where was that stuff? ... Aha!* Grabbing the plastic bottle, he returned to the back steps, shook some talcum powder onto his hands and arms, rubbed it in, curled up on the stoop, laid his head on his baseball card album and closed his eyes, a smile crossing his face as he drifted off to sleep.

He awoke the following morning to the sound of lawn mowers, the sight of an open bottle of Jack Daniels and a throbbing headache. There was a time, before Beth, when Brady could drink with anyone and was proud of it. The trick was to hold your liquor in public and your hangover in private, when the harsh light of a new day seemed to demand a forensic examination of the night before. The result was often guilt about something said or done, large or small.

But guilt would not be a part of Brady's new day. This time, as his mind replayed the events of the previous night, he felt instead a sense of satisfaction. Beth's accident, followed by her departure, had made Brady tighter than a sailor's knot. Now, his little toot loosened that steady strain and reminded him that yielding to sleep at odd hours in odd places was one of his old bachelor habits now making an encore. Brady's new status also sparked an interest in self-improvement which, it occurred to him, he could activate by building on a highlight from his youth to finally establish a good relationship with his father.

While Brady clung to the hunting memory of bagging his solitary buck, he was painfully aware that the more typical outdoor adventures were highlighted by his oversleeping, misplacing gear, burning the food and generally making himself an outdoor pariah. There was still plenty of time before hunting season, Brady decided, to push himself to learn how to handle a shotgun well enough to force admiration from his father after all these years. Of all the people he knew in Midian, Scratch immediately came to mind as the perfect teacher.

Scratch had earned his nickname through unfortunate and persistent habit. His long days in the field produced numerous bug and insect bites requiring immediate attention. His spindly arms could reach most of his body quickly and with little effort.

In budget-conscious Munson County, Scratch doubled as both deputy sheriff and animal control officer, where his duties consisted primarily of disabling wild dogs and other pests with tranquilizer darts from his modified shotgun. Scratch took considerable pride in his reputation as the finest shot in Munson County. It took no prodding for him to agree to conduct a special seminar for Brady.

"First thing to cover, I guess, is the kind of gun you want to use," Scratch said the following Saturday morning as the two of them stood in a field in rural Scofield, about 12 miles from downtown Midian.

"You mean 'weapon,' don't you?" Brady offered helpfully.

"You been watchin' too many movies," Scratch said, shaking his head. "This here's a gun, a Remington 870TA, to be exact. Now, if those clay targets we'll be aimin' at start shootin' back, then we got ourselves a weapon."

"Any particular reason you chose that gun?"

"No, not really. It chose me, I guess. My Daddy gave it to me about 20 years ago, when I was a teenager. Been real reliable, hardly ever needs any repairs, and about the most popular pump action gun there is. Haven't shot clays with it for years. Mostly use it for waterfowl, like mallards and Canada geese."

"What do I need to know to get comfortable with it?"

"Well, when you're shootin' trap, you need to know where the first target is goin' to come from and where it wants to go. Once you know that, you can shoot the targets much faster, without missin' 'em, because you can hold a bit higher and pre-plan your attack. When you're able to shoot the first clay faster, the second one becomes easier, because it's closer to you, makin' it simpler to see and point. After you get the first target, let your eyes go to the second one immediately, while your gun follows your eyes a second or so later. What you're trying to do is make the move to the second target a controlled move, rather than a lunge in that general direction."

"Is all that going to make me a better hunter?" Brady asked. "Don't forget, that's what I'm aiming for here."

Scratch lowered his gun and shook his head slowly from side to side at his impatient pupil. "If we can get you to the point where you start blastin' these clays real regular, you'll be plenty confident out in the field and be able to hunt with anybody.

"Now," he continued, returning to his lesson, "two things you want to avoid are shootin' the first clay too slow and the second one too fast, which would cause the gun to be out of control as it moves to the second target. If you can get your gun and your eyes to move to the second one at the same speed, your gun won't likely be out of control, so you have a better chance of breakin' the target."

"That all sounds good, Scratch. Let's see you put it in action."

Scratch grunted and called out down the meadow, "Leland! You ready?"

Slowly, from some underbrush in the distance, emerged a blonde head belonging to a boy who could not have been more than 12 or 13 years old. He waved back at the men.

"That's my nephew," Scratch said. "We ain't too fancy around here. Manual trap just as good as an automatic one, long as the guy runnin' it knows what he's doin'."

"Does he?" Brady asked. "He looks pretty young."

"Oh, he'll be fine," Scratch said with a smile. "He'll be fine." He then motioned for silence, raised his gun and yelled, "*Pull!*"

Immediately, a target launched about 50 yards away. Scratch fired and sent shards of clay in every direction. A moment later, a second target rose through the sky on a different trajectory, but met the same fate. The process was repeated 10 times before Scratch lowered his gun.

"If we were competin'," he said, "we'd be shooting these in groups of 25. But I told Leland to keep it to 10 for now. That okay with you?" Brady nodded.

"Good. Now, it's your turn," he said, handing his Remington to Brady. "Take a minute to get the feel of it. There'll be a little kick you aren't used to. When you shoot, try not to jerk the gun. Just slide it from side to side and aim just ahead of your target."

After a brief pause, Brady nodded, Scratch yelled and Leland released the first clay. Through the gun sight, its speed seemed faster to Brady, who hurriedly pulled the trigger. The ascent of the clay continued, unimpeded, as the recoil knocked him back a couple of feet, jerking the gun barrel skyward. A startled Brady glanced at Scratch just as the second clay took flight.

"*There* it is!" Scratch yelled. "Over *there*! It ain't over *here*!"

Brady braced himself, lowered the gun and got off a shot in the general direction of the disappearing clay.

"Get ready!" Scratch yelled. "Forget about the last shot. Soon as you fire it, start thinking about the next one."

Only the seventh target was destroyed. It was a lucky seventh and Brady knew it. The two friends took turns shooting for the next 30 minutes, with Brady hitting about as many clays as Scratch missed. Finally, Scratch yelled for Leland to hold up. A minute later, he was standing beside his uncle.

"My turn now?" he said to Scratch.

"Yup, it's your turn," Scratch said, turning toward Brady. "I told him I'd pull a few for him if he helped us out." With that, Scratch headed out to take his place at the far end of the meadow, leaving Brady to observe the youngster.

Leland was five feet tall, at most, and couldn't have weighed 100 pounds, but Brady was struck immediately by the boy's air of easy confidence as he cradled the gun in his arm while waiting for his uncle to get settled. It was clear he had spent enough time in the field to become completely comfortable around guns. Brady got the feeling he was witnessing the logical extension of an almost sacred rite passed down from one generation to the next. He was surprised to see that Leland would be using Scratch's gun. *This'll be good. I'll bet that recoil knocks him over.*

A few moments later, Leland raised his uncle's Remington confidently and yelled in a high-pitched voice toward Scratch, "*Pull!*"

A clay bird began its rise, then a shot rang out, shattering the gray disk into dozens of pieces. The boy's shoulders moved only slightly as he prepared for his second shot. It, too, found its target. After 10 shots, Leland could claim five clays, more than the total hit by Brady all morning.

"Where'd you learn to shoot like that?" Brady asked.

"Uncle Scratch and my Daddy," the boy said. "They been shootin' since they was my age. Sort of a family thing, I guess."

"Let me ask you a question," Brady said. "How'd you shoot when you were first starting out?"

"Oh, I was right terrible," the boy replied. "Couldn't hit nothin'. But Daddy and Scratch were patient with me. Kept giving me pep talks. They knew I'd get the hang of it sooner or later and I guess I have.

"Won my first turkey last fall," the boy added with a broad smile.

With that, Leland ran out to meet his uncle, leaving Brady alone with thoughts of a less patient mentor.

Skeeter: *Gotta be careful here. He's moving past the pity part pretty good. Wouldn't want to see him throw it in reverse, now that he's started moving forward again.*

Herb: *Looks to me like he's gonna be okay. He's got a goal and he's working toward it. You play like you practice, so, by the time he's out hunting with his Dad, he should be ready.*

For several Saturdays after that, Scratch, Brady and Leland continued Brady's shooting education. Each week, Brady picked off a couple more clays, though he could never seem to quite catch up to Leland. On their sixth day in the field, Brady had just shot his first target of the day when he noticed a wasp crawling into his shoe. Carefully laying his gun onto the grass, he gently unlaced his sneaker so as not to get stung, removed his shoe, then beat the wasp to death with it, picked up his gun and resumed shooting. In the process, he only missed firing at one target and wound up hitting six of 10.

"Son of a *bitch*! That's concentration!" Scratch said with a smile. "You realize what would have happened just a few weeks ago? Either you would have got that wasp or it would have got you, but you *never* would have gotten back to those clays."

Brady smiled in return and, for the first time, was feeling confident in the field. A few more sessions with Scratch and he would be ready for duck season in Wisconsin...and especially ready for the look on his father's face when Brady coolly squeezed the trigger and bagged his first bird. He was looking forward to sharing his plan the following night in Atlanta over dinner with his sister, who was flying in for an art show there.

Early Sunday morning, Brady followed his custom of swinging by the office for an hour or so to prepare for the coming week. He continued to be amazed at how his planning hour on Sunday made his Mondays much more productive, with that positive momentum often carrying through the week. It reached the point where he felt guilty when he didn't make it over on Sunday, knowing he would be less effective the following day. Before Beth left, Brady would later return home to pick her up in time to attend the Midian Presbyterian Church, a place he avoided now, partly out of embarrassment, but also out of annoyance and disappointment with the silent response of the Church, his Church, to this obvious crisis in his personal life. Broken bodies were something everyone could rally around, but, when lives were broken, this local version of Christianity favored speculating about the causes of the pain over making much effort to comfort the afflicted.

After finishing his task list for the week and prioritizing the first two days, he headed for the door, but was stopped by the sound of his ringing phone. Though his routine here was well known, he seldom received calls on Sunday and was tempted to let his machine take the message. Instead, he instinctively reached for the receiver.

"Hi, Brady, it's Sally," announced his sister. "Didn't get an answer at your house, so thought I'd try you here."

"Hey, what's up!"

"You were going to come over for dinner at 6, right?"

"Right."

"Well, my plane gets in at 1," she said, unusually quiet. "Can you meet me at the airport?"

"Yeah, I guess," he said, glancing at his watch. "What's up? Why the change?"

"I don't really want to go into it now," she said. "I'll see you at 1."

Brady set his phone down with a shrug. There was continual drama in Sally's life, so there was no telling what scrape she had gotten into this time. He wouldn't bother to speculate, knowing she would be laying it all out for him soon enough.

When he met her at Hartsfield, he took one look at Sally's eyes, red and puffy, and suggested they pause for a Bloody Mary. After two long sips of her drink, Sally exhaled slowly, looked up at her brother, then spoke.

"It's about Dad," she said softly.

"Oh, no," Brady said with a flash of recognition, picturing the man who could steamroller feelings without realizing he had even turned on the tractor. "What did he do now? Or should I say, 'What did he say?'"

"He didn't say a *thing*," she said, dabbing her eyes with a handkerchief. "Look, Brady, it happened last night. I wanted to wait until now to tell you personally."

"Tell me *what*?" he said, thrusting his hands out, palms up.

"Dad had a heart attack last night while he was out with friends and…well…"

"Well, what?"

"And now he's gone."

"Gone? *Gone?* Are you saying he's…"

"Dead, Brady. Dad's gone. I didn't hear about it until early this morning, when a neighbor of his tracked me down. I already had a reservation to come up here, so thought I might as well keep it and tell you personally. Then we could go back together."

Sally kept talking, but Brady turned his gaze out the window to the planes taxiing back and forth on the tarmac below. His life always seemed a jigsaw puzzle whose pieces almost fit, but never quite came together. Now, in the midst of his latest attempt to assemble them, Sally had swept everything off the table.

After a lifetime of reaching out to his father, Brady had begun to imagine the distance between the two suddenly closing, but Harry's death now froze the divide forever in its tracks. A private screening of a highlight reel of their lives together began to play in Brady's mind, carefully edited and spliced to show only the good times: family trips, playing catch in the back yard, going to County Stadium to watch the *real* Braves, the ones from Milwaukee. In that way, death can turn surviving cynics optimistic, if only briefly.

But all the bile that had built up over the years could not be so quickly dismissed. It would always be there, bubbling, like molten lava. If it ever erupted, it would recast forever the landscape in its path.

7

Harry Greer had spent the past five years in Florida after a lifetime of avoiding it. During his working years, he had written the state off as nothing but a bunch of sun-drenched hedonists. That view changed when he retired and decided that sun, surf and a little fishing weren't such bad ideas after all.

Still, there was the matter of where to locate. For years, he was fond of saying every Florida town should be called "Ersatz," because they were all phony in some way. Then he discovered Tarpon Springs, a small Greek enclave on the Gulf Coast with real immigrants that gave it, in Harry's view, more substance than the rest of the state. After Brady's mother died, Harry had bought a condo to winter there. In an attempt to fit in, he would make vague allusions to his own Greek heritage when, in fact, an army of genealogists would have difficulty finding it.

It was in Tarpon Springs, while stumbling through one of his own jokes over dinner with friends at Pappas' restaurant, when

Harry suffered a massive heart attack and succumbed, after finishing his scordalia, into a plate of spanakopita.

Thornton Wilder would have loved Harry's graveside service the following weekend. It was a warm and bright June day, everyone sitting erect on row after row of folding chairs. It could have been the *Our Town* set. Instead, it was Philbrick, N.H., an old mill town that was about as close as it gets to Grovers Corners, which served as the setting for the opening and closing chapters of The Harry Greer Story. Brady hadn't seen many of the relatives in years, some he barely remembered at all.

Somewhere behind those faces perhaps the key lay that might unlock the enigma that was Harry Greer. Was it held by his sister, Emily, a spinster secretary at the local phone company who had never left Philbrick? His brother, Ray, who had almost gone broke trying to run the family farm before striking it rich by selling out to developers? After Harry moved away, there had been few family gatherings and he had not spoken to his siblings after the farm was sold. Both Emily and Ray expressed their condolences to Brady, but in doing so left the distinct impression their motivation was nothing more than a sense of duty.

The funeral announcement in <u>The Evening Graphic</u> had also produced two members of the Philbrick High Class of '42, awaiting their 60th reunion. One of them, Spec Stetson, couldn't resist telling Brady his favorite memory of Harry from high school. Young Harry, Spec said, was known for being able to drive his Model A Ford with his knees, so he could wrap both arms around his date. That remained the major insight Brady received about his father's character during his funeral visit.

Upon returning to Florida to begin organizing Harry's estate, Brady was amazed all over again at his father's choice of retirement residence. Worlds of Wonder was a 100-acre geriatric theme park featuring golf, shuffleboard, swimming and table games ranging from cribbage to canasta. Each condo building was topped with a façade connoting a different nation. The Moroccan minaret, Chinese pagoda and Thai wat presented a cacophony of cultures that made any outsider shake his head at its garishness.

"You're forgetting the most important thing," Sally said as she caught Brady's disapproving eye.

"And that is?"

"That the people who live here *love* it--and that included Dad."

"I know, I know," Brady said with a sigh. "It's just that, when you hear the residents call it "WOW," instead of Worlds of Wonder, that's really pushing it, don't you think?"

"You're just a little nervous, that's all."

"Nervous? About what?"

"I saw a couple of those women in the elevator checking you out," she said with a broad smile. "You may be saying, 'Wow!' yourself, in no time."

"There are two chances of that happening," he replied narrowly, "slim and none. So, let's take a break from my retirement plans for a minute and talk about Sally. Is the artist still starving?"

"No, it's not *that* bad," she said, wrinkling up her nose the way their father always did. "Waiting on tables covers the rent and puts enough food in the fridge to get by. I just need a break with the sculpture, one small break. That's all."

"And what are you doing to make that break happen?"

"A couple of galleries have my pieces on consignment. And I've talked to the art critic at the local paper once or twice. But it's been slow going so far."

"Well," said Brady, "at least you haven't thrown yourself into the arms of a Sugar Daddy. I'm proud of you for that."

"Don't think I haven't thought about it," Sally said with a laugh and a flip of her blonde hair.

As they went through Harry's things, Brady got the uncomfortable feeling he was invading his father's privacy, especially when he came across the package of condoms in the nightstand. Dad? The Shuffleboard Stud? He slid them into his own pocket to keep them from Sally's view.

"Come on in here," she called from the bathroom. "Plenty of guy stuff here for you to look at."

"That's okay," he answered quickly. "I'll pass on that."

Brady's eyes had snapped a picture of Harry Greer in a bathroom many years ago and it would always be his most indelible image of his father. It was during a crazy Cinco de Mayo party his parents had put together in the old neighborhood to celebrate the arrival of decent weather in Milwaukee after an especially difficult winter. Harry had managed to come up with some mariachi music and a piñata and the tequila flowed freely.

Everything was traditional except the fireworks. Those went off when Brady, then a sophomore in high school, came home early from a friend's house and ran upstairs to use the bathroom. As he flushed the toilet, he was struck by the notion that he wasn't alone. Taking a hesitant step toward the shower, he pulled back the curtain and saw his father slouched on the shower floor——one hand gripping his drink and the other on the left leg of Mrs. Escobar, who lived two doors away and was his mother's best friend.

"Dad!" was all Brady could say before turning and running out of the room. "Wait!" his father called after him, then, "Oh, *shit*!" as Brady slammed the door.

Harry made an awkward attempt to bring the incident up the next time he was alone with his son a few days later, but Brady just glared at him and left the room. The subject was never raised again.

Brady never figured out exactly what his mother, Rhonda, knew about the incident, but, shortly thereafter, she began to spend most of her time cloistered in the 500-square-foot refuge her husband had built for her off the garage. It was a special kitchen for Rhonda, housing the tools of her trade: a convection oven in which she made her signature wedding cakes, a Wolf range for her to produce her *pate choux* and other cake decorations, and a reach-in cooler big enough to hold three five-tier cakes at once. Rhonda Greer was known throughout the North Shore of Milwaukee for her distinctive cake artistry. She usually delivered her creations several hours before the reception, then departed. But, on those occasions when Rhonda remained as an invited guest, her stony stare stood out like bad acne in the otherwise flawlessly-exuberant wedding photos.

So, there would be no mementos from Harry Greer's bathroom for Brady. Returning to his father's clothes closet, he tried to find something to take along, but quickly concluded he was not ready for white belts and matching shoes.

Skeeter: *Some things in life, you just got to shake off, like a sign from the catcher: You don't like it, shake it off and go on to the next one. Dwell on the bad stuff and you'll never get to the good stuff.*

Herb: *Seems like there ought to be an extra casket at every funeral, to bury the bad stuff. But, it's like George Eliot says,* *"deeds have an indestructible life, both in and out of our consciousness."*

Crossing the room to a window, Brady gazed out across the carefully cropped lawns of Worlds of Wonder to focus on another world, one very far away, where a young boy was tagging along on one of his Dad's sales trips through rural Wisconsin, listening to the Braves on the radio of the old family Ford, a Country Squire, while his dad was inside the building next door on a call. That was the day a rookie named Chuck Tanner stepped up to the plate and hit the first pitch he saw as a Major Leaguer over the fence for a home run. Brady couldn't wait to tell his dad and they celebrated Tanner's hit with a couple of hot fudge sundaes.

A moment later, Brady's mind returned to the real world, where he rejoined his sister, examining various bills and checkbooks, when they came across the key to a safe deposit box at Tarpon Springs Bank & Trust. He and Sally decided to check it out the next morning.

"Do you have any idea what's in there?" Sally asked as her brother placed the box on the table in a private room next to the vault.

"Not a clue," replied Brady, stung again by another reminder of his father never seeking his financial advice.

Harry Greer spent most of his adult life selling foundry supplies as a self-employed manufacturer's representative, working for companies without their own sales force. Harry had mentioned casually that, from time-to-time, he had chosen to take shares of a client company's common stock, instead of cash, for sales services rendered. As Brady and Sally sifted through the contents of the safe deposit box, Brady let out a gasp.

"Son of a *bitch*!" he said in almost a whisper.

"What is it?" Sally asked.

"Look at all these certificates…for…American Wheel Works?"

American Wheel was a sleepy little Sheboygan, Wis., company--until four years ago, when the founder's son took over and cut some major deals with the Big Three automakers, as well as taking full advantage of NAFTA to work with foreign auto plants based in Mexico. As a result, the company's stock had soared and split three times. The 110,000 shares they carefully—gingerly—

removed from the box had a street value, at the current price of $29 each, of about $3.19 million.

Brady let out a long, low whistle. In a dozen years as a stockbroker, he had never paid much attention to American Wheel and had certainly not recommended it to any of his clients. Too obscure; too thinly traded. In a matter of seconds, it had become his favorite company.

Skeeter: *Wow! I do believe our boy's hit himself a grand slam!*

Herb: *No, he got carried around the bases without even swinging his bat...but he ain't won the game yet. Playing with a lead's different than playing catch-up. Some guys never get comfortable making the switch.*

Brady paused for a moment to enjoy the stunned look on Sally's face. Finally, he couldn't resist, saying, "Looks like you've found your Sugar Daddy after all."

As they exited the bank into the balmy Florida morning, Brady peered past the gently swaying palm trees across the parking lot. It was a splendid spring day on the Gulf Coast, with Florida's suffocating summer humidity at least two months away. While pausing to let the welcome scent of citrus enter his nostrils, he saw more clearly than ever before that there were two ways to retire in Florida. About 20 yards to his left, there was a stoop-shouldered, sixtyish man shuffling his feet behind a cart from the nearby supermarket, full of junk discarded by others. Perhaps he could sell enough of it to raise some cash for food.

Off to Brady's right, he caught sight of a Jaguar XK8 convertible, British racing green, pulling into the bank's parking lot. It was driven by a dashing, bronzed, silver-haired man in his 60s, who looked to be arriving straight from the tennis courts at the Tarpon Country Club. Just a few minutes before, Brady was uncomfortably close to pushing his own cart. Suddenly, it looked as though he would be riding in style the rest of the way.

He had always assumed affluence would lighten his own emotional load. Instead, however, Brady's jackpot was weighing him down. Was this his consolation prize as the son who couldn't earn his father's approval? Even a six-figure inheritance couldn't fill that emotional crater.

Tuning in Harry Greer's feelings was like trying to locate a short wave radio station: there, for a moment, then gone. Those glimpses were maddening. What Brady had always wanted more than anything was to know his father as a prelude to knowing himself. Was that possibility now buried? Harry Greer had been successful, but was not one to share openly the details of his life, even with professional advisors. He had always done his own taxes and...wait a minute... what about the death tax here? What effect would it have on Brady's new fortune? The inheritance tax went as high as 55 percent, but surely Harry Greer—a lifelong Republican who labored long hours every April to minimize his taxes—had jumped through the necessary estate planning hoops to avoid giving Uncle Sam a windfall... hadn't he?

A call to Harry's attorney revealed that Harry had only set up a living trust. While that minimized probate expenses, it left every dollar over the exclusion amount exposed to the tax man. So, after Uncle Sam was paid, Brady and Sally were looking at about $800,000 each.

Though Brady was still considerably richer than he had been the previous day, the initial wave of euphoria over his good fortune began to crash against the rocky reality of its tax consequences. *A millionaire! I was a millionaire—for a few hours. Then, bang! Just like that: Half of it disappears!* He soon became agitated about the amount skimmed off the top by the government to the point where he felt he had to confront Harry's lawyer about it.

"We're not even *talking* about sophisticated estate planning here!" Brady yelled over the telephone. "A simple *trust* document would have saved the estate *hundreds* of *thousands* of dollars!"

"You're forgetting one thing," came the cool reply. "Any plan is based on the information I get from my client. The last time I saw your father, his stock was worth less than $700,000. Almost all of that would have been exempt from the estate tax.

"There's one other thing that might make you feel better," the attorney added, "the life insurance. You and Sally will be splitting the proceeds of a $250,000 policy. That pays out--tax free--as soon as the insurance company gets a copy of the death certificate. It'll take nine months to settle the rest of the estate."

"Thanks," Brady said and hung up the phone, feeling better about being back in the million dollar neighborhood, but still incredulous that Uncle Sam was the biggest winner of all here. Brady knew the quality of legal advice was largely dependent upon the same premise as that from an accountant or stockbroker: making all the data--current and accurate--available was a requisite for sound advice. Brady felt a twinge of guilt. Here he was bitching about losing money to the government that wasn't his in the first place. By any measure, his net worth was still having a killer week.

The next thought to enter Brady's mind made him laugh: it was about furniture—real antiques, instead of the bogus stuff he and Beth used to fill their houses. Quality usually appreciated over time, so that was one kind of investment he might consider.

Since Brady spent most of his days staring at a quote machine, it also seemed logical to put some of his inheritance directly into stocks…maybe mutual funds for diversification? No. Brady rejected that, knowing he would be taking cash out soon and the cost of doing so from a mutual fund would be steep. He was cautioned about windfalls years ago from a savvy client: Whenever you come into money, Brady was told, don't make snap decisions. Park it in a safe place for at least six months before you decide what to do with it. That advice helped him settle finally on a combination of Treasuries and CDs. No home runs there, but at least he protected his principal until he had a long-range plan in place.

After dropping Sally at the airport the following morning, Brady decided to escape the congestion of both his mind and the streets of Tampa Bay with a drive up the coast on Highway 19 to Cedar Key.

As he passed a large van on the Courtney Campbell Causeway heading back toward Clearwater, Brady was thinking that, somewhere in all their relocations, he and Beth had forgotten to pack up their passion and keep it moving with them. If that had been their only problem, he could have dealt with it. After all, wasn't that normal? After a while, when the passion wanes, don't two people who love each other figure out how to express their feelings in less physical ways? He would rather be dealing with that right now than the prospect of starting over with another woman.

A few minutes later, as he turned north on 19, he thought of how his marriage had been a nomadic existence--moving about like a lost tribe in search of a different home every two or three years-- but it had been important to Beth. Would more enthusiasm there have caused her to stay? But then there was her relentless narcissism...and all those mirrors. He knew that would have grated more, not less, on him over time.

Passing a bank, just north of Countryside, reminded him that T-bills and CDs were only a temporary parking place for his newfound wealth, so Brady turned his focus to reflection of a different sort: thoughts of the last interview he saw with a lottery winner. "What will you do with the money?" The responses always ranged from the noble—charitable causes or assisting friends in need—to the selfish: buying a boat, sports car or bigger house. But Brady's dilemma went well beyond that. He hadn't really won the lottery; he was, instead, now living in the No Man's Land of the partial lottery winner. Nearly a million dollars was a windfall, to be sure, but not enough to consider running away to the South Pacific. He would need to double that before he could begin to feel comfortable about not outliving his nest egg.

As he rolled on toward Pasco County, the numbers tumbled through his mind: *a seven percent after-tax return for 10 years, that would get him close to two million.* But he knew himself well enough to realize he would likely be acquiring a few creature comforts first, so wouldn't be starting with his entire windfall. He was tired, for instance, of his old Mustang and thought stepping up to a Porsche Boxster might make the world--at least his world--a better place in which to live.

He let out a sigh as the traffic eased north of New Port Richey, knowing he lacked the patience for conservative investments. Brady shared the hubris of many brokers who thought they could time the market, rooting passionately for rallies--not always for profit, but just to get back to even in their own accounts. *If the public only knew how few brokers had enough cash on hand to write a $5,000 check!* He had been much more aggressive with his own funds than he ever would be with a client's, gambling frequently on stock options that, overall, had cost him thousands of dollars. But the occasional winner kept him coming back for more.

The other way to reach his nest egg goal, of course, was through the old-fashioned device of hard work. He considered that possibility briefly, before dismissing it. In Midian, he would never earn more than $70,000 per year and would be lucky to save $10,000 from that.

Approaching Hudson, it startled Brady to find all the options before him causing rigidity, not flexibility. He imagined first a hall of mirrors--Beth would like that--then a red light district with each option awash in mascara, sporting fish net stockings. Ye, Gods! What other mirages lurked as he headed north up the Gulf Coast on Highway 19? Meanwhile, the real face he could not shake belonged to Beth.

As he continued to contemplate his windfall, Brady found himself in the mood for a cigar. His habit previously had been to settle for a Swisher Sweet. Those days were over. He could now afford to purchase a good smoke, which is what he had treated himself to in Tampa, after dropping Sally off at the airport. Reaching into his breast pocket, he retrieved a Cupido robusto, an expertly rolled Nicaraguan, rich and oily in its beautiful wrapper and quite smooth to the touch. A superbly crafted smoke. He lit it up, then rolled down the window and smiled approvingly. "Close, but no cigar" had been a favorite saying of Harry Greer's.

Brady hadn't enjoyed a good cigar--earned or otherwise--in a long time and it made him feel as though his life had now shifted into a higher gear. With each puff as he motored on toward Homosassa Springs, he felt a little more expansive and less constricted than he had only a few days before. Money in the bank might not buy complete security, but it could buy off insecurity. As Brady adjusted to the feel of the smooth robusto in his left hand and the taste of it on his lips, he contemplated the possible range and scope of the future that stretched before him, one that might be as sleek and sun-drenched as this highway to Cedar Key...or as rough as the scrub brush beside it. A good smoke would be helpful to determine who would benefit from Brady Greer's new lot in life...and who might suffer from it.

8

      Shortly after arriving home, Brady noticed two realtor business cards on the dining room table, an encouraging sign that sometime soon the right couple might tour the house and decide they had to be the next keeper of the Reynolds flame. Surveying the furniture, Brady looked forward to closing day, when those rental pieces would be gone and he could get a fresh start with his own furniture at a permanent address, one not requiring renovation.

      The thought of starting over somewhere—anywhere—with a clean slate caused Brady to begin whistling. Walking to the stereo, he inserted a CD from Frankie Yankovic and smiled broadly as the music of "America's Polka King" filled the air: "In Heaven there is no beer; that's why we drink it here." *Which was better: a sudden inheritance or the fact that it arrived right after Beth left?* She would be more anxious than he to dissolve their marriage before her baby and his booty both arrived—in nine months.

Though he was savoring these brief moments of pleasure after his windfall, Brady remained convinced he had become the favorite punch line for every joke behind every antebellum door up and down Midian's Main Street and beyond. And those tourists. What were they smiling about? Were they laughing at him, too? Leaving town for a while eased the humiliation, but it was still there to greet him when he returned home.

He decided a few more days outside the rumor mill were needed. Without his presence and any fresh revelations, the mill would soon grind to a halt and idle briefly, before new grist from the next local scandal set it to churning once again. *The Midian Rumor Mill is proof*, Brady thought, *that the perpetual motion machine does, indeed, exist.*

Where to, now? Head for the hills... that's it! The mountains of North Carolina! He repacked his bag and returned to his car. As he passed the city limits, Brady cautiously eased himself up in his seat, until he was fully erect behind the wheel. He opened the window on his left and inhaled deeply, recalling again the soothing, cathartic combination of country air and open road.

It took only a couple of breaths before he felt able to think clearly about a destination. Wherever he landed, he wanted simply to blend in with the wallpaper and be left alone. Suddenly, he remembered a little inn, The Mountain Manor, between Cashiers and Highlands. He and Beth had admired it from the highway a couple of years earlier and always wanted to try it, but had never taken the time. It would be the perfect place to disappear for a couple of days. Chances of running into anyone he knew there would be slim, indeed.

He pulled up to The Manor two hours later and found the situation even better than he had hoped. There turned out to be a convenience store at the gas station next door, so he checked in, then began the short walk for some food, when he stopped abruptly. *What am I doing here, settling for this stuff?* He turned back toward his car and was soon headed into Highlands for a baked trout dinner. *Gotta get used to having money in my wallet*, he thought, *I know I can do it...*

Though he was ready for bed shortly after returning to the inn, Brady had difficulty getting to sleep while the couple in the next room would not stop pounding on the wall... either hanging lots of pictures, or having a much better time than he was. He awoke the following morning groggy, resigned to a day in which he would need to receive energy, because he wouldn't be able to supply it. His first thought was of the Chicago Cubs, who had been locked in a tight contest on the West Coast the night before. Brady could not recall being awake at its conclusion, so immediately clicked on the sports news and was relieved to find that Chicago had pulled out a one-run victory in its last at-bat.

That called for a celebratory breakfast, so he headed downstairs to scan the Asheville paper while waiting for the rest of the guests to join him for the 8 AM seating.

It is an integral part of the bed and breakfast owner's code to be in a chipper and chatty mood each morning. Here, the innkeeper came bounding into the dining room, rubbed his hands together and announced animatedly the morning menu: a Vidalia onion and feta cheese quiche, bacon, fresh pineapple and homemade peach muffins. It all sounded and smelled tasty to Brady, so he put down his paper and prepared to dig in, when he looked across the table into the face of ...Rex?

Skeeter: *Oh, oh...we got us a problem here...*

Herb: *...but also an opportunity. How's Brady really doing? Is he moving forward or moving back? We're gonna find out right quick.*

The initial shock of this serendipity hung there in the air between them over the breakfast table, like the odor of a guest who hadn't bathed in weeks. *This'll be interesting*, Brady thought, keeping his eyes on Rex. *What'll we do now? Stand up, unzip and see who can mark his territory the fastest?*

Recovering first, Brady nodded, "Rex."

"Brady," he replied, as nonchalantly as possible.

As the muffins were being passed, Brady continued, "I never figured you for the quiche type."

Rex grunted and looked away.

"So," Brady continued, suddenly feeling as chatty as his host, "are you up alone, or...with a date?"

"Look, she's sleeping, okay?" he said, irritated. "I was going to take some muffins up to her later...but maybe I'll do that now."

"Please. Stay," Brady said quickly, holding up his hand. "Don't leave on my account. I'm fine, really."

Brady was surprised at how easily he was taking this. Before his Florida trip, his emotions at any personal meeting with Beth or Rex would have been a cauldron of confusion, quickly reaching the boiling point. Now, however, he had accepted that Beth wanted a new life. Fighting that would be foolish. Besides, Brady had learned long ago that trust was an all-or-nothing proposition: A person either deserved complete trust, or none at all.

"Look," Brady continued, "can we step outside for a minute?" The eyebrows arched above Rex's face as a startled look spread across it.

"No, no," Brady laughed as a couple of the other guests looked up from their quiche. "Not that kind of 'step outside.' Just want to have a private word with you, that's all."

When the two men had reached the porch, Brady faced Rex squarely.

"Beth tried to contact me right after she left and I never got back to her. This is an opportunity to do that, I guess. I want you to give her a message. Tell her I'm filing for divorce next week. I'll stipulate that we split the house proceeds down the middle. I'll take the billiard table and she can have whatever other furniture she wants that we own there...after I get those mirrors fixed."

"She'll like that, man. She was sick about those mirrors. That was a major mess."

Brady stared at Rex for a moment before continuing.

"Just tell her not to take anything until we get a contract, okay? The household checking account has almost nothing in it, she knows that. What's there, I'm going to use to maintain the place until it sells. That's about it. You got all that?"

"Yeah, I got it."

"Good."

"Just one question."

"Shoot."

"I thought you were really upset about all of this. You don't seem—"

"Mad? Bitter? Nope. I'm not happy about it, that's for sure. Just decided to move on, that's all. We better get back in there before all those muffins disappear."

The pair returned to the dining room just in time to see Beth take a chair at the table. It was the first time Brady had seen her since their separation and, instead of showing any signs of a pregnancy, she appeared to have lost weight. He began to sort through his emotions about seeing her again, but they were quickly overtaken by his enjoyment of Rex's obvious discomfort. There was no way he could warn Beth as Brady approached.

"Hi, Beth," her husband said.

She looked up and gasped, then glanced quickly at Rex and back to Brady. The color drained from her face as she tried to comprehend why her husband was here. And...what was he doing with her boyfriend?

"Do I at least get a 'hello?" Brady asked brightly.

"Ah...hello."

"Looks as though your memory of this place is as good as mine," he continued. "Well, I understand congratulations are in order...that you two are expecting?"

Beth cleared her throat and reached for her water glass, glancing again at Rex. "I don't know how you got that idea. We haven't...I haven't...there hasn't been any announcement."

"Well, that ought to be easy enough. You know," he said, staring at her intently, "pregnancy is like trust: it's an all or nothing deal. Can't do it half-way. So, I'll ask you: Are you pregnant?"

Now, all conversation in the dining room ceased as the eight other guests looked expectantly at Beth for her answer.

She lowered her fork, picked up her napkin and gently dabbed at the corners of her mouth. "Yes," she said quietly.

There was spontaneous applause from everyone, everyone except Beth, Rex and Brady.

"Oh, honey, that's wonderful!" said the hefty woman on Beth's left. "Is this your first?"

Beth sighed as the color came rushing back to her face. "Yes," she said again.

"Oh, that's great!" the woman gushed. "Earl and I have three." Nodding at Rex, she added, "You and your husband are gonna love being parents."

With that, Beth rose quickly from the table and rushed back upstairs.

"Is she okay?" the woman said to Rex.

"Uh, yeah. She's okay," he said as he turned to follow Beth upstairs. "Just a little tired, that's all."

As Brady sat down to contemplate his cold quiche, the woman turned to him and said, "Friend of the family?"

"You might say that," he replied. "I've known them both a while."

Skeeter: *Wow, Herbie, I can't believe how well our boy is doing! If seeing Rex didn't get to him, I was sure Beth would, but, hey, no problem!*

Herb: *You're right; that's the way it looks…but I'm with Rex on this one. Our guy seems to be doing just a little too well with this…*

Brady checked out of The Manor immediately after breakfast, wondering if his past would always be "close behind," as Dylan observed. He drove over the line into Tennessee—-where he and Beth had never been together—-until he found a motel with a hot tub, where he could try to purge some of the toxic residue he suddenly felt he was carrying. A few minutes later, he was joined by an athletic, blonde-haired man in his 40s.

"Calm down, Timmy!" he yelled from the tub to his young son at the pool. "I promise. We'll get there in time for batting practice.

"Kids," he said, smiling warmly at Brady. "We get to one Braves game each year and tonight's it. You a Braves fan?"

Old Braves or new Braves? Which do you mean? That's a complicated question. You have no idea how complex…

"No," Brady heard himself say. "Not really. They must be cursed, don't you think?"

"Cursed? You mean…like the Babe in Boston and that goat in Chicago?"

"No, not exactly. This curse isn't that specific, nor that colorful. It just is. Ever wonder how they could win all those division titles—10 in a row, I think—and only one World Series?"

"Bobby Cox can't manage in the post-season. That's what everybody says."

"I don't know about that," Brady said thoughtfully. "That's a lot of division titles. He's got to be doing something right. A lot of people were upset when they left Wisconsin. Looks like a lot of that bad karma's still traveling with them, don't you think?"

The man looked at Brady, incredulous. "But that was ages ago," he said.

"Seems that way," Brady agreed, "but it was well after the Babe left Boston and they wouldn't sell that goat a ticket at Wrigley. Don't worry about it too much," Brady said as he stepped out of the hot tub and reached for his towel. "Enjoy the game."

Your bogus Braves can't even sell out the stadium in the playoffs! he wanted to add. *They'll never have fans again as good as they had in Milwaukee. Never! In a few years, little Timmy here is gonna get his heart broken when they pack up and make their next move to...to Mexico City, or wherever...*

How many people can I make uncomfortable in one day? he thought as he returned to his room and clicked on the TV. *Anything good on?* He surfed around the channels, from one maudlin talk show to the next. *Why do these people air their dirty laundry in public, from coast-to-coast?* Brady Greer could never do that. Suffering humiliated him and was something to be done in the privacy of your own room...even if it was a rented one. He focused more intently on the TV screen in front of him. *These people are bizarre. Some of them, though, are legitimate victims. They aren't objects of ridicule, but of sympathy, the sympathy of thousands— tens of thousands—from coast to coast. Is that why they're putting themselves through this?*

Gradually, watching this cavalcade of suffering improved Brady's disposition. As each story unfolded on his screen, he found himself comparing it to his own. A sleazy love triangle? Hmmm... his situation seemed more civil than those he was looking at, but it felt every bit as tawdry. Devil worshippers? Porn stars? Racists in various shapes and sizes? As the afternoon began, he had yet to see one person with whom he would trade places. He tried to feel better about that, but could not escape the fact he was measuring himself here against a national freak show. *Who wouldn't feel better next to these people? Where do they come from? How do they feel after strutting their psychoses on national TV?*

Brady wasn't sure what he felt anymore, only that he felt strongly about one very specific habit: the daily deposit he looked to make in his karma bank. Every day, he tried to find at least one opportunity to confront directly a service employee—the kind who was rarely given a pat on the back—and give him or her a very sincere compliment. He could tell by the looks on their faces that this was something sadly extraordinary. Several months ago, he had stopped an elderly woman while she was wiping down tables at Wendy's and told her she was so good at what she did that her pride in her work was what kept him coming back. She burst into tears and he didn't know what to do. Was he going too far or were other people not going far enough?

These little interludes helped him forget for a few minutes that life, it seemed, had dealt him one setback after another--then, suddenly, it threw him a very nice grubstake for…what? He had read that many people, even the most intelligent among us, often squandered their inheritance. Doing so was said to be some twisted psychological way to get back at their parents. Brady understood the part about unresolved issues, but he didn't get what good it would do to throw money away. Just sitting on it, until there was a strong reason not to, made more sense to him.

He stared at the phone. For years after he left home in Wisconsin, it would ring every Sunday, his mother on the line. How was he doing? Was he getting enough to eat? Do you want to talk to your father? Oh, he can't come to the phone. After the death of Brady's mother, he had hoped the calls would somehow continue, but he and his father couldn't come up with enough words to construct a conversation.

Thanks to Sally, that had begun to change right before Harry Greer's death. To celebrate her father's most recent birthday, she asked various friends and family members to each write a brief recollection of their favorite memory of Harry, which she then compiled in a booklet to present to him. For Brady, that assignment was easy.

The first time the Milwaukee Braves appeared in a World Series was the only one they won: 1957. There was a frenzied demand for tickets and Harry Greer was able to come up with only one—which he gave to Brady. Young Brady was overcome with both joy and the depth of his father's sacrifice--and old Brady had no trouble dismissing the fact that they had not actually *shared* this experience--to the extent it was easy for him to write a sincere, moving remembrance of it for his father. Harry was very touched by it and surprised at the depth of Brady's sustained appreciation, nearly a half century later…but the two had just begun to move toward the point where Brady would be comfortable opening up his personal life in a discussion with his father.

By 4 o'clock, Brady had popped open his first Rolling Rock of the day to go with his afternoon snack of beef jerky and Cheetos. Soon, it was on to the local news from Atlanta, which always struck Brady as an endless loop of traffic accidents, domestic violence and courthouse squabbles. He had heard about a station in San Antonio that played classical music behind these stories to infuse them with the *gravitas* they otherwise lacked. *That's what this stuff needs*, he thought wearily, gazing at the screen, *a little Wagner to punch it up.*

The national news wasn't much more informative, leading with a piece on violence in the Middle East. *How can something that happens every day be considered 'news?' When peace breaks out over there, that'll be the real news.* Just once, he wanted to hear an anchorman say, "Ladies and Gentlemen, there wasn't any hard news today, so we'll be bringing you some features we've been keeping in the can for this special occasion."

Then it was on to the game shows. "Alex, I'll try 'Potent Potables' for $100." *We don't get to know the contestants here as well as we do on the talk shows, which is just as well. They're greedy exhibitionists who could be my next door neighbor. What else do I need to know?*

When no baseball games were on the evening schedule, it was a mixed bag of sitcoms and news magazines. Those viewers willing to endure another dose of local news—and Brady was now right there with them—were then rewarded with a few jokes and celebrities hawking their latest projects before sleep took over.

That was Brady's schedule—rinse and repeat—for two days, until the weekend arrived. He thought it might be time to venture back to Midian, slip into his office and try to catch up on his work there, rather than have his mind and body slowly ground to oatmeal by this diet of junk TV and junkier food.

That night, Brady contorted his body in various positions, in an unsuccessful quest for rest. At home, he had a routine for his insomnia: head to the kitchen at 2 AM for a bagel dog, then switch on various TV reruns to put him in snooze mode. By the time he clicked off the tube on this night, Brady had opened the window to let in the cool mountain air and decided to give sleep another try.

Maybe, from somewhere deep in his subconscious, a useful idea for his inheritance would bubble slowly to the surface.

9

The following morning, Brady awoke before dawn, suddenly convinced he would have to return to Midian to find the clue to which path he was destined to take. He was in a cranky mood, feeling as though he hadn't slept at all, and alternately looking for a directional sign, then sitting back, letting it come to him, but the result was the same: nothing. After a fitful morning of failing to focus during the drive in from Tennessee, Brady decided to run off his restless energy at a favorite refuge: his thrice-weekly, noontime basketball game at the Midian Recreation Center.

On the surface, these games were just opportunities for middle-aged men to get some exercise and, on a good day, perhaps flash a glimpse of glory from their distant youth. But Brady saw them also as a form of expression, a social system in which the interlude of skins-and-shirts stripped away inhibitions and allowed latent aggression to surface as men from various walks of life shed their professional personae and simply tried to dominate each other. Since this was pick-up basketball, there was little subtlety involved, so Brady reveled in its occasional appearance.

Jimmy Nelson, in particular, fascinated Brady. He was a local accountant packing an extra 30 pounds or so who fashioned himself as the incarnation of Michael Jordan or Magic Johnson, but his body was unable to execute orders from his brain. When his off-balance shots clanged off the rim, as they usually did, Nelson would shake his head in disbelief while his fellow players wondered anew if the reality of his game and its fantasy would ever meet.

Brady's fantasy was different. He imagined himself the point guard, the coach-on-the-floor, for a fine college team. It was his job to find out which teammate had the hot hand, then get him the ball where he liked it as often as possible. Brady had also read a lot about the art of rebounding and liked to anticipate the carom of errant shots, in hopes of keeping the ball alive for his team.

On this day, Brady delighted in guarding Nelson, working him away from the basket, then dropping back, encouraging his pudgy friend to shoot when he was well out of range, an offer that was seldom refused. Nelson's open teammates rarely saw the ball and soon began bickering amongst each other, which was almost always the harbinger of defeat. Meanwhile, Brady had only one reliable shot and he knew it: a 15-foot jumper from the left of the key. He could usually get it off at least a couple of times each game and was otherwise content to get the ball into other hands, those that could do the most damage.

It was a victorious noon hour for Brady's team, a happy experience, except for the fact that Nelson's sweat was both profuse and pungent and his team had been shirtless this day, so Brady sought fresh air on a bench outside before heading for the showers.

At rest under the warm, mid-day sun, he gazed at the youth soccer game forming on the field below. *Nobody played soccer when I was growing up* he thought. *Now, it's everywhere. Does baseball have a clue that it's being eclipsed?* In a flash, his mind transported him back 30 years, to his days as a baseball player at Lakeside High School.

Nobody could ever figure out why Coach Paul Saunders did what he did or played the players he played. Nothing about him seemed logical, but he tolerated no questions about his methods— especially from his players. So, despite being one of the best athletes on the team, Brady spent most of his three years on the varsity riding the bench, watching teammates of lesser talent participate.

During his senior season, he could take it no longer and began to openly question Saunders' judgment. While there was satisfaction in showing up the coach, it did nothing to help Brady understand why he was not allowed to participate more with the team. The young player always wondered how far he might have gone under different leadership. Even so, Brady's love of baseball was strong enough to endure his experience with Saunders. *But that can mess up a whole life* Brady thought. *A coach takes an impressionable young kid and ignores him…Why did he do that? Why was he such a jerk?*

Skeeter: *Our guy has been hanging onto this Sauders thing for quite a while, which makes me think: Inheritance usually means money, but it's really anything--good or bad--that moves from one generation to the next . Unless you stop the bad stuff, it just keeps moving.*

Herb: *When a relief pitcher enters the game, he inherits whatever the guy before him leaves behind…which usually ain't pretty, or else he wouldn't be there. You gotta beat the mess or the mess beats you.*

Brady remained on the bench, watching soccer and thinking baseball, a grim concentration forming on his face as an idea emerged vaguely behind it, then slowly began to take shape as his thoughts caromed like those ivory balls on his antique billiard table: a plan to invest his own inheritance in a way that would hunt down the problems of his past and confront them, so he could get about the business of enjoying his future. The main thing that gave Brady pause was risk—this plan took a lot of it.

As a stockbroker, he was a student of risk and found it a fascinating subject. Some clients hid from it, assured of both safety and small returns; others lusted for it, dreaming of the home run, but often striking out. The conservative investor started by weighing acceptable risk, while the gambler locked into the rich reward. Brady had seen his happiest clients weigh both risk and reward carefully before making a commitment.

It struck him that he had spent his life risking very little--with little to show for it-- and now he had little to risk: no family and no possessions he would miss—save for his baseball cards.

There were lots of places he could hide his father's inheritance. He had decided to leave Midian and start over elsewhere, so what did it matter if he were run out of town?

The reward he was after was the chance to unlock the shackles of his past, so he could move forward with a fresh start as a free man. Group therapy sometimes attempts to confront these demon proxies through role play. *But what if I could actually confront these people, face-to-face? Wouldn't that be better?* Brady decided dealing with his real demons would be worth the biggest risk of all, jail, because he was confident of being both agile and astute enough to avoid that fate.

He felt a rush of adrenaline as he rose from the soccer bench and suddenly realized he hadn't felt this alive in a very long time. Brady was focused now on a grand scheme that would require three acquisitions: an appropriate weapon and the ability to use it, a secluded holding pen and the right vehicle for gathering his quarry.

The first step on this journey would be a stop at Gene's the following morning for coffee. The café was formally known as the Dixie Diner, but those who had lived in Midian more than a few crop cycles knew it as Gene's, after its legendary founder and Georgia Bulldog booster, who had made it an institution.

Every weekday for 30 years, until his death two years ago, Gene would signal lunch time in Midian by stepping out his front door with his old army bugle onto the town square just before noon and blowing the chorus to "Glory, Glory to Old Georgia," a song Brady enjoyed mostly because it was set to the tune of "I've Been Working on the Railroad." Gene's son, Ned, now ran the café with far less flare, but it was still the place favored by the town's movers, shakers and pretenders to start their day.

Brady rarely made it to Gene's in time for the morning gossip report—figuring all the regulars who would ever become his clients had already done so—and it had taken him nearly two years to be invited to sit at the big round table up front. His habit was not to order more than coffee because anything else from the kitchen at Gene's was a cavalcade of cholesterol, with any nutritional value fried out of it well before it reached the table. The old-timers were either oblivious to that or didn't care. However, Brady was very motivated to be there on this day because he knew chances were good he would run into Scratch who, sure enough, was seated at the big table when Brady arrived, greeted by the thick scent of hot grease assaulting him from the kitchen.

"Well, well," Scratch began, breaking into his crooked smile. "If it isn't Mr. Dow Jones. To what do we owe this honor?"

"Just got hungry this morning," Brady replied, "hungry for your company. Haven't seen you in a while."

"Sheeeeeee-it!" Scratch said, reaching for his coffee cup. When Scratch was really on his game, he could stretch that word into three syllables, but it was early this morning, so he settled for two.

"Actually," Brady began slowly, "I was wondering what you're up to these days, you know, out in the field."

"Wild dogs," came the answer. "Been pissin' off a lot of farmers out in the country. Had to move 'em."

"How are you doing that?"

"The usual. Bop 'em with a dart gun, then take to 'em to the shelter."

"Mind if I tag along? Ride shotgun?"

"Hmmm…don't think the sheriff wants ya in my truck, but I don't mind if ya wanna meet me out there."

The pair met up again that afternoon, Scratch happy for the company and the opportunity to show off his dart gun knowledge.

"Tell me about your weapon there, Scratch."

"This here's a single-shot, breech-loaded, 32-gauge shotgun. Simple and reliable. An outfit over in Douglasville modifies 'em. The 26-inch barrel has been rifle-barreled and it's sittin' under a Weaver four-time scope, which is your standard rifle scope."

"What's it shoot?"

"I'm usin' reusable darts. They got yellow tails for stabilizin' in flight. Shovin' 'em down the barrel about eight inches, right in front of the blank charge, makes 'em most accurate. The needles can be straight or barbed. I'm goin' with barbed, 'cuz the straight ones like to bounce off the target. Waste a time, know what I mean?"

"Right. Uh, what's in the dart?"

"Boy, we're playin' '20 Questions' today, ain't we? Could be Telazol or Xylazine. Today, I'm usin' a combination of Ketamine and Rompin. You put in a certain amount, dependin' on the weight of the target. I'm guessin' most a these mutts are around 50 pounds, so I gotta move fast on the bigger ones. Don't sleep as long. Little ones are down for the count."

"Are you aiming anyplace in particular?"

"Yeah. You wanna go for that fleshy butt, but only from the side."

"How come?"

"I saw a guy shoot a coyote in the ass from behind once. Damn dart went right up his poop shoot, like a magnet. Those ain't much fun to take out, if you get my drift."

"That's a lovely picture you're painting there, Scratch. What happens next?"

"Well, the animal's gonna still be conscious for five minutes or so, then he should be down for about 90, plenty of time to remove 'em. He's gonna stay groggy for about 12 hours. Exact times depend upon where he's hit, what shape he's in and how full his stomach is."

"Okay, let's see you do your stuff."

Scratch pointed to a group of three dogs about 100 yards away and motioned to Brady to follow. When they were 50 yards away, Scratch stopped and whispered, "The range on this thing is 30 yards, max. Ya hit anything beyond that, it's just luck. Shouldn't be a problem here, these dogs ain't afraid a nothin."

When they had closed to about 25 yards, Scratch raised his gun as the three dogs turned toward him. Selecting the one still presenting a side view, he fired, placing the dart just where he wanted it, in the side of the left butt. The other dogs scattered, barking loudly as they went. Just as Scratch had predicted, the downed dog was motionless within minutes and he quickly secured him in the truck. Brady thanked him heartily for the education and began the drive back to town in his own pick-up, his mind racing. *Yes, a gun gets the job done nicely…but you wouldn't need one at all--just the dart--from really close range.*

Skeeter: *Now that our boy has all this dough, he's gonna spend it on animal control?? Never figured he felt so strong about that. Me, I'd go with the T-bills…*

Herb: *Hold on, Skeets. We're not seeing the whole picture here yet. He's trying to control something wild, but I don't think it's dogs.*

One of the things that fascinated Brady about living in Midian was how different it was from the surrounding countryside. The city had been infused greatly in recent years by new blood, often arriving from Atlanta, which had heightened Midian's genteel polish as antebellum homes had been renovated. The supermarket carried more gourmet items, the wine selection at the liquor store had broadened considerably and the entrenched yellow dog Democrats--who had run the town for well over a century--were now, for the first time, being challenged seriously by zealous Republicans. You could even get a good mocha latte and bagel at the new coffee shop, which made no sense to the regulars at Gene's.

By comparison, time advanced at a glacial pace beyond the city limits. Munson County was still a collection of cotton fields and dairy farms run by the same families for two or more generations. Profit margins in agriculture were thinner these days than a tractor's dip stick. When county commissioners came up with a new tax referendum, you could count on voters in the county—who doubled the number of city voters—to reject it overwhelmingly. Many dairymen, such as Clyde Boles, had turned to the poultry business to make a better living. Georgia led the nation with the production of over one billion broilers a year and there were two large poultry processing plants in Athens, just a half-hour away. As a result, the sight of large poultry houses had become a common one throughout the countryside. Brady decided their remote location and adaptability to hold more than chickens would fit nicely into his plan, so he set out to learn more about the poultry business from Clyde.

As he was driving to the Boles place, Brady's thoughts turned to all the rugged farm boys who had made it to the Big Leagues, including Andy Pafko. Another farm boy had made an impression on him, too, and that was Bob Feller.

"Damn!" said Clyde as Brady stepped out of his car. "A stock broker makin' house calls? Stop the presses!"

"Not just house calls," Brady said with a laugh, "*chicken* house calls."

"Those birds got no money. I can tell ya that right off."

"Then they won't have the pleasure of hearing my sales pitch. But I was thinking that I hadn't ever seen your operation. Got a minute to show me around?"

"Sure," Clyde said as the two men headed for the closest of the three buildings. "Ever been to one of these? It's hard for me to remember, but the smell can get to ya pretty bad the first time around."

"No, never been in one," Brady said as Clyde handed him a bright blue, paper-thin jump suit and clear plastic overshoes. "But I can handle it. I mean, how bad can it be?"

It can be *real* bad, as Brady found out the moment he walked through the door, his nostrils assaulted instantly by a stench that literally staggered him, the result of thousands of tiny birds producing buckets of chicken excrement around the clock, totaling about 60 tons per chicken house each year. Collected daily, its nitrogen and phosphate content made it excellent fertilizer for Clyde to use in his vegetable garden and sell to his neighbors, but there was no escaping the acrid aroma inside the chicken house. Once it took up residence there, it became a permanent tenant that could never be evicted.

The houses were each 40 feet wide, longer than a football field and made of wood. The sides had huge, horizontal curtains that could be rolled up to allow a natural supplement to the continual breeze provided by large fans at either end of the building. Gas-heated furnaces were used in wintertime. Temperatures were closely regulated, being set at 88-90 degrees for the first few days after the chick's arrival, then lowered a half-degree daily to reach 62-65 degrees about 50 days later, when they would be ready to leave.

"You're lookin' at over 20,000 birds here," said Clyde, motioning to the enclosed area that resembled a small airplane hanger. "They arrive in three school bus-type vehicles in plastic trays of 100 each. Takes 60 tractor trailers to get 'em outta here."

"How much do they grow while they're here?"

"They're less than a half-pound when we get 'em. Our goal is to bring each bird to at least six pounds using less than 12 pounds of feed by the time we ship 'em out."

"To where?"

"Either Miami or the West Coast. They like the large birds, instead of the three-pound variety just raised for their breasts."

Clyde raised chickens under contract with a North Georgia poultry company, which called for him to supply labor and housing for the birds, while the company provided the baby chicks, feed (about 75% corn) and immunization medicine, which was administered through the thin water pipes used to supply water to the birds. He could earn a bonus if mortality was below expectations and growth above it.

"We're tryin' to keep our losses to less than one percent of the lot during each growth cycle," Clyde said. "We check 'em all the time. If we lose more than a dozen a day, we know we got a problem."

A seven-day hiatus between pick-up and drop-off gave Clyde and his crew time to thoroughly clean the chicken houses and perhaps disappear for a few days to hunt or fish.

Getting into the poultry business with a contract partner had become a lot more reliable way to make money than going it alone in the dairy business. Clyde received about a nickel per pound of chicken, regardless of the market price for the birds, which had held steady at 34-to-35 cents per pound, making it a lot more predictable than other agricultural investments. Still, there were poultry operations that were struggling. Brady asked Clyde if he knew any that might be for sale.

"Gonna finally make an honest living, eh?" asked Clyde.

"Not starting to," Brady said with a grin, "just continuing...only just branching out into a different line of work, that's all. I'd be especially interested in something off the beaten path. Out in Scofield, for instance."

"Hmmm...only chicken operation I know of out there is the Cutliff place. But that big wind last spring took off part of his roof and wrecked the end of one of his buildings. He's been makin' do ever since with a big sheet of plastic. He'd rather sell the place than fix it, but hasn't found a buyer."

"That could be just what I'm looking for," Brady answered, trying hard to mask his excitement.

Brady arranged to meet the owner two days later at his place in Scofield, an unincorporated area in the southeastern corner of the county. Cutliff had the unkempt look of a bordello bed, though Brady guessed his life was considerably less exciting. The man hadn't shaved in over a week and his caramel-colored lower teeth announced the frequent use of chew, which occasionally found its way into the Styrofoam cup he carried everywhere. Cutliff's 40 acres featured a two-bedroom cabin near the front of the property and poultry buildings—what was left of them—situated well off the little-used county road.

"No more charm in the chicken houses, eh?" Brady asked.

"Don't know how charmin' it was," Cutliff said. "But I *can* tell you what it is now: It's a pain in the ass, is what it is. The bank owns a lot more of it than I do."

"So, you've gone on to something else?"

"That's right. Got me a job over at the paper company. If their roof blows off, *they* can fix it. Besides, I don't have to walk around smellin' like chicken shit all the time."

Part of the roof on Cutliff's chicken house was still rolled up like the lid on a sardine can. The north end of the building was gone completely. Though it had been empty for over a year, the unmistakable odor of festering fowl lingered. It suited Brady's purpose perfectly and he was able to strike a deal quickly with its motivated seller.

It had been a busy week for Brady, one he now needed to top off with another trip to Athens, this one to acquire appropriate transportation for his project. *A chicken farm*, he thought to himself as he headed north on the Athens highway, *but never a chicken farmer. That stench! How do they stand it? But, if you want to get off the beaten path, what better place? Hard to imagine anyone wanting to casually drop in. But maybe I'm missing the point here. Maybe my life is becoming a game of chicken: Take some risks and see who blinks.*

Brady knew a sport utility vehicle was what he needed, but he hated the statement they often made—"As a matter of fact, I *do* own the road"—and so was reluctant to purchase his own SUV. As a result, he drove from one auto dealership to the next in Athens, rather passively, hoping an alternative would emerge. Just when he was ready to give up and head home, he paused to peek at the latest Boxsters and was jolted upright by a sight that immediately took him back to the glorious summer between his sophomore and junior years of college.

There it stood, through the window to the main showroom of the Porsche/VW dealer: a red and white VW Microbus. Brady parked immediately and hurried inside. Approaching the Bus, he quickly saw it had split windows, dating its vintage to '67 or earlier.

Its sliding doors meant it could be no older than a '63. *Wow... '63 to '67...the Microbus sweet spot!*

Brady had never actually owned one of these, but he had spent a very memorable summer during college touring through the West in one with a flexible group of friends, old and new, whose identity often changed from week to week. In fact, he left his virginity in the back of that Bus, somewhere between Clovis and Tucumcari, when he found himself alone one afternoon with a flower child named "Peace," from Hohokus, NJ, and allowed her to seduce him. The memory made him smile as a salesman approached.

"That's a classic right there, sir."

Brady nodded.

"Carries up to nine people and the two rear seats can be taken out to transport greater loads."

"That's just...what I...was thinking," Brady said. "How much?"

"Oh, it's for show, not for sale," the salesman said. "Mr. Michaels is very fond of it."

"Is he here? Now?"

The owner, Mickey Michaels, was in his office. Brady had heard Michaels was a Georgia graduate who would have been more comfortable forming a band to follow in the footsteps of local legends R.E.M. and the B-52s. While his group did play a lot of gigs on the fraternity circuit, he did so knowing his future was in the family auto dealership. He was well-known in Athens as both a shrewd businessman and a major booster of the Georgia Bulldogs.

"How are the Dawgs looking this fall?" Brady began.

"Lookin' real good," Michaels said brightly. "Could finally grab that SEC title again. About time, dontcha think?"

"Absolutely...say, Mickey, that's one beautiful Bus you've got over there."

"That old Microbus? Thanks. I picked it up at an auction in Birmingham a few months ago. Single-owner family. They'd had it 30 years and took real good care of it. Reminds me of the old days, you know? All the music?"

"Sure, I know. What do you figure it's worth?"

"Oh, it's not for sale," Michaels said casually. "But, if it was, I could get 20 for it, easy."

"I spent some time in one of those, many years ago," Brady said. "Brings back good memories to me, too." Brady thought briefly about offering his old pick-up in trade, then dismissed the idea, not wanting to get bogged down in dickering over its value, and realizing he could get more for it with an ad in the Athens paper. In the meantime, he could park it at Flaps' place.

"I'll give you 20 for it right now. Cash," he said.

"Whoa," Michaels said with a look of surprise. "Those memories must be pretty damn good."

"Good enough to share," Brady said. "I might add some black to that red paint job and doing some tailgating at the Bulldog games this fall."

"Well…I really wasn't going to sell it," Michaels said slowly, "but…since you're a Georgia fan…I might let it go for…22-5?"

"Twenty-one is all I got."

"Done. I'd be a fool to turn down full value. You did say 'cash,' right?"

The two shook hands before Michaels walked Brady over to his business manger to complete the paperwork. In less than an hour, he was the owner of a vintage Microbus, smiling at the thought of riding into his future on the wheels of his past.

10

When Brady's world got to spinning a little too fast, as it was now, he liked to sit for a spell and think things over. His favorite place to do that was the Waffle World out by the Interstate. He had read years ago that billionaire John D. MacArthur ran his investment empire out of a coffee shop in South Florida. Brady liked to fantasize about doing the same thing from the Waffle World in Midian. He loved checking out the strange patrons at odd hours, plus the smell of hash browns after one of the waitresses belted out her order for them all the way ("I need 'em scattered, smothered, covered, chunked, topped, diced and peppered."). And it was all set to music in a most unusual way, since the owner of this particular franchise insisted that only artists in the Georgia Music Hall of Fame be allowed on the juke box. Thus, you might hear the big band sound of Johnny Mercer and TLC's hip-hop during the same cup of coffee. Brady liked to feel he was one up on MacArthur, since the Waffle World never closed. If those sassy waitresses just kept that coffee coming to the corner booth, he could envision his world running quite nicely.

"When are you gonna give me that great stock tip that'll get me outta here and into that house I deserve, the one on Easy Street?" Sheila, his favorite, asked him again with a smile as she topped off his cup.

"Hot tips can burn you, Sheila. Haven't I told you that?"

"I try not to remember anything I hear on my shift," she said. "Otherwise, the white coats would come and get me, then I wouldn't be able to deliver your pecan waffle. You wouldn't like that, now, would you?"

"No," Brady said with a sigh, "I guess not. You had any luck yet with that car?"

Sheila's '84 Pontiac Fiero had become a popular topic between them. She'd been trying to sell it for months, dropping the price steadily until it now sat with a "$1,500" cardboard sign in the Waffle World parking lot.

"There it sits 'til it sells," she said. "It was awful nice of GM to keep recalling it, but I think the word is out. That thing's had as many engines as I've had husbands. But, I swear, it's easier to get rid of a husband than it is an '84 Fiero. Everyone knows where my extra key is, but I can't even get 'em to steal it."

"Next time I stop by, we'll draw up a sales plan," he said with a laugh.

Planning was something Brady liked to encourage others to do, but he seldom took his own life advice. He was content to react to whatever curve balls came his way, which he knew didn't make sense, since he always felt best when he seized the initiative. Studying for his securities exam came to mind. That required a laser-like effort, which is what he gave it. Brady pumped himself up by setting a goal of having his knowledge of the various rules and regulations peak on exam day. As a result, he scored near the top of his class. He hadn't felt the same level of energy since…until now, now that he was focused on something big.

Everyone back at Lakeside High School in Milwaukee had pegged him as a future star. He had the world by the tail then and seemed ready to shake it any which way he wished. Instead, the world had done the shaking, dumping him out here in rural Georgia.

How did that happen? Brady wasn't sure, exactly, since introspection had never been a popular pursuit.

Shortly after leaving Atlanta, he turned his psyche over to a therapist who encouraged him to take responsibility for being so unintentional. Brady responded to this psychologist the way many people do when they're uncomfortable with a message: He fired the messenger.

When he was younger, Brady scoffed at those who painstakingly planned every career move, often under the watchful eye of a mentor, carefully chosen. Eventually, though, it was the planners who had the last laugh at the drifters who placed their bets on mere fate and lost. *"The Three Little Pigs" changes lives. Who knew?*

But he remained insistent there had been accomplices to his fate, people who had stacked the deck in a way that made it tough for him to get ahead. It was now time for a fresh deck and a new dealer. An eye for an eye. Payback would be sweet, especially if he could do it under the guise of a great social experiment.

His idea along that line was coming together nicely and he was working hard at home late that night on additional details while sipping some Gentleman Jack, when he was startled by a knock at the front door. Glancing at his watch, he saw that, in another 15 minutes, it would be midnight. *What now? Who could it possibly be?* Making his way to the front door, he peered through the pane of glass next to it to see...a disheveled Irma.

"Irma? Are you all right?" he asked instinctively as he opened the door, though he could see from the corkless bottle of red wine in her hand—some of which had landed on her blouse— and the smell of her breath that she was definitely in no pain.

"Oh, I'm *fine,* Brady Boy," she said loudly with a crooked smile as she reached for the door jam with her free hand. "Just *fine.*" After several seconds, she continued, "*Well*? Do I get an invitation to come inside or not?"

"Ah, sure, Irma" Brady said, opening the big red door wider. "C'mon in."

Guiding her into the living room, he motioned her toward the couch, while he took a seat in the chair next to it.

"What's the matter, Brady?" she said with a disappointed look. "You can come over here. I won't bite."

"Can I make you some coffee?" he asked while carefully taking a position at the opposite end of the couch.

"Coffee?" she said with a start. "Why coffee? All that would do is ruin my buzz, my *excellent* buzz."

"What's the occasion?" he asked tentatively. "Are you…celebrating something?"

"Well, I don't know," she said, putting the wine bottle on the coffee table and moving toward the middle of the couch. "When you think about it, each day's worth celebrating, right?"

"Of course, it's just that—"

"It's just that most of those daily celebrations don't involve getting *drunk*. Is *that* what you were about to say?"

"Yes, you're right. I was thinking that."

"Well, Roland's left town for a couple of days. Gone off fishing in North Carolina with some of his buddies. Did I ever tell you about the…nature of his disability from that accident?"

"Ah…no," Brady replied, shifting his weight forward to the very edge of the couch cushion. "Look, that's really none of my—"

"No action, Jackson," she interrupted, as her hand moved across the couch's equator onto Brady's cushion.

He rose to his feet, knowing there were no good choices here, only a variety of bad ones; it was just a matter of degree. He turned to face her squarely, then sat down on the coffee table to look her straight in the eye. It was time to make Irma play a little defense, so he blurted out, "How does that make you feel?"

Irma sat back on the couch. "How does it make me *feel*? How the hell do you *think* it makes me feel?? I'm a healthy woman and I'm not ready to—"

"Look, Irma," Brady said, "we can say anything to each other. I value that a lot and know you do, too. We've been really good as friends. Don't you think we'd both be better off in the long run if we just held onto that?"

Irma put her head in her hands for a long moment. She then sat up sadly, almost mournfully, looked out the window, then turned away from Brady and said softly, "There are times when I need to hold onto more than …oh, forget it; never mind. What was I thinking? I never should have bothered you."

As she rose to leave, Brady, desperate to end the discussion on a positive note, started to mention a nightcap, then caught himself.

"No, that's okay," she said, heading for the door. "I'm feeling pretty sober all of a sudden. I'd better be going."

Skeeter: *Well...just when you think you've seen it all...that was one helluva wild pitch! He managed to catch it and throw it back, but...I don't know...don't see any way you come out a winner on that one.*

Herb: *That lady made me nervous before. Now, she's flat out dangerous...free-lancing like that. No place for that kind of thing on a team—and she ain't on the team anymore, if she ever was.*

The next morning, Brady's thoughts turned toward establishing a plausible explanation for his new interest in Scofield, to keep it out of the rumor mill. He decided to say simply that he was buying the Cutliff place as a weekend retreat. That made sense because everyone knew his house on Main was on the market. After it sold, he would still want a good place to run Louie around on occasion and anyone could see Scofield fit that description. Brady would just be reinforcing the walls of one of the chicken houses to create some extra storage space. That's all.

Two weeks later, as soon as he closed his deal with Cutliff, Brady headed up to Athens to round up the sheet rock, joint tape and insulating foam he would need for his renovation. It pained him not to trade with Midian Hardware, but he felt obliged to get the bulk of his supplies out-of-town, so as not to attract suspicion closer to home. Brady had never been the handyman type—as Beth frequently reminded him—but that had largely been a result of disinterest, plus the need for the master craftsmanship required for renovation work. Standards here would be less exacting and the audience far smaller and less demanding. There was no choice but for Brady to rise to the occasion.

He divided the rear of the damaged chicken house into six rooms, each with an area of 150 square feet and opening into a walled common area of 300 square feet. Working evenings and weekends, he figured his alternations would be done in about a month. Saturday mornings were set aside for yard sales—an abundant spring tradition in Midian—where he was confident he could pick up the furnishings he needed. A water cooler and small refrigerator would also be placed in each room, so the occupants could feed themselves for several days at a time, if need be.

Brady felt optimistic about everything but the plumbing. He retained an Athens contractor to complete that first, so as to reveal as little as possible of his overall plan to the outside world.

In the meantime, there was customizing to attend to on the Microbus. It was becoming commonplace to see metal dividers installed in sport utility vehicles for transporting pets. Brady arranged to have one of these Pet Guards installed in his Microbus, only in a slightly different manner. He would be hauling larger livestock, so he removed the center seat to construct a holding pen extending from just behind the driver's seat all the way back to the rear engine. The front divider was also insulated to mute the noise from the holding pen, while allowing for a small opening through which food could be passed from the front seat. He also purchased a new bike, a 26" Columbia Patriot to strap on the roof, ready for extra mobility, once he reached his destination. Brady's expense nut for his modified Bus was approaching $25,000, but it was evolving exactly as he had planned.

The more time he spent in Scofield, the less he spent in his office, so his brokerage business began to suffer. He thought about giving it up entirely, but decided against it, mostly because his local identity was tied up in being "Brady, the stockbroker." He was not ready for it to become "Brady, the weird recluse who lives with the chickens." Besides, he had few traders in his book, so he was able to group his office appointments earlier in the day, leaving the remainder of his time free to pursue his new passion as a poultryman…of sorts. It was an activity he was surprised to find was agreeing with him.

Most of all, Brady was pleased to find himself stopping literally to smell the lady slippers, periwinkles and verbenas that now filled his life. For the first time, he was really paying attention to his world and becoming fascinated by what it included. He immediately discovered that, when you open your eyes in rural Georgia, the first thing you see is kudzu.

Brady had learned from Irma that the broadleaf green plant was introduced into America over a century ago by the Japanese and first gained favor in the South as a fast-growing, flowering vine used to shade porches. It was now early summer, but later, by Labor Day, kudzu blossoms would be filling the air with a sweet, grape-like aroma. The turning point in the life of this ubiquitous plant, according to Irma, came when a Florida botanist, unimpressed with its ornamental value as a porch vine, decided to plant it as a screen to hide his trash pile. Within a year, his trash—as well as his neighbor's fence—had disappeared under a blanket of kudzu.

Skeeter: *That probably killed 'Yard of the Month' for that guy, didn't it?*

Herb: *Came from Florida, huh? That explains a lot. Makes sense that kudzu is the out-of-control brainchild of some evil Gator...*

That initial strain of kudzu soon worked its way across the state line en route toward covering much of Georgia. It was said that the way to plant kudzu was to throw it on the ground and run. Brady decided to let the plant do the running, along his lot lines, but always kept a pair of pruning shears close at hand.

The path to his chicken house was strewn with milkweed, purple thistle and wild blackberries. He had learned from the county agent that the cedar trees growing in a random pattern along his fence line by the road were probably the result of seeds sown by the serendipity of bird deposits. While he worked, he was often accompanied by several brown thrashers and even installed a feeder and birdbath to make them feel at home. Best of all, he no longer had to jive Irma about the flora and fauna of Munson County, because he had reached the point, by actually paying attention, where he could carry on a conversation on the subject and know what he was talking about.

While he was working out in Scofield, it occurred to Brady that something happened to city people when they moved into the country that made them drop their pretenses and revert to their unvarnished selves. It was as if they had made a conscious choice of country reality over the city illusions of worthwhile cocktail parties and social standing. Country people, he decided, tended to be as straightforward as a fast ball down the middle.

A good example of that was Ernie Powell, owner of the Scofield Gas 'n Grocery, where the regulars who gathered there for coffee each morning liked to say you could get as much gas from the sausage biscuits as you could out of the pump. Ernie was a refugee from Atlanta, having owned a camera shop there for three decades before retiring a couple of years ago to the country. He bought the little grocery, because, as his wife liked to say, she had "married him for better or for worse, but not for lunch." It was a ramshackle repository--one of many found frequently throughout rural Georgia, with a lone gas pump--and known for its biscuits in the morning and barbecue in the afternoon. The constant pinch of snuff just below his lower lip helped give Ernie the country look and Brady especially liked the fact that he was a recent enough arrival in the area to not care about prying into a person's private life.

"Any rain headed this way?" Brady asked while stopping for some gas.

"Not likely," came Ernie's reply after a thoughtful skyward glance. "Been dryer than a Baptist party around here for too long. Sure could use some wet, but I don't see it 'til maybe fall. Then, when it's too late to help the crops, it'll drop on us 'til we can't stand it."

"Any hope for the Braves this year?"

"Hell," said Ernie as he spit into his ever-present Styrofoam coffee cup, "hope's all they got in the Series, if they get that far. They'll win this summer, like they always do. Probably drop like a leaf off a tree after that, though."

Might as well try out country living, Brady thought as he drove away, *'cuz I've already tried out everything else: Hot Lanta when I broke into the brokerage business, the suburbs when I tried to jump-start my career by changing firms, then what looked like the end of the line in a small town. Who knows? Country living could bring a new lease on life. Might even mount a comeback and return, triumphant somehow, to the big city. Either that, or self-destruct. Can't tell how it'll all play out. Either way, it'll be more exciting than pushing Co-Cola.*

11

Brady would have preferred some company for the road—might need it, in fact, to help with the work ahead—but resigned himself to handling this assignment alone. Just before dawn, he eased his red and white Microbus out of Midian and onto I-20, heading west. He had packed it thoughtfully, including his .32 gauge Remington shotgun, carefully wrapped in a blanket behind the front seat and his new bike covered with a tarp and tied to the roof. It was a damp and dewy Georgia morning and Brady looked forward to beating the traffic rush to the Atlanta by-pass, so he could turn north on I-75 and clear the metropolitan area well before the commuter cacophony reached its crescendo.

He could never abide the incessant chatter of drive-time DJs at this hour and turned instead to his box of cassette tapes for companionship. His fingers nimbly picked their way past Dylan, the Eagles and Jimmy Buffet, coming to rest on a rare wedding performance of Marty Zipko's Polka Band.

As the first chords of "Who Stole the Keisha?" filled the Microbus, Brady smiled at the thought of Zipko playing that song years ago at Kilroy's Ballroom, a big place in Grafton where the motto was, "Two Halls for Two Balls." But it made him sad, as well. Polka lovers were a dying breed, their children more interested in rock 'n roll. *Gotta keep it alive,* Brady thought. *That's what "The Blues Brothers" did for rhythm and blues. Polkas deserve their own movie.*

Three hours later, Brady was casting that movie in his mind as he crossed over the state line into Chattanooga and approached Nicajack Lake to begin the prettiest leg of his trip. The verdant Tennessee countryside rolled by--interrupted by the occasional, massive junkyard resting on a distant hill, just beyond the reach of the nearest zoning ordinance. Brady made his way north on I-24, climbing gradually, until the highway reached Monteagle, the highest point between Chattanooga and Nashville. He marveled how, during previous trips late in the year, the nasty weather would roll in from the north and stop abruptly at Monteagle Pass, the sun radiating clearly from there south, as though a heavenly switch was thrown routinely.

When he approached Nashville, Brady gave his polkas a rest and let the sounds of Music City radio wash over him. When he had the time here, he would spend the night club-hopping to favorite haunts like Douglas Corner and the Bluebird, listening with awe to extremely talented, eager artists who would never get a record contract. Brady was running a tight schedule on this day, however, allowing him only a quick stop for lunch. As his stomach growled, pleading with him to pull over, he noticed the familiar yellow and black sign announcing the nearest Waffle World. It was a little late for breakfast, so Brady ordered a ham and cheese sandwich and settled down with a copy of *The Tennessean* to see if there was any news he could use. A headline below the fold on page one caught his eye: "Lady Ta Ta Sought in Robin Hood Caper."

A glance at the story revealed Nashville police were pursuing a scam in which an accounts receivable clerk at the home office of Tennessee Power had been skimming off thousands of dollars each month from consumer utility bills and redirecting it as anonymous donations to a local homeless shelter, which had used the funds to replace all its furniture, build a media center and hire a recent graduate of the Culinary Institute of America to supervise its newly-remodeled kitchen. As a result, the Nashville shelter was quickly becoming a Mecca for vagrants from throughout the South.

105

Tessa Anne Hunt, 29, of Dallas—known as "Ta Ta" since childhood--was being sought for questioning by investigators, who had learned---

At the sound of sudden laughter from behind the counter, Brady looked up from his paper.

"That's one *egg-white* vegetable omelet, Sam—I know you can do that for me, cancha, hon?—a side of sliced tomatoes and wheat toast, no butter. Got that?"

The waitresses at Waffle World tended to wear their difficult personal histories on open display for all the world to consume and digest along with the greasy fare set before them. It was commonplace there to be waited on by women who tried gamely, but vainly, to conceal years of heartbreak and hard luck with a few minutes of makeup. Their clientele reflected this approach to life, along with an obvious eagerness to consume thousands of calories of comfort food daily and a reluctance to burn off the excess. Anyone trying to eat healthy instead of hardy in that context stood out like Shredded Wheat on a dessert tray.

Brady turned his head, trying to guess the identity of the egg white fan. Scanning the restaurant, his gaze fell upon what appeared to be a lone female figure in a corner booth. Her delicate facial features were his best clue regarding her gender. Otherwise, the tan jacket, Cossack hat and wire rim glasses—a John Lennon look that struck Brady as odd for the South, even Music City— could just as easily belong to a boy. She, too, was reading the morning paper. Brady guessed that the George Jones lament now playing on the jukebox was new to her. In fact, she was probably new to Waffle World, judging from her order.

A quick glance at his watch snapped Brady out of his reverie and told him he needed to get going. He stuck *The Tennessean* under his arm to finish later, then paid his bill. In a few minutes, he was back at the Microbus, collecting trash and tidying up in preparation for the next leg of his journey, when he suddenly heard a voice behind him.

"Excuse me," it said. "Could I talk to you for a minute?"

Brady jerked his head around, suddenly face-to-face with Miss Egg-White.

"Uh…sure," he stammered. "What's up?"

"Well, I noticed you were from out-of-state and was wondering where you're headed."

He was able to get a better look at her now. She was slim, about five-foot-five and definitely a girl, though she was doing everything she could to obscure that fact. Her high cheekbones, long lashes and confident bearing suggested one who would be comfortable in far tonier surroundings.

"North," he said, not inclined to be too specific. "The Chicago area, up around there."

"That would be perfect," she said, her eyes darting around the parking lot, then back to Brady. "This is probably a terrible imposition on you, but do you suppose you might be able to give me a lift?"

"A ride?"

"Yes. I won't be any trouble, I promise. All I've got is a knapsack and a duffle bag. Would you have room for that?"

"I've got plenty of room for that; that's not a problem. Isn't this kind of risky for *you*, though? I mean, what if I'm Jack the Ripper?"

She looked at him thoughtfully for a moment, then nodded toward his vintage Microbus and said, "I guess a crazy person wouldn't drive around in one of these, now, would he?"

"Back when this was new, a lot of crazy people probably drove these around while their crazy friends did crazy things in the back," Brady said with an easy laugh. "But it's an adult now and so am I, so we're both behaving."

"Well, I *would* like a lift," she said, "and I can contribute some gas money. In fact, I insist on it."

"Don't worry about that," he said. "Just grab your stuff and throw it in the back, so we can get going." A minute later, she slid into the front seat as Brady cranked up the Microbus. One of the items she brought with her was a large, three-ring binder. Brady asked her about it.

"Oh, that? You know how everyone's always saying they've got to 'keep it together?" He nodded. "Well, that's how I do it."

Skeeter: *Hey, sweetheart, that's what Brady's trying to do! A three-ring binder ain't gonna cut it, at least not for him...and I* *don't think a lady hitchhiker is gonna help much in that department, either...*

Herb: *Take it easy...this could be a good thing. Brady's been spending a lot of time—maybe too much time—alone since Beth left. She might keep him connected to the real world.*

Skeeter: *That's assuming she is, herself, of the real world. From the looks of her, the jury's still out on that...*

"My name's Brady, by the way," he said, extending his hand to her. "What's yours?"

"Tanya."

"Tanya, from..."

"Here. I've been living here, in Nashville."

The voice he was hearing didn't sound like Nashville, but Brady decided not to press the point as he headed the Microbus north on I-24.

"Okay...let me guess. You're a singer who's been performing around town, trying to get discovered. Is that close?"

"Uh, yeah...I sing," she said, "but not that well, just well enough to...to pitch my songs."

"Most Nashville songs are about pain," Brady said, eyeing her carefully. "Where does your pain come from?"

Tanya shifted uneasily in her seat. Looking straight ahead, she said, "That's a pretty personal question. I'd really rather not go there at the moment."

"That's fine, that's fine," he said with a wave of his hand. "Didn't mean to pry. It's just that I'm fascinated by the songwriting process. Seems like the early country stars sang about the tough times they actually lived. There was something raw and real about that. The current crop of country singers tries to sell those lyrics, but it's a lot harder to do when you're blow-dried and just in from the suburbs."

Tanya stared silently out the window at the highway traffic

"You know where Johnny Cash was from?" Brady asked.

"No."

"Son of a sharecropper in Dyess, Ark. Whole family worked the fields. One day, while Johnny was in school, his Daddy shot the family dog, 'cuz it was eating too much food. That's pain."

"Yes," she said, "I suppose it is."

"And Roy Orbison," Brady continued. "Death stuck close to Roy and his kin, like flypaper. And you know about Loretta Lynn. Coal miner's daughter from Butcher Holler."

Tanya gazed forlornly out the window on her right, clearly wishing to change the topic, then turned toward Brady. "How about you?" she said. "What do you do down in Georgia?"

"I grew up in Wisconsin, but I've been living in Georgia for quite a while," he said. "Make a living as a stockbroker, pay my taxes, never spent the night in jail..."

"And you're headed...where?"

"Back to Milwaukee, actually. Just a quick trip."

As they headed north on I-65, he thought of how, a few hours before, the front seat had been occupied by a cooler of Dr. Pepper, a box of cigars and a bag of various cassette tapes. It was now the territory of a struggling songwriter. Was their meeting pure serendipity or had fate introduced them to instruct each other? While pondering that point, Brady realized Tanya's presence was pulling him out of his comfort zone and it surprised him that he wasn't resisting the journey.

"Well, what have we here?" said Tanya as she reached under her seat for Brady's bag of cassettes.

"Just a collection of older stuff, I guess," said Brady, nodding toward the bag as he casually ejected his polka favorites. "Pick out what you'd like to hear. Lady's choice."

Tanya held up each artifact by the thumb and forefinger of her right hand, suddenly the curator of Brady's musical museum.

"Wow," she said slowly, a moment later. "Did these come with the Bus? 'Woodstock?' You don't hear that much anymore." Sliding the cassette into the dashboard player, the sounds of Alvin Lee and "Ten Years After" soon filled the Bus. *Go home! My babe. Go home! My babe.* Brady smiled, visualizing Lee's trademark grimace while attacking his guitar on stage. Tanya, on the other hand, stared ahead in disbelief. If there was any social value in the noise she was hearing, it washed over her without registering.

"So," she said a moment later as she gently turned down the sound of the manic rocker. "What's up in Wisconsin?"

Brady thought for a moment, uncomfortable with the focus returning to him.

"Oh, I'm just taking a few days off," he said casually, "doing a little hunting."

Tanya was apparently as unattached as he was and about as unlike Beth as it was possible to be. Brady wondered about rebounding in her direction, then tried to dismiss the notion as too reflexive. On the other hand, their lives would separate a few hours from now, after they arrived in Chicago. What did he have to risk but rejection? Any stockbroker learns to deal with that daily. But making a move suddenly struck him as an act of desperation. He did not know this woman and wasn't sure he even liked her. Besides, Beth might have left his heart, but she was still on his mind…and the episode with Irma had driven him deeper into his shell, in an effort to shield himself from the need to deal with a social life.

Brady suddenly thought of Eisenhower's farewell speech when he left the White House: *Avoid entangling alliances*. Where did that come from? How did stuff like that just pop into his head? He had no idea…in a way, it annoyed him. Why now, when he had locked in the focus of this trip on its special mission, did this attractive young woman appear on the front seat next to him, seemingly available?

When they approached Louisville, Brady and Tanya agreed that some Thai cuisine would hit the spot, so headed over to the Siam Orchid. If there was even a glimmer of romantic possibility in the air, it was quickly overcome when they both opted for garlic, she with the goong gratium and he with the ped gratium prig tai. After ordering his second bottle of Singha, Brady asked Tanya to tell him more.

"So," he began, "how does a girl like you get interested in songwriting?"

She thought for a moment and finally said, "Well…telling a story about real people and their real pain, all in three minutes. That's a challenge."

"Why three minutes?"

"I don't know…the record companies and radio stations…it's all about what they want…" Grabbing her purse suddenly, she said, "I'll be right back," and headed for the rest room.

Brady shrugged and pulled out his copy of *The Tennessean*, continuing to read about Lady Ta Ta: "The mild-mannered bookkeeper everyone knew in Nashville as "Tessa" has been estranged from her extremely wealthy family in Texas for the three years she has been in Tennessee." The head shot of Tessa with the story looked as though it had been taken right out of her finishing school yearbook. Brady was staring deep into his water glass when Tanya returned.

"We were talking about songwriting," he said as casually as he could. "How are you approaching it?"

Replying with a passion Brady hadn't heard before, Tanya said, "There's a lot of social injustice in this world. That's something I care about deeply and want to change. A strong song can become a battle cry that the people can use against their oppressors."

"Oppressors?"

"That's right. What I need now," she said, "in order to make my case musically, is the kind of life experience you were talking about earlier. You can go to all the songwriting workshops in the world, but that won't help you write something that moves people. To do that, you need to see more sides of life than I have."

Brady's eyes dropped from Tanya and locked onto the label on his Singha bottle, which he then lifted and tilted carefully, as if reading it for the first time. Liberals were curious creatures. He had read about them, but seldom encountered one. He knew of none in Midian, where politics was a passionate pastime, but real differences on issues there were ones of nuance usually invisible to the naked eye.

Setting his bottle down on the table, Brady leaned back in his chair and smiled. "Limousine liberals just go along for the ride. Are you ready to go beyond that? To join the demonstration?"

"Absolutely!" she said, indignant. "I'm not just a spectator. I'm looking for first-hand experience."

When they returned to the Bus, he handed her the keys. "I've seen Indiana before," he said, "the most interesting parts—

111

Milan, Colfax, Oolitic—are small towns away from the interstate, so I'll read my way through it this time."

Tanya suddenly found herself behind the wheel of the Microbus, guiding it north up I-65. They had agreed that the driver got to choose the music, so she placed one of her own tapes into the cassette deck.

"What in the world is *that*?" Brady said a moment later.

"Oh, that's Sinead O'Connor," she said. "She's very passionate, don't you think?"

Brady just grunted, raised his eyebrows and returned to his *Sports Illustrated*.

"There's a place up here called New Harmony." Brady said a few minutes later, after they crossed the bridge over the Ohio River into Indiana. "Ever heard of it?"

"Have I heard of New Harmony? Oh, *yes*! Are we going there?"

"Ah...no," he said, startled by both her recognition and her enthusiasm. "We can't stop there now; it's way out of our way, over by Evansville. What's the attraction there for you?"

"The Harmonists set up a communal society there 200 years ago, very progressive; it became a center for science and culture."

"But it couldn't have lasted very long, or I'd be...more familiar with it..."

"That's right. After 10 years or so, they sold their land and moved to Ohio...or Pennsylvania; I can't remember which."

"Driven out by the forces of evil?"

"No," she said disapprovingly. "Just felt it was time to move on, I guess. During the short time they were here, they accomplished a lot: the nation's first kindergarten, first free public school and first free library."

"How do you...know all this?"

"It was a...communal colony," she said slowly. "I've just done a lot of reading up on that kind of thing recently, that's all." Turning toward him, she added, "What's your interest in it?"

"Not sure, exactly," Brady said as he watched the Hoosier countryside roll by on his right. "Just heard about it years ago and it sounded intriguing. Never knew the details, but I'd like to learn more about it. I find those kind of social experiments very interesting."

"They're not just interesting," Tanya said with conviction, "they're *vital*. We need to learn from every one, success or failure, to build a better society."

Skeeter: *Okay, hold it. Stop the Bus! This is where I get off! Am I hearing this right? He's traveling back to the past, trying to sort it out, and he's got this…this commie songwriter who's supposed to be helping him?? We need the National Anthem right about now…and maybe a few fighter jets screaming through the sky overhead to restore some order here.*

Herb: *Skeets, Skeets, calm down. We don't really know what we're dealing with here and neither does he. She read about some social experiment, took place a long time ago, and it didn't work out. So? That doesn't make her a communist, Harmonist or anything else, other than curious. Tell you what I think; I think she doesn't know what she is right about now.*

A few miles later, she said, "I've got a question for you. Wouldn't it be easier if, when two people met each other, they could just say they were from the past and heading for the future? I mean, that would spare us all from having to dredge up our own tale of woe and tell it over and over, wouldn't it?"

"Uh-huh," Brady grunted without looking up from his magazine. "But some people are from the past and headed back there. What about them?"

He glanced over toward her, saw her quizzical look and a question creeping toward her lips and decided to change the subject.

"You see the turnoff for US 40 there, up ahead? It's kind of the north/south dividing line for the state. They say there are times when it's snowed on the north side of that highway, but not the south. Fascinating, huh?"

"Do you want me to turn off?"

"No, no. Nothing to see there, except maybe when it's snowing."

"Or not."

"Right," he said with a smile. "Or not."

They made good time through the Hoosier state, with Brady returning to the driver's seat to jockey for road position with the 18-wheelers that seemed to proliferate as they approached Chicago. He wanted to get through the Windy City before they stopped for the night, so they wouldn't have to deal with rush hour traffic first thing in the morning. Making Lake Forest achieved that objective, so they got rooms there--separate rooms--then headed for Buster's Seafood.

Over lobster and scallops, Brady looked across the table and said, "Well, this is where I drop you off; this is where," he paused, relishing the moment with a sip of his Rolling Rock, "this is where I say, 'Ta, ta."

Tanya, jerked her head up, shocked.

"Or, should I say, 'Ta, ta, Tessa?"

"How...how did you know?" she said, dropping her head and glancing from side to side, to see if anyone was within earshot.

"It all adds up," he said. "And I must compliment you. Nice outfit. You don't look at all like that finishing school picture in the paper."

"That was from Emma Willard and it's not—"

"I know, it's very sensitive about being called a 'finishing school.' You must have been quite the item there. Did you start a chapter of the Young Communists League?"

"No," she said with terse whisper. "It wasn't until I was backpacking in India that I realized how vast the distance was between the haves and the have-nots. It opened my eyes. When I came home, I started to see how great that divide is here, too."

"And vowed to fix it?"

"Well, no, not exactly. It's a huge problem, obviously. But each of us can make a difference, if we get committed to doing that."

"Even if it means breaking the law."

"In Nashville, the haves are in a lot better shape than the have-nots. I was just making a statement for social justice." She stopped to eye him carefully. "Does that mean you're going to turn me in?"

"No," he said, suddenly intent on watching his thumb trace the label on his Rolling Rock. "I'm not going to do that." Then he looked up at her. "It's nice to be part of someone else's drama for a change." He took another swig. "So, where do you go from here?"

"I...don't know," she said. "I'm sort of taking life on the fly at the moment."

"Well," Brady started slowly, gazing out past the fish tank, into the lobby, then back at Tanya, "maybe you can help me."

"Really? Doing what?"

"This is going to be a complicated trip for me. Back to the future…or maybe just back to the past. I don't know. Hadn't planned on taking on a passenger, but I could use some help."

Brady asked her for a minute to think. As a veteran of life on the fly, he was about to activate a very important plan, unrehearsed, and could relate well to her present position. It was true she could be useful, but only if she promised to stick with his agenda.

"You have to agree to some very specific rules."

"And they are…?"

"Number one, we will not be judgmental of each other. I'm dealing with my own stuff here. Help it unfold and I'll help you help the downtrodden—someplace far away from Nashville."

"Okay."

"Next, everything you see and hear while you're with me must be absolutely confidential. What happens here stays here. Understood?"

"Okay. We're clear there," she said. "Anything else?"

He looked at her evenly. "I can send you back to Dallas or wherever at any time, for any reason."

Tanya thought for a moment. "Do you know what they call that in psychology?" she said. "That's a negative sanction, encouraging a desired performance with the threat of something undesirable."

"That's fascinating," Brady said blandly. "What about it? Do you agree to those conditions?"

"Yes…and now I've got a condition for you. It's ironclad and non-negotiable."

He looked at her, surprised. "And that is?"

"Don't *ever* call me 'Ta Ta,' in jest or in anger. Just promise you won't go there."

"Not a lot of happy memories, huh?"

"None. We'll stay with 'Tanya,' okay?"

"That's fine; no problem. By the way, the 'Tanya' thing. Does that make you a fan of Patty Hearst?"

Tanya's jaw went slack.

"Just a hunch," he said before taking another sip of his Rolling Rock. "Didn't realize she was still a role model. Listen, remember when I mentioned that I would be doing some hunting in Wisconsin?" She nodded.

"Well, I'm going after some very unusual game. It's a person."

Wrinkles spread slowly across Tanya's brow. "What do you mean," she said. "You're, like, a bounty hunter?"

"Not exactly," Brady replied. "Think of it this way. I'm simply picking someone up to take back with me—us—to Georgia. Remember all those trucks we saw today on the highway? They were hauling cargo from place to place, same as we will be. It's all very routine, really."

"Except that ours is human," she said. "Does this person *want* to go to Georgia?"

Brady shifted uneasily in his seat. "He *needs* to be there. Yes, definitely. It may not—probably will not—be apparent to him at the time. If we all just trust the process, everything will work out fine; really, it will."

"Hmm...," Tanya said thoughtfully. "It almost sounds like a kidnapping..."

"You *could* say that," Brady agreed, "but that doesn't address the whole picture here. Let me ask you a question: How did you feel when you were living in Dallas? Dead or alive?"

"Well...I was in kind of a...coma; I couldn't wait to get out of there."

"Okay...then how did you feel when you were helping all those people in Nashville?"

"I felt...useful, like there was some purpose to my life."

"Exactly!" he said. "We're all going to be energized by bringing these people together. We'll put them back when we're finished, nobody will get hurt and this experience could become the mother lode of lyrics for you before we're through.

"Step One of the plan goes into effect tomorrow," he said as he paid the bill. "Once you see how smooth that goes, you'll be comfortable with it."

12

Brady awoke just before dawn. He was a true morning person, one who usually didn't need a jolt of caffeine to alert him to the possibilities of a new day. Typically, he would savor the sunlight advancing in stages before him, as though by time lapse photography. But today he was restless and eager to accelerate the process. A quick scan of the weather map in the *USA Today* which had been delivered to his door showed the forecast for Milwaukee was clear and mild. This was also to be the last day before a full moon, which Brady wanted to use on this mission to his full advantage.

A groggy Tanya did not understand why they had to start their day so early, but Brady was able--with the assistance of an excellent latte from the little shop across the street--to coax her into the Microbus in time for them to be on the road by 7 AM.

"Do you remember an old TV show called 'This Is Your Life,' with Ralph Edwards?" he asked his sleepy passenger as he merged the Microbus in with the rest of the early morning traffic on I-94.

"Not really," she said.

"Every week, old Ralph would surprise some celebrity, trick him into coming to the studio. Then he'd sit there while Ralph brought in a whole bunch of people from his past. It was great TV, unscripted, and you always found out some new things, things you didn't know before about a famous person."

Brady glanced over at Tanya, eager to have her share his enthusiasm, but she was not yet fully awake and could manage only a grunt in response.

"Well," Brady continued, smiling and undeterred, "this is *my* life, only it's the guests who are going to be surprised."

The first name on Brady's guest list was Paul Saunders, his old baseball coach. Brady was certain he hadn't played much back in high school because Saunders was one of those coaches who could only deal with players who did things exactly his way. Sure, Brady had been a free spirit back then, but wasn't it a coach's job to work with all different types of personalities and get them to blend together? Saunders' teams had always been as boring as their coach and, come to think of it, had not won that many conference titles, either. But they always did things Saunders' way. That seemed to be paramount. How would the old man—he had to be in his 70s by now—how would he respond to an environment over which he had no control?

When Brady stopped for gas at the first Milwaukee County exit, he found his hunch to be correct: Old coaches usually don't have unlisted telephones. Saunders' Lakeside address was right there in the book.

"Good news, Tanya," he said to his companion as he returned to the Bus. "How would you like to do some shopping today? I'll be busy with some recon work."

"Shopping?" she asked, glancing down at her black sweatshirt and black jeans. "Maybe if there's an army surplus store around here. I'd rather find a good book store. What's 'recon,' anyway?"

"Reconnaissance," Brady answered. "I've got to scout around the scene of our activity tomorrow, learn the routine of my subject. That sort of thing."

A half-hour later, Brady dropped Tanya off at the Harry W. Schwartz bookstore, on Downer Avenue. He then headed out to Lakeside, where he parked the Bus behind a row of shops on Silver

Spring Drive and removed the bicycle he had stored in the back expressly for this purpose. Brady felt odd being on a bike in this neighborhood again, some 40 years after he had learned to ride one there. One of his favorite routines as a kid was to take his bike to the Fox-Bay movie theater nearby. Suddenly, he imagined the scent of popcorn in his nostrils and a smile slowly crept across his face. Great memories, great times—or so he had thought prior to entering therapy several years before moving to Midian. His therapist had done her best to suggest that what happiness he thought he had was a mirage. Though he resisted that conclusion, her seeds of doubt about his childhood had taken root. On this day, Brady was finding, to his great pleasure, that his vivid recollection of the scent of theater popcorn in this particular place eclipsed all negativity.

Skeeter: *Popcorn…I would have figured him more for the peanuts and Cracker Jack type. Wouldn't you, Herb?*

Herb: *This guy is not any kind of type that I can see, so nothing he does should surprise us…amaze us, maybe…but I'm only surprised when he seems normal.*

In less than 10 minutes, Brady was on Saunders' street, just two blocks from the coach's house. He decided to make a couple of casual passes past the home to see if there might be a position he could take up in sight of the coach's doors. Approaching the modest, two-story home on what looked to be a small lot, probably no more than a quarter-acre, Brady noticed a driveway on the left side of the property and a walkway from the front door that snaked around a large elm tree to the sidewalk in front. He didn't have time on that first pass to take a good look across the street, so doubled back a few minutes later.

He was most pleased to see a hedge on the left side of that property that was perfect for his purpose: It would conceal his presence, while still affording him a full view of the coach's house. Riding around the block, he tried to catch a glimpse of the coach's back yard, but couldn't. He would have to focus on the front yard and decided after several more passes around the neighborhood that he was comfortable doing that.

"How'd it go?" Tanya asked later.

"Fine," Brady said confidently. "How did *you* do? I see you found something to occupy your mind. A history book?"

"A People's History of the United States,' she said, holding up her purchase. "It's by Howard Zinn."

"Howard Zinn? Isn't he—"

"No, he's *not* radical," Tanya said, rolling her eyes. "That's just what the mainstream media says. Zinn fills in a lot of the blanks, the stuff they didn't teach us in high school."

"Well, you'll have plenty of time to tell me all about it later," Brady said, rising to leave. "Let's go. We'll be having an early dinner, the 6:30 seating. I've picked out the place, Nicosia, on Prospect, an unforgettable ethnic experience."

"Why's that?"

"You'll see."

"You can never go wrong with the lamb," Brady said after the hostess had shown them to their table. "Order the exohico. It's his specialty. Lamb with feta cheese, artichoke hearts and potatoes, wrapped in filo dough. You'll love it...but leave room for dessert."

Shortly after they had finished their entrees, three masked men burst into the dining room from the front door and began firing revolvers wildly in every direction. Diners screamed throughout the restaurant as they dropped below their tables.

"My God! Brady! We're trapped in a *holdup*!" Tanya wailed.

"Don't worry," he said, hiding a grin as he crouched next to her with his hand lightly on her back.

Just then, three cooks bolted from the kitchen and began returning the fire. A moment later, the lights went out, the shooting stopped and a hush fell over the restaurant.

"What's *happening*?" Tanya asked in a nervous whisper.

"I think we'll see here in just a minute," Brady replied.

Suddenly, the lights came back up with bouzouki and baglama music filling the air. Brady looked toward the kitchen to see the smiling cooks lowering their revolvers and returning to work.

"That's terrific!" Brady said with a smile as he helped Tanya, still in shock, back to her seat. "The Greeks won!"

"Wh-what do you mean, 'the Greeks won?" she asked.

"This is a Cypriot restaurant," he said with a smile. "Each night, the Turks and the Greeks duke it out—with blanks, of course—to see who gets to present the dessert menu."

120

"You…you've got to be kidding…"

"Nope, that's what they do. When the Turks win, it's often muhallebi, which is a little bland for me. The Greeks usually deliver semolina cake. With a little brandy syrup, it's very nice."

"Brady! You *knew* this all along? You *knew* this was going to happen!? Is scaring me to death your idea of *humor*?"

"Hey, hey. Take it easy," he said, holding up his hand as dessert arrived. "I'm sorry it upset you, really. This is for old time's sake. My Dad used to take me here. It was his favorite restaurant in Milwaukee, that's all."

Skeeter: *So…now Memory Lane goes through Cyprus? I guess Brady likes being around those guns.*

Herb: *Hey, a good Cypriot restaurant is hard to find. Besides, we said before he needed to work on his change-up. Any ethnic place she tries after this will always seem more serene.*

Night had set in when they returned to the Bus and Brady walked around to the passenger door and motioned Tanya to get behind the wheel, in order to drop him off a couple of blocks away from the coach's house. As she started up the Bus, he carefully removed the Remington and a blanket from behind the seat.

"What are you *doing*!" Tanya said with a shriek.

"Take it easy," Brady said, motioning her to calm down. "This thing won't be firing bullets, just these." He produced a couple of tranquilizer darts from his pocket. "Nobody gets hurt; you'll see. It's as harmless as that shoot-out in the restaurant" …*almost*, he added to himself.

"Brady," Tanya said, composing herself, "I know what I did in Nashville was against the law, but I never, ever, physically hurt anyone. Suddenly, it seems like I'm surrounded by guns and I don't like it, even if this one's shooting some…some sort of dart instead of a bullet. This is making me *very* uncomfortable."

Brady set the shotgun down gently and looked at Tanya. He had been a stockbroker long enough for his training to automatically kick in at times like this. *Feel, felt, found: Objection Handling 101.* It started by disarming her with the words she least expected to hear.

"You know," he started thoughtfully, "you're right: guns *are* dangerous. We've all got to respect their power and the damage they can do in the wrong hands. So, I know how you feel about that; I've felt that way, too.

"That's why I've found extra precautions are necessary, for safety's sake. Can you smell the oil here?" He pointed to the gun, she nodded. "I made sure to clean it very carefully before we left. Right before I did that, I worked with a local deputy sheriff—the best shot in Midian—to hone my skills as a marksman. These darts need to be carefully placed, with just the right amount of Telazol. Did my homework there, too.

"So, you see," he concluded, "you wave a gun around like they were doing back in the restaurant, somebody's likely to get hurt. When you take the proper precautions, though, it's a piece of…semolina," he said suddenly, then smiled in appreciation of his little joke. "Well, let's get out of here before the Turks come back for their dessert revenge…which they'll be doing at the next seating."

Brady had not thought to put a light on his bike, so would now be operating on foot and would call her at the motel on his cell phone when it was time to pick him up. He inserted her number into his speed dial, then changed into a black turtleneck and jeans.

"Stop here," Brady said quietly, wrapping the gun in his blanket as they turned onto coach's street, two blocks from his house. "Remember where to pick me up and to come as soon as I call."

She nodded and drove off.

Casually walking toward the coach's house on the opposite sidewalk, Brady slowly surveyed the situation. No movement at coach's, not even a light on. After a quick check to be sure he wasn't being watched, he slid into the hedge across from coach's house, stretched out on his stomach and waited. An hour passed, then another 30 minutes. At the two-hour mark, the coach's house was now bathed in a lunar glow, without any signs of life within. Brady called Tanya to pick him up.

What he heard next was *not* part of his plan—a busy signal! "Son of a *bitch*!" he whispered to himself. "What is she *doing*?" A minute later, Brady tried the line again. This time, Tanya picked up on the fourth ring.

"What's going on?" Brady hissed into his cell.

"It's the switchboard up front that was busy. What was I supposed to do?"

"It's not important now," Brady said. "Just get over here right away."

A couple of minutes later, Tanya pulled up, precisely as directed "How did it go?" she asked as he climbed into the Microbus.

"Nothing," he said. "Zip. Maybe he's out of town. I'll give it another try tomorrow."

The following morning, Brady was about to head out for another look at Coach's house, when Tanya looked up from her coffee at the motel restaurant and said, "Since this is your old neighborhood, do any of your friends from back then still live around here?"

Brady thought for a moment. "Just one, really. Dennis was the one guy in our group who never left."

"Are you going to see him while you're here?"

"Nah, not this trip," he said on his way out the door. "Dennis is a rock, very solid, a good accountant; I'd trust him with my life…but just don't have the time to reconnect right now. Maybe next time."

Emboldened by his new familiarity with the neighborhood, Brady approached coach's house on foot, glanced around to confirm he was alone, then stepped off the sidewalk onto the driveway for a better look. As he was just about to peek through a window in the kitchen door, he was stopped in his tracks by a woman's voice.

"May I help you?"

Brady turned with a start toward the sound, which seemed to be coming from a clump of shrubs to his left. "Uh, yes," he said quickly to the shrubs, "maybe you can. I'm looking for the coach. Any idea when he might be back?"

The woman--a petite redhead, in her 50s--was standing now, trowel in hand. "I'm afraid he might not be back at all," she said. "Are you one of his former players?"

"Yes, that's right. Just stopped by to say 'hello."

"My, that is unusual," she said. "He didn't have many visitors before they took him away."

"Away? Where?"

"A rest home down in Shorewood, at least that's what I heard."

"Alzheimer's?"

"No, it wasn't that. I'm afraid your coach was just a mean old man. He yelled at everyone and threatened some of the neighborhood kids. Said he'd shoot them if they came in his yard. After he fired some warning shots from an old BB gun one day, his daughter, Evelyn, flew in from Cleveland and made arrangements to put him in a home. She hasn't decided what to do with the house. Would you like her number?"

A call to Cleveland gave Brady the information he needed. The following morning, he paid a visit to Heritage Village.

Its subdued atmosphere struck Brady immediately, quite unlike the garish Worlds of Wonder favored by his father. The nerve center here appeared to be the recreation room, where canasta, cribbage and Scrabble seemed to be the games of choice, while several women seated at a large table in the rear of the room were hard at work, trying to make sense of a large, "Where's Waldo?" jigsaw puzzle.

Monotonous as all this might seem to the outside world, older people could usually be counted upon to bitch mightily whenever any change was introduced into their carefully orchestrated routine. Brady hoped the coach was a recent enough arrival to welcome thinking about something that might take his mind off his surroundings.

"Good morning," Brady said outside coach' s door. "I'd like to talk with you, if you have a minute."

After a momentary pause, the coach's door opened slowly and he glared at his visitor. "*If I have a minute*? Is that what you said? I've got nothing *but* minutes--until they turn into hours, then I have too many of those. I suppose there's some point to my being here. Have you come to tell me what it is?"

The two men faced each other, several feet apart, "Who the hell are you?" the coach said, his eyes squinting as he tried to place the face before him. With a grunt, the old man left the door open as he turned and shuffled back into his room. Brady followed him, taking a metal chair at the foot of his bed.

Before he answered, Brady could not help but focus on the coach's hands, as he had often done years before. They were oversized for his frame, which had been almost six feet tall when Brady was in high school. Now, though, with coach's shoulders stooped as they were, it was hard to determine his true height. His fingers were gnarled like branches tormented from years of strong crosswinds. Brady remembered clearly that, when the coach demonstrated the proper technique for a throw to first, his hand would flare out, over his shoulder, but his fingers would point toward the ground, like dousing rods responding to water.

"Brady Greer," he said, meeting the coach's tired eyes directly, "Remember me?"

The coach rubbed his chin thoughtfully, then said with a shrug, "Actually, no...I'm afraid my memory's not--"

"Okay," Brady said, grimacing, "maybe this'll help: the guy who mooned the Shorewood cheerleaders."

"Son...of...a...*bitch*," the coach said slowly as he eyed Brady up and down. "Well, well. . .it's been a long time." Then, with a sneer, "What's the matter? You didn't make enough fun at my expense when I tried to coach you? Now you're following me...here?"

"Just wanted to talk to you, that's all," Brady said as gently as he could.

"*Talk*? After all this time? You don't have a telephone?"

"Look, I was in town and thought I'd drop by--"

"So we could do...what? Reminisce?"

"Maybe. We could catch up with each other. Down where I live now, in Georgia, a bunch of us have a regular basketball game. If we kept track of individual stats, which we don't, I'd probably have more assists than anybody. Does that surprise you?"

"At this point, Greer, very little--beyond your being here-- would surprise me. Anyway, I stopped being surprised by life a long time ago. Stats only have meaning if you know the competition. These guys you're playing against, are they younger than me? Do they have both their eyes? Their arms? Their legs?"

"Yes, they do," Brady said with a laugh. "In every case. Why is it so hard for you to admit I might actually be good at a sport?"

"You were an uncoachable kid, that's why. Hard-headed kids usually become hard-headed adults. Now that I think of it, though, pick-up games probably suit you just fine: no coach, no system, no discipline. Just run and gun."

"Wait a minute. That's a little unfair. If you're out of control, nobody wants to play with you, even in a pick-up game."

"But that's the beauty of the playground," the coach said. "You change teams every time you play, right? Hang around the court long enough and they'll let you in. They'll tolerate almost anyone when they need to even up the teams."

"Let me try this another way," Brady said, his facial muscles tensing . "I'm playing another sport now, basketball, three decades after I left high school, against guys my age and younger who are good athletes.   They had good high school careers; I didn't. Hell, some of them even played college ball. Why didn't I share their success earlier, at least in high school?"

The left side of coach's pursed lips began to twitch, as though he was trying to speak from the side of his mouth. It was a nervous tic Brady suddenly remembered from long ago. "I've already answered that one for you," the old man said. "You were a pain in the ass. It's funny, I've gotten to where my memory can fail me, but I remember that very well."

"And that's it with you?" Brady said, the timbre in his voice rising. "A kid is a pain in the ass, so you put him on the shelf without making any effort to work with him? We had our differences, obviously, but I love baseball, love it more than ever now. I wanted to play for you; you know I had the talent, but it didn't happen. I never had the chance to find out why, so, that's why I'm here: to hear what it was about me—and a couple of other guys, now that I think of it—that turned you off so completely."

"Well," Saunders said, the edge fading from his voice as he rubbed his cheek, "you're right. There was something.

"I don't care what anybody says, Greer, baseball's still the National Pastime. All these stupid owners and greedy players have stuck their forks in the golden goose, but they haven't killed it—not yet, anyway. And it remains the Pastime for at least three reasons: It's still played about the same way it was 100 years ago. Sure, the pitchers and hitters have both gotten better, but it's still the same distance from home to first, the pitcher's mound to the plate, and so forth. Also, it's a great team game, but there are still all kinds of personal stats you can use to weigh a player's value, even compare players in different generations."

"And the third?" Brady prompted. "You said there were three reasons?"

"Ah…right, that's right," said the coach, trying hard to recall it. "…Yes! Number three may be most important of all: no clock. You get 27 outs to win, no matter how long it takes. None of that 'kill the clock' crap you get in football and basketball."

"But what has all that got to do with me?"

"Simply this, Greer: You didn't respect the game. Remember that kid from the South Side? 'The Polish Poppi?' From Don Bosco High?"

"Sure. Kip Kapopka. Works for the Commissioner now. He's in the papers all the time.

"He played about the same time you did, probably didn't have much more talent than you--but he played something like 12 years with five teams in the Big Leagues. Know how he did that?"

"How?"

"Kapopka made a career out of making himself useful. He could fill in wherever there was a need—infield, outfield, behind the plate, even pitched a little spot relief here and there. No matter the challenge, he never backed down. Always had a positive attitude. "Kip the Kameleon" the papers called him and he was proud of that."

"And what does that have to do with me?"

"You were the opposite of The Polish Prince: a smart ass and, like I said, also a pain in the ass. The game is a gem and you treated it like a piece of gravel. If a kid didn't respect the game, he didn't play for me. It was that simple, but not always easy to get through the thick head of a 17-year-old."

Brady gazed out the window at the closely-cropped grass for a long moment. The coach's words stung, because they were on target—*then*, in high school, but he *understood* now. It had taken a long time, but now he got it; he adored the game *today*, probably as much as Saunders.

"You're right, Coach," he finally said softly. "I didn't respect the game then, but I love it now. Guess it's a little late for that to do any good, though, huh?"

"Maybe not, Greer," said Saunders, again rubbing his cheek and carefully eyeing his visitor. "It's in a damn crisis right about now. It'll take a smart ass to save it. That's what you've been for a long time. Maybe you're the guy."

When she picked Brady up out front a few minutes later, Tanya was anxious for details, but he was still replaying it all in his mind.

"You know how old people can get irritable and cranky?" he said finally.

"Yeah."

"Well, Saunders was that way a long time ago; nothing's changed there. What never registered with me before was how much he loves baseball. I love it, too. As different as we are, we share that and we also agree that the game's broke and needs to be fixed."

"How's that going to happen?"

"I don't know, but it would be nice if it could happen in the next couple of months. His daughter told me the coach has cancer and that's about all the time he's got left."

"And you care that much about the coach? I thought—"

"It's hard to explain, Tanya," he said, looking out the window, trying to see the future as the Milwaukee skyline receded into the past, "but closure is important. When people die before you can get there, well, then the best you can do is find someone to take their place. Who knows? Maybe there's still some way to make the Coach a happy man."

13

"Where to tonight?" she asked.

"I'm not in the mood to stop," he said. "Let's just drive straight through to Georgia. We'll take turns behind the wheel 'til we get there."

It was just after midnight when they approached Chicago, so they avoided the by-pass, taking the interstate through the heart of downtown. *A resting heart*, Brady thought. *That's what it does now, rest on the third shift, so it can get back on the treadmill at dawn and run like a sonofabitch again, 'til closing time.*

As the city skyline passed on their left and dropped into the background, Brady gazed out onto the working class neighborhoods on the South Side and wondered what stories they could tell. *Immigrants come to America dreaming of a better life. How many of those hopes were realized? How many dashed by insensitive people in a position of influence? Oafish teachers? Coaches?* A total count would always be elusive, because each little story tended to spin in its own orbit.

After they turned south in Gary, leaving the heavy truck traffic behind, Brady slid behind the wheel as they resumed the next leg of their journey. He couldn't read his way through Indiana this time, even by the light of the full moon, so he might as well drive. He actually enjoyed guiding the Bus south on I-65. Radio reception was best in the darkest night and it still amazed Brady, though he'd been doing it for years, that he could pull in 50,000-watt stations from as far away as Pittsburgh and New Orleans. On family trips when he was a kid, Brady would rest his chin on the back of the front seat of their station wagon late at night, listening to "The Green Hornet" and other radio mysteries, while his Dad drove and his Mom and sister slept. There was the appearance of closeness to his father then, but the two were really as isolated as a pair of dateless moviegoers and—

"Brady?"

"Yeah?" was all he could manage as she snapped him back from his reverie.

"We need to talk."

"Gee, I've never heard that on a first date before," he said with an impish grin. "That usually comes several months down the line."

"I'm serious," she said, eyeing him with impatience across the dark expanse of the Bus cab. "You wanted to remove that man against his will from his home and take him across several state lines, back to Georgia. How many laws that breaks, I'm not sure, but, as the driver of the getaway Bus, I deserve more information on the big picture here."

"Since when did laws start mattering to you?"

"Breaking a law on my own is not the issue here," she said. "What matters to me at the moment is that I'm doing illegal stuff without actually seeing the point. I think I deserve to know what's going on here."

Brady raised his hand, requesting a moment to collect his thoughts. If she didn't like what she heard, she might opt to return to Dallas or hide out elsewhere, by her own choice. He was surprised at how much he suddenly didn't want that to happen. Did he not trust her? Or, had he glided over the hurdles to closeness without realizing it to become more emotionally involved? Either way, he had to state his case convincingly.

"Look," he said slowly. "You're right. I haven't given you the big picture here and I apologize for that."

"Thank you," Tanya said with a quiet nod as her facial

muscles began to thaw. "I can't recall the last time I heard a man apologize for anything."

"Have you ever felt you deserved something," he said, "but had it denied to you in an irrational way?"

"Hmmm," she said thoughtfully, rubbing her right cheek. "I haven't really felt that in my own life. I've seen it in other people, though. Seems like some people have it easier than they have a right to deserve, while others are born into almost impossible situations."

"That's my point!" Brady said, his voice becoming more animated. "If your effort in school, in athletics or on the job is being judged fairly by those in control, then, of course, you accept whatever happens. But what if those key people in control are mean, stubborn or just plain ignorant? You don't get the grade, the playing time or the promotion on grounds other than true merit. What then?"

"You try to bring justice where there's injustice?"

"Exactly!" he said. "When kids are victimized by adults, the kids usually can't just pick up and move. They're stuck in their school, in their city, and don't have the choice of where to live. They can only sit there and eat the injustice, day after day. You can't ask for a replay or have the film reviewed. There is no appeal."

"Which somehow brings us to this Bus on this road on this night, I have a feeling."

"That's right," Brady said as they entered the outskirts of Indianapolis. "I got jerked around by a bunch of people when I was younger and that made it tough for me to get ahead. Unlike many in that position, though, I acquired the financial means to reconnect with these people and get them to answer for the way they treated me. That's what was on my mind when I first approached the coach."

"And now?"

"Now I realize that would just be wallowing in my own bile. When you see old people walking down the street, it's not too hard to pick out the ones doing that. I'd rather not wind up that way."

"So, what's the alternative?"

Skeeter: *I feel the famous "Plan B" coming on here...*

Herb: *There better be a Plan B, because Plan A was looking pretty shaky. You got to start with a plan; that's important...but you also got to adapt when things change. Stay flexible; that's just good game management.*

Skeeter: *...and, if you can spin the change as a plus, that's even better.*

"The alternative," Brady said, "is even better than the original plan, which was just dealing with my personal issues. Now, we can sink our teeth into something big, much bigger than ourselves."

"Have you decided what that something is?"

"Yes, as a matter of fact, I have. I don't know if you buy the notion that each of us has a destiny, but I find that idea intriguing. Maybe we each have a destiny, one which is often unknowable. Sometimes, though, we can figure it out, and that's what I did after talking to the coach."

"Tell me all about it."

"Well," he began, laboring mightily to be sure this would make as much sense to her as it did to him, "My destiny—the reason I was put on this planet—is to save baseball."

"Save it from...what?"

"From whom, actually: The cretins and charlatans who are running it."

"Do I get to ask *how* you're going to do that?"

"Whoa, Tanya! I just figured out my destiny. Give me a little time here to revise my plan for how I'm going to get there. It's really starting to register with me how much life is about choices. Everyone chooses whether to live a life of drama or one of consciousness. People who don't realize that—which would be most people—are stuck in their daily drama, just trying to make it through each day into the next. One of the things I like about you is that you looked at your life, didn't like what you saw, and are trying to change it. Am I right?"

"Never thought about it quite that way, but, yeah, that covers it."

"And, I'll bet if you could see right now a lot of kids you grew up with in Dallas, they'd look like hamsters in a cage, running through their daily dramas on one of those little wheels to nowhere."

"But the cage is safe and getting out of it is risky. I know why I got out: I just couldn't take it anymore. How about you? What you're doing here is real risky. Why are you doing it? You talk like you're running toward something, but I think you're running away, too."

Brady sighed and shook his head. Those few times he had opened up to bare his soul, it had been to someone who was paid to listen. He barely knew Tanya, yet that fact, plus the exhaustion from the day now setting in, lowered his defenses. *What the hell...*

"I've played by the rules for nearly 50 years and where has that gotten me? I haven't accomplished anything meaningful, because I've only taken a bunch of little risks; I've refused to take a big risk, to step outside my comfort zone. Yet, when you look at history, most every major accomplishment was made by someone who dared to be different. Security, alone, is a pretty empty reason to exist. Big opportunities are worth big risk and that's what we have here."

"The opportunity or the risk?"

"Both," he said. "It's like this: Staying caught up in your own drama can make you feel dead after awhile; choosing to be conscious is energizing, but I made some lousy choices before that, when I was just bumping along."

"Such as?"

He looked at her, wondering how deep she planned to drill into his oily past.

"College, career, busted marriage, the usual stuff."

"Tell me about your marriage."

"Beth and I were married for six years, happily, I thought. But...I don't know...sometimes love just isn't enough, I guess..."

"Any kids?"

"Nope."

"So, how long have you been divorced?"

"It isn't final yet."

Tanya looked at him, eyes widening.

"Don't worry," he said quickly, "everything's in the works, no disagreements on the terms, should be a done deal in the next couple of months."

"And she—Beth—is where?"

"Still in Midian, but planning to move, from what I hear.

Look, my marriage busted up, then my Dad died and that all put me in a tailspin. This just seems like a good time to take a look at where I've been and where I'm going."

"And that logically leads to…kidnapping people?"

Brady paused to collect his thoughts. For years, he had been embarrassed by his impulsiveness. He typically plunged his own money into stocks or options with the hubris of a professional, but without the forethought he urged on his clients. It was often an expensive mistake. But it also made him feel like a player, making life more exciting. Planning, for Brady, had been only the vaguest of concepts, but one he needed to summon now to help figure out the best way to proceed.

"I spent a lot of time, Tanya, running away from my past. Then, I resolved to confront it. At first, I thought this was going to involve bringing a lot of people into my personal journey, thus the interest in social experiments. But now, after meeting you and talking with Coach, what I do will involve fewer people, but will have an impact way beyond just my life, touching the lives of millions—in a positive way. This hamster is out of his cage, so to speak, and he feels good about it."

"Hmm," she said thoughtfully, "sounds as though you've decided that making your omelet justifies breaking a few eggs."

"I could tell you I'm just borrowing the eggs, not breaking them," he said, "but I respect your intelligence more than that, so here's the truth, Tanya: kidnapping is a crime, a felony, for which a person could be sentenced from 10 to 20 years—more if there's a ransom or bodily injury."

"Wow," she said as her eyes grew bigger.

"Yeah," Brady said quickly, shooting a look toward her, "that might even trump embezzlement, grand theft and forgery, but not by much."

Tanya stiffened and turned away from him, looking out the window on her right. Brady paused to let his words sink in even deeper before continuing.

"This is big now, Tanya," he said, "bigger even than your Robin Hood caper in Nashville. But, remember what I said about big risk: It's worth it, if it's matched by a big reward. If we can figure out a way to save baseball, we'll have the gratitude of millions."

"And you'll be patching a blow-out in your past."

"Yes, I will—but not just for myself. How many kids out there have been messed up by bad coaches, ignorant teachers or just plain mean adults? Tens of thousands, easily. You don't read about us. We're all expected to just suffer in silence."

"It's like our own Viet Nam," he said. "The focus there is on the almost 60,000 who died and that's understandable. But there have to be several times that number still walking the streets, still trying to cope after all they saw over there. They don't get a memorial and probably don't want one, but their lives have been messed up, big time. They deserve more acknowledgment than they've had. So, you see, Tanya, what I'm really doing here is speaking up for a lot of people who haven't been able, for whatever reason, to be heard."

Skeeter: *Now he's going to represent emotional cripples everywhere while slaying his own dragons…then bail out Major League Baseball, is that it?*

Herb: *Yes…that would appear to be where we're going here…but the most fascinating thing, at least to me, is that he seems to be doing this all on the fly, making it up as he goes, which sounds like the longest of long shots--but baseball does need a wake up call, so good for him.*

Skeeter: *Herb, you're a journalist: No rooting.*

Herb: *I'm not a reporter here, I'm a commentator…so I'm… commentating… whatever…*

The Bus cut through the black Hoosier night in silence. "Well," she said finally, exhaling slowly, "it seemed there for a while like we were just trying to snatch some poor old guy from his yard. But you've obviously given this a lot of thought. The idea of this whole thing being socially useful certainly makes me feel better about it."

The trace of a smile crept across Brady's face as they drove onward toward Kentucky. Several miles later, he suggested that Tanya get some sleep, so she could pull the graveyard shift behind the wheel.

After they stopped at dawn near Chattanooga for coffee, Brady resumed driving. Guiding the Bus back onto the interstate, he decided this would be a good time to educate Tanya about the mores and folkways of the South.

"Would you like to know a little bit about where we're going?" he asked.

"Sure," she said. "But is it really that different from anyplace else?"

"Well," Brady said. "You can judge that for yourself soon enough. First of all, when you die, you don't want to do it in North Georgia."

"Why is that?"

"Because that's where they'll take your money for cremating you, then never get around to actually lighting the fire."

"So they bury you instead?"

"No," he said, matter-of-factly. "They just stack the bodies up for a year or more, like cord wood. Don't do anything in particular with them beyond that." He let that sink in for a minute before continuing.

"And people like to say, 'Y'all come see us.'"

"That sounds very nice," Tanya said.

"Yeah, but they don't *mean* it," he answered. "It tends to be vague and non-specific by design. After you hear it enough, you'll be tempted to ring their bell in the middle of the night, just for spite."

"Hmm, that *is* a little strange…"

"But here's my favorite," Brady said, relishing the moment. "What's the meanest, nastiest thing you can say about anyone?"

"Hmmm…let me think," she said slowly. "Well, when I first got to Nashville, I was a waitress for a while. That place had a cook who was really mean to me, nasty and rude. He made fun of me when I couldn't get the orders right. Besides that, he smelled like he didn't bathe but once a week."

"Okay," Brady said. "Here's how you convey that thought in the South--even to his next of kin--without being offensive: 'You know, Bubba's got a bit of a mean streak in 'im and he might be needin' a bath a little more often, *bless his heart.*"

"Bless his heart?"

"That's right," Brady said proudly. "Put that at the end of any sentence and it's amazing what you can get away with. You still get to trash somebody, but it takes the edge off."

"Wow," Tanya said as she reached under the seat and produced her large three-ring binder. "I guess you were right. The

136

South really does sound different."

"I've been meaning to ask you more about that," Brady said. "Whatcha got there?"

"This?" she said, looking at the binder. "Oh, that's my special book. My own words to live by, you might say."

"Looks like it's been around awhile," he said. "How long have you been keeping it?"

"Since I started college, I guess," she said. "I began by rearranging the books of the Bible so they'd make more sense. After that, I decided there were parts of the Bible that just didn't work for me, so I took 'em out."

"A lot of the Old Testament?"

"Right. That and Revelation. Then I would come across stuff that did work for me, like Nietzsche, so I'd start adding that. Now I've got my very own book, a living document. It expands and contracts as time goes on."

"Did you say 'Nietzsche?' He's in there, too?"

"Yup. 'Morality is the best of all devices for leading mankind by the nose.' That's what he said. Makes sense to me, so it made the binder."

Brady thought for a long moment. "So, you're giving the world 'The Book of Tanya,'" is that it?

"That's right!" she said. "That's what I call it. How did you know?"

"Just a lucky guess."

"I've got to write that 'bless your heart' thing down," she said. "I know that'll come in handy.

"You know," she said moments later, sliding her binder back beneath the seat, "I think most people live their lives by their own book, they just don't always like to admit it. I think it's easier to keep it all together, in a binder. "

Brady stared far into the distance down I-75. Somehow, he got the feeling Tanya and the Deep South might get along rather well.

He started to think about what his own book would look like: lots of cross outs and erasures, interspersed with plenty of blank pages. In short, an unintelligible mess. He reached for the cassette bag. There had to be something soothing in there. He smiled when he came upon The Beatles' "Rubber Soul." That would make him feel better.

It was after the evening rush hour when they approached Atlanta, but Brady still marveled at the traffic mess on the Perimeter Highway there--drivers darting from one lane to another at 70 MPH at all hours of the day or night without a glance in their mirrors, as if the laws of both physics and the road were useless abstractions. But there were many large skid marks and gashed abutments that said differently.

As Brady turned the Bus east onto I-20, they were just an hour outside of Midian, "Tomorrow, you'll get your real introduction to the Deep South," he said. "So far, it's just been highways. Interstates look pretty much the same everywhere, but there's no place quite like IPCOT and Munson County."

"IPCOT? Don't you mean 'EPCOT?'"

"Nope. I've got a little operation out in the county that I like to think of as the Innovative Penal Colony Of Tomorrow. For you, admission is free. You'll find it interesting."

14

Brady was down at Gene's the following morning, greeting the new day with a glass of orange juice and trying to plan his next move.

"Not much of a breakfast," Scratch said, swallowing his gravy biscuit and nodding toward Brady's OJ. "Ya oughta get the grits, at least."

Brady had tried without success to cotton to Southern cooking, but Scratch had a point about the grits. They were said to be the best in town. "Seasoned as we go," Ned liked to say. "If you wait 'til they're done, they got a whole different flavor."

With a sigh, Brady asked for an order, discretely including a request for some bacon and cheese on the side. Maybe, with a touch of Tabasco, he could learn to like them.

"Damn," said Scratch as the order arrived. "That's the most loaded up mess o' grits I ever seen. Ned must have a jar of peanut butter around here somewhere. You want some o' that? Too bad this place ain't a little fancier. We could get you some ground pepper."

"Okay, smart ass," Brady replied as the chuckles reverberated around the table. "I'm trying to get with the program here, but I'm doing it my way. Let me ask you something. You ever play any sports in high school?"

"Yeah, sure," Scratch said. "I played ball. Everybody plays football down here, unless they're feeble or some kinda nerd."

"Tell me about it."

"Well...let's see...what's to tell? The coach took one look at me, tall and thin, the first day of practice, and he says, 'You're a wide receiver.' Only problem with that is I ain't got hands worth a shit, so I didn't play all that much. Funny thing is, I would have been better off as a defensive back."

"Why's that?"

"Well, that's where they put me in practice against the first team offense. Every time they'd run a pass at me, I'd knock it down. Hardly ever picked one off, but I had a knack for knowin' where the play was goin'. I'd just step in front of the guy and bat it away. Used to really piss the coach off. He'd cuss me out and yell at me for stealin' the plays somehow, but it never occurred to him to use me there in a game."

"How come?"

"I didn't look like a defensive back, I guess."

"That must have really made you mad," Brady said eagerly.

"Not really. As my Daddy likes to say, 'You can't polish horse shit.' This guy was a horse shit coach. Anyone could see that. Word was he had saved the life of the principal's wife years before at a summer camp where he was the lifeguard. As long as that guy was principal, our coach had a job."

"But you could have been a *star* on defense!"

"Woulda, coulda, shoulda," Scratch said with a shrug. "If 'ifs' and 'buts' was candied nuts, we'd all have a Merry Christmas. Gotta go. I hear my wild dogs callin'."

Brady stared out the window, across the town square, thinking that the real Silent Majority had nothing to do with politics. Instead, it consisted of the legion of raw talent that might, under proper guidance, have been steered toward success. But, for every star who found the spotlight, how many talented Scratches were there in the shadows, waiting in vain for their skills to be recognized and nurtured?

Brady decided to seek refuge at his office in the train depot. The market was up and down these days, just like his emotions. His reverie was broken by Irma's knock on the door.

Skeeter: *Oh, oh…be careful…this woman is toxic.*

Herb: *I don't think she's that bad. Remember, Brady shares her secret about those little jaunts to Atlantic City. Midian's a small town. They need each other…maybe in kind of a twisted way, but they do need each other.*

"How's my money man?" Irma said with forced cheeriness as she entered the depot. "I hear there's a new lady in your life. Now, tell Irma all about it."

"Where did that come from?" Brady replied, startled both by the question and the sight of Irma, whom he hadn't seen since her midnight visit.

"Come now, dear boy. This is Midian. News like that moves faster than one of those freight trains outside your door."

"Just a girl I met up in Tennessee," he said casually. "She's doing some research for a writing project. Probably be around for a week or two, then head back home."

"But, in the meantime, bunking at your place?" Irma said with a devilish grin.

"She's my houseguest, yes," Brady said, "while I'm fixing up a little place I've got out in the country. It's my retreat—away from the prying eyes of Mother Midian."

"Oh, my!" Irma exclaimed in mock anxiety. "I didn't mean to pry…"

"You most certainly did," Brady said, grinning back at her, desperately wanting   everything between them to revert to where it had been before her midnight call, but sensing that was going to be very difficult.   Irma was now pickin' at him, as they said in the South, a popular parlor game that lasted as long as its subject allowed.

"So, what can I do for you?" he said finally. "I'm sure you wouldn't make a special trip over here just to traffic in gossip."

"Oh, no," Irma lied. "I should *say* not!" After a couple of perfunctory questions about her utilities, she was gone.

Brady's talk with Irma made him wonder anew about Tanya. They had not become friends, exactly, only fellow travelers, but he enjoyed her company. They could continue on together for a while, helping each other search for…what? Happiness? Contentment? What then? Did they have enough in common to build a lasting friendship? Brady thought he had those questions answered after dating Beth for several months, but he no longer trusted his judgment with women, which was why getting involved with a socialist socialite from Dallas now made as much sense to him as anything else.

"So, what are your first impressions of Midian?" he asked her when he returned home later and found her scanning the latest issue of the *Monitor*.

"It's a beautiful little town," she said, "but it seems very…I don't know…*bourgeois*."

"Really?"

"Yes," she said, looking up from her paper. "Just walking around downtown, talking to some of the shop owners, I get the feeling money is much more important here than ideas."

"Hmm…can't argue with you there," Brady said.

"And this Sherman guy must have really been something. People still talk about him as though he might turn up any minute, strolling down Main Street. How long has he been gone, anyway?"

"About 150 years."

"Wow! Everyone seems pretty proud of the fact that he didn't burn the town down."

"If he had, we wouldn't have all those pretty houses to look at on Main Street. You know, they re-enact the Battle of Kolb's Farm every April, less than 30 miles from here."

"Why? Was that a big Southern victory?"

"Depends on how you look at it. The South gained some ground, driving Sherman back a little, but lost three times as many men as the North in the process. Finally, it got dark. That ended it, much as anything."

"Why would they celebrate that?" she said. "I mean, they took heavy casualties. Don't you usually celebrate clear victories, instead of defeats?"

"How about the Alamo?" Brady shot back at Tanya, the Texan. "As I recall, we came out on the short end of that one, but the guys on our side became folk heroes."

142

"That's right," she said thoughtfully. "Guess you got me there."

"Even though the South lost the war," he said, "its people remain convinced their genteel lifestyle is superior. I mean, look around. What looks better to you? Midian, urban sprawl or some faceless suburb?"

"I've never seen a town like this anywhere else," she said. "It's like a movie set. All it needs are petticoats and parasols."

"Precisely! You can't beat the *look*, but some of the stories behind those beautiful antebellum doors aren't so pretty."

"What do you mean?"

"Well, let's take booze. Seems like every other person here is a Baptist, but I've never seen people drink like they do in Midian. It's the oil for the social machinery every weekend and there are some pretty prominent people who get lubricated a little too much on a regular basis. But it's all done behind closed doors. Restaurants are always trying to get a liquor-by-the-drink law passed, but it hasn't happened, because that would be bad for our image and we couldn't have that."

"Yes, I guess not…"

"Don't get me started," he said. "Midian is quirky, quaint-- maybe even kinky--but we'll have plenty of time to get into all that later. Let's jump in the Bus. I'll show you around."

"You see that church up ahead?" Brady said as he drove south on Main Street with her from the town square. "That's the Baptist church, the biggest building in town after the courthouse. But it's only one of 'em."

"What do you mean?"

"You see over there, a block west of us?"

"Yeah."

"That's the other Baptist church, the black one."

"But I thought—"

"I know," he said. "You thought segregation was over. It is, legally. But this is the reality: Two great big ole Baptist churches within a block of each other--one for the blacks, one for the whites. You like music. Guess which one's got the better music?"

"Hmm…the black one, I'd guess."

"Isn't even close," Brady said. "It rocks. Everybody's really into it, singin' and swayin.' At the white church, you get a dirty look if you're off-key. I always thought they should swap choirs for a while. That'd loosen everybody up."

"Sounds like a good idea."

"If that ever happens, it'll be in the next century," he said with a shrug. "This is *not* the land of sudden change. When shifts do occur, the impetus tends to come from the outside."

"So that's what you are? Sand in their oyster?"

"Yes," he said with a grin, "guess that's me."

"So, when do I get to see IPCOT?" she asked.

"That's where we're headed.'"

Brady drove slowly through the countryside, past cotton fields and peach orchards, out to Scofield. Turning into IPCOT, he could not help but notice the thriving bougainvillea and wisteria. The place had never looked better.

"So," Tanya said, looking around as they left the Bus, "you're in the chicken business, too? You didn't mention that."

Skeeter: *No, what he's really doing is playing chicken...with reality.*

Herb: *Now, Skeets, let's give him a chance here. The man aims high; got to give him that. Says he has a plan to hit that target, so let's see what he's got.*

"Follow me," he said, "and let's take a closer look."

Unlocking the gate, he ushered her into a courtyard, off of which there were a half-dozen separate rooms.

"Ugh! Those chicken really smell," she said with a grimace, "but I don't see any."

"Once they've been here, the odor just becomes a permanent fact, even after they're long gone."

Tanya eyed the six rooms surrounding the courtyard. "Okay...so, the coach's room stays empty. Who's next on your list?"

"To understand the importance of our next guest, you have to know what's been going on in baseball. Do you follow it at all?"

"No, not really."

Brady motioned for her to join him on a bench in the shade before continuing. "For about 100 years, the club owners ran the game with an iron fist. They made a lot of money and kept most of it. In 1970, St. Louis attempted to trade its center fielder, Curt Flood, to Philadelphia, but he shocked baseball--and America, for that matter--by not only refusing to go, but by suing Major League Baseball and its reserve clause."

"What's that?"

"Well," said Brady, picking up a small rock and bouncing it in his hand, "it was what the owners used to bind a player and his contract to a single team for life. Baseball faced legal challenges before, but never had a player of Flood's caliber attacked the game's sacred clause. He accused baseball of violating the 13th Amendment, which bars all involuntary servitude, including slavery, and he did that in 1970—which was the last year of segregation in Midian, by the way."

Tanya looked around the courtyard, then back at Brady, incredulous. "And you're going to get this Curt Flood guy and bring him here?"

"No," Brady laughed as he dropped the rock, picked up a stick and threw it toward the center of the courtyard. "I couldn't do that if I wanted to. Flood died a few years ago. I'm just trying to give you some background. He basically sacrificed the rest of his career, spending a couple of years in court to get this thing thrown out."

"And, when he did, he became a hero, right?"

"No, he was seen more as a pariah at the time for exploding a bunch of myths about baseball. In fact, he fought the issue all the way to the Supreme Court, where he lost."

Tanya thought for a moment while lightly drawing a line in the sandy courtyard floor with her right foot. "Then, why is he important?"

"It's tough to be the first guy to challenge something that big and he was willing to do that, to become the battering ram that beat on the door. It took a few more years and a few more challenges to get the door to cave in. That's when players got their freedom to move to other teams by their own choice."

"And that's a good thing?"

"Depends on where you sit. The pendulum has swung from total owner control to the point where the baseball player's union is now the iron fist. It's become the strongest union in sports."

"Aha!" she said triumphantly, rising from the bench and throwing her hands into the air. "So, the working man wins!"

Brady eyed her narrowly. "Well...*technically*, that's

right—except these working men aren't punching a clock, they're making millions…even the ones who have trouble punching a single out of the infield."

"Which leads us…somehow…to this empty courtyard here at IPCOT…"

"That's right. Baseball is in another crisis at the moment. There's even been talk of a strike before the World Series, unless someone can knock some sense into the thick heads on both sides."

"And that 'someone' would be…"

"Me, your traveling companion. That takes care of the 'who.' It's the 'how' that's…evolving. I know a college professor who understands the labor movement very well. He'll be joining us soon, so we can map strategy for our new plan."

Tanya returned to the bench, this time with her legs folded beneath her. "And is he aware of that?"

"Uh…no. At the moment, he isn't."

"How can you be sure he'll help?"

"It's the only way he'll ever get back to Kansas City," Brady said with a smile.

"Kansas City? That's where we're going?"

"First thing in the morning."

15

"You'll like Kansas City," he said as they started west on I-20 that afternoon.

"Where everything's up to date?" she asked. "That's hard to believe."

"That is pushing it, I agree, but it's a lot more up to date than people realize who haven't been there. That old image of a glorified stockyard, a Cow Town, is long gone. You'll have time to see some of the sights and we'll also have time to take care of business. Have you ever studied much history?"

"I had to take some to get through school, but I dreaded it. All those names and dates. Memorize this, memorize that. Very dry stuff. I had a hard time keeping it all straight."

"The names and dates, alone, are boring. Can't argue with that. But once you get beyond them and really understand some of those names and how they interacted with each other to change the course of history, well, that can be very, very interesting."

"So, we're going to Kansas City to study history?"

"Not exactly. We're going to meet up with one 'Dr. B. Wright Conger,' an expert in the field by his own admission."

"And with a doctor-sized ego, as big as all outdoors?"

"Almost. Dr. Conger *is* a very bright guy. That part's legit. But he also has a very narrow view of history. If you share it, great, you get along fine. If not, he can make your life really miserable."

"Let me guess," she said as they approached the Atlanta perimeter. "You fell into the latter category."

"That's right," Brady said with an approving sideways glance. "I walked into that class liking history so much that I thought about majoring in it. After a semester with him, though, I ran for the exit and never went back."

"What made him so unbearable?"

"Well, for openers, he saw everything through the prism of class struggle. That, in his view, was the real civil war in America. The other Civil War—the one about slavery that got all the attention—that one irritated him, because he felt it detracted too much from the more important conflict between the owners and the renters, the haves and the have nots."

"That sounds very refreshing to me," she said. "Didn't that make for lively class discussions? I mean, different points of view should have been pretty stimulating."

"Only when they're encouraged by the person running the class. Dr. Conger never asked anyone else for their opinion, because he didn't want to hear it. His style was to lecture, both inside the class and out. If you figured out his point of view and fed it back to him, you did fine. But venture an opinion at variance with his and he'd cut you off, then dismiss your observation—usually in a most demeaning way."

"Boy, that sounds pretty stifling. How'd he manage to get away with doing that?"

"One word: tenure. It protects the good teachers, but it's also a refuge for egomaniacs like Conger. After he got tenure, he really cut loose. He became a favorite guest on radio talk shows in Kansas City, because he was unusually liberal for the area and loved to lord it over everybody. One local caller became incensed and said, 'I want to compliment you guys for being able to get Almighty God to appear on your show.' Conger responded by saying, 'Well,

I'm humbled, but I won't deny it."

"He said that *publicly*?"

"You bet. Right on the air. A bunch of people got together and brought a billboard downtown that said, 'Wright is Wrong.' He loved the attention and the station loved it even more, because its ratings went through the roof every time he was on."

The shadows lengthened in the late afternoon as Brady guided the Microbus north on I-75 toward Chattanooga. Listening to Lyle Lovett and his quirky impressions of Texas life filling the Bus from the cassette player, Brady's thoughts drifted far and wide. A few minutes later, he turned to see Tanya had dozed off while working her way through the *Atlanta Constitution* crossword. He admired her spirit and her sense of serendipity in being willing to follow him to who-knows-where.

And where was all this going to go? That was a question Brady only allowed himself to ponder while on the road. Living in the moment was supposed to be an important ingredient for happiness, but that was damn sure easier to say than do. It was Brady's natural inclination to agonize about the past and fret about the future. To revel in the present required a degree of focus he had yet to master. Sharing his life with Tanya, if only briefly, had been a pleasant step in that direction.

"This one's got me stumped," she said, moments after snapping out of her light sleep. "Four letters for 'The actor, Ray.' What do you think?"

"Hmm...Ray Liotta? Ray Milland?" Brady said. "I don't know of too many more Rays."

"The first letter has to be 'A.' Does that help?"

"No," he said after a thoughtful pause, "that just makes it worse. Wait a minute...how about Aldo Ray? Could 'Ray' be the last name?"

"That works," she said. "But I never heard of Aldo Ray. Who was he?"

"An old-time actor. Could have been from silent pictures, I don't know. And I couldn't tell you specifically anything he did. That name's pretty unusual. It just stuck with me."

Skeeter: *Wait a minute...silent pictures? He wasn't that old...husky guy, with a raspy voice. Didn't he do a bunch of war movies with John Wayne and James Coburn?*

Herb: *He touched a lotta bases, that's for sure: "The Green Berets," "Battle Cry" and "The Naked and the Dead"...even worked with Bogie in "We're No Angels." But he also did "Riot on Sunset Strip" and "Frankenstein's Great Aunt Tillie," so he had his hits and his whiffs, just like everyone else...*

"My, my," she said with admiration. "You are blessed with total recall of the truly obscure, aren't you?"

"Bless my heart," he said with a straight face. "Don't forget that."

They exchanged knowing smiles, ones borne of the mutual understanding that comes from shared experience, however brief. Piece by piece, a bridge was being built, but Brady was still unsure about crossing it.

When they reached Monteagle, an hour north of Chattanooga, he decided it was time to stop for the night. It would be a full day's drive tomorrow, but he felt they could make Kansas City. The old Monteagle Inn was steeped in local charm and provided the perfect antidote to the droning predictability of the hotel chains dotting the interstates from coast to coast. The owner was obviously a big Tennessee football fan and the lobby was a shrine to the undefeated National Champions of 1998, including a tribute read into the Congressional Record by Cong. John J. Duncan, Jr. ("Mr. Speaker, I have often said that, in my district, the colors orange and white are almost as patriotic as red, white, and blue...")

Settling into his room full of Volunteer memorabilia, Brady mindlessly clicked on the TV, searching for a baseball game that might help him launch his nightly journey through the various REM stages. No sooner did he find a game than his reverie was interrupted by a knock on the door. It was Tanya, dressed in a blue windbreaker over what looked to be a red and black cotton nightshirt and a pair of rubber pool sandals.

"Well, well," Brady said as he slowly admired the scene before him. "What have we here? The homeless of Monteagle?"

"May I come in?" she said. "We need to talk." Without waiting for a response, she crossed the room to an armchair by the window and seated herself. She removed her windbreaker, revealing the familiar University of Georgia Bulldog logo above the screaming headline, "Hunker *Down*, Hairy Dawgs!" across the front of her nightshirt.

"You better be careful wearing that around here," he said with a smile. "We are definitely not in Bulldog country anymore."

"Do you have anything to drink?" she asked nervously.

"No," he said. "Just water from the tap. Are you okay? You don't look well."

"I'm fine. Could you turn that thing off and come over here?"

Brady clicked off the TV and took a seat on the edge of the bed opposite her.

"I have something to ask you," she said, "and I don't quite know how to do it, so I'm just going to come right out and say it, okay?"

"Sure," he said. "Fire away."

Taking a deep breath while locking her eyes to his, she said, "Brady Greer, how many miles does a girl need to travel with you before she at least gets a kiss?"

Suddenly speechless, Brady could only stammer, "I don't know...I didn't know... that's...what you wanted."

"Let's forget what I want for a moment. I guess my real question is, 'What do *you* want?"

"Well, I want to get to Kansas City," he said lamely, groping for humor, which had often been his salvation. But there was no mirth in her eyes, only her lingering question.

"Look," he continued, trying to regain control of himself and the conversation, "I'm a guy, you're an attractive girl. Of course I'd like to get together with you. I guess it's just that, once that happens, there are complications...complications and expectations. I haven't had the time to really sort all that out, is all."

"You're telling me," she said in amazement, "that Brady Greer, who doesn't strike me as the cautious type, has to plan an entire potential relationship before he makes the first move? Is that what I'm hearing here?"

"You heard it," he said softly as he reached for her hand, "but you don't have to believe it." He gently pulled her toward him until she was seated on his lap. Slipping his right arm around her slim waist, he slowly leaned toward her until their lips met uncertainly, then tenderly and then with increasing intensity.

A minute later, he released his grip on her and rose to his

feet. "This," he said, "calls for a celebration!"

"Where are you going?"

"You wanted a drink, right? Well, I'm going to get it. I'll be right back.

"By the way," he added as he reached for the door, "that shirt. Not from the 'Victoria's Secret' catalog, I'm guessing."

"No, no it's not," she said defensively. "It's all the rage in Midian, though. That's what they told me downtown."

Brady hustled down to the front desk of the Inn, shaking his head as he went. He approached the leathery desk clerk to inquire how far he would have to drive to find some liquor suitable for the occasion.

"I got the best damn stuff for that right under this here counter," said the old man from behind his corncob pipe as he produced a Mason jar full of a liquid with a rusty hue and what appeared to be a piece of fermented fruit at its bottom. The hand-printed label scrawled on its front said, "Uncle Jack's Lightnin'."

"We don't carry this in our gift shop, if you know what I mean," the clerk said with a wink, "but we always keep some around for special occasions. I seen you drive up a while ago with your lady friend, so I reckon that occasion's special enough."

"How much," asked Brady, trying not to look the old man squarely in the eye.

"Ten bucks'll do it," he said. "Yessir, that should do the trick just fine."

And it did.

16

The following morning, Brady again lined his pill bottles up for their daily roll call. There was a good multi-vitamin, backed up by garlic, bee pollen complex and extra calcium. He was still playing basketball when most others his age had given it up and he credited that as much to the boost he got from these daily supplements as to anything else. He was now grateful to have that extra energy to deal with Tanya, who started off behind the wheel that morning, while Brady studied *The Tennessean*.

"You know what's amazing?" he said. "One or two editors decide a certain story is full of human interest and, 'Bingo!' everyone's off chasing it. The press zeroes in on some of these disappearing people and ignores the others. It's a real lemming mentality; they'd follow each other over a cliff, rather than go off in a different direction. You do that, then you've got to explain yourself."

"You really think they discriminate?"

"Yup. Advertisers pay the bills at newspapers and they need customers with lots of money to spend. If the subject of a story is young, cute and white, people with money are going to read it. If you're old, black or Hispanic, that audience will most likely turn the page, unless there's some quirky human interest angle involved."

"That sounds pretty cynical."

"Maybe it is, but newspapers aren't charities. They're big businesses, trying to make a buck. We think forking over our 50 cents makes us the customer, but the big bucks come from advertisers."

"I can't believe you're going to read that," she said with a nod toward the supermarket tabloid on his lap.

"Why not? Legitimate news gets boring after a while. "Yup," he said with a puckish grin, "I have a need to know what Elvis has been up to lately."

Their route would take them back to Nashville, then cut northwest to Paducah, Ky., and across Southern Illinois to St. Louis, then due west to Kansas City. All in all, a good 12 hours, including various stops along the way.

Brady tried hard to affect an air of nonchalance, as though nothing had changed between them. But they were now connected on an entirely different level and only time would tell whether it was a truly deeper one.

Brady shook his head ruefully as he stared down the interstate. So what, exactly, had happened the previous night under the influence of some surprisingly smooth moonshine? What in the hell was going on here? He dropped his newspaper and turned to look at Tanya. "Can I ask you a question?"

"Sure."

"We haven't really talked about *you*. I know a certain name is out of bounds, but I think it's reasonable to want to know more about how the person behind that name became Tanya."

"Well," she said after a thoughtful pause, "okay. My parents have a lot of money and they threw it at me in every way imaginable: toys, clothes, vacations, cars. After a while, I realized they were giving me everything but time. My Dad was always cutting some big business deal and Mom, well, Mom had too much time on her hands."

"Which was a problem."

"Right. Everyone thought of her down there as this great society hostess, which she was, but, in the process, she drank a lot—too much, actually."

"But got help?"

"Yeah, 'help,'" she said sarcastically. "You can't imagine how tough that is to kick until you've seen someone try to do it. She went to treatment centers several times. During one of those trips, her best friend helped herself to my father.

"Anyway. . .I've seen a lot of people who have too much money. The more I learned about those who don't have enough of it, the more I thought the world might be a better place if things evened out."

"So you became Robin Hood."

"I took action. Look, I know it was against the law, but there are a lot of poor people in Nashville living a lot better today because of what I did. You know what really gets me? The Bible is full of passages saying you've got to help the poor to be a good Christian. Those yahoos who think the most important thing in life is to build a moat around their stuff, then raise the drawbridge, should spend less time thumping the Bible and more time reading it."

Brady continued in silence. *'Thou shalt not steal' is in there, too, isn't it?* Finally, he said, "So…you're breaking ground for a new branch of Christianity?"

"No, not really. Christianity sets the bar pretty high. I don't think I know anyone who clears it all the time. But there has to be value in just trying to be Christian—whether or not you actually get there—otherwise, most churches would be empty. When you get right down to it, I agree with you: It's all about choices. Most people choose what parts of the Bible they're going to follow and what they're not."

"Thus, the Book of Tanya."

"Right," she said with a smile. "Some people start with the Ten Commandments; I start with helping the poor. That's what free will is all about to me."

Skeeter: *Wait a minute…first, she's kind of a commie, now she's kind of a Christian? Is this woman ever gonna fit in anywhere?*

Herb: *Why do labels matter so much, Skeets? She's trying to find her own truth in life. When she gets there, she may not squeeze into one of your tidy little pigeon holes. You may find that annoying, but she finds it liberating. Good for her.*

Skeeter: *Don't you start with that commentating stuff on me ...*

Brady stared out the window for what seemed like a very long time. It was rare for him to open up to anyone, much less such a recent acquaintance, but he found himself now in the mood to unload. Finally, after a loud sigh, he folded his hands in his lap and looked straight ahead, trying to excise his emotion and be merely analytical.

"Dads can be tough," he said. "My Dad showed very little emotion. When he was unhappy with me, he just turned cold. He could really turn on the charm for other adults, but either couldn't or wouldn't for me. There was one positive to that, though, and that's the sense of humor I developed to make him laugh. He would crack up every once in a while and that would really make my day. Most of the time, though, he didn't seem to care much whether I was around or not.

"Why do you think he was that way?"

Turning to look at her, he said, "I don't know, Tanya. I just don't know. I guess that little chestnut got buried when he did."

They drove on in silence for another minute or two, when the Microbus suddenly swerved onto the shoulder of the interstate and Tanya brought it to an abrupt halt before jumping out the driver's door.

"Hey!" Brady yelled after her as he rose to the edge of his seat. "What are you doing?"

"I need some help here," she said as she opened the sliding door behind Brady and entered the caged area. Unbuckling his seat belt, he exited his door and followed her into the back, where he looked up and saw her beginning to undress.

"What are you *doing*?" he repeated.

"You better slide that door shut," she said very softly. "All that talk about rejection made me think about acceptance. Are you ready for some?"

"Right here? On the interstate?"

156

"Why not?" she said. "Have you ever noticed how serious you are? In the 60s, people drove these things naked. This feels like a good time to honor our heritage by shedding some of that baggage you've been carrying around...along with whatever clothes you happen to have on at the moment."

Brady glanced at the sign outside, 20 yards in front of the Bus, "70 MPH." *Was there a speed limit inside?*

It had been a very long time since he had made love in the morning light, even longer with such an eager partner. Within minutes, he had lost himself in her wonderfully taut body as the Bus swayed gently from side to side. The spell was broken when Tanya opened her eyes to the sight of flashing lights reflected on the Bus ceiling.

"Oh, shit," Brady said, looking up just in time to see the silhouette of a Tennessee State Trooper approaching the Bus. "It's the police!"

"Stay here," he said, covering her with a blanket as he threw on his sweatshirt and jeans. "I'll handle it."

There being no way directly into the front seat from the cage in the back, Brady had to exit through the sliding door and retrieve his shoes from the front seat before facing the trooper with his registration papers and insurance card.

"Is there a problem, officer?"

"I was about to ask you the same thing," the lantern-jawed trooper replied. "These old buses usually start to shimmy at about 65. Yours was doing it standing still. Amazing, isn't it?"

"No, I mean, 'yes," Brady stammered. "I guess, after a while, you guys see it all out here on the highway."

"Yes, I guess we do," he said, without expression. "Sometimes, we're happy to see what we see keep moving, right on toward the state line. That's where you're headed, right? Kentucky?"

"Yes, sir."

"Well, just keep on moving and everything will be fine."

As the officer returned to his cruiser, Brady slid behind the wheel of the bus and turned to a laughing Tanya. "Things are a little less exciting when I drive," he said, "but I'll take it from here."

We were lucky it was a trooper, Brady thought as their journey resumed. *County deputies patrol the interstates, too. What*

157

were we looking at then? An indecent exposure rap? That would look interesting in <u>The Midian Monitor</u>: *"Broker Buck Naked in Nashville."*

Skeeter: *Well, it's nice to see him scoring again. His runs seem to come in bunches these days, don't they?*

Herb: *Yes, they do. Maybe she is good for him. Our guy is wound a little tight at times and she appears to have the knack for loosening him up. It can be tough to figure these things out on your own. Sometimes, a person crosses your path who can show you the way.*

The fine line between the rational and the irrational had always fascinated Brady. In the wake of Beth's departure, he had experienced days when that line was invisible. The appearance of Tanya was motivating him to focus. *To become the hunter of something more than his past?* Brady was giving this some considerable thought as they approached the outskirts of Kansas City, stopping for dinner in Independence.

"This is Harry Truman's town," Brady said. "Too bad his museum's not open. It's a very interesting place."

"Does the buck stop there?" she said with a smile.

"As a matter of fact, it does, right on the desk he used in the Oval Office, and our friend, Dr. Conger, lives nearby, so we'll be stopping there, too.

"It's also a good baseball town," he said. "It was such an important part of the black game that the Negro Leagues Baseball Museum is located in K.C. The A's came here from Philly before they wound up in Oakland. Now, they've got the Royals."

"Why so many changes?"

"Money, basically. For both players and teams, it seems as though they're always ready to pull up stakes and head for a bigger payday."

The Kansas City climate had always intrigued Brady. Its humidity in summer could cling to you like an unpaid debt. Winter temperatures hovered within a few degrees of freezing, yielding sleet in steady doses. Springs and falls were brief. You had the worst of the four seasons here. How many places could make that claim? So, even though the sun had gone down, it was the kind of damp July evening that made you want to find a reason to get indoors and stay there. While Tanya watched TV in their motel room, Brady phoned the front desk, inquiring about directions to the Independence Mall.

Shortly after dawn the following morning, as Tanya continued sleeping, Brady dressed quickly and quietly and made his way down to the lobby, pausing briefly to pour some orange juice at the continental breakfast bar, before easing himself behind the wheel of the Microbus and heading for the Mall.

Conger was a disciplined man who had carefully constructed his daily routine over many years. During his college days here, Brady had heard him speak often—pontificate, actually—on how the best way to maintain his daily exercise regimen in the summer without wilting in the heat was to walk briskly several times around the interior perimeter of Independence Mall in the early morning hours, well before the stores opened. Conger had even gone to the trouble of purchasing a pedometer—a talking pedometer—that announced at various intervals how many steps he had taken and how many miles he had covered. Thirty years before, when Conger would have been in his 40s, he would laugh about the older mall walkers who couldn't keep up with his brisk pace. Brady had a hunch Conger was still at it, covering the Mall's circumference each morning, only now at a pace consistent with his retired peers.

After parking the Bus in the virtually empty lot, Brady casually approached the front entrance to the Mall, not wanting to be noticed by any of the morning marchers. Moving through the main doors, he decided to take up his position on a bench in the center of the Mall on its main floor, at the bottom of the escalators, and wait.

He was slowly becoming mesmerized by a pair of maintenance men guiding their floor polishing machines in a wide arc over the empty expanse in front of him when Brady noticed some movement out of the corner of his eye and turned slightly to see a half-dozen gray-haired marchers heading his way. Fearing he might be recognized, Brady kept his head down while glancing sideways at this ambling pack of erstwhile striders.

The cacophony of colors before him assaulted his eyes to the point where he had to rub them. There were peach shorts with mauve tops, stripes with Hawaiian shirts and seersucker shorts with what appeared to be Madras tops. Had they all gone blind? Was

159

insensitivity to color a requisite for becoming a senior citizen or did that status simply mean you had earned the right not to care anymore?

He could see there were two women, one slender and one plump enough to require more years of mall walking than she probably had left on this earth before she would be in shape. There was an intensity on the faces of the men that reminded Brady of pictures he had seen of Olympic speed walkers, determined to heel-and-toe their way to victory without ever actually lifting their feet off the ground.

The man in the middle, the one with his peach shorts seemingly pulled up to his armpits, was undeniably Dr. B. Wright Conger. His crazy thatch of red hair, still uncombed and unbrushed, now had plenty of gray to go with it, and his lanky frame appeared less so with stooped shoulders, but that crooked, amber smile was just as Brady remembered it, the product of too many Pall Malls over the years. Could he still be smoking them when he wasn't walking?

The group hurried past Brady's position, just 10 yards away from him at its closest. Checking his watch, he noted that it was 8:30. They won't be much longer, Brady thought, planning to clear out well before the stores opened at 10 AM. He decided to trail them from a discrete distance. At 9 AM on the nose, they were finished. Brady watched as Conger made his way out of the Mall and across the parking lot, away from the others, to his red Volvo wagon. Just had to get those few extra steps, eh? *That'll cost you tomorrow*, Brady thought as he watched the Volvo disappear into morning traffic.

Mindful of the free continental breakfast back at the motel that wasn't worth the price, he picked up some fresh bagels at the corner coffee shop on the way back to the room. Tanya was awake and watching the morning news.

"Out taking your morning constitutional?" she asked with a smile.

"Not *taking* it," he said, "more like watching it. You should see those retirees hustling around the Mall. It doesn't look too pretty, but they're breaking a good sweat, getting a great workout."

"Hmm," she said with a frown, "you could break a sweat just standing in this heat. I hope we have more exciting things on our agenda today."

"Yes, in fact, we do. I want to take you to the Truman Library, then show you around Kansas City. We'll top it off with dinner at Arthur Bryant's."

"What is that? A fancy place?"

"Not exactly," he said, "but it is one of KC's best-known restaurants. A jug of their barbecue sauce is one of the most coveted souvenirs here."

He couldn't bring himself to tell her that drinks at Bryant's came self-serve, from a vending machine, but she would get over that, especially if they visited J.C. Nichols Plaza first. It had a variety of sophisticated shops that often surprised people on their first visit to Kansas City, expecting little more than stockyards and steak houses.

Shortly after dawn, Brady was in the parking lot of their motel, securing their luggage to the roof of the Bus while Tanya slept. Conger was a legendary creature of habit; his students had always joked about that. Brady figured picking him up would be easy, a job he thought he could handle alone.

After a cup of juice in the lobby, he made his way over to the Mall. As Brady had hoped, the Volvo was parked by itself at a considerable distance from the entrance. He pulled the Microbus into the space next to it, climbed into the cage behind the front seat and waited.

Of the several things that made him uncomfortable about his current mission, the one that troubled him most at the moment was that it was being done right here in Captain Harry's back yard. What would the old haberdasher—the product of a black-and-white world that could yield the decision to drop the hydrogen bomb, followed by a good night's sleep—what would he think of the quixotic Brady Greer?

A few minutes after 9 AM, Conger emerged from the Mall and began walking toward his car. As he approached it, whistling and reaching for his keys, Brady pushed open the sliding door. Just as Conger turned to respond to the unexpected noise, Brady took careful aim at the professor's butt and pulled the trigger, thankful that a silencer at the end of the gun barrel muted the sound.

"Holy *shit!*" Conger exclaimed as he fell to one knee and reached around to feel the dart. "I've been *shot!*"

17

Brady jumped out of the van, onto the back of the prostrate Conger, and covered the professor's mouth as he continued to protest. A couple of minutes later, the professor's body grew limp and Brady released his grip. Conger had become 180 pounds of dead weight and had to be positioned carefully on Brady's shoulders, before he could be gently deposited in the back of the Bus. Once that was accomplished, he closed the sliding door and circled to the other side of the Microbus to enter it, glancing quickly around the parking lot to be sure no one had seen or heard Conger's capture.

"I got the package," a sweaty Brady said nervously as he returned to the motel room. "Let's go."

As they turned east on I-70, it was becoming apparent that another sultry summer day was unfolding. Brady's favorite form of air conditioning was the natural kind, so he reached down with his left hand to crank open the manual window of the old Microbus and welcome the rushing wind in from the highway. Since he was behind the wheel, it was his turn to select the music and he fumbled through his pile of cassettes, searching for something to match his mood, which was one of nostalgia.

While his run-ins with Conger had often been painful, they could never eclipse the good times he recalled from his college years. Of all the capers he had pulled, the one that still amazed him most—and now caused a broad smile to creep across his face—was the panty raid that had caused his suspension during his sophomore year. A *panty raid*? How retro was *that*? So tame by today's standards that he would never admit it to his friends in Georgia, but the administration at his small, Midwestern college back then had been scared to death, the virginity of their sweet, young coeds being at stake.

Actually, the big prize from that panty raid hadn't been a pair of panties, but an enormous, gag bra--one that had to be at least a size 50 with a "D" cup---that a friend of Brady's had retrieved from the Kappa Alpha Theta house. One cup gold, the other black. A real trophy.

"Brady?"

"Huh?"

"Brady, where *are* you?" she asked.

"What do you mean?"

"You have the goofiest look on your face. What planet are you on now?"

"A good one," he said. "An old, friendly one." After pausing a moment, he asked, "Have you ever been to Graceland?"

Skeeter: *Hold it...tell me we're not getting Elvis involved here...*

Herb: *Why not? Brady lives in the past more than the present. If we're headed back to the Fifties, who represents that better than The King?*

"No, I haven't been to Graceland," she said. "That's in Memphis, right? Is that on our way?"

"It's not a matter of where we *have* to go," he said, "but of where we *need* to go."

"Well, I'd *love* to go there," she said, eyeing him carefully, then nodding toward the back, "but what about our 'package?"

"I think I can arrange for our passenger to be napping in Memphis and it's really not that far out of our way to go there. Besides, you've been a good sport about going along with my agenda. It's time we did something for the songwriter."

Tanya peered around the front seat, into the Pet Guard cage and its unconscious passenger. "Power Bars and bottled water. Isn't that diet a bit…spartan?"

Brady continued pawing through his cassettes, knowing he didn't have an Elvis and searching for a proxy. "It'll do until we get back to IPCOT. Don't worry, he'll get real food once we're home…there it is!" He withdrew a Johnny Cash cassette, another product of Sun Records. That would do nicely for traveling music, even if they weren't on a train. Just listening to Johnny Cash, though, it would seem as though they were riding the rails.

Conger refused to cooperate during the first rest stop, when Brady exited the interstate, found a deserted country road and told him he could only leave the Bus handcuffed and blindfolded.

"Okay, Conger, have it your way," was Brady's response.

An hour and a couple of bottles of water later, Conger begged him to pull over. This time, he quickly agreed to Brady's terms and relieved himself—at length—without incident.

Several hours later, they pulled into Memphis. Tanya was looking forward to all the Elvis memorabilia, but this was Brady's second visit and the attraction to him was more the state of Graceland: frozen at the moment of Elvis' death in 1979. Some of the rooms, with their black-and-white TVs and jungle furniture, harkened back to an even earlier era. Walking through Graceland, listening to the guided tour on tape, Brady felt he was back in the '50s and that made him very comfortable, indeed. *To really appreciate Graceland*, he thought, *you had to see the shotgun shack where Elvis grew up, in Tupelo.* But there would not be time for that this trip.

"Hey, Brady," Tanya said, glancing at a couple of Elvis CDs. "Look at this. Elvis wrote hardly any of his own stuff."

"He didn't have to," Brady said. "RCA had a huge investment in him, so they made sure he had access to the best songwriters. See? That's all you have to do: Discover the next Elvis, then start feeding him great material."

A few weeks from now, in mid-August, thousands of people would descend upon Graceland for the anniversary of Elvis' death. Brady had understood, but never accepted why Elvis remained so big—bigger in death than ever. He wondered how much it had to do with the connection Elvis gave people to the happiest decade of the last half-century, the years between the end of the Korean War and the Kennedy assassination.

Everywhere Tanya saw Elvis—his Vegas outfits, army uniform and gold records—Brady saw, instead, life before Dallas: big AM radios, Formica tables and retro furniture now worth far more than when it was new. It made him feel the warmth of the Hardy Boys, "Ozzie and Harriet" and sandlot baseball.

After exiting Graceland, they crossed the street to the parking lot and checked on Conger, who was still out cold from the last shot of Telazol, so Brady headed the Microbus north on Elvis Presley Blvd., toward the interstate. It was this sudden return to strip malls and their weather-beaten signs that snapped him out of his reverie and made him start to feel a cool resentment toward progress and its cynical edge.

Skeeter: *You know, the '50s really was a magical time...*

Herb: *...unless your civil rights were being violated. The fifties was also McCarthyism, Little Rock and Birmingham, in addition to Korea, bomb shelters and the launching of Viet Nam and Castro...and it gave us three great cultural phenomena: fast food, the "vast wasteland" of TV and the modern marketing of politicians.*

Skeeter: *Easy, Herb...such a killjoy! You get your sweet and sour with any decade. Go ahead and dwell on the dark side. I still say "Laverne and Shirley" and "Happy Days" got it right...both set in Milwaukee, by the way...*

"Do you know what Graceland calls for?" Brady asked. "When was the last time you had a milk shake?"

"Hmm...I don't know..."

"We've got to be able to find one around here...I'll be damned! There's a Dog 'N Suds up ahead. Anytime you can find a shake and a car hop at the same place, that's a definite bonus."

Thus fortified, Brady and Tanya resumed their trek out of the '50s and back to Georgia, resolving to drive straight through. The following afternoon, they arrived at IPCOT and Brady slid open the side door to address the task of moving Conger into his new quarters. The professor was still groggy from his last shot and Brady was not looking forward to again hoisting the dead weight. With a grunt and a muffled curse, he lifted the professor onto his shoulders and put him to bed. After checking Conger's quarters to be sure there was a new bottle of water in the cooler and plenty of food on the shelves and in the fridge, Brady returned to town for a good night's sleep.

The following morning, he looked in the mirror and saw a few more pounds on his frame than normal. He was letting himself slide into milk shake shape. That was his signal to get back on the basketball court and run off some of that excess baggage.

Brady arrived early for the noon game, partly to work on his shot and partly to get some of the ribbing out of the way that he knew would result from his recent absence. After the game, he was able to take his attorney, Steve Bennett, aside.

"Steve, let me ask you something. What did you major in as an undergraduate?"

"Well...let's see...that was a long time ago. I was a history major. Thought it would be good preparation for law school and it turned out that it was."

"A good department?"

"Yeah, I guess you could say that. Oddly, the guy who taught con law was the only weak link. Had a brother he hated who was a lawyer, so he hated the law. Don't know what he was doing teaching it, under those circumstances. Name was Dick. When I got to know him a little, though, I felt sorry for him. His lawyer brother was clearly the fair-haired child in that family. Dick was smart, but just a very unhappy guy."

"So, you worked around him?"

"Yeah, you could say that. Had to take his course, so I dealt with him as best I could. Why do you ask?"

"Oh, I don't know...I've been thinking about teachers lately and the impact they have on us. Just curious about other people's experiences."

"Well, you spent more time on the basketball court than I did. That's obvious. Did you play in college?"

"Nope. Just a late bloomer, I guess."

On the way back home, Brady tried to imagine how Conger was reacting to his new surroundings. Highly agitated, no doubt. Perhaps walking off his anxiety, since that was his favorite exercise. Brady wanted to give him time to calm down before questioning him. Wasn't that one of the benefits of being in the country? But people that age could be easily irritated even when their surroundings were familiar. Taking Conger way beyond his comfort zone might move Brady closer to his own destiny, but it clearly wasn't going to be improving Conger's humor.

Brady agonized about his next move. He recalled his first experience speaking before a group as a young broker, when he became gripped by the sensation that the collar on his shirt was becoming smaller as he spoke, his voice becoming squeakier with every word. He wasn't buttoning his shirt much these days and rarely wore a necktie. Still, that memory returned every time he faced a situation where he didn't know quite what to say.

As a youth, he had enjoyed a wonderful sense of spontaneity that society later spoiled by labeling it "ADD." It was then reduced to an illness, something to be treated with the *drug du jour* and commiserate about at cocktail parties.

He had reacted initially to the news of his financial independence by doing what new heirs often do: binging, only his was a binge of mind, not wallet, thus his hangover could not be so easily treated. But now he was on a mission: to figure out how to save his favorite sport from the messy business it had become.

Brady had affected a taste for Birkenstocks during the humid Georgia summers, partly for comfort, but also because they made a statement: He was the only one in Midian who wore them, sending a message to the locals that they could be more comfortable, too, if only they weren't so stuck in their ways to try something new. But it wasn't the locals who were on his mind at the moment. His audience had become baseball fans everywhere in a desperate attempt to save the game before time ran out for his old coach. Somehow, he thought Conger might hold the key to doing that. Brady picked up his phone and called Cleveland.

"Evelyn? Brady Greer. Just thought I'd touch base and see how the coach is doing."

"About as well as can be expected, I guess. The cancer's gotten to his bones and he's in a lot of pain. He spends most of his time in bed now."

"Well, make sure they're taking good care of him. I'm still hoping to give him something to smile about."

He gave Tanya a lingering kiss as he left the house, then started up the Microbus and pointed it toward Scofield. Try as he might to organize his thoughts and plan for this conversation, Brady knew he would ultimately just be winging it. When he had gone about a mile beyond the city limits, he pulled over to the side of the road in an effort to think it all through carefully. He had done that a lot before he met Tanya, just pulled off the road—-mostly to sleep--—but sometimes to jot down his thoughts so he would not forget them.

As much as he tried to stay focused on baseball and its labor issues when thinking about Conger, his mind kept returning to Yulia.

Yulia Estrikova was the beautiful exchange student from Volgograd who had been Brady's steady girl in college—-until Conger decided she needed extra attention, which she soon received from him around the clock. It wasn't too long before she didn't have any time for Brady, who initially refused to believe he had been beaten out by a rival as physically unattractive as Conger. But he soon learned that women find beauty in many ways and that the professor had connected with her mind in a manner no college student could hope to match.

Skeeter: *Oh, no...has our guy ever had a relationship that worked?? How many different train wrecks can one guy survive?*

Herb: *That's the key, Skeets: different. You keep having the same wreck, pretty soon you don't walk away. But like I've been saying all along, you mix things up, you keep learning...one day, it all comes together. That happens sooner for some, later for others...*

The two had never married. Brady knew that much. But he didn't know what had become of her and that was one of the questions on his agenda for this afternoon.

Arriving at IPCOT, Brady unlocked the courtyard door and was greeted by screams from the professor's room. As he approached it, the sound of the old man's cursing brought back memories of the similar tirades Brady had heard as a student years before. Then, it had been ranting about Richard Nixon; now, Brady was the object of his scorn. He knocked and waited. There being no answer, he slowly opened the door and began to step into the room.

The professor rose from his bed and moved menacingly toward Brady, then stopped for an assessment. He squinted for a moment, then took a step back. "Who the hell ARE you?" Conger thundered, "and what the HELL am I DOING here?!"

"I'm disappointed you don't remember me, professor. Brady Greer."

"Greer? I don't recall…were you a *student* of mine? What in the HELL is going on here? "I want YOU," his finger now in Brady's face, "to get me out of here IMMEDIATELY!"

"Professor, calm down; you're not going anywhere. You're my prisoner, if you insist on looking at it that way. At least you are now, until we've had a chance to talk. You can rant all you want about that or just accept it. How you deal with it is up to you."

The wild look in the professor's eyes softened ever so slightly as he weighed Brady's words before responding.

"But, *why?*" he said finally. "What the *hell's* the purpose-- after all these years--of sticking me wherever the hell it is that I am?"

"We all have demons, professor. I'm sure you have a few. I just found myself in a position where I could collect a useful one to deal with it face-to-face."

"So I'm your *demon*, eh? How the hell did *that* happen?"

"Well, I loved history when I got to college, but your very narrow view of it wasn't exactly a secret. Ever wonder how many times you poisoned the well during those 25 years? How many kids you turned *off* to history with your manic bullshit circus act?"

"Everyone has his own style, Greer," the professor said, returning to sit on the edge of his bed. "Too many people spend too much time trying to be someone they aren't. I was honest in my classroom. You apparently weren't there very long, but you obviously found me memorable. The bland don't register quite that well, do they?"

"The 'bland,' as you call them, don't strut and scream. They realize it's supposed to be about the material, not about them. An egomaniac in the classroom poisons the process, the same way a reporter does when he gets in the way of a story or a referee does by interfering in a game."

"Where did this wealth of expertise come from, Greer? Have you ever taught anything?"

"Uh…no. It comes from sitting through a lot of lectures, good and bad."

"What did you wind up majoring in, anyway?"

"Poli sci."

"Hah!"

"What's wrong with that?"

"Poli sci: What a wussy major! Politics is hardly a science. Any idiot knows that. Did you ever find any connection between political theory and what actually happens in the real world?"

"Of course. Theory doesn't become practice every day, but those who understand theory are usually in a better position to make the system work for them. I got quite a bit out of it, actually---and was certainly better off than the kids who got history shoved at them through the narrow funnel of the New Deal. What the hell would you have done if you had taught before FDR came along? Tell us how wonderful the Bolsheviks were?"

"The ones who stayed around got a pretty good education, Greer. I'm sure your poli sci degree was useful to you in your field. By the way, what is your field?"

Not wanting to hear Conger's views on the brokerage business, Brady changed the subject. "That's not important. The point is that you wanted clones, not students, so I walked."

"So, now I'm on some sort of Elba, because you didn't like your neat, little world view challenged, is that it?" the professor asked with a sneer.

"No, actually an issue's come up that requires a little radical thinking and it occurred to me you might be just the man for the job."

"Let me get this straight: You kidnapped me, now you want me to help you?"

"Actually, you could be helping yourself. As I recall, you loved antagonizing people on the radio in Kansas City. This might give you a national audience."

"An audience of crackpots, like you? No thanks!"

"How about an audience of every baseball fan in America."

"What are you talking about?"

"The players and owners have a horrible relationship and there have been work stoppages before. Now, the players are talking 'strike' again, before the World Series."

"So what? The owners are swine...except Angelos. He's defended the working man; he gets it."

"Wait a minute: The owners aren't the only ones at the trough here. The Players Association is the strongest one in all of professional sports. Salaries have gotten so ridiculous that marginal players can easily make a million or more each year."

"And whose fault is *that*? The owners, of course. They're throwing money and the players are catching it. If you're trying to outlaw stupidity, good luck!"

"It's a matter of balance, Conger. It wasn't good for the game when the owners dominated it and it's not any better now that the players are in control."

"So, who are *you*? The guardian angel of baseball? When did *that* happen?"

"I'm an activist. You remember the Sixties. I'm guessing you did your share of protesting then. Well, I'm doing mine now."

"And breaking the law in the process."

"I'm not the first protester who broke a law and I won't be the last. We rebels justify that in the name of the greater good. Surely, you remember—"

"Yeah, I remember. Look, Greer, I *hate* baseball. Bores the hell out of me. Hockey's my game."

"You don't have to like it to help it."

"And what if I don't want to?"

Brady glanced slowly around the austere surroundings for effect. "Then this is home until you do."

"*Fuck you*, Greer!"

"Professor! I'm disappointed," Brady said, shaking his head as he started for the door. "That's what people say to add heat to a discussion, instead of light. Think about it. We'll talk more tomorrow."

18

Over the past few weeks, Brady was finding it difficult to get a good night's sleep and wanted to believe that was not due to fear of the possible consequences of an interstate kidnapping, but, instead, mostly to the adjustment necessary to again sharing his bed. There was just enough breeze up here on the second floor to remain comfortable with the window open, but Tanya had closed it, preferring the air conditioning and its background hum. The most jarring aspect of that to him, beyond the change it represented in his well-defined routine, was that it prevented him now from hearing the plaintive burst of his beloved train whistle gently piercing through the muggy Georgia night.

But there was one habit he could not break and that was the occasional nocturnal trip to the Waffle World when sleep became elusive. As he threw on a pair of jeans and a sweatshirt, he would shake his head in wonder at Tanya purring in repose. How could anyone sleep so deeply?

Brady liked to pause in the driveway, just before starting up the Bus, and think about "Stagger Lee," one of his favorite rock 'n roll classics: "The night was black...and the moon was yellow...and the...*leaves*...came...*tumb*-ling...*down*." It was August, so the leaves were safe for a while longer, but Midian was quite black in the middle of the night at any time of year. In fact, Midian was a city in which black and white were the operative colors. Beyond the racial divide, that applied also to your social position. You either had it—through birth or money, preferably both—or you didn't. Politically, you were expected to be either Republican or Democrat; independents were annoying, the ants of the political picnic. Something wasn't quite right with those oddballs. Why couldn't they just figure out which side of the fence they were on and stay there, like everyone else? A popular parlor game was guessing which party a professed independent *really* called home...late at night, when his doors were locked. Brady figured the Civil War had thrashed and beaten this form of gray out of Midian and it hadn't been seen there since. Perhaps that was what made him feel most like an outsider. The distinctions in Brady's world never seemed as neat and clear as they were for those around him.

He knew a cup of Waffle World coffee at 3 AM meant he wasn't going back to sleep, but it often helped clear his head for a few minutes, which always seemed to be worth it at the time. Sometimes, just before he rose to leave the restaurant, the state editions of the morning metro papers would arrive. Brady liked the feeling of reading his paper while the rest of Midian slept. On this particular morning, he reached for a fresh paper and noticed immediately that there had been another kidnapping. This time, it was on the West Coast, some 3,000 miles away, yet there it was, the lead story in his Georgia newspaper. There suddenly seemed to be a rash of these going on, but it always seemed to be the young, attractive female victims who got the publicity. There had been nothing, for instance, about the disappearances of Brady's IPCOT guest in any newspaper he had seen. The balanced coverage preached in journalism schools had, in practice, morphed into a motor skill: pushing emotional buttons. Editors around the country decided quickly that abducting a young woman was news, while nobody wanted to read about missing old men. If Brady kept targeting that group, it looked as though he would be flying safely beneath the media radar.

Sitting there in his midnight confessional—his favorite booth at the Waffle World—Brady tried to justify the kidnapping in his mind and convince himself he had seized Conger for his knowledge of labor history that might be brought to bear on baseball. That was a tough sell and it was making him uneasy. What if Conger refused to cooperate? What would he do with him? What would keep him from pressing charges after he was back in Kansas City? The professor's presence, however, also rekindled thoughts of Yulia and Conger as the randy old goat who had spirited her away.

That was not, of course, how Conger had appeared 30 years before. Then, he reveled in his status as a cult figure around campus. His radio appearances—even when his arguments proved obtuse to all but Conger—made him the best-known personality at school. To be sure he stood out even more, Conger took to loping around the grounds with his head stuffed into an Irish Donegal walking cap and a trench coat covering his shoulders like a cape. When he approached you thus attired and with his carved blackthorn walking stick leading the way--a gift from Local 608 of the International Brotherhood of Carpenters and Joiners--you couldn't help but notice…especially if you were a very impressionable exchange student from the Communist Bloc, a place where Conger found many kindred spirits.

In a way, Brady had been Yulia's first American mentor. Needing a little spending money, he had agreed to help out in the registrar's office the week Yulia arrived from Volgograd with what seemed like a million questions. He was only too happy to provide the answers. Often, this was done while he gave her a guided tour of Kansas City, usually ending up sharing a six-pack on the hood of his '59 Cadillac hearse just beyond the end of the north/south runway at the old KC airport, watching the planes make their final approach seemingly within reach of the Muehlbach Hotel downtown. The hearse had become the party vehicle of choice among Brady and his friends, both for its ability to carry a crowd and the hidden compartment it contained in the back that could snuggly store a case of beer.

There were, of course, parties in Russia and hearses, as well, but the concept of meshing the two was daring to Yulia. She quickly developed an admiration for this American creativity and its chief proponent, Brady Greer, who was still gestating in his Midwestern cocoon and had never met anyone as exotic as this five-foot, seven-inch Bolshevixen with eyes greener than poison ivy.

Skeeter: *The ball can look a lot better when it leaves the pitcher's hand than it does by the time it crosses the plate. You think maybe Brady's figured out "exotic" doesn't last, no matter how exciting it is at the start ? We need to find him a nice American girl...*

Herb: *He has to find her on his own. Just be patient...if he can learn from the past, he'll be ready for the future.*

Yulia's father had been one of the finest hockey players in Russian history and her mother curator of the People's Museum of Art, in Volgograd. Yulia had inherited her father's nimble grace and auburn mane. Her discerning eye for art came from her mother, who would show her daughter big, coffee table art books, then read them aloud to her when Yulia was still a toddler. She looked forward to majoring in history, with a concentration in art, and playing volleyball in college. She excelled at both effortlessly, always smiling and seemingly carefree.

"But for my father," Yulia had confided to Brady then, "it was so difficult. When he could no longer play hockey, he did not know what to do, so he drank. Mother supported us with her work at the Museum, but the strain was very great and she became anxious about everything when her age began to show."

Mirror, mirror on the wall, thought Brady. *They're everywhere.*

The resulting tensions at home caused Yulia to try to outrun her emotional baggage by studying in the States. She became Brady's wounded angel and, in the process of trying to nurse her back to health, he would lose himself repeatedly in her emerald eyes, often forgetting where he was in the process. It wasn't long before Brady was also losing track of why he was in college, preferring instead to major in his own social studies.

Prior to that year, Conger had been openly contemptuous of art history and the nuisance course in it he was required to teach. Suddenly, however, he reconsidered that position and found a new fascination in art, one he was anxious to share with his prize student. This called for frequent trips to area museums as part of an independent study course that had been fashioned solely for Miss

176

Estrikova. It was a different Kansas City than Brady knew and Yulia soon became swept up in the surprising diversity of local culture and flattered by the attention of the knowledgeable and articulate Professor Conger.   The campus grapevine soon had them down as an item, which might have torpedoed the career of a lesser light on the faculty. Conger, however, had become the face of the college throughout Kansas City and had, in the eyes of the administration, simply become too big to confront. Ultimately, though, he proved the old adage that there's no fool like an old fool when Yulia abruptly dumped him in the spring, shortly before her return to Volgograd.

So Brady and Conger had shared for years the dubious bond of the Hurricane Yulia experience and presently shared the same zip code. But what of Yulia? Her entrance into a room had a way of making other women in it recede into the wallpaper, so Brady guessed she was still a presence somewhere.

He gazed out of the Waffle World onto I-20 as the first glimmer of day broke to the east.   It was already mid-day in Russia and she was out there, beyond the sunrise. Perhaps she was running an art museum. Probably had a house full of kids by now.

"My, my, what planet are we on tonight?" It was Sheila, his favorite waitress, bringing him back to Earth.

"Planet Waffle," he said with a sigh as he turned to face her, "and it's awful."

"I beg your *pardon*," she replied with mock indignation.

"No offense," Brady said with a smile. "Just doing a little heavy thinking. It's amazing how far away you can get on a cup of that coffee."

"I'll say. I was about to ask for your passport. Anything you want to share with Dr. Sheila?"

"I don't know," he said. "Maybe some day you can explain to me how women think."

"That ain't too hard, Bubba. Just remember that, when they're with a man, they want him to really listen to what they have to say. Don't just 'yes' 'em. And, when they talk about a problem, never, ever, give 'em advice unless they specifically ask for it."

"I don't get it," Brady said. "If they're going to bring up a problem, aren't they looking for a solution?"

"Yes, of course," Sheila said, shaking her head, "but they ain't really wantin' it from you. What they really want to do is talk it out and figure it out themselves. Most men don't get how easy their job really is. All you have to do is listen, really listen. Let her know she's being heard. That'll make her feel better, whether she figures out her problem or not."

"So, being heard is more important than being helped?"

"You got it! Men think they have all the answers and women are just dying to hear them. Wrong. Women want to be heard *by* them. The man who understands that suddenly becomes a very smart man in their eyes."

"Thanks," Brady said as he doubled the size of his usual tip. "It's nice to know a doctor who pulls the night shift."

"Wouldn't have it any other way," she said with a rueful smile that had seen too many years of human nature unvarnished by sleep. "The days are dull. I'd much rather deal with crazies like the one I'm talkin' to."

"Crazy? Me? Not crazy enough to drive an old Fiero. I see you're down to $1,200, by the way. Any nibbles?"

"You leave that old sled alone, now. It's gettin' more attractive. May even be gone next time you come around."

As Brady returned home, he gave up on the idea of getting any sleep and flicked on the TV. Looking back at him was the early market report from Asia. There was a time when he would consider it carefully, sensitive for signs of early trends in that day's trading on Wall Street. But that was a world removed from him now. Between his satellite dish and the Internet, he could access more news than ever before, but this torrent of information was making him feel somehow less connected to world events, like a stranger overcome by the cacophony of a new city.

Was it just information overload causing his circuits to fuse or was it the weight of his own world that was grinding him down? Brady contemplated such questions frequently now, but never seemed to arrive at conclusions. As he started the process again, he heard a sleepy voice from the bedroom doorway.

"Brady? Aren't you going to get some sleep?"

I'll sleep when I'm dead, Brady thought to himself, wondering for an instant if there would ever be another Zevon devotee in Midian.

"No, I guess not," is what he said. "Just doing a little thinking. Went out for coffee, 'cuz I didn't want to bother you."

"That was very thoughtful of you," she said as she took a seat across from him. "Anything you want to talk about?"

"Not really, but thanks anyway. I just need to focus on spending some more time with Conger. I'll be fine."

Tanya rose from her chair and smiled as she squeezed his shoulder before disappearing into the kitchen to put on a pot of coffee. Some women were wrapped up in themselves and some were happiest wrapping an arm around others. Though Brady was quite familiar with the drawbacks of narcissistic women, his pattern had been to yield to their temptation repeatedly, preferring them over...champions of the working class from Dallas.

When he was operating on little sleep, Brady thought he could function reasonably well until mid-day before it would catch up with him, so he headed out to the farm to have another talk with Conger. In doing so, he was feeling encouraged that he had, in this case, overcome his habit of doing things on the fly. This time, he had a game plan: Get the principals involved together in...sort of...a...binding arbitration to set the game he loved back on a healthy course. Conger's knowledge of labor history made him an important piece of the process...if he would only agree to cooperate. All Brady needed to do was spend enough time with Conger to convince him to play ball.

"*Greer!* You son of a *bitch*," Conger thundered upon seeing him again. "There are *laws* against kidnapping. You *do* know that, *don't* you?"

"Don't worry, professor," Brady said soothingly. "You're not slated to be a long-term guest here. I need to learn as much as possible about labor negotiations as quickly as I can. The sooner we cover that, the sooner you can go home."

"You *could* have just sent me a letter. Did you ever think of *that*?"

"That was never an option," Brady said evenly. "I'm going to be as blunt with you as you've been with me."

"Well, good; it's about time."

"My life has been out of control for years and I had the opportunity to seize the reins, so I took it. Now, are you in the mood to talk or should I come back in a few days?"

179

Conger pursed his lips for a long moment as his eyes surveyed his bleak room. "Talk," he said.

"Okay. Let's start with how you formed your view of history and your impatience with--"

"Right, my patience--or *lack* of same," Conger snapped. "Let's get right to it, shall we Greer? I'm only going over this once, so pay attention.

"I grew up in Chicago. Kenilworth, a very fancy suburb. Does that surprise you?"

"Well, I…"

"It doesn't matter. Anyway, that was a rhetorical question. My father owned a foundry, a big one, on the South Side. Employed over 200 people. Made metal castings for companies from Detroit to Duluth, all over the Midwest. Our family—I had a sister, too—had a beautiful summer place on Lake Geneva. Mom had a cook and a live-in maid. Life was good, very good. In fact, we had no idea how good…until…"

"Until what?"

Conger looked away for a long moment, gazing at the far side of the courtyard before he continued. "Until one day, it was a Friday, I had just arrived home from school and was looking forward to the weekend. My Dad was going to take me fishing. Instead, two policemen knocked on the door and asked to speak to my Mom. The three of them went into the den and, being a kid, I tried to listen through the door and heard my Mom sobbing—not just crying, but really cutting loose like I'd never heard before. Turns out my old man had driven out into the country—that's what it was then; it's just another suburb now—put a gun in his mouth and pulled the trigger."

"Why?"

"Well, it seems he had taken all the cash he could find, then borrowed to the max against our two homes and company assets to take a big piece of a very speculative stock deal that went bust. We were wiped out and he couldn't face the consequences."

Being a stockbroker, Brady knew the answer to his next question, but couldn't resist asking it: "But why would he take that kind of risk?"

"Just a case of hubris, pure and simple. Up to that point, he was Midas; everything he did in business seemed to work. But this was overreaching and he lost his balance. It was a long fall."

"Leaving you...where?"

"Damn near on the street is where. We had to sell everything to pay his debts. Can you imagine what it's like to go suddenly from a mansion to a small apartment? The shock? The disgrace? You can't, unless you've had that experience, which I wouldn't wish on anyone—even you. Mom scrambled to get a job when she hadn't worked her entire married life. None of my friends needed to earn their spending money, while my sister and I worked after school to help make ends meet. But that wasn't the worst of it."

"What was?"

"One day, a couple of weeks after we buried Dad, I cut out of school early--I was in eighth grade--and took a bus to the South Side. I just had to get another look at my Dad's foundry."

"What did you find?"

"Just about everybody had been laid off, except his bookkeeper, Opal. She'd been with him for years and was glad to see me, but the news was grim. She was less than five years from retirement, but her plan was wiped out. The same for everyone else, both in retirement and health benefits. A lot of loyal people put their heart and soul—and their trust—in that company for years and all they had to show for it was a pink slip. If you could see the look I saw, the devastation, on Opal's face that day, you'd know why I feel the way I do about worker's rights. Ever since, I can't look at the kind of wealth you see in Kenilworth without feeling it's hollow. You know the old saying, 'Where there's money, there's trouble."

"What is that? Marx? Engels?"

"No, actually that's Crawford, Broderick Crawford. Didn't you ever watch *Highway Patrol*? A great TV show. They don't make 'em like that anymore. He used to close each week's episode with a little aphorism. 'Where there's money, there's trouble. This is Broderick Crawford. 10-4.' That was always my favorite."

Skeeter: *Did Conger—a college professor—just tell us he's living his life according to the Gospel of Broderick Crawford? Is that what I heard?*

Herb: *That's right...let's see: Aldo Ray, Broderick Crawford...we're keeping some pretty macho company here. Lt. Dan Mathews—that was Crawford's character—also said, "Leave your blood at the blood bank, not on the highway" and "Reckless driving doesn't determine who's right—only who's left." Truly, a wise man...*

"If classic TV commentary isn't lofty enough for you," Conger continued scornfully, "then you might want to consider Aleksandr Solzhenitsyn's exposé of the Soviet gulag. He learned there that the object of life is not financial wealth, but the maturing of the soul. Just another way of saying, 'Where there's money, there's trouble,' I suppose..."

Brady just stared at him, wondering if he was finished.

"So, how am I doing?" Conger asked finally. "Am I any closer to getting out of here?"

"Well, now I know more about *why* you think the way you do. How about some insights on labor relations, negotiating, that sort of thing?"

"Hell, Greer, *books* have been written about that, lots of them, but I guess kidnapping's easier than reading for you."

Brady just stared impassively at the professor.

"There are always at least three basics," Conger continued, "bargain collectively—lots of strength in solidarity, you just got to keep everyone together—don't make a threat, like a strike, that you can't back up and never give back anything you've gained without getting some concession from management."

"Hmmm...now I see why the players are so strong."

"That's right. From what I've read in the papers, the union leaders have kept players from breaking ranks, at least publicly; they've shown they're willing to strike and have leverage there, since they can afford a walkout and are specialized enough that management can't bring in scabs; and they don't give up concessions, once they've earned them."

"So...how do we break the union?"

"*We*, kemo sabe? I don't think *we're* going to do anything. Frankly, I admire what they've done. If all unions were that strong, the world would be a better place."

Brady stared at the professor, then rose to leave. "Oh," he said as he turned to go, "I do have one more question."

"Which is…?"

Brady made sure his eyes were locked squarely into Conger's before uttering his next word, "Yulia."

"Yulia?" Conger repeated with a quizzical look. "What about her? Wait a minute…is *that* what this is all about? Tell me you didn't hijack me just because you're still hung up on that Russian Roman Candle. Come *on*, Greer! She's quite the piece of work, I'll grant you that, but she was hardly in Kansas City long enough to unpack. I assume we both moved on with our lives. At least, I know I did."

"No, she isn't the reason you're here," Brady said, suddenly nervous about bringing her up. "I was just thinking about her the other day…"

"Hell, I haven't talked to her in months," Conger said casually.

"Months?"

"Yeah, she's in Washington now. Calls me from time to time for advice on this or that. I'm still the father figure, I guess. She's got a job with one of those mail order bride outfits. There's a lot of pretty women in Russia after Western guys. Sounded like she was doing pretty well."

"Is she married?"

"Don't know about that. Never mentioned it if she was. Hey, what's the matter with you? You don't look so good."

Without answering, Brady closed the door behind him. *Yulia? Here? In the States? Why was it always so damn hard to focus? Focus, got to focus, shut out the crowd noise and bear down; just keep pitching. Working on a* very *big game here and this is* not *the time to let a woman get in the way*…But Yulia is the type who never just crosses your mind, she always lingers, looming ever larger, until all other thoughts are totally eclipsed.

19

Brady struggled to keep his leaden eyes open and on the road as he drove back to town. It was hard enough for him to process this new information and think about his next move without also having to fight through exhaustion. Should he have parked his inheritance in CDs or T-Bills? Just followed his clients into Co-Cola? Hopefully, everything would be clearer on the other side of a good nap.

Opening the door to his house, he was greeted by an excited Tanya.

"How did the morning go? Did you two have a nice talk?"

"Fine," he said blankly. "Yeah, I guess you could say it went pretty well."

"Good. I was down at the library. Your boy Conger is a very opinionated guy, quite the expert."

"Really? How so?"

"He's written a lot of articles and a couple of books. Known as 'the champion of a more egalitarian socioeconomic structure.' Says it would close the chasm between rich and poor."

"And you agree?"

"Absolutely! That's what I was trying to tell you before: Too much wealth in too few hands. I've seen people get crazy with too much time and too much money. It's disgusting."

"And your prescription to fix it is…what?"

"It's got to start with a commitment to fix it. That's half the battle right there. Without that, the 'chasm' as Conger calls it, between the haves and have nots, will just keep getting wider and deeper. Ultimately, of course, it would fix itself."

"Meaning?"

"Meaning the have nots will get so desperate that they take to the streets and we have another civil war."

Brady looked out his front window, toward the Confederate War Memorial, where the Daughters of the Confederacy continued to place fresh flowers once a week. "We're still recovering from the last one," he said quietly. Turning back to Tanya, he continued, "And I'm feeling pretty drained at the moment. Got to get some rest." Was delirium setting in or was he actually going to learn enough from the past to improve the future? That was his last thought as his head hit the pillow.

Brady awoke with a jolt several hours later, disoriented for a moment, as he always was when he grabbed his shuteye at odd hours. This time was a little worse, however. His hands and brow were moist with tiny pearls of perspiration because a dream had transported him to another land, where he found himself in an old, wooden dance hall with large ceiling fans overhead. It was a scene right out of the Fifties, with several dozen eager women with their picnic baskets on one side of the hall and a similar number of hungry men on the other. There had been some sort of random drawing to see who would be feasting with whom and Brady had approached his partner, clutching her number with great anticipation. At first, she was turned slightly away from him so he couldn't make out her features. As he moved to within a few feet of her, she turned suddenly and Brady found himself greeted by…Yulia…no, it was Tanya…then Yulia, now Tanya. Back and forth they went, as if alternating pictures on a hologram.

After Brady recoiled in horror, he looked again and, this time, saw several faces laughing at him heartily. All of them belonged to Beth.

He would leave it to his two favorite analysts—Sheila and Stretch—to figure out what all that meant. But he needed no help in concluding that Yulia, once again, had burrowed her way into his brain when he least needed a distraction. He wanted desperately to remain focused on baseball, but...she wasn't a half a world away, as he had always assumed, but right *here*, just a two-hour plane ride from Atlanta! How best to deal with that?

Complicating matters was Tanya. Here she was, an attractive, younger woman who didn't see him as the bizarre recluse he might well become, but instead a modern knight errant, willing to take an unconventional approach to slaying past dragons in an effort to improve his life.

As he was considering all this, the bathroom door opened and through it stepped Tanya, wearing a towel, a smile and a gleam in her eye. Extending her arms skyward, as if in celebration, the towel fell to the floor and she paused long enough for an approving look from Brady before slithering between the sheets and snuggling against him.

"Just thought you'd like some company," she purred.

His response was to turn and face her directly and, with arms gently massaging her back, begin kissing her, softly and slowly...here, there and everywhere.

When they had finished, she lay in his arms without speaking for what seemed like several minutes. Finally, she turned toward him and said, "Are you in the mood to talk?"

"I'm in the mood to listen," he said with a smile, deciding this would be a good time to take Sheila's advice for a test drive.

"Well, I'm wondering about something," she began slowly, with Brady listening   hard enough to pinch up his nose and furrow his brow. "Your body was here just now, but your mind was somewhere else. Am I right about that?"

"I...I'm not sure I know what you're talking about," he said, stalling until a more plausible answer popped into his head.

"When you get to know the way someone is when you're making love, you can tell when they're not all there."

"Ah, yes. Amazing that we've achieved that state so quickly. But it's not like we've been together for years. I think we're still new enough with each other that there will be some surprises along the way."

"I certainly hope so," she said while Brady turned to see her earnest and unsmiling. "But I trust my intuition and it tells me this is more than that. What, exactly, is it?"

Brady propped himself up on his elbows and slid back to the headboard, where he came to rest on a pillow. "Well, Tanya, it's like this: Some things have come up in my talks with Conger. I'm thinking about heading out of town again."

"Oh, another pick-up in the Bus?"

"No, not that kind of trip. This is a quick plane trip I need to make myself. Be sure Conger's got enough food and water while I'm gone, okay? I'll be back before you know it, not just with my body, but body, mind and spirit. I promise."

"I'll look forward to that," she said softly, swinging her feet onto the floor and grabbing her towel. Then she entered the bathroom and closed the door.

Skeeter: *Remember what Flaps said about Rex? How he could get into a batter's head? Looks as though Yulia's been studying those moves here.*

Herb: *Brady can't go on being a free swinger the rest of his life. He's got to learn when it makes sense to take a pitch.*

The first time Brady saw Washington it had been through the eyes of a high school senior on his class trip. He had arrived in an old, yellow school bus after 1,500 miles on the road from Milwaukee, convinced politicians answered a higher calling than most and that the gears of government tended to mesh smoothly, routinely producing enlightened legislation for the benefit of everyone. Then came Viet Nam, Watergate, cynicism and a major reassessment.

He had been back a few times since high school, choosing on each occasion to focus instead upon the beauty of the place, with a special affection for the cherry trees down by the Potomac because they never seemed to blossom during Cherry Blossom Festival, making them kindred spirits, maverick independents in an otherwise partisan and scripted town.

Stepping out of the airport, Brady was immediately bathed in a cloak of humidity, reminding him again that the city had been built upon a swamp. Why? He had never understood, exactly.

Something to do with its location astride the Mason-Dixon Line, he figured. Finding the real answer might call for investing a few hours at the Smithsonian, but there would be no time for that on this trip. His focus now was history of a very personal sort.

As soon as he checked into his room downtown, Brady opened the telephone book in search of a listing for "Yulia Estrikova" and found that surname, but no "Yulias" or initial, "Y." He then turned to the Yellow Pages and marveled at the number of dating services he found there. To his amazement and relief, the name of one on K Street—"From Russia, With Love"—virtually jumped out of the book at him. He dialed the number and the pleasant, but unfamiliar, voice on the other end was happy to give him an appointment the following afternoon.

Dating services had always made sense to Brady, though he had never used one, assuming that his location in Midian made him geographically undesirable. Now, he prepared for his interview like any other prospective bachelor: putting his best foot forward. In this case, that included a quick trip to the hair salon in the lobby, the tailor-made sport coat he rarely wore in Georgia, his best Italian loafers and, to top it off, a $50 silk necktie purchased at the tony men's store next door. Brady had never paid that much for a necktie before and would have little use for it back in Munson County, but there was a high gloss to downtown Washington that was a welcomed counterpoint to rural Georgia and he wanted to feel a part of it, if only briefly.

Arriving at "From Russia, With Love," he was impressed immediately with the warmth of the surroundings. The Chesterfield leather couches, earth tones and Delacroix lithographs on the walls made him feel as though he were in someone's den and in a way, of course, he was. Brady tried to pay attention to the receptionist while simultaneously scanning the offices for any sign of Yulia. There was none.

After watching the introductory video and completing his questionnaire, Brady was handed three large photo albums and invited to take his time in the conference room to search the pictures and profiles. He had planned to do exactly that, scanning each page very deliberately while gazing periodically over the albums and through the glass windows for any sign of Yulia. As he did so, he was impressed by the number of beautiful blondes, brunettes and redheads he saw on the pages before him from throughout Russia, the Ukraine and Lithuania. Though their addresses were for sale individually, it soon became apparent to Brady that the goal of this operation was to sign men up for "Love Tours" of the old USSR— at $3,000-to-$4,000 each.

With still no sign of Yulia after he had finished the second album, Brady decided to slowly make his way to the water cooler at the rear of the office. Turning from it with cup in hand, he came face to face with a slender, red-haired woman, statuesque...suddenly, he saw those eyes. Yulia? Could it really be? Yes! She had put on about 10 or 15 pounds since her college days, but still carried it like the athlete she was. She gave him only a perfunctory smile as she reached for a cup.

After she had filled it, she turned slowly back toward him.

"Excuse me," she said, "you look a lot like a guy—"

"Yulia, I *am* that guy. It's me, Brady!"

"Oh, my God!" she said, putting her right hand to her mouth as her left hand dropped, water dripping from her cup. "Is it really you? What are you *doing* here?"

They each took a moment to square their memories with the realities before them. Some laugh lines had begun to radiate out from Yulia's eyes and mouth, the kind women hate, but men appreciate. Her magnetic smile and flashing eyes were still very much in evidence. Her hair was shorter than he remembered, but the biggest change, he thought, was the way she was dressed. Gone was the cheap cotton skirt and sweater that had been her uniform in college. Instead, she was now decked out in a very stylish magenta silk pants suit, accompanied by an expensive necklace, gold bracelets and, most importantly, an emerald ring on her serious finger that did not appear to signal permanent attachment.

"I heard you might be having a back-to-school special on Russian brides," he said brightly. "You know me. I hate to pay retail."

"Are you *serious*? You're one of our customers?"

"As of about an hour ago. Now, let me ask you a question: What are *you* doing here?"

"This is my business," she said proudly. "I own it. That is, my partner and I own it."

"Congratulations," he said. "Looks like business is

booming."

"That's right. No complaints about that. So, what about you? Are you living here in town?"

"Uh…no. Actually, I'm living down in Georgia. Just in town for a day or two on business. Don't have any plans for dinner tonight. Care to join me?"

"Hmmm…tonight's tough," she said thoughtfully. "But I could do for a drink after work…"

"I don't know…," he said slowly, with a straight face. "My hearse is in the shop…"

She gave him a quick, quizzical look, then blurted out, "Brady Greer! You haven't changed one *bit*!"

"Yes, I have. The hearse is gone. Died one day right in downtown Kansas City. Had to have it towed on its final trip to the auto graveyard, so we'll both be walking this time. I'll meet you in the lobby of my hotel, the Mayflower, at 5:30."

Skeeter: *This is no contest; if it were a fight, they'd stop it. She's got serious stuff—all the pitches—and he's still a banjo hitter in the minors. I smell a shutout here…*

Herb: *Take it easy, now; give him a chance. He's a contact hitter, not someone swinging for the fences. All he wants to do is start a rally.*

Skeeter: *He's already got a game going—back in Midian. What he's in danger of starting is a circus.*

With a new bounce in his step, Brady returned to the conference room, gathered up the photo albums and handed them to the receptionist. Heading for the elevator, he turned and smiled confidently at her, saying, "I won't be needing these anymore."

It had been a very long time since Brady worried much about his wardrobe, but here he was--for the second time in a single day--fretting about what to wear. He finally decided to replace his dress shirt and tie with a simple black tee shirt under his sport coat for cocktails. This wasn't a real date, he had to remind himself, just a couple of former lovers getting together for a drink. *Calm down, relax. Stay loose.* He had given himself pep talks in the past to generate enthusiasm where none existed, but could not remember the last time he felt the need to rein himself in. Suddenly, he recalled again his brokerage training: two speeches in every sales call. Give yours first, you lose the sale; give yours second, you close the deal.

Brady waited by the lobby elevators as patiently as possible as the minutes ticked by...5:35, 5:40...5:45, 5:50. It was almost 6 o'clock when Yulia swept through the revolving door at the front entrance.

"Sorry I'm late," she said with a slight smile as she shook her head. "One of the drawbacks of doing business in too many time zones: Customers call at all hours and expect us to be there."

"No problem," he said, guiding her toward a booth in the bar off the lobby. "No customers, no business. Gotta take care of 'em."

After she ordered her vodka Collins and he his Rolling Rock, she turned to him, exhaled slowly, and finally said, "Okay, I feel like I'm relaxed for the first time today. So, tell me, what are you doing in Georgia?"

"It's a long story. That's where the music stopped, so I grabbed a chair. But let's get back to the water cooler for a minute. How did you get into the bride business? I'll bet that's much more interesting..."

"Well," she said, drumming her fingers lightly on the mahogany table, "I knew a lot of girls in Volgograd who were complaining all the time about Russian men. They drink too much and run around. Sometimes, gambling's the problem. A lot of them just don't know how to treat a woman. One night, a bunch of us were having dinner and they asked me about American men. I had a lot of good things to say, then I remembered that you guys complain a lot about American women. Too high maintenance and so forth. A little light bulb went off and I decided to make it easy for unhappy women to get together with unhappy men and, hopefully, produce some happy couples."

"How long have you been doing that?"

"We're in our fifth year. We've got offices now here, in the U.K. and Europe. So, tell me, when did you decide to look for a Russian woman?"

"Well, I didn't run through everyone in America first, though sometimes it seems that way. Actually, I had some rather fond memories of a certain Russian woman," he said with an impish grin, "so thought it might be a good idea to fish in that same pond, so to speak."

191

Yulia rolled her eyes and smiled. "No special ladies down in Georgia? I hear Southern girls are very pretty."

"Yes," he said, "there *are* pretty ladies down there. In fact, I was married to one, but it didn't work out, so I thought I might find someone special up here." He glanced away for a moment, then returned his attention to her. "How about you? You must have had plenty of opportunities to meet your match, especially in your line of work."

"That's true," she said thoughtfully, after sipping her drink, "but I travel a lot, so don't have much time to devote to a relationship."

"No one in your life at the moment?"

"Well, yes, there is… Remember, I mentioned my partner?"

"Right."

"Well," she said with a laugh, "Don and I have done a really good job of mixing up our personal and business lives for several years now."

"Without getting married?"

"It's pretty hard for other people to understand, Brady. We're each married—to our business. We don't spend much time together in the same city. I've already gone through one divorce and decided I wouldn't think about marriage again, unless my life was in a really stable place. I haven't been able to say that for a while. In the meantime, there's a lot of satisfaction in matching up pretty Russians and rich Americans."

"Rich? That's a requisite?"

"Rich' is relative. Anyone from the States looks wealthy to most of these girls. They don't feel appreciated by Russian men; American men don't feel appreciated by American women. So," she said with a shrug, "we're in the business of getting people together who appreciate each other."

"And you're doing this full-time?"

"Well, mostly. I'm an entrepreneur, Brady. After the Wall came down, I think it exposed more entrepreneurs than roaches. In the era of *glasnost*, you never know what opportunities will emerge in the East-West business...which often involves risk…as a matter of fact…" Yulia resumed drumming her fingers on the table before glancing at her watch. "Damn, Brady! I've got to go. How long did you say you'd be in town?"

"Just...until tomorrow," he replied. "Gotta get back to Georgia."

"Let's stay in touch," she said, picking up her purse as she rose to leave. "You never did tell me what you're doing down there."

Craning her neck to make out the wording on his business card in the dim light, she said, "A stockbroker, eh? Hmm.... Maybe I'll give you a call for some advice." As they both rose from the booth, she leaned toward him, gripped his elbow, then kissed him lightly on the cheek and said, "I'm really glad we ran into each other; maybe you can help me," and hurried away.

20

When Brady wanted to do some serious thinking, he got behind the wheel. So, he canceled his flight back to Atlanta after he returned to his room and, the following morning, rented a car and headed for Georgia.

On the way out of Washington, he pulled off I-95 for a cup of coffee and a quick look at the morning paper. The All-Star game had been played in Milwaukee the night before and Brady was eager to see how his hometown had done under the spotlight. The verdict on the evening, overall, was positive. The city and the Brewers had pulled out all the stops to stage a first class event, which it appeared to have been…with one notable exception: The game had ended in a tie at 7-7. *A tie? How could that be? Was there a curfew? A power outage?*

No. Next to a photo of the Commissioner conferring with umpires, the story explained that both sides had run out of pitchers. The stadium announcer had been directed to tell the crowd at the start of the 11th inning that, if the game was not decided in the next six outs, it would be declared a draw. That bulletin was greeted with hoots and jeers by the Commissioner's supposed friends and neighbors, the Milwaukee fans. Already derided as a meaningless exhibition and almost eclipsed by the home run derby preceding it, the All-Star game had descended now to the level of farce.

Though the decision to call the draw was not entirely the Commissioner's fault and was endorsed by both managers, the awkward picture it painted for the national television audience was an instant reminder that this was the man who did, seven years before, what two World Wars and the Great Depression could not: cancel the World Series.

Brady took a closer look at the photo. There was someone else there, just behind the Commissioner…still visible, but not identified in the caption. Brady recognized the broad face and big smile easily: Kip Kapopka, "The Polish Poppi" from Milwaukee's South Side.

Suddenly Coach's words came back to Brady: "Kapopka built a career out of making himself useful." He continued to cash in on one quality: He was popular with both players and owners and moved easily in each camp. Kip had been a three-sport star at Don Bosco High School at about the same time Brady was riding the bench at Lakeside. He was later selected in the first round of the Major League draft as a high school senior. Though he was never a star after that, he built a Big League career by developing the ability to plug leaks in the lineup. Due to injuries or trades, a sudden need could crop up anywhere and Kip could be counted upon to hold the fort until a more talented replacement was found. Playing Kip Kapopka was always a popular move with the fans.

But, staring at Kip's picture there on the counter of the coffee shop, Brady didn't see "Kip The Kameleon;" he saw, instead, a self-made man who had become--through sheer diligence and positive attitude--the person Brady might have been. That was all the more remarkable to Brady when he considered that he had been born on second base, at least, while Kip started life in the dugout…yet Brady had not advanced, while Kip had already crossed the plate.

Herb: *"It's never too late to become who you might have been."*

Skeeter: *Hmm… how can you be sure of that?*

Herb: *That's George Eliot's line, not mine, but I agree with it. Some games are won in the first inning, others in the fifth and still others in the bottom of the ninth. You have to believe there's always that chance everything will come together. Otherwise, you might as well just concede defeat.*

Skeeter: *That's the second time you've mentioned Eliot. The guy must be a big fan.*

Herb: *Actually, Skeeter, Eliot was…well, I guess you could say Eliot was a fan of sorts, a fan of the game of life.*

Each time he landed with a new team, Kapopka had taken the time to study its ownership. How had these horse breeders, stock traders, car dealers, high tech entrepreneurs and oil men made enough money to afford buying a baseball team? Though their baseball decisions could be questionable—even stupid—they had done something else really well to earn a seat at the owner's table and Kip Kapopka made it a point to study their successes.

That knowledge came in very handy during contract talks, when the South Side journeyman was typically offered a modest contract. "You know I'm worth more than that," he would bluff to the general manager, "but I'm a team player, so I'll tell you what I'm gonna do. I'll sign for it…if the owner will agree to put another 10 percent of what I make into his next deal, in my name."

At first, even though his piece of the resulting business deal was extremely small, Kip was surprised at how readily the team went along, the owner enjoying a player who recognized his business acumen. Later, Kip would shame an owner, if need be, telling him the other owners wouldn't understand if one of their number suddenly refused to do business with Kip outside of baseball.

So, as the years rolled by, Kip found himself viewed as both employee and partner. Even though that meant being a very limited partner, he was able to build up a potential annuity—whenever the general partner would let him cash in his share—and seize the opportunity to observe first-hand how money makes money. After his playing days ended and communications between players and owners became increasingly bitter, Kip Kapopka emerged as the one man both respected and trusted by each group. In his amorphous role as Special Assistant to the Commissioner, he became the glue binding the two sides together with fragile agreements.

Brady looked up from his paper and gazed out the window of the coffee shop. He remembered well when baseball was a rock, a refuge to which you could return periodically when other aspects of life—jobs, relationships—were uncertain. The All-Star game mattered when Milwaukee first hosted it in 1955. He knew that first-hand, because his Dad had taken him to it. Since the two never talked much, those kind of shared experiences loomed larger in defining the relationship in the son's mind as the years rolled by. Brady looked again at the Commissioner's picture. Brady believed this man loved the game, yet he had become a lightning rod for many of its problems. *An enigma, just like Harry Greer.*

That '55 game had also gone extra innings, but with a different result: Stan Musial—now *there* was a Polish ballplayer— Stan the Man led off the bottom of the 12th with a home run, completing the biggest comeback in All-Star history, as the National League overcame a 5-0 deficit to win, 6-5. Brady grunted loudly. "Hell, *Musial* would have pitched if he had to! *Anything* before accepting a *tie!*"

"Excuse me?"

Brady glanced up from his paper to see his waitress looking back at him quizzically, then quickly felt the gaze of the others at the counter.

"Ah…never mind," he said hastily. "Just got a little too involved in the sports section."

As he reached into his pocket to pay his bill, Brady felt a hand on his arm and turned to see the face of the elderly man seated next to him.

"Did you say 'Musial?" the man asked hopefully. "Is he planning a comeback?"

"I doubt it," Brady said with a laugh and started to add that the old Cardinal slugger must be in his 80s by now, but caught himself. A wave of sadness had washed over the elderly man, as though he had almost rediscovered something precious, only to see it slip again from his grasp. The man's mind had evidently traveled a great distance and Brady decided to leave it there.

A few minutes later, he was back on the highway, headed south through rural Virginia. Brady used to think life in these small towns was a lot less interesting than in the bigger cities. But that was before he moved to Midian. He now knew from personal experience that many of these apparent hayseeds were much brighter and more successful than they chose to reveal. Since they avoided the hassles of urban gridlock, both physical and emotional, in favor of small town serenity, they were confident in their superiority to their big city brethren, to whom they offered quiet pity, instead of gloating.

Though he was trying to use the open road to clear his mind, it kept filling up with thoughts of Yulia. In keeping with the mysterious and conflicted nature of her native land, she was somewhat available, yet somewhat taken; ostensibly free, yet also hostage to inexplicable forces.

Brady's response to that struck him as appropriate, since he was somewhat interested, yet also hesitant. Did it really matter? Yulia was based hundreds of miles away from him and traveled frequently. It was a bad time for him to think about relocating anywhere and he was not sure if, given the opportunity, he would choose to live in Washington.

And then there was Tanya. She had seemed to him a budding revolutionary when they met. As he got to know her, she appeared more like the coltish scion of a powerful family determined to jump its emotional fences. If she ultimately failed, she could always revert to the comfort and safety of high tea, shopping sprees and domestic help. But, if she succeeded in establishing her independence, she would become a far more interesting person. Brady doubted Tanya had the strength to break away on her own. To do that, she would need to draw energy from someone else.

He didn't think anything through to completion during the trip back to Georgia, simply finding something so very soothing about solitude on the road. The mellow state of mind he was in upon his return home was tested immediately when he walked into an empty house.

About two hours later, Tanya walked through the door with a star-struck schoolgirl look on her face that Brady recognized immediately.

"Hey, welcome back!" she said with a hug. "How was the trip?"

"The trip was fine," he said. "How's the professor? How's he doing?"

"He's *amazing!*" she gushed. "I never realized there was so much history that never made it into textbooks."

"So, you two have been getting to know each other?"

"Yeah…a little bit, as best we can through that courtyard gate. Oh, Brady, Dr. Conger is *so* interesting," she said. "He and I have been reading the same book and he's using it as a text in one of his classes."

"Let me guess: Howard Zinn?"

"That…That's right," she said in amazement. "How in the world did you know?"

"An educated guess. Look, Tanya," Brady said, feeling his blood rise, "you were just supposed to be taking supplies out there, not signing up for one of his classes."

"Well…I had some questions about his stuff I read at the library and he certainly had plenty of time to answer them. I just thought, you know, while you were away, I would try to--"

"For*get* it!" Brady glared at her. "Stay a-*way* from that old son of a bitch, okay?"

Tanya, clearly stunned, gaped at Brady momentarily, trying to summon something to say. Finally, this:

"Sure, Brady, sure. It's not that big a deal, really. I hate to see you… so…worked up."

Skeeter: *His control's a little wobbly here, Herb. I'm getting worried about him…*

Herb: *He'll be okay; he just needs to go into "time out" for a while. Let's see…I wonder how a grown man would do that…*

The following morning, Brady stopped briefly at his office before heading up to Athens to visit Flaps.

"Hey, stranger," his friend greeted him. "I've been wondering how you felt about that All-Star game. I thought the Commissioner just wore ugly ties, now he's given one to everybody. Not a good night for baseball, eh?"

"Terrible," Brady agreed, shaking his head in disgust. "A golden opportunity to showcase Milwaukee as a great baseball town and it turned to tin."

"What's on your mind today? You buying or selling?"

"Neither, actually," he said. "Just wanted to say, 'hi.'"

"I'm flattered."

"Well, there is one other thing…"

"And that would be?"

"The card. Just got to see it."

Flaps flashed a knowing smile as he moved several steps down the counter and unlocked the display case protecting his most expensive merchandise. Mostly, those were the rookie cards of Willie Mays, Mickey Mantle, Sandy Koufax and other legends of the game. But none of them interested Brady as much as the card Flaps now gripped gently between his thumb and forefinger as he removed it before placing it carefully on the counter.

Topps was the most venerable name in baseball card collecting. The company had its first big success with a set of cards issued in 1952, numbered sequentially from one to 220. Brady and most other kids of that era organized their cards in order, keeping them all together with rubber bands. As a result, the first and last cards in the set were usually in rough shape, which diminished their value considerably. On the other hand, it made the exceptions— those cards that had somehow escaped rubber bands, bicycle spokes and other hazards of youth—valuable for their scarcity.

Mothers were famous for tossing these cards in the trash, regardless of their condition, after their sons left home and long before they became desired by collectors. Brady remained thankful that his mother could part with nothing from his childhood.

In 1952, Topps selected Andy Pafko, then of the Brooklyn Dodgers, to be on its #1 card. A '52 Pafko in pristine condition had been auctioned in 2000 like a rare painting, bringing the gavel down at $83,870, more money than Pafko made in any of his 17 seasons as a player--despite sporting a .285 career batting average that would make him millions today. There were many copies of the card still in circulation, but each typically had rubber band marks, a dog-eared edge, was off-center or carried some other common blemish. A combination of these flaws could drive the price of the card down to $200, which was the approximate value of the one currently in Flaps' possession. It had well-defined rubber band marks, each of its edges was frayed and the picture of the smiling Slovak was slightly off-center.

There were a couple of reasons Flaps had acquired his battered copy. Most of all, it was because he knew how much it meant to Brady. There had been other days, like today, when Brady had made the one-hour round trip from Midian just to see it. Beyond that, there remained the hope in the heart of the dealer that, one day, Brady would tell Flaps he had to acquire his very own perfect Pafko. That would be a big payday for the card shop, which was having its own cash flow problems.

In the meantime, Brady was resolute: Baseball cards had lives, just like people. Cuts and bruises were common to both along the way. The notion that a man's worth could be contained in a two-dimensional card of his past achievements--and de-valued exponentially with every nick, scratch, and flaw--fascinated Brady. For a person to survive decades unscathed was impossible, but the occasional baseball card could make it. When that card was a #1 Pafko, a special space on the lofty pedestal of Brady's childhood memories was reserved for it.

He had no desire to own the '52 Pafko in anything less than flawless condition. The fact that Brady could now afford to make that acquisition was not the point. Just knowing that the perfection of Pafko was something valued by thousands of collectors gave Brady a great deal of satisfaction. Most of them had never seen Pafko play and, thus, could not know what the genuine joy and all-out hustle of the farm boy from Boyceville meant to a young kid growing up in Milwaukee in 1953. That, Brady fantasized, was a kind of secret just the two of them shared. It was on days like this that Brady needed not to own perfection, but to remain driven by the knowledge that it was out there, somewhere, and that the time would come when he deserved to acquire it. Only he would know the hour of its arrival.

Brady took a long look at the card on the counter before him. Pafko broke in with the Cubs in 1943 and became an All-Star outfielder. When Stan Hack, a five-time All-Star, retired in '47, Pafko was moved to third base without complaint. Years later, in the twilight of his career, the veteran tutored a young outfielder named Henry Aaron to succeed him. In between, Pafko had the best view of the most famous home run in baseball history when Bobby Thompson hit "The Shot Heard 'Round the World" over his head in 1951. Brady liked to think of Pafko as baseball's Forrest Gump, always crossing paths with various legendary figures.

He glanced around the shop. There were football cards, basketball cards, hockey cards, even Hollywood cards promoting various movies.

"Do you still get the gum these days?" he asked Flaps.

"Huh?"

"You know, the gum. It used to come in all the packs."

"Kids don't care about gum these days," Flaps said. "In fact, we don't really get that many kids in here. It's mostly adults, looking to buy low and sell high, just like the stock market. Every time a decent rookie comes along, I got people in here, loading up on their cards, planning to sock 'em away until who knows when, then make a killing when the boy wonder has a Hall of Fame career."

"And when that doesn't happen?"

"Which is most of the time, of course. When that can't-miss prospect blows his arm out or can't hit the curve ball, well, then you got yourself a stack of cardboard nobody wants."

"Does anyone get attached to these little pictures anymore," Brady asked softly, "or are they just another commodity?"

"Well, I got some customers always interested in the big names. You know, Mantle, Mays, that sort of thing. Got others just looking to fill out a set from a certain year. Nowadays, though, with free agency and all, you got players moving all over the place. The days of a top player sticking with one team for his whole career are about over. Personally," Flaps continued, playing to his audience, "I liked it better when we didn't know how much everyone was making. Now, seems like money drives everything, you know? Makes it tougher for the fan to bond with his hero, you might say."

Brady took one last look at Pafko. *We will always be bonded*, he thought, before handing the card back to Flaps.

Refreshed, somehow, by his time machine excursion, Brady was ready to deal again with the present and get back to his office before the market closed for the day. Along the way, he would pick up something for Tanya, a peace offering after snapping at her like a cur dog. *Why had he been that way?* Brady felt detached from himself, as though he was remaining rational, but some evil twin had suddenly appeared to behave badly.

A recent rally in the market had made his time away from the depot lately less noticeable, but he still relied on his telephone to stay in touch. He listened casually to the dozen messages waiting for him when he returned from Athens. Only one snapped him to full attention.

"Hi, Brady," it began. "It's Yulia. Really glad we ran into each other up here. I had no idea I'd be getting down your way so soon, but I'm going to be in Atlanta next Tuesday. Want to get together? Let me know."

Sinking slowly into his leather chair, he hit the "play" button a second time, then a third, etching her words deep enough into his mind to begin the customary forensic examination. *"Glad." Glad is good. No, wait: It was "really glad." Even better. A casual, off-hand tone. Very appropriate.* After all, they were hardly an item now, just an old college couple trying to catch up with each other's missing years. Would it become more than that? Did he want it to be? The answer would require more field research.

21

   The more he thought about Yulia's call, the warmer Brady felt. He recognized it quickly as the same sensation she had given him the first time she registered on his radar in college. Being with her was a habit both exotic and mysterious that was tougher to lay off than a good slider, low and away.

   It struck him that the two women in his life were heading in opposite directions: Yulia was now rejecting her Russian roots to enjoy the fruits of capitalist success, while Tanya had shed her Ta Ta persona and all its materialist trappings in an effort to join the proletariat. Brady suddenly felt out of step. He, too, was running away from something. In fact, reality was disappearing over the horizon as he attempted to steer his mind into the past.

   He decided the next step had to be another meeting with Yulia. In the meantime, what to do with Tanya? He had considered chocolates or a thoughtful little knick-knack as a peace offering, but settled on flowers. Brady was truly contrite after raising his voice and arriving back at the house with a dozen red roses in hand appeared to be the best balm he could apply to the abrasion he had caused.

"Oh, Brady," she cried as she greeted him with a hug. "They are absolutely gorgeous! You are *so* sweet!" When he mentioned later that he would be heading over to Atlanta one night the following week for dinner, she encouraged him to take care of business.

Since Yulia's taste was refined, that business was conducted at the Four Seasons, where Brady was impressed most by the check he insisted on grabbing. Living large for even one night was a welcomed escape from his reality...especially when that evening was shared with an animated and radiant Yulia.

"We've struck gold, the real mother lode, with these Southern men," she said with a grin as their salads arrived.

"How so?"

"Well, they tend to be well-groomed and well-mannered— very courtly. But they continue to have traditional views about gender roles. You know, Daddy brings home the bacon while Mommy's barefoot and pregnant in the kitchen."

"Hmmm...I don't know about that," Brady said. "I know a lot of Southern women who are committed to their careers."

"But don't you see?" she said, poking her salad fork into the air. "That's my point, exactly. Old customs down here die hard. These men don't accept independent women as much as they just tolerate them. Given a choice, they would still rather be what you Americans call, 'the breadwinner.' That's what we do: give them that choice. Over half the guys on our next trip to Volgograd will be from the South. That Southern charm and willingness to take charge is very attractive to our girls."

"Put 'em together--our charm, your girls--and you get Olga O'Hara, eh?"

"What?"

"Never mind. Look, I'm happy to hear your business is going well. But what do you do when you're not working? Do you have a life *away* from the office or is your office wherever you happen to be at the moment?"

"I *do* have my own life," she said defensively. "I have several close girlfriends, here and in Europe. We get together or I read, work out…maybe catch a movie. But it's true that most of what I do relates somehow to work. I love my job. It's a big part of me…and I've made a lot of people happy."

"How about Yulia?" he said, as casually as he could. "Is she happy?"

She paused for a moment to dab her lips with her napkin. "Yes," she said. "I think so."

Unconvinced, Brady pressed on. "You haven't mentioned your partner. Is he part of that happiness?"

Yulia shifted uneasily in her seat and stared at her plate. Finally, she looked across the table and said softly, "Brady, I thought we would be two old friends here, having a nice, quiet dinner, not two participants in an inquisition."

"Well, the feelings over here are running a little stronger than just 'friend,' he said. "Very frankly, I'd like to know if I have a shot with you to be more than a friend."

Yulia put down her fork and reached across the table for Brady's hand. It was a gesture that looked affectionate to anyone else in the restaurant, but he got the feeling immediately it was meant more to prepare him for words he did not want to hear.

"Brady, I have always cared about you and always will. But, you have got to realize, I travel a great deal. I just don't stay in one place long enough to…to work on a single relationship."

"So, it's a time and distance problem, is that it?"

"Well," she said, releasing his hand and leaning back in her chair, "that's a big part of it."

"Leaving…what? What else?"

Yulia paused for a sip of her pinot noir, then continued. "Well, I do make time for some social life, but…"

"But what?"

"Those girlfriends I mentioned?" Now she lowered her voice and eyed him carefully. "With a couple of them, I am *very* close, especially close."

The boy from Milwaukee took a moment to let this message register. He had known some gay men over the years, but had never met a woman who was openly queer. And, of all the women he had ever known, he would probably pick the one sitting across from him to be the least likely lesbian.

"You're not…serious," was all he could muster.

"Oh, yes," she replied. "Indeed, I am. But it's not just other women. I still date guys, too."

A switch-hitter? That concept, applied here, left him speechless. He cursed to himself the debasement of the term used to describe those few players willing and able to learn to hit from either side of the plate.

"Look," she continued softly, "some guys find that a turn-on. I didn't know how you would feel and talking about it, like we're doing here, is the only way to find out."

He cleared his throat. "I can honestly tell you, Yulia, this is one of those subjects that has just...never...popped up...on my personal radar. I mean, I come from a place where everyone was straight, at least as far as we knew. I just, uh, never considered this, that's all, so I can't give you a flip answer. This comes as a...surprise...so I'm going to need to...think about it."

Skeeter: *Oh, boy...hittin' from both sides...lotta great ones did that. There was Mickey, of course...Pete Rose, Eddie Murray...*

Herb: *I think Willie McGee hit over .350 one year doing that...*

Skeeter: *But, you know, most of them still do better— sometimes, a lot better—from one side.*

Herb: *Hmmm... I wonder if Yulia--"*

Skeeter: *Let's don't go there, okay?*

"That's fine," she said with a relaxed smile. "Remember back in college? Everyone seemed to have the same romantic assumption then: Find that one great partner for the rest of your life. Well, I figured out that doesn't work for me. Different partners fill different needs. You just ended a serious relationship, which is always difficult. But maybe that's an opportunity, too...an opportunity to figure out if you still need one person, or maybe several. Either way," she said brightly, dabbing her lips with her napkin, "let me know where you come out on that, then we can figure if we'll just be friends--and there's nothing wrong with that-- or maybe something else, okay?

"There," she said with a satisfied sigh as she leaned back in her chair. "Don't you feel much better now that we understand each other?"

On a normal evening, the one-hour ride back to Midian would be filled with music, with Brady often singing along with one of his favorite CDs. But his definition of normalcy was becoming increasingly elusive and it was absent on this night as Brady made the drive in his silent Microbus, trying to sort out his feelings.

He thought sex with Beth had been normal and it seemed to be satisfactory at the time, but now...was her need to push the envelope one of the things that drove her away? Tanya was restless and aggressive in bed, as though she were trying to unleash the demons within. Brady could understand that and was, in fact, enjoying it. It reminded him of some memorable nights with Yulia in the back of the hearse, many years ago...could it be that way with her again? After all, she wasn't asking him to join her and one of her "close friends," only to accept that Yulia would be working both sides of the singles street.

What did *he* want? An exclusive relationship with Yulia was not going to be the option he had hoped for. And it sounded as though being with her on her terms was going to drain what little mental energy he had left. Brady exited at Midian and decided to see if a cup of coffee at the Waffle World would clear his mind. Sheila was off and so was the price on her Fiero—down to $1,000 now. In the absence of conversation, he busied himself by flipping through some syrup-stained newspapers left on the counter.

Picking up the sports section, he saw that home runs were again flying out of various ballparks at a record pace. *Some of these mashers weren't so beefy just a few years ago. Takes more than weights to get that bulk. Why doesn't baseball do something about that?*

Brady was startled to find a kindred spirit right there on page three, just below the fold: "Shorter Says 'No' to Steroids." While preparing for a road race up in New England, Frank Shorter, the former Olympic marathoner, was asked about recent reports of steroid use in baseball. As the head of something called the U.S. Anti-Doping Agency, the article quoted Shorter as saying Major League Baseball had called to ask him about dealing with steroid use, but refused to follow the lead of professional football and basketball and ban them. Why? Shorter did not know.

Meanwhile, the same paper reported the MLB Player's Association had set an August 30 deadline—three weeks away—as its strike date, if its demands were not met by owners. Brady felt disgust welling up within him. *Who the hell's in charge here? Are the inmates running the prison?*

Gazing out the window, watching the parade of truckers rolling down the interstate, Brady saw a familiar face in the foreground, hanging there, disembodied, above the parking lot: Kip Kapopka, the symbol of the The National Pastime's veneer of strength masking its ennui and impotence...and the low expectations and low results that seemed to characterize every renegotiated contract between players and owners. *Why don't those bastards* do *something? The game's becoming a national* punch *line!*

He grunted to himself as he headed for his Bus. Waffle World had worked its wonders again: He'd stopped thinking—for the moment, at least—about Yulia, the problem accompanying him when he walked in the door. Instead, though, Brady found himself increasingly agitated about the health of his favorite game.

Arriving back at the house, he slipped into bed next to a smiling Tanya, closeness and contentment easily within his grasp, yet unreachable. For nearly 45 minutes, he shifted about—from stomach, to back, to side—yet sleep never arrived. Though he wasn't hungry, Brady gently eased himself out of bed and made his way lightly into the kitchen. Munching on Triscuits and peanut butter and washing them down with a bottle of Rolling Rock, his mind traveled back through the decades to Milwaukee County Stadium, home of the Braves, when a team's entire roster didn't turn over every three or four years and the fans didn't know or care about player salaries. The drugs of choice back then were nicotine and caffeine and striking was not an option, because...well, because the players weren't organized, for one thing. Beyond that, everybody seemed to respect the game too much to sully it with a strike. That was unthinkable, as unthinkable as swinging both ways outside the batter's box.

Other sports had long ago recognized the wisdom of revenue sharing and adopted it seriously as a means of leveling the playing field among all teams. Yet baseball was content to just inch along in that direction, allowing the few clubs that were flush to keep most of their huge local television revenues and thus continue to dominate the many teams of meager means, most of whom knew before the first pitch on Opening Day that their chances of reaching the playoffs were as slim as a blade of outfield grass.

Somewhere after his third beer, Brady Greer reached the inescapable conclusion that baseball needed shock treatment, a catalyzing event to stun it to its senses. By dawn, he had determined what that jolt would be.

22

"Brady, are you all right?" Tanya asked as she squinted and turned on the kitchen light at 6 AM. Glancing at the empty green bottles of Rolling Rock, lined up on the table like soldiers standing guard on St. Patrick's Day, she said, "That must have been some meeting if it drove you to drink all night."

Lifting his swollen eyes toward her and running his tongue over teeth that had turned tacky from inattention, he replied, "It wasn't the meeting. I've been doing a lot of thinking, Tanya...a whole helluva lotta thinking."

"About?"

"Destiny. You know, what we talked about before? I knew what mine was then, just didn't know how to get there. Now, I know. You've probably been wondering about the overall plan out in Scofield. It's coming together now and just involves one last trip in the Microbus. We'll leave in the morning and be back in a few days."

"Those are the broad strokes," she said. "You need to paint me a better picture. You've already got one very unhappy guy out there. What are you trying to do, grab a group of nine so you can field a team?"

Instead of responding, Brady's mind somehow clicked into Eddie Feigner, who toured for years as "The King and His Court," barnstorming throughout the country with just three other players. One of Feigner's favorite stunts was to pitch on his knees—from second base! Still, they beat practically every local team who challenged them. But that was softball....and it had no other relevance whatsoever to the conversation Tanya was trying to have with him here. *Coffee. Gotta get some coffee.*

"Hello? Earth to Brady! Are you going to tell me what's going on?"

"Huh? Oh...sorry. Look, my batteries are a little low right now. Tell you what, you put on some coffee, I'll tell you what's happening, then it'll make sense to both of us," he said hopefully.

A couple of jolts of caffeine cleared Brady's mind and loosened his tongue.

"Baseball is in a ditch right now," he began, "and I'm going to pull it out."

"What do you mean?"

"Well, there are problems that threaten the health of baseball, but there's too much mistrust between labor and management to confront them, let alone solve them. Even when it takes a strike to reach a deal, the real problems are never addressed, just get put off until another day. In the meantime, a few teams are competitive every year and the rest don't have a realistic shot at winning consistently."

"And what do you propose to do about that?"

"Players and management are each operating in their own little comfort zones. I figure, knock them out of those zones, into a space that's new and uncomfortable, then there's a good chance real progress might result."

"How are you going to do that?"

"There's just one guy on the planet that everybody involved in baseball's labor talks trusts and that's Kip Kapopka. He's the one they count on to eventually make some sort of peace, however temporary or unsatisfying. Remove Kip from the process and maybe the talks move to another, more serious level."

212

Tanya's eyes widened. "You're going to make this Kip guy a...martyr?"

"No, no," Brady assured her, "nothing like that. Just a hostage...a hostage for progress."

Tanya managed to keep whatever enthusiasm she might have had about this idea in check, but he sensed she had become comfortable enough to at least go along with it for the time being. That was another one of Sheila's lessons he was struggling to master: Include a woman in your plans and she is far more likely to be a willing participant. Giving her input was even better, but that was still an advanced concept for Brady Greer.

.   They were on the road later that afternoon, deciding to drive straight through to Milwaukee. Their target was a little more difficult to scout this time, since the terrain was foreign to Brady. The South Side of Milwaukee might as well be the dark side of the moon to a kid growing up on the North Shore. Brady had driven over it many times--on the freeway to the airport--but had never paused to know the streets below. Lots of immigrants down there, is what he had heard... mostly from Eastern Europe...bringing traditions with them he didn't understand. Blood sausage? Pickled pigs feet? And the one that really grossed him out: tongue sandwiches?? *People really* eat *that stuff?*

Just after dusk the following night, they reached Milwaukee. This time, Brady exited into the wilds of the South Side,.guiding the Microbus west from the freeway.

"Wow," Tanya said, looking up at an enormous clock, fully-lit, about a mile way. "What's the story with *that*?"

"That's the four-sided Allen-Bradley clock," he said, "17 stories up, bigger than Big Ben. Each face is 40 feet high. Boats navigate by it out on Lake Michigan. It's so bright at night, they call it the Polish moon...uh, that is, *we* used to call it that. I'm...not sure if... *they* call it that...down here..."

They headed north to Lincoln Avenue, then west again toward what he was sure would be the Polish community.

"I don't understand," Tanya said as they passed block after block of modest homes on cramped lots. "I thought you said this

213

guy was a big shot baseball executive. Why would he be living *here*?"

"This is where he grew up; it's where his people are. They've been following his career all the way from high school to the Big Leagues. That's rock star stuff on the South Side. He could afford to move out; I'm sure of that, but he's a hero here…and they love him even more because he stayed here."

As they continued west, toward Kosciuszcko Park, Brady was becoming confused. He had made some phone calls before leaving Georgia to confirm that this was, indeed, Milwaukee's Polish neighborhood, but he wasn't seeing signs of that. Instead, they had passed several Mexican restaurants, bars and *panderias*.

"I never saw so many bars," Tanya said finally. "They're on every corner…but a lot of them seem to be Spanish…are you sure we're—"

"Don't worry; we're headed in the right direction," he said confidently. "Neighborhoods change a little bit over time; that's natural...and those aren't just bars, they're *taverns*, mom 'n pop operations…the social centers of the community, you might say. Years ago, they weren't just on the corners. If you look closely at the houses in the middle of some of these blocks, you can see they were originally taverns."

"Wow…that's amazing…how could they support all those bars—taverns, I mean?"

"Same way all those coffee shops make it in Seattle, I guess: become indispensable to your neighborhood clientele."

A few minutes later, when they stopped at a red light, she looked up at the street sign and said, "Cesar Chavez Drive? Uh…what part of…Poland…was he from?"

"Southern Poland," Brady said as he turned left, looking for an opportunity to double back. "Lots of produce down there. Okay…maybe we did overshoot our target just a bit here."

"Did I just hear you admit a mistake?" she said in mock amazement. "I love it when you do that."

One more left turn and several blocks later, they arrived at Kosiuszko Park, pulling up right in front of the statue of George Washington's brigadier general on horseback.

"There he is," Brady said. "One of America's first Polish heroes, from the Revolutionary War."

"But he didn't die in battle," Tanya said.

"What? How do you know that?"

"All you have to do is look at the statue," she said casually. "When all the hooves are on the ground, that means he died naturally; front hooves up, he died in battle."

"But one leg's up…"

"That means he died in some sort of accident."

Brady glanced at her skeptically. "Where did all that come from?"

"History class," she said with a smirk. "You're not the only one who picks up trivia, you know. You were so busy seething at Conger, you probably missed his lecture on statues."

"Are you telling me those rules are followed *every*where?"

"Yup. It's part of The Sculptor's Code of Solidarity …probably one of the earliest unions."

"That's it," Brady said, throwing his hands in the air. "Time to head back to familiar territory and find a room on the other side of town. We can get a better look around here in the daylight."

"How are you going to find him?" she asked the following morning over coffee at their motel, 10 miles north of Kosiuszko Park. "Do you have his address?"

"Nope, but that shouldn't be too difficult. Everybody down there knows where he lives. The trick is going to be finding out without raising suspicions."

Returning to the South Side, they headed west on Mitchell Street, in search of just the right place to make their inquiry. Shortly after turning onto Windlake Avenue, they found it: Klub Muzyczny, a white frame corner tavern with a "Blatz" sign over the door, looking as though it had been open for business well before Kip Kapopka made his Major League debut. Brady stopped the Bus, opened the door and asked Tanya to meet him back there in an hour.

"Well?" she asked when he returned to the Bus. "Mission accomplished? Did you get the address?"

"I got it," he said, as a painful look crossed his face, "but my stomach's gonna pay the price."

"How so?"

"The woman behind the bar had just finished making a pot of stew when I walked in, so I figured the best way to establish some quick rapport with her would be to try a bowl."

"That makes sense; what's the problem?"

"Once I asked for it, I had to eat it. That's the problem. Sauerkraut is one of my least favorite things and that's what I was looking at, that and plums and some kind of mystery meat."

"Brady, that really doesn't sound so bad..."

"Wait; it gets worse. All the regulars were knocking back shots of vodka."

"At 10 A.M.?"

"Right...so I joined them. It wasn't regular vodka; it was brown. Tasted like honey."

"Well, you can't drink and drive—especially before noon—so, tell me: Where are we going?"

"Not far from here, apparently. The houses are a little bigger south of Oklahoma Avenue. That's where he lives."

Tanya guided the Microbus away from the neighborhood of three-story, brick and frame Polish flats, arriving several minutes later in a cluster of larger, single-story brick homes, surrounded by enough yard to provide a pleasant buffer between houses.

"That's it," Brady said. "Up ahead, on the right."

Tanya pulled up in front of the largest home on the block, distinguished also by the uncommon sight of a garage in back.

"We're here. What now?"

"I'm guessing he's at work. The Commissioner's Office is officially in New York, but he and Kip both live in Milwaukee—at opposite ends of Milwaukee—so they spend most of their time here. The Brewers are in town this week, so I think our timing's good."

Later that afternoon--after a nap had helped him recover from brunch at Klub Muzyczny--Brady and Tanya drove back to Kip's neighborhood, parked the Bus at the end of his street and waited. It was just after 6 PM when a silver Chrysler 300 turned into Kip Kapopka's driveway.

"Is that him?" Tanya asked.

"Think so, but don't know for sure. Let's give it a little while longer to let him show us some more of his routine."

Ten minutes later, a heavyset man, about six feet tall, emerged from the front door of Kapopka's house, accompanied by a Scottish terrier on a leash.

"Bingo!" Brady said, eyes widening. "That's our boy."

"Looks like a pretty big 'boy' to me."

"You're right about that. The Kipster hasn't missed any meals lately."

"That limp is pretty severe," she said. "He must have had some sort of accident."

"Just another chapter in The Legend of Kip Kapopka," he said as he started up the Bus. "He was in a bad car accident a few years ago. Drunk driver came right at him, going the wrong way on the freeway. He managed to swerve to avoid taking the hit head-on, but they still had to cut him out of the wreck. He was pretty busted up. Looks as though his leg hasn't been the same since."

"Wow…uh, where are we going?"

"We're done here for the day. The pick-up will never work in this neighborhood. You can sleep in tomorrow, while I do some more scouting."

The following morning, Brady returned at 6 AM, parking again at the end of the block, to see what opportunities might be presented by Kip's morning routine. An hour later, the Chrysler slowly backed into the street and headed north, trailed at a discreet distance by the Microbus.

The first stop was the one Brady was looking for. After Kip had gone about a mile from his house, he turned down a side street off Lincoln Avenue, then pulled into a parking lot behind a small wooden building, Peploski's Bakery. Kip was in and out within minutes, carrying a white sack. After the Chrysler pulled away, Brady entered the parking lot, examining it carefully. Twenty spaces, with only a couple of them open.

Skeeter: *What do you suppose he's cookin' up here, Herb?*

Herb: *I'm not sure…just so it's not half-baked, that's the main thing. One of these days, we got to have us an idea that stays in the oven 'til it's done.*

"This is going to be a little tricky," Brady said excitedly to Tanya when he returned to the motel, "but I'm sure we can do it."

"What's the plan?"

"Kip strikes me as a guy who's grooved into his routine. We can tell food is a central part of that, so it won't surprise you to know that he starts his morning with a bag of *paczkis*; they're like jelly doughnuts, only richer. The lot behind his favorite bakery is

217

hidden from the street. When he pulls up tomorrow morning, the Bus'll already be parked there. When he comes out of the bakery, you'll be standing next to the engine in the back with the cover popped open and ask him for help. Tell him you've got some tools in the Bus, walk him around to the side, then I'll open the door."

"Then…what?"

"He gets a dart in the neck, I drag him inside and we're off."

"No, *you're* off—off your *rocker*! That's the craziest thing I ever heard! You saw how big he is. How are you going to get him inside?

"You overlook the element of surprise. You push, I'll pull. He won't be expecting that. All you have to do then is slide the door shut."

"I thought you said it takes four or five minutes for that stuff to knock him out."

"That's true…so I'll tie him and gag him before he gets the dart."

"What about his car?"

"You're going to drive it a few blocks away, then park it on the street. I'll be following, to pick you up."

"This is the first time you've done this in broad daylight, Brady. Are you sure it's going to work?"

"Yup…and I'm feeling good about it. Only way I'd abort this mission is if there's other people nearby when he pulls up. So don't worry; we'll only go ahead with it if the coast is clear."

The following morning, Tanya shook Brady awake just before dawn.

"Brady! Brady?"

"Uh…what? What's the problem?"

"Don't you *hear* it? It's raining!"

"What?"

"It's *raining*. What's your plan now?"

Brady groaned as he pushed himself up off the mattress and ambled to the window. "Yup," he said, opening the curtain, "raining it is—and raining hard."

"Well??"

"Take it easy, Tanya. This isn't really a problem. In fact, it could be good for us."

"How do you figure?"

"Well, I thought it would be enough for him to stop and help a young woman by herself. The fact that our Bus—your Bus—is gonna break down in the rain just makes it that much more likely that he'll stop to help."

"And get soaked on the way to work? I don't think so…"

"You're gonna help prevent that by covering him with your umbrella. Once he's out of his car, he'll go wherever you lead him, which, of course, will be right to the sliding door."

"I'm using the umbrella I don't have?"

"And latex gloves," he said. "Don't forget that; that's even more important. Be thankful for those giant Wal-Marts, the really big ones; they're open all the time." Glancing at his watch as he slipped on his blue jeans, he added, "You know, I never really cared for Wal-Mart, intellectually speaking. It just smothers the business of the mom 'n pop stores in small towns all across the country. But, when you need an umbrella and latex gloves at 4:30 in the morning, it's a lot less objectionable."

About 45 minutes later, Brady returned to the room and shook off the water as he set down the umbrella and a bag of supplies. "The return trip was a lot drier," he said. "This'll all work great; you'll see."

A few minutes later, they were hurrying down the expressway. Peploski's opened at 6 and Brady wanted to grab a parking space early, as well as the one next to it. After they positioned the Bus near the back of the lot, Brady produced two "props," as he called them--large, orange rubber cones--from a construction site near their motel, and placed them in the parking space next to the sliding door of their Bus. Within 20 minutes, the rest of the parking spaces filled up. Sipping coffee as they strained to identify oncoming traffic through the rear window in the downpour, Brady and Tanya waited…

Suddenly, 30 minutes later, Brady yelled, "There he is!" and jumped from the Bus to scoop up the cones. Moments later, the Chrysler eased into the vacant space and Kip exited, limping as fast as he could to get into the bakery.

"Why aren't we getting him now, rather than when he gets back?" Tanya asked.

"We had an important choice to make there," Brady said, trying to convince them both that this was just one of many careful calculations. "Do we get between Kip and his pastries or Kip and his job? I think there's less urgency when he's on his way to work."

A minute later, when they saw Kip emerging from the bakery, Tanya exited the Bus with her umbrella through the sliding door and made her way to the back, where she popped the engine cover and waited for Kip to approach.

"Yes, of course, I'd be happy to help," Kip said as he began to peer into the engine.

"Wait," Tanya answered, "let me show you my tools inside, out of the rain." Holding her umbrella over his head, she guided Kip to the sliding door. Brady could hear her make a couple of muffled references to the distributor cap. When they reached the sliding door, she stopped, opened it and Kip obligingly peered in, out of curiosity and in search of a brief respite from the rain.

With that, Brady grabbed the shoulders of the startled Kip and yelled, "Now!" Tanya then gave a light shove. "Harder!" Brady commanded. This time, Tanya pushed as hard as she could into Kip's back, knocking him off balance and into Brady's arms. Brady took over from there, sticking a Telazol dart into the neck of the stunned Kapopka as he pulling him into the van…almost. Kip quickly recovered, recognized his predicament and began flailing at Brady as he thrashed his legs, desperate to regain balance.

"The legs! He yelled back at Tanya. "Get 'em in here!"

As Brady tried mightily to twist the sputtering Kip onto his back, Tanya grabbed both of his ankles and pushed them up, to clear the track on the sliding door, before ramming it to the right.

"Ow!" Kip yelled as his right ankle was crushed by the door. Tanya pulled the door back a few inches with her left hand, while applying a heartier shove to the ankle. This time, the ankle retreated all the way inside before Tanya's next try to slide the door shut, which was successful.

Meanwhile, Kip was fighting Brady to a draw and beginning to land some punishing blows to his head and ribs, when he suddenly went limp from the dose of Telazol lodged in his neck.

"Brady? What's going on in there?" Tanya yelled. "Are you all right?"

"Ooof!" came the muffled reply as Brady struggled to crawl out from under Kip's dead weight. Fishing into his captive's pocket, Brady hooked his car keys, opened the door and threw them to Tanya, yelling, "Go! Get rid of the car!"

"Brady! My God! *Look* at you!"

"I'll be okay," he said, staring at the blood on his sleeves, then wiping his face with his right hand, which was then smeared red. "Just *go*, okay! We've got to get out of here." After quickly catching his breath, Brady applied duct tape around Kip's mouth, then secured his legs with clothesline before handcuffing his hands behind his back.

A few minutes later, Tanya parked the car on Mitchell Street and returned to the Bus.

"Is that a good place?" she asked with a nervous glance over her shoulder at their new passenger.

"Yeah, fine. It's fine," he said, putting the Bus into gear.

"I can't believe you used handcuffs," she whispered.

"Like I told you," he said grimly. "Wal-Mart's a great place."

"And the duct tape. Isn't that a little rough?"

"A few years back, when Tampa Bay first came into the league, they did a 'Salute to Duct Tape' promotion. Everyone who brought duct tape to the stadium got in free, as I recall. So, I thought that was a nice touch...say, is Kip's bag of *paczkis* back there? A fresh doughnut would taste good right about now. Jump out and check at the next stop sign, okay?" When the Bus rolled to a halt, Tanya exited, then slid open the side door.

"C'mon! C'mon!" Brady said. "Get those doughnuts up here!"

"Brady...there are no doughnuts..."

"What are you *talking* about?" he asked, turning his head toward the cage as she raised the open bag for him to see.

"Son of a *bitch!*" he said in a loud whisper. "Nothing but *cash!*"

Tanya grabbed the bag and several loose bills that had spilled from it, slid the door shut past their snoring cargo and

returned to the front seat. As the Bus pulled away from the
intersection, she began her audit.

"Wow…" she said, a minute later, "there's almost $800 in
here, all of it in small bills."

"That's very interesting," Brady said. "Looks as though our
friend Kip is even more of an entrepreneur than I thought."

"Meaning?"

"Meaning I'd bet that money isn't his. He's made a career
out of being a go-between and I'll bet that bag was on its way to
someone else."

"You know," Tanya said, suddenly pensive, "there are
almost as many Catholic churches around here as there are taverns.
You see that big one up ahead? Pull up there, okay?"

"Tanya…this is *not* the time for sightseeing. Maybe some
other—"

"No, Brady. I want to stop *now*. It'll just take a minute."

As they pulled up to St. Josaphat's Basilica, Tanya grabbed
the bag, opened her door and jumped from the Bus.

"Tanya! What the *hell* are you doing??"

"Shhh," she said with a smile as she put her finger to her
lips and began to run up the steps. "Wait here. I'll be right back!"

Several minutes later, Tanya reappeared, jogged down the
steps and jumped back into the Bus. "Okay," she said with the
biggest smile she could muster. "Let's roll!"

"Uh…Tanya? The *bag*? Where's the *bag*?"

"The bag," she said, "and its contents are now in a place
where they can help people who can't help themselves. God, what a
rush! You can't *believe* how good that feels!"

"But, Tanya," Brady said, exasperated, as he headed the
Bus toward the freeway, "that money wasn't *yours*!"

"That's right," she said with a nod toward the rear, "and it
wasn't his, so now it's theirs."

Brady shook his head as he gazed into the distance, toward
the on-ramp of the freeway. He wondered if that bag was the kind
of trouble that would sprout legs wherever you set it down, just so it
could always walk back to you.

23

The rain began to ease as they approached the Illinois state line and stopped completely as they entered Chicago. Brady wanted the return trip to Georgia to go as quickly as the trip up, but for a different reason: He had finally snatched a person whose absence would make the papers. How long would it take before Kapopka would be declared missing, his car located and the whole thing trumpeted in every sports section in America? Brady was guessing he had no more than 24 hours before Kip became radioactive.

He would prefer to get back to Scofield before everything hit the fan. Driving straight through again, he could keep that timetable, but he had to make one important stop en route.

Though the heavy rain when Kip was picked up made chances of a detailed description of the Microbus license plate remote, there was a far greater likelihood that someone might recall enough information about the vehicle to make Brady's life uncomfortable.

So, he resolved to get rid of it during this trip back home, just as soon as he could find a suitable replacement, which he decided to seek on the South Side of Chicago. Right after exiting off the Dan Ryan Expressway onto 71st, Brady pulled the Bus to a stop on the road's shoulder.

"What are you *doing*?" Tanya asked.

"There's a lot of grunting going on back there," he said. "I think our passenger's getting pretty agitated."

"What are you going to do?"

Picking up his shotgun, he said calmly, "I think this should put him in Dreamland, at least until Louisville." Taking careful aim, Brady then fired a dart into the side of Kip's left buttock. Turning back toward the road, he put down the shotgun and resumed driving west on 71st, to Pulaski.

After 30 minutes of cruising through the south side, Brady gave up and eased back onto the Dan Ryan. Soon after the highway merged with I-80, they headed east, into Indiana, and Brady suddenly got the urge to buzz downtown Gary, turning off again at Exit 3 of the Indiana Toll Road, where I-80 comes together with I-65 and Hwys 20 and 12.

Before they reached the third stoplight, Brady saw it on the lot at Big Earl's Auto World: a vintage black, Cadillac hearse that he guessed to be about a '64, which would have made it nearly new when Brady was 500 miles away, becoming acquainted with hearses as a college student in Kansas City.

It turned out to be a '66, which was even better. He had to have it and quickly made the deal to swap it for the Microbus with Earl's sales manager, Cedric, who assured him that the hearse, with only 40,000 miles on it, was in fine running order. While Tanya guided Cedric back inside the office, asking a series of thoughtful questions about the oppressed people of Gary, Brady drove the hearse to the far side of the lot, backing it up to the sliding side door of the Bus. He then opened the door, slid the somnolent Kip onto his shoulders and—being careful to bend his knees—lifted his passenger carefully, before depositing him gently into the rear of their new ride.

"I don't get the fascination with hearses," she said, as they headed south on I-65 and she shifted uneasily in her seat. "Isn't that kind of macabre?"

"I can see how people might feel that way," he said, "but it's not negative to me, it's a positive, a positive trigger, you know? Here's another example: pineapple. You go to Hawaii once, have a good time and pineapple's never the same again. It's always special, because it reminds you of Hawaii. That's how I am about old hearses: They remind me of some very good times in college."

"That's an interesting perspective…"

"And here's another reason to appreciate hearses," he said. "For a lot of people, it's the nicest car they'll ever ride in, but they won't be able to enjoy it. They'll never be able to say that about us, though, because here we are, healthy and able to absorb the entire experience."

Skeeter: *Hearses? Pineapples? That sounds a little weird to me. You got any triggers, Herb?*

Herb: *Yes…as a matter of fact, I do. Cold beer equals baseball for me…always has, for as long as I can remember.*

Skeeter: *Good. That's more like it; that's a trigger I can understand.*

Brady, meanwhile, was somewhat concerned with how the old hearse would handle the steep incline at Monteagle, in southern Tennessee, but it came through fine. Approaching Chattanooga, as they drove into the emerging sunrise, he kept the radio tuned to sports talk, waiting for the breaking news bulletin he knew would be inevitable. There was plenty of discussion about the various demands of players and owners as Major League Baseball moved closer to another strike, but no news about Kapopka.

After they stopped for breakfast at the Georgia border, Brady gave Kip another shot before they all headed for Atlanta. The hearse was running well—in the longest continuous trip it had ever made—Tanya was starting to relax and everything was proceeding as smoothly as Brady could have possibly hoped…until smoke suddenly appeared from under the hood. Brady immediately began to tap the brake and guide the car to the shoulder of the interstate, where the smoke from the engine became even more intense. *Shit! What is it now?*

When he popped the hood, the rest of the smoke was released in a giant, billowing mass that lifted a good 50 feet above the morning rush hour traffic before dispersing.

"What is it?" Tanya asked as she exited from the right side of the car.

"The radiator," Brady answered, somewhat relieved. "With a little water, we can get back on the road again."

"Where will we get that?"

"I'll keep the hood up and somebody'll stop. In the meantime, you need to cover Kip's head with something and put your suitcase in front of him. We can't let anyone see him through the front window."

Fifteen minutes later, a car did pull up—from the Georgia Highway Patrol. Out of it, stepped an officer who looked as though he could have lined up at linebacker right then and there. Instead, the big man walked toward the hearse, focusing more on Brady than the car as he approached.

"You don't look like you're on your way to a funeral," he said, "but do I need to call a priest for your car?"

"No," Brady said with a nervous laugh, "Don't think so. Radiator got a little too hot, that's all. Do need some water, though. Have any?"

"As a matter of fact, I do. I keep a can in the trunk for special occasions."

After the two men had filled the radiator, the trooper looked at Brady, nodded toward the hearse and asked, "Where do you find one of those, anyway?"

"Oh, it takes a little digging around," he said breezily. "You just have to know where to look. One thing you can always count on is that they haven't been driven too hard."

"Or too long," the trooper said as he headed back to his car. "Take care of that radiator."

Brady slid back behind the wheel and had to compose himself before continuing.

"I thought we were flirting with death enough just by riding in one of these things," Tanya said. "That was a little too close for my taste."

"Mine, too," Brady said, catching his breath. "We've just got to take it easy and remember this baby isn't used to distance driving."

Two hours later, they pulled into Scofield. Brady asked Tanya to keep Conger occupied while he managed to maneuver the somnolent Kapopka to his solitary room at the far end of the courtyard.

Returning home, Brady showered and crawled into bed, ready to make up for the sleep he had missed. As he did so, he habitually reached for the channel changer, to get a few headlines and maybe a couple of jokes before closing his eyes.

Clicking over to sports, Brady's attention was suddenly riveted to the following bulletin: "We have just received a report that Kazmir "Kip" Kapopka, the key figure in Major League Baseball's labor negotiations, has not been seen since leaving a bakery in Milwaukee early yesterday morning. He was expected at his Milwaukee office yesterday, but, instead, his abandoned car was found late this morning, parked on a South Side street."

Brady fought for a few minutes to stay up, but it was no use. The details of this new story would be there, waiting for him when he woke up.

A couple of hours later, Tanya gently roused him. "You've *got* to see this," she said.

Clicking on the bedroom TV, Brady saw a spokesman for the Player's Association in the process of giving his take on Kip's disappearance to a sports reporter:

"As I said, we're all just hearing about this today, so we don't know all the facts, but, if this turns out to be some cheap trick on the part of the owners to push back our strike deadline, it will represent an all-time low in labor negotiations. The issues we have with the owners should be settled at the bargaining table, not in the media."

"Are you saying you suspect the owners might have staged this disappearance to strengthen their bargaining position?"

"No, let me clarify: What I'm saying here is that our members don't have a great deal of trust in the other side at the moment. We are not going to accept anything at face value. Instead, we will reserve judgment until all the facts are known. We are, of course, following this story with a great deal of interest, along with the rest of America. We hope Mr. Kapopka will be located quickly, so we can resume bargaining with the owners."

The scene then shifted to Chicago, where another reporter was interviewing a spokesman for the owners.

"This is a very tough time, most of all for the Kapopka family," he said. "First of all, our thoughts and prayers are with them. Beyond that, the owners have asked me to emphasize their position that the absence of Kazmir Kapopka in no way changes their position on the issues at hand. We expect the Player's Association to continue to bargain with us in good faith."

"The suggestion has been made," the reporter said, "that Kip Kapopka's disappearance may be part of a negotiating ploy on the part of the owners. What's your reaction to that?"

"That," the spokesman said, his face turning crimson, "is the most despicable thing I have ever heard! We are going to assume Mr. Kapopka's disappearance has nothing to do with these negotiations until proven otherwise. I would suggest the player's time would be better spent studying our proposals, rather than dreaming up such idle fantasies."

"Oh, boy!" Brady said as he clicked off the TV and rubbed his hands together. "You know what we've got here? We got us an old-fashioned, Cold War meltdown!"

"What are you *talking* about?" Tanya asked.

"Don't you see? It's simple: When Russia and the U.S. each had their fingers on the trigger during the Cold War, anybody else—Pakistan, Peru, you name it—could have dropped a bomb on one of them and that superpower would have been convinced the other superpower did it."

"And then retaliated, only against the wrong country."

"Right. And that country would, of course, have to fire back and, presto! You've got World War III."

"Are you telling me we've started a World War here?"

Skeeter: *Ah, yes...that's what we need now...the global perspective. I would have put my money on striking a match in the Middle East to start the next World War, but, who knows? Might happen right here.*

Herb: *...with a man from The Town Sherman Refused to Burn doing the honors. That's almost more irony than I can stand...*

"No," he said. "That wasn't our objective and that's not what we've done. Remember, what we're trying to do here is fix the sport for the good of everyone. We fans are the only ones who see it from that overall perspective. Labor and management are operating only to protect their own narrow interests. A couple of days ago, each side was dug into its respective position and a strike looked inevitable in a couple of weeks. Kip's disappearance was like throwing dynamite on concrete: some of it was bound to get dislodged."

"Okay, Einstein—or is it, 'Machiavelli?' What's next?"

"I'm going to give Kip a few more hours for that last dart to wear off. Then, first thing tomorrow, I'm going to have a little fun with him…before we get down to business."

Before heading out to Scofield the following morning, Brady stopped in downtown Midian to check the headlines in the various area dailies. Atlanta had the Kapopka disappearance on page one, while Athens and Augusta were playing it prominently on their sports fronts, each side hurling charges at the other.

After arriving at the farm, Brady approached the room of his newest guest and gave the door a hearty knock. No answer. He knocked again. Silence.

"Kip? Hello?"

There still being no answer, Brady stepped forward, slowly turned the knob and opened the door. There, before him, sat Kazmir Kapopka, on the edge of his bed, staring nervously at the wall, clad in the white dress shirt he had been wearing since the bakery and a pair of boxer shorts.

"Well?" Kip said, finally.

"Well, what?"

"What's going on? Why am I here?"

"How long did you think you were going to get away with it?"

"Away with *what*?"

"Skimming the take" Brady said in his most sinister voice. "You know The Man won't put up with that."

"What are you TALKING about?!" Kip yelled, leaping off the bed. "I *never* stole from him. Not *once!*"

"Take it easy," Brady said, holding up his hand. "Sit down and relax."

Kip eyed Brady carefully. "Wait a minute…you don't look like one of his guys. Who *are* you, anyway? If it wasn't for that drunk bastard who plowed into me, I would have beat the shit out of you back at Pepi's. You *do* know that, right?"

"Right," Brady agreed, unwilling to argue the point.

"Good," Kip said in the measured voice of a man who had experienced enough tense negotiations to know his odds of success were better when his emotions were in check. "I *still* might do that, by the way. As it is, though, looks like I already got a good piece of your face.

"Now that we've got all that straight, where the hell am I and what am I doin' here? I have *no* idea what this is all about, but I can tell you this: The cops'll go easier on you if you let me go *immediately*."

"You're in no position to make demands, Kip. The cops would be just as interested in what you're doing carrying bags of cash out of a bakery first thing in the morning."

"Ain't you *listenin'* to me? I pick up the cash; I drop the cash. That's it. Don't know nothin' beyond that and don't wanna know."

"We know where you get the money. Where does it go?"

"Look…that's a touchy subject I don't talk about with just anybody. I'm gettin' the feelin' here you didn't grab me for the money, anyway. Why don't you tell me who you are and what you *really* wanna talk about…and that's not a demand, just a question."

"Okay…fair enough. Baseball. This is about baseball."

"*Baseball*? On whose authority?"

"The fans, that's who. We're upset, distressed with the direction our game is heading and we're trying to save it before you, the owners and the players drive it over a cliff."

"The *fans*? What do you mean, 'The Fans?' Who *are* you?"

Brady had given that question considerable thought, concluding that an army—even if mobilized only in his mind—would be the most impressive answer.

"Look, Kip, the players are organized. They've got the strongest union in sports. Hell, maybe it's the strongest one in the country. And the owners are organized—not as tight as the players, but working together. But the fans have no power, because they've been too spread out, with too many voices—until now."

"The fans? Organized? When did *this* happen? *How* did it happen?"

"Details," Brady said with a wave of his hand. "Not important now. What *is* important is that we fans have come together and insist on being heard…and we'll go to extremes, if need be, to that."

"Which includes kidnapping."

"Desperate measures for desperate times. You are a guest of the SLA."

"The SLA?? Wait a minute…wasn't that the outfit that kidnapped Patty Hearst? I thought they all died in a shootout years ago."

"We are *baseball* guerillas," Brady said proudly, "inspired by our fallen comrades from the '70s. We are the Sandlot Liberation Army."

Kip looked at Brady for a long moment of disbelief. "Give me a break…"

"No, Kip, we're quite serious. Chapters of the new SLA have popped up all over the country. Our Sandlot Army has tens of thousands of foot soldiers who still revere the game in its purist form. We plan to liberate the bastardized baseball you play in domes, on plastic grass and with designated hitters, where greed has eclipsed everything else."

"And you have a plan for that?"

"Yes, we have a plan and you are its centerpiece."

"Look, I don't know or care what your plan is, Mister… what did you say you name was?"

"I didn't. You can call me 'Cinque.'"

"Okay, Cinque, what I *do* know is that we have barely two weeks to go before the players are gonna strike. If that happens, the fans will be a lot more pissed than they are--than you say they are-- now. I need to get back to those negotiations to keep that from happenin'."

"I read the papers, Kip. Both sides have foxholes so deep they can barely see each other. Seems like it's been that way for a long time and past agreements--the ones you've helped reach--only paper over deeper problems that have to be addressed sooner or later."

"So, how're *you* gonna change that?"

"You are the hostage and the ransom is sanity for baseball, a new paradigm in which all teams can compete on an equal footing."

"Sanity through insanity, is that it?" Kip said with a grunt. "You really are nuts. It'll never work."

"There's only one way to find out," Brady said, "and that's to field test the theory. So, now you know what's really going on here. Now it's your turn. What's the deal with the bag of money, just between you and me? "

"What if I don't feel like tellin' you?"

"Suit yourself. I'll just empty the bag out on the highway somewhere, then cut your food off for a few days."

"You really are a son of a bitch, you know that? Okay…let's start here: You know what a Polish flat is?"

"Ah…no."

"It's a three story house, where different families live on each floor, but they're all related. You know, aunts, uncles, in-laws…all of that."

"Okay…"

"They're very common; you see 'em all over the South Side. Anyway, everybody dreams about havin' their own place, right? When one member of a family gets enough money together, he helps the others get their own place—"

"In a neighborhood like yours."

"Right. Well…sometimes these relatives think you're loaded, when you really ain't. Nothin' can talk 'em outta thinkin' that. So, when you're a good guy—like Pepi—you find a way to help out, even if you don't have the cash. That's what he did…for years. Kept borrowin' on his own house, his business…then his wife gets sick, he gets nailed with some huge bills—you should see those suckers; we're talkin' really big—and, all of a sudden, he's in a big hole."

"And you're filling that hole…how?"

"With cash. We found a guy who's givin' Pepi money—he calls it a "bridge loan"—and we're payin' him back with receipts from lottery sales in the bakery."

"Wait a minute. His piece of the lottery business couldn't be big enough to generate the kind of cash you had in that bag…"

"Well…we got a wrinkle--that's what Pepi calls it--that's makin' all this work, at least for now. He figured out a way to set up his machine to sell the lottery tickets, but not report the sales, so all the take is goin' to cover the loan."

Brady's jaw went slack as his eyes widened. "He's booking the lottery *himself*? My God! What's gonna happen if he ever sells a winning ticket?"

"We figured the odds on that are pretty long, so he's willin' to risk it. Besides, we're gettin' a good deal on the bridge loan."

"How good?"

"He's just chargin' us one percent interest."

"Wow, that is good. Wait a minute...one percent...how often?"

"Every week."

Brady glared at Kip in disbelief. "Kip, you aren't paying one percent—you're paying over 50%! That's usury! There are *laws* against that!"

"It's the bottom of the ninth," Kip said quietly, "and it's the only option he's got left."

"I just have one other question," Brady said. "Why don't *you* help him—beyond being his bag man, I mean? Everybody knows you made all those sweet deals with your owners over the years."

"That's the problem: 'everybody knows.' I got my own family to deal with about that. Besides, you ever heard of limited partnerships?"

"Sure, sure I've heard of them."

"Well...when you go to get your money out, you find out how limited they can be. I'll tell you how long term some of that stuff is: My kids stand a better chance of seein' it than I do."

That night, Brady took Tanya to dinner at the Last Resort Grill, his favorite restaurant in Athens, and tried not to think about his talk with Kip...but his thoughts kept drifting back to the weary baker, taking huge risks to support his extended family.

The following morning, Brady felt better and found himself in the mood to visit Gene's and perhaps even give grits another try.

"Hey, Stranger, you're just in time," Scratch called out as Brady walked through the door.

"In time? In time for what?"

"Well, shoot, everybody here's got an opinion on this baseball mess. So, we might as well hear yours, too."

As Brady eased into the empty chair next to the deputy, Scratch added, "At least they know who scooped up the Kipster."

"Wh-What?" Brady said, trying very hard not to sound anxious.

"Haven't you heard?" Scratch asked as he dug into his grits. "Some society dame from Dallas. If that doesn't beat all..."

Brady reached for the sports section in the middle of the table and pulled it toward him. There it was, two pictures of Tessa Ann Hunt, of Dallas: one a debutante photo and the other a snapshot from her ex-boyfriend in Nashville, who, the story said, was also looking for her...

24

When he returned home, Brady grimly threw the sports section on the kitchen counter, in front of Tanya. "Congratulations! You're a *big* celebrity now--coast to coast."

Her facial features froze in unison, as if reacting in concert to being electrocuted, while she sank slowly into a kitchen chair and considered the picture before her.

"How in the hell did that *happen* so fast?" he said. "I mean, how in the *hell* could that happen *at all*?"

"Oh…my…God!" was all she could say. "Oh, my God…"

"Well?"

Putting the paper down on the table beside her, she leaned back in her chair and looked up at Brady. "Remember that company I worked for in Nashville? We all had to get fingerprinted when we started there. They must have those prints in some federal file, in Washington or wherever."

"But you were wearing gloves. I remember. We talked about that before."

"Well. . ."

"*Tanya*? 'Well' what?"

"I put them on just as *soon* as I got in the car...right after I adjusted the mirror. My hands *never* touched the wheel; I'm *sure* of that."

"But they damn sure touched the MIRROR! Shit! I don't *believe* this! Another mirror…"

"Don't you *dare* yell at me, Brady Greer! I've *never* done *any*thing like this before. It was raining; I was in a hurry..."

"Well, Tanya, your little Robin Hood caper in the Music City made you something of a cult hero there. Now, however, you're a household name—which, fortunately, is not connected to your current appearance. If it were, the feds would already be beating down our door. Oh, and your old boyfriend. The paper said he was looking for you, too. What's *that* all about?"

"Well," she began with a sigh, "my experience in Nashville was a little more... complicated...than I've…had a chance…to mention. The apartment I cleaned out was one I shared with Carter Collingsworth. He's from New York and a passionate activist for the homeless."

Brady grunted. *Two Trustafarians, slumming for the underdog.* "Go on."

"Well…everything was fine, or seemed to be, until Carter became aware of what I was doing. We had big blow ups about it and he kept threatening to expose me to the Power Company. The last time he did that was the night before I met you. He sounded more serious than usual, so I left."

"And took some of his stuff?"

"Some of our stuff. Look, that's not important at the moment. What are we going to do now? That's what matters."

"For starters, we've got to make you look even less like that debutante picture. One trip to the drug store and I can make you a redhead. That and some glasses should buy us some time…"

"Ugh. I hate glasses."

"That's precisely why they're a good move. Anyone you ever knew in Dallas—and Nashville, for that matter—will be asked about you. Somebody--your old roommate, for instance--is bound to mention that, which might help. . .a little."

"Then what?"

"You need to get out of Midian—preferably, out of the

country."

"But, what about—"

"We don't have the luxury of thinking about anything else right now, not until I'm done with Kip. We can always meet up again after that."

Whatever self-assurance Tanya had acquired as a child of upper class Dallas seemed to melt away when she looked at Brady and pleaded, "But where will I go?"

With all the confidence he could muster, Brady replied, "Don't worry; this wasn't part of the plan. We both know that. I'm going to take care of you. You're going to be okay. Just give me a little time to think this through." With that, he kissed her on the forehead and headed out the door.

Brady was operating under three deadlines now: the planned baseball strike loomed just a couple of weeks away, federal bloodhounds would soon be picking up a trail to Georgia and his old coach was fading fast. It was time to let the world know that Kip Kapopka was safe and why he was being held. Who better to do that than Kip, himself?

Brady knew—America knew—Kazmir Kapopka had gotten his nickname from his love of kipper snacks, so Brady made it a point to pick some up in Athens before returning to IPCOT. He also had a script in hand he had composed for Kip to read into a tape recorder. The tape would then be sent to the perfect media outlet that would guarantee maximum attention to the cause of the SLA.

"I'm not reading that," Kapopka said later that morning. "No way."

"You're not even going to *look* at it?"

"No, I'm not," he said firmly. "The most important thing I own is my reputation with both the owners and players. They trust me, because I've always been straight with both sides. Besides, any cooperation with kidnappers only encourages them; I've read that all my life. The only thing I would say is to urge them *not* to cooperate with you in *any* way. If they did that, there would be nut cases all over America lookin' for opportunities to take hostages for every half-baked cause you can imagine."

"But, Kip, everything I've written here is a statement of fact. Besides, don't you want your family to know you're okay?"

"Not on your terms. I refuse to read it."

Skeeter: *Wow, Herbie, I'm impressed. Didn't expect Kip to stand on principle...especially after Brady got a look at his cash 'n carry sideline.*

Herb: *Remember what Conger said: You make a threat, it's got to be credible. Let's see how far Kip is willing to push this...*

Until that point, Brady had been determined to make Kip as comfortable as possible, including providing him with special meals of kielbasa and knockwurst from a butcher shop Flaps had recommended in Athens. But now he wanted to play hardball? Brady was ready to join him.

"I need you to read that statement, Kip," he said, "but it's up to you. Until you cooperate, there's going to be a change in the way we handle your food service. From now on, you're going on the Dick Gregory diet."

"The *what*? What the hell is *that*?"

"Lemons and water—all the water you want—every day. That and 1½ cups of maple syrup. That's it, nothing more. If you're going to protest, you can fast like a protester."

"Aren't you forgetting something?" Kip asked.

"What?"

"The players. Their union is...formidable, you said so yourself."

"*Formidable?*" Brady said mockingly. "Let's not sugar-coat it, Kip. The Players Association calls the shots, pure and simple. Every time it sits down to bargain, it seems to win."

"And that's your problem," Kip replied. "If you don't control them, you're wasting your time--and mine."

"I realize that, of course," Brady said as Kip eyed him with contempt. "But I do have *you* and sometimes that's all a guy can do: go with what he's got."

"Now, I *know* you're crazy."

"Not necessarily. Even though we both know you are basically just the public face of the real bargaining process, you're still the one man trusted by both sides. As long as you're in captivity, I don't think there'll be a strike. Your situation knocks everyone out of their comfort zone—not just you, the players and owners—but the media and public, too. When you disappeared, the stories, at first, were all about you. Now, though, everyone's weighing in with opinions on what's best for the game. It's interesting. Baseball has an unusual opportunity to win one for itself here. I'm betting it makes the most of that chance."

"But you strike out without my help and I refuse to be a party to this."

"We'll see about that."

Brady now turned his attention back to Tanya. She had helped rekindle his energy and carry out his plan thus far and he was grateful for that, but…staying together now could hasten jail time for both of them. He had an idea to keep that from happening. Though it was a long shot, it was the best he could do at the moment and started with a call to Yulia.

"Brady! How nice to hear from you so soon. Are you going to be up this way?"

"I'm looking forward to seeing you again, Yulia, but, no, I'm afraid I won't be up there again anytime soon. What I need to do at the moment is ask you a favor."

"Sure. What can I do to help?"

"Well, this is awkward for me…but I have a friend who's going through kind of a rough patch at the moment. She needs to get out of the country for a while and I was wondering. . .you mentioned you were involved in various businesses. . .is there any chance you might be able to get her a Russian ID and passport?"

"Does it have to be Russian?"

"Well...no, I guess not."

"Good, that helps. It'll take at least a week, maybe two. Will she need a place to stay?"

"Yes, a place to stay would be great, if you can swing it," he said, not expecting the offer to deal with another problem. "We're under some, uh, time pressure here, Yulia, so if they could be on their way in a week, that would be great."

"Did you say 'they?'"

"Right...she has a friend who needs to move, too. Can you handle two people?"

"Just overnight their pictures to me, then I'll get right on it."

Brady headed immediately for the Midian Pharmacy, where he picked up a pair of cheap glasses, then examined the array of hair care products, finally opting for Clairol's Radiant Ruby. After that, camera in hand, he paid a visit to IPCOT for another chat with the professor, who was in the mood to vent.

"Look, Greer, it's about time you told me what the *hell's* going on here! You asked me to talk and I did. Then you disappear for a while and I start hearing all this damn commotion in the courtyard. Actually, I don't *care* what you're doing; I just care about getting out of here. *When* is that going to happen?"

"Take it easy, professor. That's what I came to tell you: I'm making arrangements for your release. Looks like it'll happen in about a week."

"*Arrangements?* What the hell 'arrangements' do you need to make? Just open the damn gate and let me walk!"

"It's a little more complicated than that. You'll have a traveling companion...which I'll tell you about in a minute. First, though, I need to ask you a question." Conger simply glared at his captor, so Brady continued.

"When labor and management are dug in on opposite sides of the bargaining table, what determines the outcome? What are the key factors in the victor's success?"

Conger stared at the ceiling for a long moment and shook his head. Returning his focus to Brady, he said, "You could have just read one of my books, Greer. Or, hired me to consult. I don't know why—"

"Look, Conger, I *know* I had choices, okay? A lot of my life has been out of control and I had the chance to correct that, if only briefly, so I took it. It's also about risk. Remember what Churchill said? 'Nothing is so exhilarating as to be shot at and missed?' Well, I haven't been shot at yet, but this is still the biggest risk I've ever taken—a lot bigger than the stock market, that's for sure. I feel more...*alive* when I'm risking something important."

"Unless it kills you."

Skeeter: *There are some good ways to get that rush without breaking the law, aren't there? Why doesn't he just jump out of an airplane?*

Herb: *Could be, Skeets...but you got to pull that rip cord at some point. Our boy doesn't like to pack a chute. If he even owns one at the moment, I haven't seen it...*

"So, how about it?" Brady asked. "How do you bargain to

win?"

"You can boil it down to two things, Greer: stakes and will. Count on the people with the highest stakes to put the most energy into the process and they'll do that--at least initially. But these things can drag on. Then, it becomes a matter of will: Who has the guts, the fortitude, to hold out longest for what they want? That ought to be the side with the most at stake, but sometimes it isn't. That's what makes it interesting."

Brady studied the professor thoughtfully. "But," Conger continued, "that isn't the most intriguing part of it. That would be the credibility, or lack of same, in the threat."

"Meaning?"

"The threat is the heart of any negotiation. It's why we have our nuclear arsenal. An enemy has to believe we would resort to using it in an extreme circumstance, otherwise it's worthless. On a smaller scale, the baseball players are credible when they threaten to strike, because they've actually done it before. When you threaten to do something in a negotiation, the other side has to believe you might take that action. Whether or not you would is, of course, another matter. Bluffing," he added with a smirk, "can be done with or without a poker table."

Brady rose to leave. "Thanks for the lecture, professor."

"Wait a minute, Greer. What about this 'companion' business?"

"I'm sending a student along with you, for company."

Conger rubbed his chin thoughtfully as creases crossed his brow. "Tanya?"

"A lefty pitcher and a lefty catcher," Brady said as he headed for the door. "Should be a game there somewhere."

25

Patience was never one of Brady's virtues and that was apparent in abundance the following week. The papers continued to highlight the bickering between players and owners—the billionaires and millionaires—as the strike deadline loomed closer. Tanya nervously obeyed orders to remain in the house. She tried to fill her days with reading and watching TV, but was driving Brady crazy in the process. At the same time, he empathized with her. She had been a loyal participant in his adventures and the thought of her disappearing from his life as suddenly as she had entered it saddened him. When Brady became conflicted in this way, his favorite escape became the corner booth at the Waffle World. On one of those visits, Sheila took a seat with him, which she did only when she had an item hot off the vine she wanted to share quietly.

"You haven't said much about your new lady friend," she began.

Brady gave her a surprised look. "What's to say?"

"Well," Sheila continued, lowering her voice, "there's been other folks doin' plenty a talkin' while you been clammin' up."

"Oh? Such as?"

"Such as one Irma Arnold," Sheila said. "She's been down chattin' with the old dog bonker, tryin' to get 'em interested in your lady friend."

"Really?" Brady didn't bother to ask how Sheila knew that. Every good rumor made it to her ears, sooner rather than later.

"Way I heard it, your friend has fancy tastes, at least when it comes to antiques. She was down at Ethel's a little while back and made a bee-line to one of her pricier pieces, pickin' it up, checkin' it out. Handled it like it was familiar."

"She didn't *steal* it, did she? C'mon, Sheila. This sounds pretty tame."

"There's more, stock boy, but I got to get back to work. Come back in a while and we can finish our little talk."

Brady needed a drive in the country and decided it was a good time to see if Kip's mood might have changed about cooperating. Everywhere he looked during the drive out to Scofield, Brady was reminded of the simplicity of country life. About two miles out of town, there was a pond—an honest-to-God, old fashioned swimming hole—where he frequently saw kids squealing as they dove off the wooden raft anchored in the center. A few minutes later, he waved to Doc Landis, a retired Navy surgeon who now enjoyed watching the world go by from a stationary deck: his front porch. A little farther down the road was a tidy acre belonging to Margery Mason, a puckish widow who had two mail boxes: one at eye level and another 10 feet higher, labeled "air mail."

Brady knew there were some folks in the county who liked to brag about the length of time they could go between trips to town, an echo of their parents and grandparents before them. He marveled at that ability to remain anchored at home while the rest of the world sailed on. Arriving at IPCOT, however, Brady's reverie was ended abruptly by the raspy voice of Kip Kapopka.

Propped up on one elbow, he turned his pale face toward Brady from his prone position on his bed and said, "You...are...a...real...scumbag."

"Sorry you feel that way. Kip, but I understand. We do need to get this deal done, though...not just for baseball, but so you and I can get back to our lives."

"You...know...my...life," Kip said. "Tell...me...yours."

"Uh...mine? Not much to tell there. Soon as we get this done, I'll be closing up shop here and...moving down the road, I guess."

"Family?"

"I...uh...that is, I'm unattached at the moment. No wife, no kids."

Kip brought his second elbow around his body, using it in concert with the first to push off the bed and sit upright, his feet brushing against the floor. Looking intently into the eyes of Brady Greer, he said, "You...have...no...life."

Brady, stunned, returned the stare silently for several seconds before recovering, saying, "Kip, I'm going to read you that statement we discussed, so you can see how straightforward it is:

'This is Kip Kapopka. I want my family and friends to know I am being treated well by my captives, the SLA—the Sandlot Liberation Army—a group of baseball fans who insist on protecting the game of baseball and making it more competitive. They have established three demands for my release:

1. 100% revenue sharing, to make the game more competitive;
2. A minimum salary level of $70,000,000, which every team must meet to ensure that owners invest their revenue share back into their teams;
3. A new drug policy: Any player testing positive for performance enhancing drugs will be suspended for the following 12 months. A second positive test will result in a permanent ban from baseball

My captors have assured me I will be released as soon as these conditions are met."

"It won't work, Kapopka said slowly, after a long drink of water. "The players won't go along with total revenue sharing, the owners will balk at a minimum salary level and that drug policy? Ridiculous! That's tougher than the minor league policy the players have rejected already."

"Let me ask you something, Kip. Is doping as big a

threat to baseball as gambling?"

"Well, it's a problem, that's for sure. And it challenges the integrity of the game, so…I don't know…they're probably two of the biggest problems we've got."

"And you don't get a second chance when you gamble, so why should dopers--guilty cheaters--get more than a second chance?"

"I just know the players won't go for it, that's all."

"We'll see," Brady said. "The owners and players have to be forced to compromise to get the game back on a rational footing. That's what this is all about."

"I'm going to say it again, Cinque: It's pretty low to starve someone to get your way."

"You're not being starved, Kip. You have been fasting, fasting for peace between the warring factions in your own tribe. Think of yourself as the American Gandhi."

Kip stared back at Brady, incredulous. "The part about my 'being treated well," he said with disgust. "I won't read that."

"Very well. That comes out."

"Give me the damn script and get your tape recorder. Let's get this over with."

That afternoon, Brady drove up to Athens for a special visit to Flaps. It felt right, finally, to own the special Pafko card he had always wanted, so it gave him great pleasure to place that order. Brady then returned to the hearse, wiped the small, cassette tape package carefully for prints and paused to savor his next move. He now needed a megaphone for his message and was sure Enzo "Wheels" Baleno would provide it.

Twenty years ago, Baleno had retired from baseball as holder of an obscure, but impressive record: He was the all-time leader in inside-the-park home runs. These were not just round-trippers, he liked to point out, they were hustle trips, or simply *hustles*…and he was especially proud that his new career mark of 60 matched Babe Ruth's famous record for total homers in a season that had stood for decades.

"Hell, a lotta guys can bop it out, then jog around the bases," he would tell anyone who would listen. "How special is that? Show me a guy who gets a hustle with the ball *in* the park;

now *that's* special." On slow news days, sportswriters loved to call him up and get Wheels going on his favorite subject. Eventually, he figured he might as well get paid to talk and started his own sports show on a local radio station in Pittsburgh, his hometown. It wasn't long before it caught on enough to become syndicated in key baseball markets around the country.

But part of Wheels' appeal was his notoriety. An investigation shortly after the end of his career had shown his gambling style extended well beyond the base paths. Specifically, Wheels Baleno was betting on games in which he played and, for that, had been banned from baseball. A coterie of fans had remained active, urging that the ban be lifted, so he might become eligible for the Hall of Fame. Wheels fanned that flame with the sound of his voice for two hours every weekday morning, broadcasting from a special studio designed for him at the Alloy Grill in downtown Pittsburgh. Brady appreciated Baleno's high public profile and zeal for reinstatement. They combined to create, he figured, a riveting platform for his message from Midian, so Brady headed for the post office, where he dropped off his cassette package for overnight delivery in an envelope addressed to Wheels at the Alloy Grill.

This program was broadcast daily, 10 AM to noon, on its Atlanta affiliate. Brady was listening to it the following morning when he heard a car pull into the driveway and glanced through the window to see that it was Scratch.

"Tanya! Stay upstairs!" he called up to her. "We have a visitor from the Sheriff's Department."

"Hey, Buddy," he said as he opened the door. "C'mon in. What's up?"

"Not much," Scratch said as he casually surveyed the hallway. "Hadn't seen you in a while and thought I'd just stop by and say, 'hi.'"

"Great. Got time for a beer?"

"Gotta pass on that one, pardner. The wife's waitin' dinner on me. Heard about your new lady friend, though. Seein' as you're afraid to bring her by the competition down at Gene's, thought I'd just take the initiative, c'mon over and introduce myself."

"Gee, Scratch," Brady said with a smile. "You're making me feel bad. I promise you'll meet her as soon as she feels better, but she's in bed at the moment, trying to shake a nasty cold."

"Sorry to hear that."

"She ought to be back on her feet in a few days. Then I'll be sure to bring her around."

"Good," Scratch said. "Oh, you wouldn't have a...picture of her by any chance, would you?"

"No," Brady said with a nervous laugh, then lowered his voice and leaned forward. "Look, Scratch, she's nice looking; trust me on that, okay?"

"Well, guess I'll just take your word 'til I see for myself," he said with a smile as he turned to leave. "Hope she feels better soon."

Brady waited until Scratch's car was out of sight, then returned to the Waffle World. Being supper time, it was busy, so he waited nearly an hour before Sheila could take a quick break.

"Shoulda brought roller skates today," she said. "Second shift is always like that, which is why I like the graveyard, but one of the new girls up and quit--"

"Sheila," Brady said urgently, "what *else* were you going to tell me earlier?"

"What? Oh, that. Let's see...your gal's from Tennessee; that's what she's been sayin'. Irma seems to think she looks an awful lot like the society dame that snatched that baseball guy."

Brady buried his head in his coffee, trying to shield his surprise.

"Irma's trying to get Scratch to dust that old umbrella stand or whatever it is for prints, but he ain't done it...yet. Told Irma he knew you were a little goofy—hell, we all know that—but he doesn't think you're crazy enough to start datin' felons."

A moment later, Sheila was back on her feet, tending to new customers, so Brady paid his bill quickly and left, pausing behind the wheel of the hearse. *What am I gonna do? Tape gloves on her, so she never takes them off?*

It was two long days for Brady before he heard Wheels open his radio show with a careful summary of his recent conversations with the Commissioner's office and the Pittsburgh office of the FBI, both of which had verified the tape's authenticity. He then played the tape in its entirety for his listeners.

It caused an immediate sensation as callers phoned in from around the country. Representatives from the Players Association and management both said essentially the same thing: They were glad to hear Kapopka was alive, but that the demands stated would have no bearing on labor negotiations. *We'll see about that,* Brady thought.

Later that day, a plain, brown envelope arrived at his home from Washington, D.C. In it, Brady found a pair of photo IDs and Austrian passports. *If Ta Ta keeps this up, she's gonna have more business cards than Jim Rockford.* There was also a note from Yulia, suggesting that Brady purchase two tickets to Vienna, departing from Atlanta early the following morning.

After he bought them on the Internet, Brady waited until dark, then returned with his gun to IPCOT.

"Turn around," he ordered as he entered the professor's room.

"Wait a minute, Greer. What are you doing? Where am I going?"

"You don't have to worry about a thing. Tanya will explain it all to you when you wake up. Now, *turn around*!"

Before Conger could continue his protest, the Telazol lodged in his buttocks and began to spread throughout his body. After Conger collapsed on the floor, Brady struggled again to get Conger's dead weight distributed evenly across his shoulders, straightening his knees to carry him out to the hearse. It was slow going, but Brady was eventually able to deposit Conger through the vehicle's rear door.

Returning to the house, he picked up Tanya and headed west on I-20, toward Atlanta. She complained of a vicious headache, the product, he guessed, of her world spinning faster than it ever had before: from anonymous bookkeeper to embezzler to subject of a nationwide manhunt for kidnapping...and soon to be ex-patriot, all in the matter of a few short weeks.

"I...I don't know what to say..." she began.

"There's not much *to* say," he said. "You haven't found your destiny, yet, Tanya, that's all. But you're trying to get there. You deserve a lot of credit for that. A lot of people never even try.

"I'm working on something big," he continued, "but, who knows? Maybe you'll wind up doing something bigger. Maybe the world's ready for a different kind of government. Somewhere between Vienna and Volgograd, you and Conger might find it, write a book about it and change the world. I'm just on the national stage, but you're going global."

"That *could* happen, I guess," she said quietly. "But I'm pretty sure the day will come when I won't want to be global anymore. I know I'll want to come back eventually. What, then?"

"You'll have three things working for you: the statute of limitations, the best legal talent your father can buy and the possibility that, a few years from now, maybe the government won't be willing to devote the time and money necessary to prosecute you. Hell, Kip Kapopka may come out of this a hero in the baseball world. We've done him a favor; we should send him a bill."

Brady started to laugh, then turned to see tears forming in Tanya's eyes as she gazed far off into the distance. They rode in silence the rest of the way to Atlanta.

"Get some sleep in the motel, Tanya," he told her after checking in, "while I keep an eye on Conger in the hearse. He can't be unconscious in the morning, but I've got to be sure he's really drowsy, so he doesn't make any trouble before he gets on that plane."

"This is really a mess," she said, "and it's my fault."

"Don't be too hard on yourself," he said. "Surprises usually pop up sooner or later in any plan. It's how we react to them that counts. How are you set for money?"

"Okay...I guess. I've still got almost $3,000 in cash from my last check from my trust."

Brady reached under his seat and handed her an envelope. "Here's another thousand. Conger will be ready for some new clothes when you two get to Austria. Just promise me one thing."

"What's that?'

"Promise you'll help pick them out, okay? He seems to be a little challenged in the mix and match department."

"I'm really sorry how this all turned out," she said. "Are you going to be okay?"

"Don't worry about me," Brady said. "I'll be fine...and I think you will be, too. It's time you got a look at how socialism works, or doesn't, in everyday life. The professor will be an excellent tour guide."

Skeeter: *Well...good riddance; one Bolshevik down and one to go.*

Herb: *One game doesn't make a season, Skeets. Exile can be a good career move. Look at Stalin. He was exiled seven times. Made a helluva comeback.*

Skeeter: *So...that's what we have to look forward to? The Age of Lady Ta Ta? If there's ever any demand for that product, I don't want to be around to see it.*

The following morning, Brady dropped off Conger and Tanya at Hartsfield International. It was one week until the strike deadline, so he was ready to put some extra pressure on the baseball establishment. Early that afternoon, he paid another visit to Kip, who was beginning to look much healthier, having ended his involuntary fast and resumed his steady diet of sausage, cheese and plenty of beer. This time, Brady arrived with his shotgun and another dart.

"Get over there, with your hands against the wall!" Brady barked at his startled captive. Taking careful aim, he then shot the Telazol dart into his target's right buttock.

"God! I've been shot!" Kip screamed as he reached down to feel the dart.

"Relax, Kip, you're not going to meet your Maker just yet," Brady said. "That's how you took your first nap after I picked you up. It's time for another one."

"You mean, finally, I'm going back home?"

"Not quite yet, but soon. 'The short-term pain is worth the long-term gain.' Wasn't that one of your boss's favorite expressions back when he canceled the World Series?"

A confused look crossed Kip's face just before he slumped on his bed, unconscious. Brady approached him, then hesitated. He was already on the wrong side of the law; there was no doubt of that. In a way, that had been an easy decision. Brady weighed the risk and decided to take it. But now, now there occurred a question of common decency: How far was too far? He took another look at Kip's limp body, then shrugged. *Come this far, I just got to go through with it.*

With that, Brady drew a cotton swab and a bottle of rubbing alcohol out of his bag and proceeded to cleanse the inside of Kip's left forearm. He then inserted a syringe and extracted enough blood to fill it. Then he filled a second syringe. An hour later, Brady was back at his house, dipping two official, Major League baseballs into Kip's blood. As soon as they had dried, he packaged the balls carefully with a note: "We are serious. Cut the deal or he loses all five pints," and made the trip back to Atlanta, to FedEx it to Pittsburgh.

When he returned to Midian around dusk and approached his house, Brady was startled to see three police cars crowded into his driveway: one each from the city, state and Georgia Bureau of Investigation. Turning quickly down a side street, his heart raced as he tried to make sense of the picture he'd seen. *What had they found? What did they know?* One thing was certain: The hearse had become an instant liability.

26

Brady headed toward the Interstate on a back road, until he reached the truck stop and parked the hearse behind it. As night fell, he crossed the street to the Waffle World, where he never thought he would be so happy to see Sheila's Fiero. He approached it and reached carefully under the left side of the front bumper. Brady's fingers slid back and forth, until they came to rest on a rusty, little metal box--just where Sheila said it would be--held magnetically to the inside of the bumper. After a couple of tries, he managed to slide the box open to reveal a tarnished ignition key. *It's like putting your house key under the mat. You might as well leave it in the ignition.*

Brady slid behind the wheel and grabbed the cardboard sign--which now said "$900"--from the back window. Just before he turned the key in the ignition, it occurred to him why the car might never have sold: the ashtray was full of cigarette butts, the floor was covered with garbage and the upholstery was stained and badly worn.

Shaking his head, he eased out of the lot and turned quickly toward Scofield. *Had the cops been out there? Damn! So close to pulling this off.* A quick drive past IPCOT showed no activity, so Brady motored back slowly, then parked. Grabbing his gun, he hurried into the courtyard and raced to Kapopka's room.

"No!" Kip yelled as soon as he saw Brady. "Not again!"

"Good news, this time, Kip: We're leaving. Turn around!"

As soon as Kip was unconscious, Brady manuevered him into a wheelbarrow and raced back to the Fiero. The forward trunk in the small, mid engine car was a very tight fit, but Brady managed to squeeze Kip into it, then backed out onto the road.

Brady could have kept going, driving away from the maelstrom suddenly swirling around his Midian home. Instead, however, he drove toward it. There was something back there, a magnetic force a lot stronger than the hidden key box, that pulled him toward the eye of the hurricane he had created.

A few minutes later, he was cruising up and down Main Street, past his house. It was dark now and the police had left...or had they? He noted the parked cars and weighed the odds. *It would only take a minute. Should I risk it?* Very reluctantly, he concluded this was one risk not worth taking and pulled away from downtown, heading north.

When he reached the outskirts of Athens, Brady stopped at a pay phone and placed a call.

"Brady!" Ross said. "I don't *believe* this! Do you realize you're the object of a manhunt?"

"Yes, Ross, I'm afraid I do, which is why this call will be brief. I need to ask you a favor."

"Well..."

"Don't worry, I'm not going to ask you to break the law, just bend it a little bit."

"What do you need?"

"In my den, just to the right of the fireplace, you'll find my baseball card album on the bookshelf. Somehow, I'd like you to figure out a way to get it."

"I think the house is being...uh...watched."

"That wouldn't surprise me. Get in there with the realtor if you have to. Just grab that album and hold it for me, okay?"

"Yeah...sure, Brady. I can do that. Are you...okay?"

"Being followed keeps me awake, but I'm fine. Keep this call just between us. Thanks for the help, Buddy."

As he turned to leave, Brady stopped suddenly, realizing there was one more call he had to make. He dialed Evelyn, in Cleveland, but there was no answer, so he tried Heritage Village, in Shorewood, and was told the coach had been moved to a nearby hospice several days before.

"Mr. Saunders is resting at the moment and cannot be disturbed," the voice on the line told Brady. "Are you family?"

"Yes," Brady lied. "I need to speak personally with one of his caregivers. It's very important."

"This is Craig," he heard a moment later. "May I help you?"

"Yes, Craig. How is Mr. Saunders doing?"

"He's resting comfortably."

"Good. I want you to promise you'll do something very important for me. Make sure he sees the sports section of the morning paper every day this week. Can you do that?"

"Well...I don't--"

"Craig! This is very, very important. What, is there a chance he might not *make* it until tomorrow?"

"We never know, Mr...what did you say your name was?"

"I didn't. Look, Craig, you're a responsible guy, I can tell. I'll be calling you back when I can to be sure he sees those sports sections."

Brady returned to the road. His original plan called for releasing Kip a couple of hours north, in Greenville, SC, but the sudden appearance of the police necessitated a change to...Plan B, a Plan B that had not yet crystallized in Brady's mind. While trying to develop this alternative, he now thought perhaps a cabin in the Smoky Mountains would be a suitable place to hide out and wait. He drove through the night, stopping only to sedate Kip as necessary and wary of being recognized by the publicity he knew his narrow escape from Midian would generate.

His worst fears about that were realized the following morning when, keeping his head down, he purchased gas, coffee and a newspaper at a convenience store in Bryson City, N.C. Returning to the car, Brady opened the paper to see large pictures of himself and Tanya—now dubbed the "Baseball Bandits"--and Kip spread across page one. It was reported ominously that the abandoned hearse had been found, but Brady had not yet been connected to the Fiero. *There'll be a breakthrough, soon as my latest package arrives. Can I make it 'til then? Will...got to have the will to gut it out.*

Brady pulled out of the parking lot and headed down the first side road he saw, just driving now, with little regard for any kind of grand design and a focus instead on avoiding capture until the negotiators in New York took bold action. He dared not show up in any store, and thus relied on the radio for updates on the nationwide manhunt for him and Tanya. It amazed Brady to hear which of his Midian friends and neighbors had been willing to comment to reporters about him—often, people he barely knew. Meanwhile, Brady gave thanks for the silent friendship of Ross and Melanie.

Most curious to him was the prominence of Irma's voice in the coverage. He had been "troubled," she said (she had seen the signs) and "never really fit in" with the rest of the community. Kip's family and various baseball officials made pleas for his return, but there hadn't been a peep from the family of Tanya, whom the media had cast as the second coming of Patty Hearst. *I wonder how she and Conger are doing. Are they getting any of this?*

The Fiero was on a dirt road now and soon came to an abandoned barn, where Brady pulled off onto the grass next to it, parked and opened the trunk.

"It's okay, Kip," Brady said as he removed the duct tape from his mouth. "You're not going to get hurt—that is, unless you do something stupid. I've still got my gun here."

"Where are we?" Kip asked, squinting into the sunlight.

"We're taking a little vacation in the mountains," Brady said as he led Kip into the barn. Checking to be sure the rope securing Kip's hands behind his back was still taut, Brady smiled to himself: *binding arbitration*. "This will be our home until I turn you loose," he said. "We're both prisoners here 'til that happens."

Reaching into the bag he had set on the ground, Brady offered Kip some peanuts, which he refused indignantly.

"They're not so bad, Kip. Hell, when you fly Southwest, they call that a meal."

Brady secured Kip to the side of the barn, then made him as

comfortable as possible on a bed of hay. As Kapopka watched, Brady pulled from his pocket two pieces of glass only slightly larger than the card pressed between them. A confused look crossed Kip's face.

"That," said Brady lovingly, as if answering a question, "is an Andy Pafko Topps '52 card, in mint condition. It's #1 in the series."

"I know," Kip said quietly. "I've met Andy; he's a great guy. Do you know what that's *worth*?"

"I know," Brady said evenly. "Other than some cash I've got, it's about the only thing of value I own at the moment, at least the only thing I can get my hands on. I also know you share my appreciation for the worth of Pafko, the person, as well as the value of his card. Next time players and management sit down to negotiate, they won't have a hostage to motivate them. I wish they would somehow keep guys like Pafko in mind--guys who played with exuberance, for the love of the game--while they're carving up the financial pie."

After staring at the card for another long moment, Brady put it back in his pocket and allowed himself to drift off into the deepest sleep he had enjoyed in nearly a week.

Skeeter: *It's finally starting to register with me...why the magnetic pull of those little pieces of cardboard. Back then, all we knew about the guys was on the back of their cards: "bats right, throws right; height, weight." Now, everything from what they ate for breakfast to their favorite kind of underwear is reported around the clock. Nothing's left to our imagination.*

Herb: *Don't forget the pictures. They're always young on those cards and, while we're looking at them, so are we.*

When Brady awoke, he checked the news on the car radio, finding there had been no progress in New York. The following morning, however, there was an abrupt change when it was quickly announced--without the usual public posturing from either side--that an emergency negotiating session would convene at the Plaza Hotel, in New York, the next morning. *No mention of the impetus for this session. The phone lines must be burning up between Pittsburgh and New York.*

After 24 hours of continuous bargaining, spokesmen for each side went before the microphones to announce their negotiating teams had reached a special, one-year agreement for the following, 2003 baseball season. It stipulated there would be 80% revenue sharing (up from 20%); a minimum team payroll of $60,000,000 for each Major League team and a new drug policy mirroring that used in the minor leagues: four random drug tests per player each year, a 15-game suspension for the first positive test and a lifetime ban for the fifth positive test.

When Brady heard the news, he let out a whoop, momentarily forgot where he was and thrust his fist into the air— right into the ceiling of the Fiero. But it would take much more than a couple of bruised knuckles to dampen his enthusiasm...which was heightened further when he thought about patrons in sports bars from Pittsburgh to Kansas City, whooping and hollering with delight. After years consigned to the competitive wilderness by baseball's economic imbalance, their teams suddenly had not only the opportunity to compete, but the mandate: The revenue windfall each small market team was to receive could not be pocketed entirely by ownership. A large portion of it had to be invested in an improved product on the field.

Finally, action had been taken that was truly in the best interest of the game, where, just a few weeks ago, there had been little hope. He knew he was not going to get everything he demanded, but significant concessions—enough to restore hope for the future of the game—had been made on every point. Brady clicked off the car radio as a pall fell over the Fiero. He could now declare victory and go...where? He had his reward, but his risk remained--and would heighten as his story and picture were printed in newspapers from coast-to-coast. *Can you pitch a game and take both the win and the loss? How is that possible?* The cold truth was hitting Brady like a Louisville Slugger to the back of his head: Instead of bringing him closer to the principal players in his recent drama, victory had illuminated the great chasm between him and the rest.

Brady knew about outlaws being captured years— decades—after committing their crimes. He had made the choice for a life on the run, hoping to avoid that fate, but always looking over his shoulder. While everyone else could revert to their former lives, as though nothing had changed and events of the past few weeks were just an aberration, there was no turning back for Brady

Greer.

"The deed is done," he told Kip back in the barn. "Everyone's going to spring training next year with a decent chance to win--even the Brewers. What do you think of *that*?"

"That's hard to believe," Kip said, refusing to give Brady the satisfaction of even the whiff of a positive reaction. "How do you know that's for real? It could all be just an act to get this over with?"

"That could be," Brady agreed. "They said it was just a one-year deal. But now that they've publicly agreed to it, they'd look stupid to renege."

"Can I go now?" Kip asked wearily.

"I'm not going to shoot you again, Kip. I'm getting as tired of that as you are. But I do need to get you back in that trunk just a little while longer."

Brady now reverted to his original plan, which was to cross the line into South Carolina and deposit Kip in Greenville, on the ball field next to Brandon Mill, once the employer of the legendary Shoeless Joe Jackson. Jackson was another player banned from baseball for life for allegedly betting on baseball, despite being acquitted by a Chicago jury in 1921 of any involvement in the 1919 Black Sox scandal. Jackson maintained his innocence for the rest of his life. *Shoeless Joe deserves to be reinstated. Maybe leaving Kip here, where Jackson played his sandlot ball, will help call attention to his case for the Hall* .

The sun was beginning to set on the deserted old ball field as Brady led a blindfolded Kip into the infield. Suddenly, he stopped. "We're standing on home plate," Brady said with awe.

"So?"

"Shoeless Joe once stole home twice in one game. Did you know that?"

"Here?" said an annoyed Kip. "Who cares? Wherever we are, it's bush league."

"No," Brady said, "not here—though he might have done that. He did it in the Bigs, with Cleveland, in 1912. He shares the Major League record with several players for stealing home the most times in one game, but nobody's done that twice in almost 50 years."

Brady gently handcuffed Kip to the chain link fence behind

home plate at what was now Shoeless Joe Jackson Memorial Park, then paused to look around the diamond at dusk. *How many dreams had been born on similar ball fields across America over the past century?* Reaching for the duct tape that would ensure Kip's silence long enough for a getaway, Brady stopped suddenly.

"How many people total is Peploski supporting?"

"I...I don't know," said a startled Kip. "15? 20?"

"How about you? How many people count on you?"

"Let's see...a dozen, at least."

Brady gazed at the empty bleachers behind home plate, then slowly glanced again around the diamond, his eyes following an imaginary runner circling the bases. Then he laughed. *Peppi and Poppi. Sounds like a couple of guys you'd meet at a prep school reunion.*

Gingerly, he reached into his pocket and produced the pristine Pafko. Clasping its corner tightly between his thumb and forefinger, he raised it above his shoulder, turned to face Kip and said, "Andy was always pretty good in the clutch, wasn't he?"

"Yeah...sure...he was good in the clutch."

"I've wanted this card for as long as I can remember," Brady said, "since I was a snot-nosed kid bringing my glove to County Stadium, hoping to catch a foul ball. Now that I have it, though, I realize I don't own it; it owns me. By giving it away, I'm a free man in my heart. Nobody else can change that, even if my body is captured."

"What are you *talking* about? You're ...giving... *me*...your perfect Pafko? Are you *serious*?"

"No, Kip, I'm nuts, but I'm not *that* nuts. I've just been thinking...I don't have a dozen or two dozen people depending on me; in fact, I don't have anyone counting on me at the moment. So, I'm going to send it to my friend, Dennis, in Milwaukee, and tell him to sell it to the highest bidder. Then, I'm instructing him to use the proceeds to set up an account to buy that bakery back from the loan shark, so your buddy, Peploski, can go back to running it like the sober business it used to be—one that didn't book its own lottery bets. Dennis will make sure you and Peppi don't get in over your heads again."

"What about you? What are *you* gonna do?"

"First thing I'm going to do," Brady said as he began

wrapping Kip's mouth with duct tape, "is get out of town and find a good place to watch the World Series."

When he had ripped off the last piece of tape, Brady paused for a moment to admire his work. Then, leaning into Kip's ear, Brady said in the lowest voice he could muster, "Just remember one thing: Where there's money, there's trouble."

Brady then turned with a laugh, trotted down the first base line, tapped the bag and continued out through right field, until he reached the street. Returning to the Fiero, he began to drive toward the local train station. Just three blocks away, however, the engine coughed hard several times, the car shook once--violently, from side to side--and the Fiero expired. Instinctively, Brady glanced at the gas gauge. Seeing it was far from empty, he slammed his fist into the steering wheel and cursed Detroit before shifting into neutral and pushing the car to the side of the street.

He then began hiking toward the old Southern Railway depot. One mile later, at the end of Washington Street, Brady arrived at the nondescript Greenville station, a rectangular box totally lacking the character of his Midian office--not even any dogs in sight. *The ultimate architectural criticism: The mutts ignore it.*

Inside, however, Brady noticed a picture on the wall of the former station on this site that had been torn down years before. Aside from the brick being red, instead of yellow, it looked identical to the one in Midian. *Why do they do that? What have they got against the past?*

Greenville was now an Amtrak stop on the route between New Orleans and New York and the northbound Crescent was due in soon. Brady figured that, dressed in the baseball cap and sweatshirt he purchased in the gift shop, he should be able to remain anonymous as far as Union Station, in D.C. En route, he was confident some sort of plan, pointing him toward the next stop in his own new harmony, would reveal itself. If it required adopting a new identity, that was one base he already had covered.